Could it be Tdo's out-fit? He sounded . . . s, sooth-ing . . .

"Almanzo thought he'd give us some time alone together," he said, moving closer.

Willow backed away slightly. "Oh? And why would I want to spend time alone with a desperado?"

"Because you're one yourself," he whispered. *"Desperada."*

Why was he looking at her so intensely? She could feel his bold gaze beneath the lowered brim of his dark sombrero. He reached out slowly and gently, seizing her wrists. He whispered her name . . . and she knew. Then his lips came to hers, tasting, moving, the roughness of his unshaven chin heightening her sensitivity. Willow's entire body quivered with the torrent of need his kiss unleashed, and she moaned as Talon Clay's kiss deep-ened, became more demanding. It was like coming home.

Finally, he drew away and touched her hair softly, breathing into her ear, "Am I pleasing you?"

Willow closed her eyes and sighed. "Are you?" She lifted her face to be kissed again.

But first she whispered, "Do birds have wings?"

DISCOVER DEANA JAMES!

CAPTIVE ANGEL   (2524, $4.50/$5.50)
Abandoned, penniless, and suddenly responsible for the biggest
tobacco plantation in Colleton County, distraught Caroline Gil-
lard had no time to dissolve into tears. By day the willowy redhead labored to exhaustion beside her slaves . . . but each night
left her restless with longing for her wayward husband. She'd
make the sea captain regret his betrayal until he begged her to
take him back!

MASQUE OF SAPPHIRE   (2885, $4.50/$5.50)
Judith Talbot-Harrow left England with a heavy heart. She was
going to America to join a father she despised and a sister she
distrusted. She was certainly in no mood to put up with the insulting actions of the arrogant Yankee privateer who boarded her
ship, ransacked her things, then "apologized" with an indecent,
brazen kiss! She vowed that someday he'd pay dearly for the lib-
erties he had taken and the desires he had awakened.

SPEAK ONLY LOVE   (3439, $4.95/$5.95)
Long ago, the shock of her mother's death had robbed Vivian
Marleigh of the power of speech. Now she was being forced to
marry a bitter man with brandy on his breath. But she could not
say what was in her heart. It was up to the viscount to spark the
fires that would melt her icy reserve.

WILD TEXAS HEART   (3205, $4.95/$5.95)
Fan Breckenridge was terrified when the stranger found her near-
naked and shivering beneath the Texas stars. Unable to remember
who she was or what had happened, all she had in the world was
the deed to a patch of land that might yield oil . . . and the fierce
loving of this wildcatter who called himself Irons.

*Available wherever paperbacks are sold, or order direct from the
Publisher. Send cover price plus 50¢ per copy for mailing and
handling to Zebra Books, Dept. 4214, 475 Park Avenue South,
New York, N.Y. 10016. Residents of New York and Tennessee
must include sales tax. DO NOT SEND CASH. For a free Zebra/
Pinnacle catalog please write to the above address.*

SONYA T. PELTON

LOVE'S LOST ANGEL

ZEBRA BOOKS
KENSINGTON PUBLISHING CORP.

ZEBRA BOOKS are published by

Kensington Publishing Corp.
475 Park Avenue South
New York, NY 10016

First Printing: July, 1993

Printed in the United States of America

For Lisa and her Lost Angel:
  May that Love fly back
to you one day . . .
  On velvet wings
like the swiftest hawk
  in the Dakota sky.

Many thanks to all who coaxed and inspired the author into the writing of this third book of the Sundance story. Many of you picking up this book will remember the first two:

Texas Tigress and *Captive Caress*.

You all wanted more of Talon Clay and Willow.

The author hopes she has not disappointed any of her friends.

And the best and the worst of this is
  That neither is most to blame,
If you've forgotten my kisses
  And I've forgotten your name.
          —Swinburne, *An Interlude*

Prologue

He walked alone this time in Wild Horse Desert. His feet were bare, his long yellow-white hair braided. The earth surrounding him seemed full of golden halos and streaks of violet blue, and he appeared to be breathing a thick amber haze reminiscent of mist rising from a meadow. He could see his breath clearly as if he were walking in wintry cold, puffs sparkling before him like golden motes. Then he saw her. Willow Margaret stood naked, ankle-deep in a bubbling spring, so wondrously transparent that the golden sun seemed to shine clear through her body like white opal, catching shimmers and gleams. Her gilded hair was braided Indian fashion, the glints in it like strands of fire cast in bronze. Her arms stretched above her head as if she were in ecstasy, while glistening crystal drops fell from her fingers. Her body was riper, her curves and face more mature, and the light of the sun touched her pensive, beautiful face as she turned to look at him.

Talon Clay moaned fitfully in his sleep and rolled to his right side.

This time Willow Margaret was frowning and her

arms did not stretch out to greet him. Her face was not a testimony to her joy, but dark with frustration. Then, while the sun faded all around the glade, Willow vanished, taking with her, inside her, the one thing Talon wanted most in this world: His son.

Talon Clay came awake with a strangled cry of anguish. He lifted himself with a groan, looked to the bedside table in the hotel room, and saw a tall, smoky bottle of tequila, half-full. Another lay on the floor, empty. He coughed, reached for his pack of cheroots, cussed, then crumpled the pack and tossed it onto the floor, deciding to quit a habit that had troubled him for three years straight.

If only he hadn't been dazed with drink and passed out the night before, he thought as he walked across the wooden floor of his rented room.

He became very still. Sideways, carefully, his eyes rolled; nothing else moved, but his muscled body tensed for the coming revelation. He touched a tongue to dry lips. A pump rattled somewhere below and then began a rhythmical creaking.

His head snapped to the side, his raw-honey hair spilling across his forehead, the taut planes of his face flinching as he looked to see if—just by any chance—he had not been alone in the bed.

Relief sent him back onto the rumpled sheets, but with the grinding urge to become sick he got up and ran to the open window for a breath of fresh air. He felt clammy, but thank God he wasn't going to be sick after all. A man never knew what he'd wake up to, drinking himself stupid like that. . . . He stared at Willow's most recent letter lying open on the floor where he had flung it the night before.

Back on the bed, he hung his head, raked his fingers

8

through his thick hair, then reached down to snatch up the much-read letter. The paper had become velvet soft from all the handling, and the ink was blotchy in some spots. There were no words of love, only words of anger. A sharp, nostalgic pain pierced him to the quick as he stared at Willow's neat schoolteacher's handwriting: *I am going away. Please, do not come looking because you will not find me. I am sick of you insulting me, saying I am dowdy and fat. As for the other women, you can have them all, and good riddance!*

Talon gritted his teeth, clenching his jaw. "Fat! Other women! Where did she ever hear such a bunch of lies? I haven't bedded another woman in five or six years!" He bent to pick up his buckskin vest and brush it off, thinking he must have been really drunk and fuming last night because his clothes were strewn everywhere . . .

His eyes shifted and he groaned. *Be Jaysus,* there it was, the damning evidence—a woman's colorful Mex shawl. "I'm really sinkin' low," Talon snarled, yanking his pants and boots on and reaching for his ranger badge. "How can I divorce you, woman, if I can't even find you? God, I haven't even seen you for over four years!" He stared down into the dusty street of La Grange. "Where are you, Willow, and why are you hiding my son from me?" He snatched up his .44, slapped on his black Stetson, and looked into the cracked mirror at one sorry Texas Ranger. "Oh, my Lord," he said with a short laugh. "What are you planning to do, man, pin that badge on your naked chest?"

Talon's stomach was growling. He was late for the breakfast he'd been promised with his board—salt pork and eggs, fluffy biscuits—and instead found his timing was closer to the noon meal.

Downstairs in the kitchen, the proprietor's Indian wife had prepared a kettle of venison and dumplings and a Dutch oven of biscuits for the "nooning." She grinned as she heaped the Ranger's plate with meat and dumplings and gave him a tin cup of tasty broth. For a man who'd survived for several weeks on meat alone, the meal was tasty, though not the delicious fare of Sundance Ranch where Miss Pekoe did the cooking.

Yellow sun was pouring everywhere by the time Talon Clay Brandon, Texas Ranger, rode out of La Grange without a notion where to begin the search for his estranged wife and green-eyed son. That's all Willow's second letter—four years later!—had told him: *We have a boy with green eyes.* And: *Get a divorce, Talon Clay!* Something did not fit, he thought, but he couldn't put his finger on it. The second set of words didn't click and the handwriting seemed different.

Was she going to begin to leave him little clues as to where he might find her? A note here, a note there? Torture, that's what it was. Women! First Garnet, now Willow.

A gun at his hip and his dyed-black leather vest open disclosing the shoulder holster of a second gun, Talon narrowed his eyes. He halted his horse at the edge of town and stared at the empty range before him, hazy blue in the distance. A Texas Ranger was supposed to be brave and powerful, a shrewd and expert brand of lawman able to stare death in the face. They were even said never to give up on anything, able to ride straight into hell. *Whenever there was trouble a Ranger wasn't far be-*

hind. . . . Well then, why the heck hadn't he been able to find his own wife all these years? He answered his own question: *He had been too absorbed in his work with the border command to seek out Willow's hideaway.* Ambition and recognition? Had he desired those things? Wasn't he a Texas Ranger because it established his sense of honor and fairness? Or had he only been trying to correct past mistakes and make up for being an outlaw?

Damn, if only he'd known, four-and-a-half years ago, that Willow was going to have his baby . . .

"Hola, amigo!"

The Ranger's eyes widened suddenly. What the—? There, riding toward him on a dun-colored mare, was Willow's sixteen-year-old brother, Sammy Hayes.

Hester Tucker and her companion stood in the shadows of a dilapidated storefront. When Hester saw Sammy Hayes she pulled Nat back against the building, almost slamming her head to the wood.

"What are you doing, Hester? I want to see the Ranger . . . he's magnificent. I almost got him into bed, too, he was so drunk. I was wearing a Mexican shawl."

Hester pinched Nat's arm. "Did you change the words in the note the way I told you to?"

"Of course! I mentioned *divorce* on the added line. He will believe his wife wants a divorce now, just like you wanted. Won't the lady boss be mad about that?" Nat tossed long blond curls spiralling down in unruly fashion to narrow shoulders. When her companion failed to answer, she brushed it off, saying, "Oh *shoot,* I left my Mexican shawl in his room when I was sneaking around. He was passed out like a drunken Mex."

11

"The Ranger's too close. Come on, we've got to get to the boy before the Ranger does; Sammy's messing things up. Keep your pants on, and let's run!"

"I wish I could wear a silky dress," Nat complained. "Are you sure they'll get a divorce?" When her companion nodded, Nat added, "I don't care about the money this Garnet's paying us. All I want is that big handsome hunk of a Ranger."

"You talk too much, Nat, and quit acting like you're dizzy in the head. I thought you had some brains behind all that blond hair. Come on! We've got to cut your hair for this job."

"What?" Nat screeched. "I ain't cutting my hair!"

"For the Ranger? To make darn sure he don't get back with his wife, Willow Margaret?"

"Oh. All right. I'll do it then and it can always grow out. It grows fast anyway." Nat sank back into the abandoned store at the edge of town and they crept like salamanders to the old shed out back. She stopped suddenly. "No, I won't do it. I have to have long hair. Hank Rountree said that was a big part of my allure. That, and my big blue eyes, big breasts and . . ."

"Nat," Hester said with her contrived New Orleans drawl—just like her cousin's, only Fleurette's was real— "Your nickname should not be 'Nat' Lacey, but 'Big' Lacey."

"All the better for that Big Bad Ranger."

Hester predicted then and there that Nat was not going to *live* to see the day she could get Talon Clay as her one and only. She might not get him for herself either, because Willow had a real good hold on that handsome lawman—even if she didn't know it yet!

12

Child let me grasp your hand,
Child let me grasp your hand.
  You shall live,
  You shall live!
Says the father.
  A'te he'ye lo.

Ghost Dance Song

I feel ... The link of nature draw me:
flesh of flesh,
Bone of my bone thou art, and from thy state
Mine never shall be parted, bliss or woe.

                                    —*John Milton*

Chapter One

"I *am* too plump," Willow said to her reflection in the mirror as she turned this way and that, her striped yellow and blue calico making a gentle rustle as she moved. "Oh, why can't I lose this extra weight?" She pouted at her face and pinched her cheeks.

"You are not too plump," Juanita said as she bustled into the room, carrying fresh linens. "You just think so, Margarita, and your wandering husband is full of beans to say so!" Juanita chose to call Willow by her middle name, giving Margaret the Spanish variation.

Then why, Willow wondered, had her husband been ashamed of her just before she had discovered her second pregnancy? She had been under the misapprehension that he had loved her, for better or for worse, and that all the ghosts should have been laid to rest, never to arise and plague them afresh.

Still doubtful, Willow turned from the mirror to face Juanita, the lovely Spanish woman who cared for her son while Willow was busy teaching three different grades at the schoolhouse. She snatched up the colorful shawl. "I have to go soon, or I'll be late for the first and second graders."

Stepping in front of Willow, Juanita tilted her head and flung out her slim arms, sighing. "You are active, attractive, and healthy; only your husband is missing and that is not so bad or sad. You are like a pink, carved cameo, and dainty like a porcelain doll. Where is this fat you speak of? I see not an ounce of it!"

Giggling, Willow said, "Stop, Juanita, you are making me laugh, and you know what happens when I start." When Juanita got her going, Willow's silly mood lasted for hours. Juanita was so good for her that Willow believed God must have sent this wonderful person to care for her and her son. "Now, where is my son? Have you left him in the kitchen with Jorge again? Oh Lordy be, you know how those two get into things!"

Now it was Juanita who laughed. Then her dark eyes grew wide just as a crash sounded from the kitchen and she rushed with Willow right behind her, both wondering what in the world the boy and big Jorge had gotten into this time. They pulled up short, unblinking at the powdery sight in the hallway. Willow's hand covered her mouth, her other resting lightly on Juanita's shoulder.

With a gasp, Juanita said, "Angelo, what have you done now?"

"Michael!" Willow giggled, beginning one of her fits of laughter again. Living with Juanita and Jorge was like a circus, all day long; that is, when Willow could pull herself away from the schoolhouse since so many children needed her there. That, and thoughts of Talon Clay and how wonderful it used to be between her and her husband.

16

"We must go and see!" Juanita exclaimed as more noise erupted from the kitchen.

Willow and Juanita rushed into the kitchen. Michael and a big shaggy dog were covered from head to foot with white flour. The huge tin lay on the floor beside them, emptied of its contents, while the four-year-old gazed wide-eyed up at them, green eyes in a very white face. Jorge barked once, wagging his tail and sending up a cloud of dust that settled thickly. Juanita blinked at her many-leafed plants and indoor flowers. *Por Dios!*

"What have you done, baby boy?" Juanita asked, bending down beside the pair on the floor. She placed her hand on the boy's tawny head and Jorge proceeded to lick her fingers happily.

After a cough and a sneeze, Michael said very seriously, "We got it down from the cupboard for you, 'Nita." He clapped his hands. "Make cakes 'n' syrup, 'Nita, 'cause me and Jorge are hungry. Real hungry." Michael patted the dog. "Right, Jorgie?"

Jorge barked and licked a spot on the boy's face clean of flour. Michael giggled with glee.

"I have to go," Willow murmured, leaning down to plant a kiss on Michael's forehead. "Hug," she said.

Standing up in a cloud of flour and a sneeze, Michael hugged his mother, then ran off to fetch the broom and dustpan from the closet; Jorge padded right behind, sending up another flurry of white as his tail wagged with happy mischief.

"Love you!" Willow called out.

"Me, too!"

Grabbing an armful of textbooks, Willow turned on her heel and sped out the door, the yellow bun at the back of her head the last thing Juanita saw with a flash

17

of the bright shawl. Juanita turned just as the two dusty mischief-makers arrived, Michael with broom standing at his side like a soldier's rifle, Jorge with dustpan clamped between his huge jaws.

"Dios." Juanita sighed and resignedly set to work as Michael and Jorge found a toy to play with at the edge of the puddle of flour.

Walking briskly to the schoolhouse, her serviceable brown shoes kicking up dust, Willow began to slow her steps. She tensed and looked over her shoulder, wondering why she had felt as if she were being watched. There was no one, she thought, as she studied her surroundings and walked along the hard-packed dirt street deeply rutted by wagon wheels. Bountiful did not have all the conveniences like the larger Texas towns did, such as properly maintained streets and lights at every corner.

Still, the main street offered most of the necessities of life: general store, post office, a livery stable, blacksmith, saloons with dance halls, and a sheriff. There were a few hotels and a clothing store, too, plus a telegraph office where trains arrived and departed, usually right on time.

Again, Willow had that feeling of being watched, but she relaxed as she saw Sammy walking toward her, his hat slouched low over his forehead, reminding Willow for a moment of Talon Clay when he was much younger. Yet, where Talon's hair was blond—having turned a bit darker over the years—Sammy's hair was bright red like her sister Tanya's.

Walking off to the side of the road, Willow whispered, "Sammy, what did you find out?"

18

"You don't have to whisper, sis, there's no one around." Sammy looked over one shoulder, then the other while Willow watched, a corner of her mouth twitching. "I delivered the note to Talon Clay and I even saw him walkin' down the street to fetch his horse at the livery where it was—"

"Sammy, just tell me! How is he? How does he look?"

"Well," Sammy drawled in his recently-developed deeper voice, "He looks like Talon Clay." He shrugged. "Well, not the old Talon Clay who used to be an outlaw." Again he gave a shrug. "You know, like a Texas Ranger. There was this Mex gal who was eyein' him like she knew him when he was walkin' down the street ..."

Sammy went on, but Willow chose not to hear the rest. Suddenly she was seething inside. So, he was whoring around with dark-eyed females again, she thought, recalling how he'd favored Mex women before he had married her. Was it Conchita again? Maybe she was trailing him like a camp follower or leading him around like an Indian scout. She would have laughed, if it weren't so serious. At times, when she was anxious and overwhelmed by the worries confronting her, she had to laugh or go crazy.

"You delivered the note then," Willow said and Sammy looked straight at her in exasperation. "You said you did and I believe you. Sammy, did you read my note to Talon Clay?"

"Yeah," he replied, tapping his hat upward so more of his forehead showed, "but what I don't understand is why you told him about Mikey and then asked for him to get a divorce? What're you doin', sis, tryin' to get him to come lookin' for you so's you can tell him to git? Rangers can travel across Texas like their mounts got wings and be somewhere lickety-split. Whenever there's trouble, a Ranger ain't far behind."

"I know, Sammy. You state the obvious often. But I believe the Rangers are going to become ineffectual with this war that has begun. They still have their border patrols and fights for law and order, but that won't last long, either."

"Women—" Sammy said with a shake of his head. "I just don't understand them. Rangers'll always be."

"Sammy," Willow began with concern, "have you already been messing with—" She shrugged. "Well, you know . . . females."

When Sammy blushed, Willow said, "Forget it."

"Sis—" Sammy looked serious now. "Talk about messin' with someone. Whew! I bet you got Talon Clay madder than a wet hen!"

Willow couldn't help laughing. "Sammy—you should say *rooster.*" Her expression darkened with rancor. "Yes, definitely. Talon Clay is a big banty rooster."

"Yeah?" Sammy sneered. "Then how come he looked so worried when he was walkin' down the street in La Grange?" He looked toward the schoolhouse and then swung back to her. "Willow—" He only called her that when he wanted her full attention. "There's goin' to be trouble when Talon finds out where you been hidin', I'm warnin' you. You don't cross a man like Talon Clay and get away with it."

Willow's mouth dropped open. "Well, listen to you. You sound just like a man."

Sammy stood straighter, prouder, pulling his shoulders back. "I think I'm just about all grown up now, sis." His voice had become deeper suddenly, his face as stern as a Texas Ranger's. "Yup, you can call me a man, if you want, and I'm plannin' to be a Texas Ranger just like Ashe and Talon Clay."

Trying not to laugh, Willow looked toward the schoolhouse at the end of the road, already seeing several children waiting on the steps, and yet another group running toward the white building. "Sammy—" she began, still not looking at him, but at the children. "Did you tell Talon Clay where I'm hiding?"

For a moment Sammy appeared sheepish, then said, " 'Course not, sis. Why would I do that?"

Studying him hard for a moment, Willow answered, "I just thought you might, that's all."

"And go against my sister's wishes?" Sammy's face was even redder, his mouth tight, his reddish-gold eyebrows fierce.

"For a Texas Ranger maybe." She laughed at his expression. "You men stick together." Willow almost wished that Sammy *had* told Talon where she could be found. She asked herself now if that was the true reason she'd sent him that letter, to find out if he still loved her and would come. He *could* have gotten the papers for a divorce already, couldn't he? He *could* see his son . . . occasionally, couldn't he?

Divorce!

"Sammy, what is this about a divorce? I never mentioned divorce in the letter—"

"Sis," Sammy said evasively, "you better get on to school." He grinned. "The schoolteacher shouldn't be late, you know."

Willow looked toward the schoolhouse again. One little girl was pointing toward the bell-rope, hunching up

21

her shoulders, giggling. A freckle-faced boy walked up to the rope, touched it, and drew back as if burnt, then ran away laughing in the bright Texas sunshine.

Willow wished she had brought her straw hat along, since the spring day promised to be a scorcher by noon. She looked at Sammy, praying again that he would not run off and join the Texas troops. Thousands of boys under eighteen, and thousands of men up to sixty and beyond, joined the Stars and Bars. The one great contribution of Texas to the Southern cause was men, and in each county, landowners raised unit after unit, many armed and equipped at their own expense. They filled most of the posts from captain to colonel, while the ranks were filled with tough farmboys. The rock of both armies, Blue and Gray, was this horde of small farmers.

"Sammy," she said, knowing she employed the lesser of two evils, "would you keep up the good work and go on spying on Talon Clay for me? I don't want him to find me because, as you said, there'd be hell to pay."

"Why do you send him notes then?"

With a blush, Willow replied, "We'll just let him keep guessing. I have to go now. You go on to the house and have Juanita feed you. And you can have the bigger room upstairs this time; not the one in the front where I do my writing, but the second largest."

Sammy's face brightened. He loved that room because it looked out over all of Texas and the rivers. "Wait a minute, sis."

"Yes?"

"What did Talon Clay do to deserve all the punishment he's receivin'?"

"I'll tell you someday, Sammy." She started for the

schoolhouse then stopped and turned. Sammy had not moved yet. "Am I too . . . plump, do you think?"

"Plump?" Sammy snorted. "You're too skinny if you ask me."

She laughed. "I did." When Sammy blushed again, making his freckles stand out more, she said, "Thank you, Sammy. I needed that."

Skinny, hmm?

Willow moved behind her desk to sit down. She looked the children over, seeing that they were busy with the task she'd assigned. Usually she loved teaching school, but lately all she could think of was her philandering husband and how she wished he could be here with her. Where was he now? What was he doing? she wondered. Was he even thinking of her? He must be, even if briefly, since he had received her note . . . but what was this Sammy had mentioned about a divorce? Was this what Talon Clay wanted, to divorce her? Would he try to find her? He had been the one man she loved more than life itself, but his restless spirit had proved time and again that one woman was not enough. Talon Clay needed a copious supply. If he did come for her, how could she ever live with his philandering, and the fact that he'd said she was dowdy and fat?

Everyone said she was still thin and lovely, so why did she see a plump and dowdy young woman in the mirror? Was she merely perceiving what Talon Clay had said she had turned out to be? No, she thought, they were only being kind and gentle. Hester Tucker had told her the same, that Talon did not identify her with the same young woman he'd married. As if that wasn't bad enough, she herself had seen Talon with Hester again, watched as he'd touched her bright curls and flirted with her in the woods near Sundance. That had been the straw that broke the camel's back, making Willow leave her beloved home shortly after she'd found she was pregnant with Talon's child. She had lost the first baby, and then become pregnant again a year later.

Resentment filled her again as it so often had in the four years since she had left Talon Clay and hidden herself and her child here in Bountiful. She felt no self-pity, no destructive revenge, only this bitterness. Michael came first; he was all she could think of now, and she had to stop feeling resentment, because that too could turn to self-pity. But she would not let it, she would keep going and make a life for herself and her child. But how could she stop thinking that she was to blame somehow? What did I do to make him wander? she asked herself. Was I really fat and dowdy four and a half years ago? She had been three months pregnant, so it was that long since she had seen Talon Clay. What has he been doing all this time? If he truly loved her he would have come looking for her.

Watching the children, the sun on their bowed heads, she recalled the Christmas when she had revealed her first pregnancy, the baby she had sadly lost soon thereafter . . .

Willow had a surprise for Talon Clay. He had turned to pull her beneath the spreading arms of a huge cottonwood. It was nice and cozy, with rays of pale yellow sunshine wrapping them in a delicious blanket of warmth.

24

"I have something for you," Talon murmured against Willow's forehead. He kept his eyes trained on her face as he brought his hand up with a package wrapped in brown paper.

With a tinkling laugh, she had replied, "I've been wondering what you've been carrying in your hand all this time." She looked up at him flirtaciously from beneath her long, tawny lashes.

"Well." He tapped her hand when she hesitated. "Go ahead, open it."

"First," she said softly, laying it aside to reach up and wrap her arms about his neck, "I want a kiss. I've been dying to have you kiss me all day long, Talon Clay."

He murmured something deep in his throat, and, moving closer, much closer, he said, "I'd be more than happy to oblige you, sweet Pussywillow."

When their lips made contact, thousands of tiny shock waves tingled along their flesh. The breath-robbing kiss deepened, and then he placed scalding kisses tenderly across her face, down her throat—and then her bodice was being opened with a swift hand. He returned to her lips, and the sun-warmed kiss went on forever, so sweet and wild that it shook the very ground they stood on. Hungry for more, Willow pressed her soft body nearer to his, feeling with delight his hand slip beneath her skirts and then across her belly. He gasped then and tore his lips from her bruised ones. Powerful currents of desire pulsed through his loins. She could feel it, too. They were like one—every thought, every feeling the same lustrous love.

"Willow . . . please, I have to have you . . . now." He gave her no time to answer, peeling her dress off over her head and pulling her gently down to the grass. Talon

25

kissed Willow until she was weak with desire, so weak that when he penetrated her the force of his entry triggered a huge explosion inside her. His manhood reached like tongues of fire deep into her. The joy of ultimate ecstasy burst over them, imprinting itself forever and ever on both their hearts. She joined with him so quickly this time that Talon could hardly believe it, for he'd thought she would never keep up with his ardent passion.

When it was over he cupped her chin in his big hand, his eyes like huge, sparkling emeralds, framed by soft brown lashes. Their faces were mere inches apart when he slid his hand across her stomach. He smiled into her eyes.

"What is your present to me?" As he said this, his hand rested on the tiny, rounded lump beneath her belly button. "Can I guess?" While he questioned her, his hand gently massaged her. She nodded, her eyes growing larger. "Let me see . . . you've been sick most every morning for the last three weeks, ah, give or take a few days. Ah . . . you have strange cravings in the middle of the night . . . your sister Tanya has told me about that one. I wouldn't know, because you've been recuperating at her house since our ordeal in the caves when Carl Tucker met his end." Lovingly he gazed into her eyes. "When will you come and live with me and . . ."

Be my love? Was this what he'd been about to say to her before he bit off his words? Talon must love her . . . he just had to! There was only one way she could find out . . . if he wasn't going to tell her.

When he finally let her go, she gathered her clothes and began to dress, hurrying now that she had to go and see something for herself. When she realized he was

26

still sitting there, naked as the day he was born, she knew the truth had to come from her lips. But he knew it already!

"I am having our baby!" She stood, whirling around to announce it to the whole world—even though they were alone in the green glade.

"I knew it," Talon said with a gasp, pulling his pants up as he stood, then jerking them on and racing along with her. She seemed to have a single purpose in mind and was already breaking out in a run up the hill from Strawberry Creek. "Wait! Willow . . . what the heck . . . where are you going? Damn . . . woman, wait till I get my pants up!"

When Talon had finally caught up with her, she had been standing in the doorway of the bedroom in Le Petit Sundance; as he came up behind her and she detected his presence, she broke away and ran to the bed. She had knelt on the mattress and pressed her hand to the beautifully executed carving on the headboard, tracing the names imprisoned there forever in the huge, curving heart. Happy tears had come to her eyes as she had stared until her eyes burned: *Talon Clay loves Willow Margaret.*

Now Willow looked up and found the children staring at her, probably wondering why she had been gazing out the window for so long. "I see that you're almost finished, children." Stacking some papers abruptly, she cleared her throat. "Yes, Susan, that's very nice. Keep working." She looked over at the clock in the corner of the room near the double doors.

Tilting her head, Susan blinked and looked at the

teacher just as she was folding her hands over her desk; she was getting that "funny look" on her face once again. Willow was still staring at the clock, beginning to feel tense for some reason. Suddenly, as she closed her eyes, a great wind blew up, setting the mists of her mind to dancing. The wind swept through the gnarled trees, and around the back yard of the house, she seemed to hear sounds of despair. Was that Juanita in her mind's eye? She appeared to be crying. Her baby? Now, there were only the rushing mists, and the roaring of wind and lost voices ... *Talon's? Or Michael!*

Willow's eyes flew open!

Just then Sammy burst in, gesturing wildly for Willow to come at once. Closing the door, she looked at Sammy and suddenly her heart gave a lurch. "What is it, Sammy?" By the look of him, something terrible must have happened. "Talon Clay." He must have been hurt, or worse.

"He's gone," Sammy blurted.

"Talon, gone? That doesn't make sense, Sammy, when I haven't even seen Talon for years—how could he be gone?"

"Mikey!" Sammy almost shouted, waving his hat in the air. "Someone's *taken* him!"

"Michael—yes?" She had not wanted to believe it; she had forced it from her mind since she'd seen the blue mist in her mind's vision.

"That's what I said. Not Talon Clay. I don't even know where that Ranger is."

Like a mantle of ice, cold fury settled around Willow. She decided aloud, "Talon." Talon must have taken him. She spun away from Sammy.

Walking with a calm she didn't feel, Willow went

28

back into the schoolroom to tell the children school was out for now, then rushed after Sammy while the children gathered at the top of the stairs, watching their teacher. They gawked and blinked. In a very unladylike fashion, the willowy blond schoolteacher jumped onto the back of Sammy's horse and raced down the street holding onto her brother's shoulders for dear life.

At the house, Juanita rushed into Willow's arms, crying, "They have taken him, our little Angelo! I am so sorry. I should have watched him better when I went out to hang clothes on the line. He was playing with Jorge in the corner of the yard when they—"

"They?" Willow pushed Juanita back gently. "What do you mean, Juanita? How many men were there?"

Wringing her hands, Juanita cried, "I only seen one, riding away on a horse ... he must have had Angelo with him. This man was skinny and not very tall in the saddle."

"Where was Sammy all this time?" Willow asked as she ran about searching the rooms for clues, coming up with nothing.

"I sent him to the mercantile for some things," Juanita said as she followed close behind Willow. "When Sammy returned I rushed out to meet him, to tell him what had happened. Oh—oh," Juanita moaned again.

"Where is Jorge?" Willow said, feeling anger well up inside of her again. Juanita looked at her blankly and, as Willow was about to question her again, they both looked up as they heard someone come in the back door.

They stood together tensely, Willow wishing she had

29

the gun Talon Clay had given to her; she'd left it behind at Sundance.

Walking into the house just then was Sammy, carrying the big, shaggy dog. Jorge was whimpering, opening one eye, the other swollen shut. "He has a big lump on his head," Sammy said. "Someone hit him a good one."

"Oh ..." Juanita sobbed out loud, rushing to stroke Jorge's fur. "They have taken baby Angelo! What are we going to do?!"

"Calm down. You keep saying *they*, Juanita." Willow stooped to pick up one of Michael's toys. "How many were there?"

Juanita shrugged, dabbing at her eyes. "I mean the horse and the rider—I did not see more than that. The horse raced away and Angelo could have been in front of the man ... oh, he kidnapped the boy, I just know it."

"There must have been more"—Willow held the toy and walked to the front porch—"because one must have snatched up Michael while another hit Jorge over the head."

Juanita stopped her moaning and frowned. "I saw only the one horse and rider."

After laying Jorge on the end of the sofa, Sammy placed a hand over his gun and holster. "I'm going lookin' for them."

Willow turned to Juanita. "I'm going with my brother, Juanita. You stay here in case a message comes." From Talon Clay, she was thinking with hope.

"What will you do?" Juanita asked, wringing her hands in the folds of her apron.

"We'll get the neighbors to join the search." Willow was shaking from head to foot, trying to gather her wits.

"Oh," Juanita moaned weakly. "I will pray for you."

Willow said angrily, "We'll find Michael, even if we have to ride into the next county—"

"And then some," Sammy added, jamming his hat down onto his head, already looking like the fierce Ranger he fervently wished to become one day.

Back in the kitchen, Juanita stared at the roast beef and fresh vegetables she had been preparing for the noonday meal. She couldn't help the grief and worry that plagued her.

Then she sat down and cried and cried.

Two gates the silent house of Sleep adorn:
Of polished ivory this, that of transparent horn:
True visions through transparent horn arise;
Through polished ivory pass deluding lies.
—Virgil, *Aeneid, VI*

Chapter Two

At daybreak Talon Clay rolled out his blankets, built a fire, then made coffee. As he leaned back against his fine California saddle of hand-tooled leather and sipped the hot brew, only the vaguest sort of plan formed in his mind. He had been relieved of the border command for the time being, so he had plenty of time to go fetch his wife and child back to Sundance Ranch, where they belonged. From now on his actions depended much upon the actions of Willow and the boy.

The Ranger stared away at the hills, remembering so much, worried, uncertain, wondering again about Willow's words. What did she have in mind? Why had she been hiding out with the child? Why had she left him in the first place? Before she had run away they had had a difficult conversation; now, he recalled it.

"What are you thinking of, Willow?" he'd asked. "You're always so silent. You seem so bitter sometimes, as if you resent something I've done. It couldn't be my past; we have that all resolved. Is it my being a Ranger that bothers you? I can never understand what's in your mind because you won't talk to me."

"I'll talk to you, Talon. Just when I thought you'd begun to love with your heart, it's only your body that speaks again."

"Isn't it normal for a man to lust after his beautiful wife?"

"When you love me with your heart, Talon Clay, then you'll know there's nothing left for me to want."

"You said that before. Haven't I proved over and over that I love you, Willow?"

"Yes, but now it's different again. *You* are different again. *It's* happening all over again."

Then she had walked away and he hadn't seen her for over four years! He had been so angry he had not even gone to look for her.

It's happening all over again. It.

Just what in blazes had she meant by that? He had not only been beaten, he had been made to look ridiculous. Willow had run away pregnant, given birth to their son, and then hid him away for four years! *Blast it,* he would have appeared even more ridiculous had the family known of her pregnancy!

Talon stood, saddled Cloud again, sheathed his .44 Winchester rifle and holstered his Colt .44 pistols. In the past four years he had put Willow out of his mind, fought rustlers and Comanches, Apaches, Sioux, and Blackfeet. He wouldn't fight the Kiowas, they were his friends; their blood flowed in his veins. Now he had nothing to show for it but a few scars here and there and memories of hunger, thirst, cold, hard winters and dry range and long, dusty chases into canyons after Mexican bandits. All it had brought him was trouble, hard riding, little pay, and a sore butt. He had become a Ranger, still was, but his decision was made: By God, he was going to *ride* for himself and *fight* for himself *and* his family.

He wanted peace, and seeking it he had come to find his own war, within a land at war, brothers against brothers—and now it was going to be man against woman. It would have to be a deeply painful confrontation. Nothing had ever been peaceful between him and Willow.

As a Ranger, he already saw himself as a conqueror. Problem was, he was usually lucky at cards, and everyone knew what that meant!

Willow was tired and her body was sore from hard riding. The night was very still. There was the sound of a night bird but all else was quiet. Another day without Michael would soon be dawning. The sheriff and his deputies were still out searching, but Willow had the awful, sinking feeling that they would not return with him on one of their saddles.

She could not sleep. She could not eat. Her energy was depleted. The sheriff had arrived at her house right after she had returned, following a futile search with Sammy, combing the area and the outskirts until they had been ready to drop. Dealing with all the routine questions had drained her. The sheriff thought it was unlikely that Ranger Brandon had kidnapped his own child; *however,* he had added, *not entirely impossible.* These things did happen upon occasion, he had said, patting her hand to comfort her and she had only looked back at the sheriff with miserably blank eyes.

Wandering restlessly outside, Willow stood under the Texas stars and moonlight. It was a magical summer night, shimmering beneath the high moon, shadows moving languidly as tree branches swayed. She hugged herself, tears smarting, so afraid and sick that Michael, her baby, was lying dead and cold somewhere. If not dead, then crying, lonely, afraid ... so afraid without his Mommy. And whoever had him, was he being treated badly? Gently? ... *What?* her mind screamed. Was he hungry? Would he even eat, or was he crying his heart out, looking at his abductors with huge green eyes, shivering like a little leaf? Her baby, *her baby,* how she feared for him. It was a twisting ache inside, as if her body consumed itself in huge chunks of rage and loneliness.

And Talon Clay, she was missing him now, too. But he had shattered her contentment. Just when she had begun to believe they could build a life together, he would come along and destroy all her hope. All those women! She should have known better, that there would come another, and yet another, and Garnet's ghost evermore between them. She and Talon Clay had always been strangers at heart. Nothing real or lasting had come from their marriage.... No, she was lying to herself now. She had Michael Angelo; he was their sum and substance in this marriage ... soon to be a divorce. His last name was Brandon. Just like Ashe and Talon Clay, he would be a Brandon man some day. Could she ever forget *that?*

Divorce. How could she think of a release from matrimony at this time? And Talon should be contacted ... she should send him a telegram. *Huh!* If she could find him. He moved like heat lightning, and Sammy had caught up only because he'd been trailing Talon for days upon days, watching and waiting secretly until

Talon took a room. Sammy could hardly walk up to his campfire and deliver her message, could he? No! Talon would capture Sammy in a flash, and no telling what Talon would do to her brother; she did not know Talon Clay any longer, did not know what he was capable of now. For all she knew, he had gone back to being an outlaw. . . . No, Sammy had stated that Talon Clay was pure Texas Ranger.

Willow thought back to a gentle morning in springtime and an elusive butterfly that had flitted past her shoulder. And then . . . he was standing there, in Sundance yard, across from her, undeniably rugged, unbelievably handsome, virile, everything a young man should be to make a girl's heart flutter. She was in love instantly. Talon Clay's deep drawl and his hair, not quite as long as hers, but it had swung forward to brush his shoulders and he'd shown her a white grin in a sunbrowned face. He'd said he was just "passing through." Then he had disappeared, this young man with the dusty clothes and low-slung hat, gone like the mist, her handsome, rugged stranger. She had hated to think he might be an outlaw as he'd led a horse from concealment and, in one fluidly skillful motion, hopped aboard the buckskin's back, then vanished into the dark camouflage of trees.

In love . . . what had it meant? Eager, magical, innocent, paradise. The whole world had been new for her, just by staring into a pair of green eyes. Was *in love,* she wondered now, the same as caring, sharing, and sticking together through thick and thin? In love, she believed now, was *In trouble.* Had she become cynical since then? How many times could a man break a woman's heart before she had to say: This is it, you are no going to keep putting me through hell; it is finished, over, take your ghosts somewhere else ...

"What are you doing here on Sundance property?" she had asked. Talon Clay Brandon. A *Brandon* man? How could she have known that back then? He had been hiding from the law at that time, had avoided her question. She had stood, shaking like a windswept leaf, and her heart had pounded like an Indian drum. After that—he and three other partners in crime had been hiding a stolen safe that day back at Clem's bunkhouse. It had not taken her long to figure out that Talon Clay Brandon was an outlaw.

Willow gazed at the stars, a flood of memories keeping her rooted to the spot; worst of all was the thought of Talon Clay and her mother. He had been in love with Garnet—in love—a carnal love, possessive, unaware, and uncaring of who got hurt. That had been before her father had brought Tanya, Sammy, and herself to Sundance, only to find that his wife, Garnet, who had come to work for the Brandons, had already passed away. Willow did not remember her mother; she had been too young when Garnet had abandoned them in California. Talon had been a young teen when Garnet had seduced him while his own father, Pete Brandon, had been "looking the other way." Her own mother, Garnet, worldly and cheap, had stolen his heart and put the lad in the cruel bondage of lust. A loose-moraled woman who had seduced not only Pete Brandon into marriage but his two sons, Ashe and Talon Clay, into a world of jealousy, opposition, bewilderment, and hatred. They had learned all that from one beautiful, wicked woman. And had Talon Clay been lying, in his heart, when he told Willow she had "healed" him and wiped away the memory of Garnet completely? Then why, if he was so "well," had he been chasing Hester Tucker around in the woods again?!

Her own mother . . . she had to compete with her own mother's ghost for Talon's love! Just the thought had driven both her and Tanya almost crazy, and then they'd had to strive to wipe the woman's memory from their minds and hearts. Ashe and Talon were men, handsome, virile men, with damaged emotions. It was a tragic drama, and a woman had to struggle forevermore to keep such a male healthy and happy. Especially when it was her own immoral mother who had done the injurious seducing in the first place!

Now, still under the stars, feeling a little disoriented, Willow sat on a bench, holding her head in her hands. Before they had become man and wife—long before— Willow had tried to get Talon to notice her. Oh sure, he'd noticed her, but *not* in the way she desired. She had yearned for his touch and had not understood what kept him from coming close. Then she had learned Talon was in love with a woman named Garnet. . . . *Well,* at that time she had not known it was her "deceased mother" because no one had ever informed her of her mother's name, certainly not her father; he'd never wanted to speak *her* name. Or had he, and she was not listening at the time? Too busy? The name *Garnet* did not ring a bell in her memory.

Willow had found the rubied yellow dress—Garnet's dress—and worn it in order to seduce Talon Clay. But he could not even see *her* for imagining he was seeing Garnet all over again. In the little house at Sundance he had tried to make love to Willow, believing in his dazed state, early in the morning gloom, that she was Garnet.

39

At first she would have let him, but she was so afraid when he became rough and he was not the Talon that she knew. She had always thought she would be able to go through with it, but when the time came she was scared, even as the passion between them gathered a compelling power of its own.

She had told Tanya her feelings: "It was lust that frightened you, Willow," Tanya had begun. "Not love. True love is never frightening. Lust steals from a person. Love gives. You both want to give and give to each other, with all your heart, soul, *and*—body." And Willow had confessed to Tanya, "I—I wanted him to desire me and I thought I could get to him if—if I looked like Garnet." Maybe it was Willow for whom Talon had been waiting all his life, not Garnet, the cheap worldly woman who had gone after every man she could get her hands on. Tanya had confessed her shame that her mother had been like that, but that had been Garnet's carnal way.

It had become time to reveal the story to Willow. Tanya had admitted that she should have told Willow months earlier, when she had first discovered the truth herself. "Willow," Tanya began as she had picked up Willow's dainty hand, threading her fingers through her sister's. "Garnet was . . . she was," she raced on, "she was our mother!" Willow had reacted violently, not wanting to hear the truth. But she knew how closely she resembled the woman in the locket, in coloring and facial features, and that everyone, especially Talon, thought so, too.

"Tanya," Willow had replied slowly, "how is it that Garnet came to live here at Sundance before Pa and us kids? And how was it that we were not here with her?

40

Why did she go away and leave us when Sammy and I were so small? I'm nineteen now, so I must have been very young when Garnet up and left us with Pa in California." Tanya hadn't had all the answers, but maybe their father, Rob Hayes, had been trying to find Garnet, because the woman did live at Sundance before they—Tanya, Willow, and Sammy had come along. Garnet had married Pete Brandon on the heel of Martha Brandon's burial—the woman who had been Talon and Ashe's mother—and Garnet had been the Hayes' children's real mother. Sad, but true.

Willow remembered being suddenly afraid that Talon would kill her, that was how much he had come to hate Garnet Brandon, née Haywood; Haywood was Garnet's maiden name or one she'd taken to further the falsehoods of her wicked and corrupt life. Then Tanya had promised Willow that she would not let Talon in on their secret. Willow was going away and there wasn't a thing Tanya or anyone else at Sundance could do about it. That had been the first time Willow had run away from the only home she'd ever known. The California town of her childhood had been her first home, the name she could not recall. All she remembered was that the temperature had soared very high, the town lingering in her mind as dry, gray, and weathered, like a ghost town.

California, Willow thought now, seemed so far away. *California* . . . why did it stick in her mind? Garnet was dead and buried, so she could not have had anything to do with the kidnapping of her son. And their enemy, Carl Tucker, was dead. That left only Talon and, though the sheriff had his doubts, Willow was beginning to believe it was just what Talon would do: kidnap her son.

Suddenly Willow came to her feet, hurrying into the house to fetch her clothes and boots. Out of her pigskin trunk she lifted a white shirt and rust and red skirt, shaking the wrinkles out. She proceeded to dress, splashing some cold water onto her face at the wash-stand. The laced bodice of the loose-fitting white shirt crisscrossed in a vee down to her breasts, its length spilling onto a wide-hemmed Mexican-style skirt. Choosing a pair of turquoise earrings, she put them in her pierced ears. After pulling on her old soft boots, she tucked a small handgun into the deep, double-placket pocket of her skirt. She looked at her knife lying on the table, deciding to bring that with her, too. Of late she had become careless, because in the past she had never forgotten to bring along the Toledo steel blade Little Coyote had given her; it was an old Indian war relic.

Willow spun to face herself in the mirror, gun in hand, straightening her arm to shoot. She grinned, then relaxed her weapon.

"C'mon, Ranger," she said with a swagger, "I'll fight ya. Do you want it right between the eyes—or the legs?" She blinked. "The legs? Well then, seein' as that's where you're gonna take it, I'll hafta tell ya there ain't gonna be no more diddling with the gals. And you better hand over my son . . . else yer gonna get it at both ends. You'll be a blind lover-boy what can't do nothin', not even pee from that thing with its hat missin'."

She could just see Talon Clay, standing with his son tucked behind him—big blond Ranger, dangerous and proud, hands on hips, guns slung low. Willow grew pensive at the handsome image, drawing her tawny brows together in a fierce frown.

The sun was just rising above the town as Willow

42

made a fervent vow: No man, not even her husband, was going to drag her son around, not into gambling dens, not into whorehouses, not even back to Sundance. No sir, *not without her!*

It was high noon, hot and still in the afternoon sun. The Ranger paused at the edge of town, then rode into the dusty streets of Bountiful. He wondered if this was just a wild goose chase, with Sammy in on it with Willow. Better not be, he thought, but then again, he'd always thought Sammy had looked up to him and Ashe, even when he himself had been a desperado. Sammy was all right, and some day he'd make a good Ranger ... that is, if any Rangers existed after this war got going. And he believed it would be a hot one. Just like this summer day. Hot. He felt feverish and excited just thinking of seeing Willow very soon now. His wife. He just hoped Sammy's words rang true, that Willow was eager to see him, even though she wouldn't admit it. How was she going to react when she saw him walk into her life again? And would she still want that divorce? She had a surprise coming on that reckoning.

Willow saw the Ranger coming. She was tired and dusty, having ridden far, joining with the deputies in search of her lost son. The deputies had returned to the sheriff's and she was just about to remove the saddle from her mount's sweaty back. Heart pounding, she looked around. Where was Sammy? He had not joined them—or if he had, she just hadn't noticed, because she

43

had been in a daze wondering if she might find Michael dead somewhere in the tangle of mesquite.

Sliding off the saddle-blanket, keeping her eyes glued to the Ranger who rode by, tall in the saddle, Willow hurried and then rushed into the house. "Juanita! Where are you? Juanita!" Rounding a corner, she bumped into the young woman. "Oh, Juanita! Talon Clay is here . . . Ranger . . . he's here—" She gulped and slapped her forehead. "I am going to faint, Juanita. I am, I just know . . . I am."

"You will not faint, Margarita. Here, I will get a cloth—" She spun back to the washbasin—"I will wet it first."

"Juanita, stop sounding so nervous . . . you're making me feel nervous, too." Willow's stomach rolled so much it felt like a tumbleweed. "I don't need it . . . I never faint, I told you, Juanita."

"She always faints," the deep voice drawled from the kitchen doorway.

Juanita and Willow gasped, both standing stock-still as the Ranger swaggered into the room. Juanita had never seen such a tall, fair man, such a loose-hipped walk—except on Chaco, a Mexican bandit her brother knew—and her eyes widened further; they flew to Willow with the question: *This is your husband? aiy, aiy, aiy!*

Juanita drifted to Willow in a trance; Willow snatched the damp cloth and swiped it across her brow. When Talon Clay finished his brief search of the room, the pantry, and the hall, he returned to the kitchen and his former laconic stance at the doorway.

"Where is he?" Talon looked Willow up and down.

"Where's my son? I've ridden far to see him." He didn't say anything about her.

Juanita and Willow exchanged glances, then Willow licked her lips, saying, "He's not here." She shrugged, looking up at Talon and feeling like butter melting under intense heat. "Michael is . . . gone." After a long silence, she went on quickly, "I know you don't believe me . . . but he's gone . . . *he really is.*"

With a curl of his mouth, Talon muttered, "That so. Think I'll just have a look around, if you don't mind." Squinting under his black hat slouched low, he shot a look to Juanita, who instantly shrank back at the threat in his green eyes. "You wouldn't want to save me the time, would you, Juanita, and just tell me where the boy is?"

"I d-don't know." Juanita stammered, her heart astir. "I really don't know. Like Willow said—he's gone."

"You look as dumbfounded as your friend there with the pussywillow eyes." Walking to the curtain, he let it drop and disappeared behind it.

His old name for her! Willow blew at her hand, fanning her face as briskly as possible to get some circulation going . . . so she wouldn't pass out, then have him walk back in and catch her foolish feminine weakness. No sir, she wasn't letting Talon see he turned her into jelly. All she had to do was get used to his presence, then she would stand up to him. And he'd be gone soon . . . wouldn't he? Funny, she was all tingly and aglow inside. Was this the way he used to make her feel?

"Of course," she said aloud, her hair swirling and shimmering about her shoulders as she turned, "he's a Ranger, and he's busy. Uh-uh, he won't be able to stay long."

"Margarita, you are shaking your head with much vigor and—who are you talking to?"

"Who?—" Willow's voice was oddly strained—"Oh, I was just assuring myself, that's all. Juanita, have no worry—he won't stay. . . . Shhh, I hear someone coming."

His voice again. Yes, he was coming into the room. "I see you have an extra room or two." He nodded to Juanita, sliding his gaze briefly over Willow. "I'll be taking the front one." He winked at Juanita. "I like the view."

Lecher! *Damn lecher!* Willow folded her arms and tossed one bent leg upon the other after Talon had walked out.

Juanita stood there, looking as if she were the one in need of that wet cloth. *Aiy, aiy, aiy. Mucho macho!* That was one lean and mean Texan!

Nice comfortable house for a schoolteacher's wages, Talon thought as he returned to the room upstairs after fetching his bags from the porch. He had stabled his horse and come back, only to find Willow and the Mexican woman gone. He examined his surroundings, pushing the cream lace curtains aside to look below, then walking slowly around the big bedroom. Opening a drawer, he pulled out a book that looked to be a journal of some sort. He sat on the edge of the bed, leafing through the pages—and his heart went still.

Willow's perfect schoolteacher's handwriting. Her book, a personal accounting, a diary of some sort. As a Ranger, he was inquisitive about everything. As a husband whose wife had cruelly abandoned him, he was thoroughly interested in the contents. Leaning back on the bed, one hand supporting his head, he leafed through it, going back, back to four years ago when she'd left him. The words leaped out at him: *Sometimes I wish Talon Clay had never come into my life.*

For a long moment he stared, a profound sorrow weighing him down, and he felt a squeezing hurt around his heart before he tossed the book into the drawer and slammed it shut. Suddenly he felt very tired. It had been a long ride . . .

A knock came at the door just as he was drifting off and he shot off the bed, automatically reaching for his pistol. The door creaked open and there stood Willow. He looked directly at her, whirling back in time and comparing her with the lovely girl he had first met eight years ago. She was definitely a woman now, with fuller breasts, shapelier hips and thighs. The woman in his recurring dream. Willow, the woman. Willow, his wife. He thought "Lover," then brushed the thought aside, then snatching it back, like leaves swept back and forth by a changeable wind.

"Talon, we must talk." She entered and closed the door behind her. "I need your help . . . Michael is gone. You must believe me when I say that."

Holstering his pistol, Talon looked up and faced her squarely. "Willow, I want to see my son. Where have you hidden him?" His eyes narrowed dangerously. "Quit what you're doing, Willow, and bring him to me, or else it's going to get nasty between us. You want a divorce? Granted, but we'll talk about that later—"

"Stop!" Willow shouted, coming closer. "I know

47

what you're up to, Talon, and it won't work. You took him, right? I think it is you who are playing games with me. But you will not come out the winner. I want him back and you better tell me where you had him taken, Talon Clay!"

Talon snorted as a cord of anger tightened in his neck. "Get your haughty chin out of the air, Willow. We don't play games anymore; we're grownups now."

"Oh?" She sashayed into the room, her Mexican skirts swirling colorfully. "Is that what we used to do—play games? That's right, Talon, all it was to you was fun and games. You always did twist everything around ... *didn't* you?"

His green eyes darkened. "Let's not argue, not again. I just want to see my son and then I'll be on my way."

"You are always *on your way,* Talon Clay Brandon. You never settled down long enough for us to be a family ... no, the other women always came first." She tossed her head, making her earrings jiggle. He stared for a moment, mesmerized.

"You left me, woman, not the other way around. And you took my baby in you when you went. Now you want to keep him from me." Eyes flashing, he glared at her. "Then again, maybe there was no baby at all, and Sammy was just trying to get us back together and you're the instigator—"

"That's not so, Talon Clay ... I would not have you back if you were the last man in Texas!"

"Hey, listen to you! You're supposed to be the perfect Christian lady and prim-and-proper schoolteacher. What's this all about, Willow? You want a divorce? I told you—you can have it. Just let me see my son and I'll be on my way—as I said." He stared at her as she

48

went still. "You're more beautiful than ever, you know that? Especially when you're spitfire angry."

There it was: he mentioned divorce. "We're not getting anywhere. You—again you called me fat and dowdy in that letter you sent to me."

"What letter, Willow? I never sent you a letter saying cruel things." When she pretended to look confused, he went on, "You're hiding from the truth, Willow."

"What do you mean?"

"I never did call you those names. You've always been slim and lovely. Just look at you. The truth is—" He thought for a moment, looking away from her, then he sent his gaze back. "The truth is . . . what is the truth, Willow? You're hiding it, not me."

"Women."

"Women?" He shook his head. "That again?"

She would not mention Hester Tucker—that was the ace she was saving for later. She added, "And ghosts."

"Ah—one ghost, you mean."

"I don't want to talk about my mother again. Not ever. She's dead and buried . . . but not in your mind and heart, Talon Clay." She paused. "You don't feel as if she's dead, do you?"

"At times." He sighed deeply. "Especially now, when you look like her. More than ever, I feel she's still walking this earth and doing her evil—through you."

"You didn't care if I was dead or alive."

"What do you expect? You up and leave, you abandon me, and I'm supposed to jump on my horse and come looking for you? That's a bit difficult when you hide yourself better than the worst desperado in Texas."

For a moment Willow saw the old Talon, the laughing, gentle, outlaw-turned-mustanger who had told her wild, funny stories and discussed horses with her, making her feel happy and carefree. She had seen him change twice now, this quicksilver man, who had been a savage-looking Indian a little over six years ago. Now he had become a Texas Ranger—ruthless and dangerous. Once again, she decided he was utterly incapable of compassion or mercy. He had shown neither when he forced her to become his bride at Black Fox's Kiowa Indian camp. And now he had arrived so unexpectedly, throwing her emotions into turmoil once again.

The Ranger relived the feel of Willow in his arms and knew again the passionate desire she could rekindle. Just looking at her, oh Lord, yes, how he could remember, and feel as if he were already holding her. He wanted her badly, he confessed to himself. She was the only woman who had ever made him experience such confusing emotions; even her mother had not had this devastating effect on his heart and senses.

His gaze mocking, Talon scoffed sarcastically, "What do you say now, Willow? Sticking to the same story?" He looked at her as if searching out the secrets of her soul.

Shaking all over, fighting to escape this precarious situation, Willow retorted, "I'm serious, Talon. Michael is gone. If you don't believe me, just go and see the sheriff—he'll tell you we've been searching for Michael for two days now. Sammy is still out there right now, and I'm not sure he has slept a wink. None of us has had much sleep—"

"Why, after four years, did you tell me about the boy with green eyes, Willow? Why, if you will not allow me to see him, my own son? Were you feeling guilty about hiding him from me for so long? And why mention divorce? Did you really want me to serve you papers? You wanted me to find you, so why hold out now, Willow?"

"What?" Willow frowned up at him. "I never asked you for a divorce in that letter."

"Oh, come on now, Willow. What do you think we've been talking about all this—"

Just then a banging on the door interrupted them. It was Sammy, and Willow let him in. She swung her gaze back to the irresistibly handsome Ranger, then turned back to her brother. "Tell him, Sammy. He doesn't believe that Michael is gone. He has this crazy idea I'm hiding him now that he's come to take him away."

Talon's mouth dropped as his gaze took in her angry expression. "Take him—" He never finished because Sammy stepped forward and put an end to their angry repetitions.

"Believe it, Talon. He's gone all right—and it was a *woman* who took him!"

I won't; I can't; I better not. Willow told herself she would not faint in front of Talon as she habitually did in the past.

And thank God she didn't this time!

Even in laughter the heart is sorrowful.
Proverbs 14:13

Chapter Three

"Now do you believe me?" Willow almost shouted at Talon. Still he did not react, only waited to hear more. Talon Clay had not changed; she could not believe it. Everything in her world seemed so different, but he was the same. He was an experienced Ranger now, but he, the man, was the same—his arrogant assurance, his deep male voice, his blond hair, his almost-perfect features, his long eyelashes. Her eyes widened even as he watched. What Sammy had said struck her tardily, and she whipped around, blinking. "What, Sammy? You said a *woman* took Michael?"

"Yeah, the sheriff said so. A little girl was playing down the road and told the sheriff she saw a woman riding out of town with a child strugglin' an' cryin'. She couldn't tell if it was a girl or a boy, 'cause she said there was a shawl over the kid's head. I just went to see the sheriff after searching the outer areas for Mikey to see if I could find some clues."

"Mikey?" Talon queried, looking confused.

Willow's head snapped up. "That's your son, Talon."

"My son." Talon looked at Willow as if begging an

apology from her, but she remained cold and stiff. *"Our son,"* he added.

"Michael Angelo Brandon," Willow put in. "And as it turns out—" she went on, sniffing a little sadly—"he loves to draw and paint pictures—especially in flour dust."

"In what?" Talon's eyes met Willow's for a moment, and then she looked away as if she were suddenly embarrassed.

Willow looked down at the ground and then back up at Talon. "Never mind that for now. You have to talk to this little girl who witnessed the kidnapping, or else get an accounting from the sheriff."

The Ranger was all business now. "I have to get a description of Mikey—I mean, Michael."

Juanita entered the room just then. "He's four years old—" She held her hand up from the floor at Michael's height. "And has beautiful green eyes just like his Papa—" A dog barked and bounded into the room. "And this is Angelo's best friend!"

Looking at the huge dog and feeling an unmistakable mist start in his eyes, Talon said, "Right," then snatched up his clothes and weapons, putting them on as he raced out the door.

"Where you goin'?" Sammy called after the Ranger.

"Where do you think?" Talon snapped, slamming his .44 into the holster at his hip. "The sheriff's office, where else?"

Jorge barked and bounded after Talon. "No!" Willow shouted after the dog. "Come, Jorge!"

The huge, shaggy dog disobediently raced off, running up to the Ranger and sitting immediately when the tall man suddenly halted. "Good boy," Talon said, scratching the dog beneath a floppy ear. "You want to come?" Jorge barked. "Must see something of the boy in the old man, huh?" Talon asked and Jorge whined restlessly. "Let's go then, and find out what happened to your pal."

Juanita looked at Willow, who looked at Sammy. All three shrugged as the unlikely pair—Jorge and Ranger—walked out the door and sauntered down the street together at a brisk pace.

Shaking the dust from her feet, Willow ran in her stockinged feet to find her boots. "Wait up, sis," Sammy called after her, very importantly snapping up the rifle he'd left standing near the front door. "We'll find him now," Sammy assured Willow as he walked beside her to the sheriff's office. "Yup, now that there's a Ranger in town, there ain't no need to fret, sis."

Willow wished she felt as much confidence in the Ranger as her brother did. Maybe it would take time, that's all. All of a sudden Willow stopped in her tracks. "Sammy, I can't go to the sheriff's ... you and the Ranger go."

Sammy nodded, waiting.

Thoroughly unsettled, Willow sniffed, searching in her pocket for a hanky. "I have ... suddenly I have this terrible urge to cry ... *Ohhhhh!*" Willow ran back to her room as Sammy stood there snorting, "Women! Why do they always have to cry when the goin' gets tough." Then he shrugged, muttering aloud, "Guess I'd cry too if I lost a kid and my husband—or wife—shows up after four years!"

* * *

It was close to suppertime when Sheriff Somers looked up just as the Texas Ranger walked in. Hot food was ready and fresh coffee was being brought in from the back room by the lean-faced deputy, who also saw the Ranger. The sheriff walked around his desk and shook hands with Talon briefly.

"Ranger Brandon, I've been expecting you."

"News travels fast," Talon answered, eyeing the meal as the deputy set it down. Then he looked at the sheriff and smiled, wondering how the man could eat that much for supper and still appear so trim in the waist and stomach.

Frank Somers was a big, handsome, neatly-dressed man with a certain amount of polish and an easy way with folks. He was perceptive, and saw before him a tall, wiry, fair-haired Ranger with catlike movements and the light of intelligence and alertness in his eyes. Unusual eyes, the sheriff thought, green and sharp, seeing right through a man. "Let's get down to business, Ranger Brandon. Oh—" he said, looking down at his food, "want a plate? We've got plenty. Man needs to eat to keep strong in desperate situations." When the Ranger declined, the sheriff took a few bites, then pushed the plate away and picked up his napkin. "We've been searching for your son," he said, "with no luck." He ended with a deep-felt sigh, tossing his used napkin aside.

"How do you know he's *my* son?" Talon Clay asked.

"Sammy Hayes, of course." Sheriff Somers chuckled. "That boy's known around these parts as a sharp-witted kid who can travel as fast as a Texas Ranger. Wants to be one, you know." He saw the Ranger nod, unaware that Talon knew Sammy's character almost better than

56

anyone else. "Sammy's also Texas's biggest little gossip."

His gaze easing over to the entrance, Talon lowered his voice. "He's right outside the door with Big Jorge, so I wouldn't say that too loud, Sheriff." He heard the man chuckle again. "Now, about my son, I'm really eager to get looking for him. Tell me what you know, what the little girl said, and anything else that might be of significant help to me."

After Talon got the information, he returned to Willow's house and ordered her to stay put. "I mean it, Willow. Searching beyond this town and outlying areas is too dangerous for a woman. After talking with the sheriff I believe Michael is far from here by now. Seems to be a fact that he was indeed kidnapped by a woman," he added tersely.

Staring at the lean Ranger, her voice tight, she asked, "How can you believe a mere child?" Turning away, she flung her arm up against the wall and leaned her forehead on her wrist. "And what do you mean, *for a woman?*" She spun about to face him as he sat quietly at the kitchen table fortifying his strength before going out to search. "A woman can do anything a man can . . . why, just look, it was a woman who took Michael!"

"You're not going. And that's that." Talon dished up the meat, bread, and beans, then sat sipping his coffee, squinting at the heat of Juanita's strong brew.

Willow gave Talon a startled look. "You can't tell me what to do."

"I just did."

Barely controlling her temper, Willow hissed, "I'm

not going to sit by while you go and look for Michael!" She would need a bigger and better gun, she reminded herself as Juanita brought more food for the Ranger and Sammy.

"Yes, Willow, you are." Talon chewed a piece of bread, swallowed, then looked up at her as she resumed her pacing.

"No, damn it, *no!*" Her resentment and fury increased as she ran from the kitchen up the stairs to get ready. She stopped and looked down at herself. She almost laughed at what she was doing. "I'm already ready," she said, slumping against the wall. "Oh, God," she prayed softly, "please help. I just don't know which way to turn anymore . . . and Talon here . . . I just have to leave it in your hands, dear Lord. I must find my son."

Juanita stared at the beguiling Ranger as he rose slowly from the table to follow Willow up the stairs. A cord of anger tightened in Talon's neck even as he felt an ache deep down inside, an ache for the son he had never seen.

"You don't have to worry about my following you," Willow lied as Talon came up the stairs toward her, "because I won't!"

Halting halfway up, Talon frowned, wondering about those words and how much truth was in them. Willow rolled on her left hip and stayed there, her palms resting on the wall as she studied Talon where he stood below. Shaking his head, he advanced on her; Willow backed up at the look on Talon Clay's ruggedly handsome face. There was something different in his expression, something frightening to look upon. He kept coming. Now he was standing too close for comfort.

Talon was silent. Willow, who was trying to quiet the turmoil within her, let the silence go on.

"Don't worry, Pussywillow," he said, his voice abruptly softer as he touched her cheek. "I'll find Michael for you." *For you,* not for us, he'd said. He watched as she slid her eyes to peek at him. "Willow." Talon gazed back at her, pleasurably envisioning her riding with him across the wildness and beauty of the Texas landscape, sharing meals, streams, and bedrolls. He shook his head—she couldn't come with him. Her life must not be placed in danger along with her son's . . . *their* son's.

"Why do you say my name and then shake your head?" Willow asked and wondered at the faraway look in his eyes. She could almost see the play of the velvet blue skies and endless grasslands, hills, cottonwoods, the rugged beauty of Sundance . . . in their poignant sparkle.

Years back . . . Talon was traversing a path in his mind, recalling the look in Hester Tucker's eyes when he had walked with her in the woods and Willow had known, had seen, them set out. Why did Hester come to mind just then? Her lips had pressed ungently against his, and at that moment he had envisioned a pair of haunting pussywillow eyes. He had wanted to tear Willow from his heart, had gone deeper into the woods with Hester, ordering her to take her clothes off . . .

"Talon, what's wrong with you?" Willow was straightening away from the wall to shake Talon's shoulders. "Why are you looking at me like that?" She shrank back from the wild look in his eyes.

As Talon Clay had waited for Hester's answer, he thought of the way Willow had kissed him earlier and pressed herself cautiously, innocently against him, and his loins tightened now as they had then. Willow had wanted him, and he had sent her away. He had looked at Hester in a new light, clenching his jaw, looking right through the "easy" woman before him and envisioning the one he wanted more than anything he'd ever wanted in his life. Not Hester, but Willow. He wanted to fill Willow with pleasure, until she screamed out her love for him. Hester had thought he'd meant herself, when he had mentioned the word "love" out loud while daydreaming of Willow. The empty-headed blonde had been stupid, silly, and Talon had turned and walked away from Hester leaving her alone in the woods.

Talon shook the memory of Hester from his mind and, moving as quickly as possible, he had Willow trapped in an instant. Pressed as she was, she could not find an avenue of escape.

"Willow." The Ranger splayed his hands on the wall above her, pressing his body close. "It's been so long . . . you're my wife. . . . But why, why did you run away, for God's sake?" His eyes had hardened.

"Talon," Willow begged, trying to move the solid rock of a man. "We have a child to search for . . . *don't*, Talon, you're making me feel shaky . . . just like you always did." She twisted about but only came up harder against the Ranger's body. "Talon, Talon . . ." Her mouth was close to his, their breaths hotly mingling. "We can't . . . not—"

"Not now—" Talon shook his head, saying quickly, softly, gently—"I know, Willow, I know. I'm pushing it. I do that a lot when I see you."

"You haven't seen me in . . . so . . . long."

Bodies pressed close, even for a few seconds, and

Talon's face contorted with pain and Willow's vision blurred. This man and wife were painfully aware of each other. It was a live thing between them. In silent communication, they stared. Talon Clay's mouth curved into a sad half-smile, the rest of his face rigid, his muscles tense.

"You're shivering again," Talon said as he pushed a little against her, wanting to kiss, nibble, inhale her sweetness, caress and enter the enticing realm of her womanly paradise to spiral up and down, becoming mindlessly lost in the exploding heat of mutual ecstasy.

To her, his voice sounded like a tremendous roar in her head, a sensuous shaking, a muddling. She answered, "I know. As I said, you always make me shaky." Just as quickly as it had come over her, the spurt of desire vanished.

Pushing back from her, Talon said disjointedly, "I . . . have to go . . . *now*—" He cleared his throat. "Willow, you stay put, you hear?" He held her chin in a pinch, then let go. "You better listen," he said over his shoulder, "else I'll bare your ass and give you a lickin' you'll never forget, woman." For a moment she grinned like the mischievous Willow of old. "I mean it. I'll be sending telegrams and you better be here."

He was going. Already!

Willow ran after him, catching up with him in the yard where Juanita was patting the dog on the head, holding him on a leash. "Jorge is not going with you." Willow took him from Juanita and held the huge dog back as Jorge barked, trying to get to the Ranger. Then she tied him in the yard and Talon watched as she gazed up at him with her all-fired woman's stubbornness defying him outright. How could he fight that look? He sighed heavily and mounted Cloud.

"Wish me luck, Willow." He spun his white horse around; then, after a half-circle in which he'd tipped his black hat intrepidly, he was away just as Sammy was mounting up in the shadows while nobody watched.

"Luck ..." Willow called out, but by now the thundering hooves had drowned out her one little word uttered too softly in the first place.

She frowned worriedly as Talon rode out of her life once again. But then—he hadn't asked her to promise that she'd stay put, right? Right!

It was seven o'clock by the time Sammy caught up with the Ranger. Up ahead in the dusty road, Sammy was languidly mounted on his horse, arms folded over the horn of his saddle, grinning like the freckle-faced imp Talon had always remembered.

Halting Cloud in the bend of a creek among some rocks, the Ranger sighed and slowly asked, "What are you doing up there, Sammy? And how'd you get ahead of me?"

"My horse's got wings—he can get out and go, lickety-brindle. I told ya I was going to be a Ranger someday." Sammy kneed his mount down the incline. "What are you doin' down here, Ranger? Come on, Talon Clay—we got to find Mikey before somethin' bad happens to him!"

"You'll be plain wore out by the time morning comes, lad. Nice and easy wins the race, didn't you know?" Talon drawled, reining his mount in another direction, away from the one he'd been traveling—north.

Sammy looked and saw the shadows lying in the folds and creases of the country, dying sunlight on cottonwood leaves and sparkling reddish on the creek bed. "Where you goin', Ranger? I wouldn't go this way; it ain't the right way, I tell ya." Sammy caught up, skirting the prickly pear, watching as the Ranger leaned over while holding his horse's mane. Among the tumbleweeds his fingers found a bright handkerchief with the initials "NL." Righting himself, he showed Sammy what he'd found.

"Yeah!" Sammy beamed. "And lookit there! You're right, Ranger, there's broken branches and tracks in the creek sand leading west. No wonder you been takin' your time, ridin' with your head sideways like you was nappin'!"

"Yup, Sammy. Never fear when a Ranger's near—" He grinned. "He'll always make it clear."

Suddenly, Sammy's hand streaked for his gun, and instantly, the Ranger moved. A grin broke on Sammy's face, and Talon said, "Very good, Sammy. But what were you trying to prove?"

Sammy's gun exploded in the next instant, causing Cloud to leap away from the deadly snake that had been about to strike at the horse's leg; Talon looked down to see the rattler's head blown clear off. "Like I said, Sammy, and I repeat—" Talon leaned across his saddle after he'd retrieved his Ranger's hat from the ground. "You and your wonder horse are very good."

"Damn right!" But Sammy did not see the grinding ache in the Ranger's eyes as they set their mounts into motion. He was hunting now, and there was no mercy in him.

* * *

Early the next morning Willow rode to the next biggest town, Paradise Valley, twenty miles this side of San
Angelo. She had asked the housekeeper not to tell
where she had gone and Juanita had promised she
wouldn't say a word to Talon Clay or anyone else. She
saw the color rise in the morning sky and felt the loneliness and pain tearing at her. It seemed that more turmoil had entered her life after she had been married.
Marriage was full of violent passion and unpredictable
emotional feelings; it made one more sensitive to life.
Sometimes she thought marriage was like war. Love and
war. They seemed to go together. Talon Clay and she
had always struggled to get along and love each other.
Little enough of happiness had come her way until Michael came along. Now her baby was gone, and the
thought of it was almost too much.

What if she had never left Talon Clay? Would Mikey
be with them still? She thought so. After seeing Hester
and Talon talking and walking together, she had warned
herself that she might not make sensible choices, and
still, she had become angry and jealous. Her judgment
had been impaired by jealousy. There was only one path
her mind insisted she take: she should have postponed
that big, dangerous move, leaving Sundance and Talon
behind. But wasn't he always leaving *her* to go traipsing
off on another adventure? Of course he had to make
money. All men had to, with whatever honest methods
were available. Now she was rambling again. She
should have stayed at Sundance; had she done that, she
would have had far less anxiety. Had she not made her

64

hasty decision to flee to another part of Texas, clearly her child would still be with his parents.

No matter, her mind was made up and she was going to search for her son!

Willow rode directly to the livery and had her horse stabled, unaware that she was being stared at by a few strangers. One took special notice of her. His black hair hung around his ears and there was a feather in the band of his hat. He wore two guns, tied down for action, and a buckskin shirt, dark from dust and sweat. His boots were run down at the heel, with jingling spurs and huge silver rowels.

Walking straight ahead, carrying her light baggage down the street to where the man at the livery said she'd find a hotel room, Willow thought of nothing but a nice, warm bath. Again she was stared at, not caring, feeling only frustration and anger eating at her insides. All humor was gone; she wondered if she'd ever smile again, ever. *Only if she saw Michael.* She checked in, then headed straight for the mercantile, walking past the land office where men leered at her.

Two men were lazing in a pair of wooden chairs outside the mercantile, tipped back, just outside the door. Inside, Willow bought a hat, .44 and holster, strips of white material, and a carpetbag which she stuffed with odds and ends of all kinds.

The storekeeper tallied up all the things she bought, his eyes racing as she quickly worked at her task. "You stuff that bag faster than some lawmen can shoot, little lady. You purchased a gun, too. You know how to use it?"

"Of course I do." First old Clem had taught her how to hold and handle a gun; then Talon had taught her how to shoot. Outside again, Willow stepped out of the way of a freight wagon as the driver hooted and whistled, seeing the lithe blonde with the huge bag slung, in an odd fashion, across her shoulder.

An hour before the usual suppertime Willow ate at an almost empty cafe, with a chatty waitress hovering, one who took Willow's mind off her troubles. Willow headed back to her hotel room, meaning to take a bath before turning in.

Just as she feared, once Willow put her head on the pillow she saw the horribly frightening images of Michael lying somewhere dying of fear and neglect, or even already dead. One of them would find Michael— herself, Talon Clay, maybe even Sammy; she knew he had followed the Ranger. Too, she knew Michael was still alive. He's not dead, her mind kept telling her, because if he was she would feel it, know it as certainly as her heart beat this very moment.

Right before falling asleep, Willow knew she was going to dream of her husband and when they had first made love in the Indian camp.

The song of the spring danced along Willow's nerve ends and the water sparkled with the new moon as, hypnotically, she walked with Talon/Lakota to the water's edge. Millions of silver stars shone in the vast bowl of the night sky. She had felt a strong sense of danger earlier, standing next to Lakota, becoming his wife. In a gentle voice he coaxed her, led her to the blanket, gazing at her for long moments as he cupped her face in his hands. His eyes had made sweet love to her before he bent his head to brush her lips tenderly, tasting the corners of her mouth. The sky and stars above spun when he cupped her buttocks, bringing her against the proof of his desire. At the water's edge, Lakota stripped down to his nakedness, and Willow choked down a gasp at the sight of his exposed maleness. At the thought of being ravished by the huge, pulsating manhood, sheer terror washed over Willow. She had protested, but he had soothed her. In the moonglow he undressed her reverently. She told him she had once wanted him as Talon Clay Brandon, but now, as a bronzed skinned savage, he terrified her. Calming her, promising not to hurt her, he told her he would be inside her before she knew it. In the middle of the bubbling spring, Lakota prepared her with his preliminary lovemaking and, afterwards, carried her to the river bank, stretching out full length. He had hurt her at first, and then went easier, caressing, kissing, stroking, tasting, until pure longing, and a warm wetness, began in the core of her. Moans and mewls tore from her throat as he tasted her between her thighs. Cries of ecstasy poured from her when he entered her at last, thrusting full length . . . and then she was climbing with him . . . with him . . .

Now, seven years later, Willow awoke from her dream, from the reality, sobbing, terribly unhappy, horribly unfulfilled. Oh Talon, Talon, my shining knight, my fair-haired Ranger, find our son, find him, Talon, find Michael for me . . . for us. She sat up suddenly, wiping at her tears. "We *will* find him, my bright Ranger. If not together, then apart; but one of us will succeed, damn it." Biting her lip, she had another, additional, thought: That same night, when they had first loved, Talon had told her something. With jarring vividness, she remembered:

"It was about a year ago I told you about all the other women I have bedded and warned you to steer clear of me. Am I right?" Talon/Lakota had said. She had responded with a small "yes" and breathlessly waited for more. He went on: "It is true that I have not had another woman since I met you ... those women were sluts, darling, and meant nothing to me. Loose-moraled women, always getting just what they were looking for. One of them got into my blood, but that's over with now. Her memory has been replaced with a love so pure and shining that nothing can ever erase it. Never."

Never? Willow wondered. What in the world had he been doing with Hester Tucker in the woods *again?* Lying back down onto her pillow, Willow thought as she stared out at the huge Texas stars: I may just find my lost son ... and the truth about "Talon's undying love." Two discoveries at once; it would be like paradise to have them both back in the circle of my love. Forever, in paradise. Paradise Creek, she thought, slowly closing her eyes, that was the name of the town she was in ... sleeping ... she hoped soundly ... soon.

She overslept. It was one o'clock by the time she walked through the sunny town and entered the saloon. She ordered a whiskey to try to calm her nerves. She was not used to hard liquor and was not in the habit of imbibing anything except a beer or lemonade on a hot summer day. She sipped slowly, trying to relax and gather her thoughts, making her plans. She had spotted a stranger from her window and would wait and see if he would come into the saloon; he might be able to help. As for the one who'd resembled a desperado, with black hair hanging down straight and a feather in the band of his hat, she had not spotted him in town since the first time.

The stranger. Willow could only think of him as Black Feather, like an Indian name, and she knew he had some of that blood. Maybe Apache, or Kiowa? she thought with a shiver. There had been a strange, somber, almost lonely expression in his eyes. The hunger in them when she had looked up suddenly and met his gaze across the dusty street! Willow flushed, remembering it, willing herself to forget.

Hester Tucker fed the horses and stood silent near the creekbed, looking around at the rocky hills and deep valleys. The sun was high, and only a few tufts of cottony cloud floated in the wide Texas sky. Her gaze went to the boy sleeping beneath a stand of scrub pine. Talon Clay's son. He's going to look like Talon, Hester was thinking. Handsome, lean, with stunning green eyes, blond hair a loose silken flow in the breeze, slim face with high cheekbones. Even when Talon gritted his white, even teeth in anger he was handsome. He had made her excited even when he swore at her all those years ago. . . . "Stupid *puta!*" he had snarled—and she had loved it. Everything about Talon Clay excited her: his smile, his anger, his arrogance, and yes, even his hatred. He had a lot of that in him.

"Ma told me your pa was a half-breed—he had Kiowa blood," she had informed Talon Clay several years ago. Her ma, Janice Tucker, knew everything about everybody. Her heart hammering away, Hester had stared at his bare, bronzed chest, but before she could mutter another word, Talon had stepped close to her again, his warm, angry breath fanning her cheeks. "You and your ma are plain loco, you know that."

Hester continued to spin back in time as she watched Michael Brandon sleep. "Talon Clay, how can you say that about Ma, when she took you in like you were her own kin?"

"Yeah. And all she ever jabbered about when I lived at Saw Grass was Sundance and what a shame it was that my own folks didn't want me there."

"They *didn't*," Hester had taunted. "At least *she—*" Hester had gotten no further because Talon Clay had clamped a hand over her mouth and snarled softly, "Don't. Don't ever say her name around me—ever. Now, you just sashay back home and tell your ma she's full of it."

When she had spun about to do exactly as he said, Talon's hand had shot out and he had grasped her by the wrist. "Ouch! You let me go, Talon Clay!"

He had taken hold of her and stared as if she had grown two heads. "Hey, you been calling my ma a whore. Martha never slept with any other man but Pete Brandon, my pa, and she certainly didn't sleep with any half-breed like you been telling me! So, you just get on home and see you don't come whoring around Sundance again! You do, and I'll round up a passel of guys that'll pump you over real good, hear?"

Frowning, Hester leaned down, picked up a stone, and sent it skidding across the water. "Damn Willow! I just bet she killed my brother after he tried to ravish her in the schoolroom." Even if Carl did, so what. Willow always had that hot look in her eyes.

Nat Lacey came up behind Hester. "This Willow we

stole the kid from, *she* killed your brother? How did she do that?"

Hester stared at another bright stone. "I don't know the whole story, Nat. Hey, those pants look mighty good on you." Hester didn't know it, but she was beginning to look and sound just like her mother, Janice Ranae Tucker. "Ma knows where to get stuff. Only thing, she never knew how to get Talon Clay for her daughter." Hester pouted and frowned.

Looking worried, Nat whined, "But you said you don't want Talon Clay any longer. All you want is revenge for your brother's death and that's why we're bringing the kid to this Garnet. I can't wait to meet her. Is she really Willow's mother? You told me that, but I can still hardly believe it, *her* mother. Ghost-town Garnet." She chuckled, tossing her blond head, her eyes huge and blue and vacant of any thought but men, especially one tall Ranger in particular, one who wore tight black pants.

"That's not her name, Nat—" Hester began in a warning tone. "And she won't like hearing you call her that. The ghost town is her hideout and her boys, the gunslingers and bounty hunters, keep it that way."

"Oh. Sorry," Nat Lacey said with a shrugging of her narrow shoulders. "How did your ma Janice Ranae find out where Garnet's hidey-hole was? Does your ma have guys working for her, too?"

Hesitantly Hester knelt and brushed the boy's hair from his cheek; she looked back up at Nat. "Like I said: Ma knows *everything*. She has her ways and I help out a lot, too, now that my brother Carl's dead. Willow had something to do with Carl's death, and I believe Talon Clay was just about to tell me how it happened . . . but then *she* came along spying on us again." Hester smirked, pulling at a yellow strand of her hair as she stood up. "Willow never let Talon Clay alone and after he moved out of our house, we never got any time to be together without 'Miss Busybody' finding out! I don't know what hold Willow has on Talon Clay, but it sure ain't love . . . at least I don't believe it is. Talon's had too many women to know what real love is."

"I wish I would've got a look at this Willow," Nat said, blowing on her cotton-buffed nails. "Then I'd know what I'm up against. No matter, I'll take him away from her, now that I seen Talon Clay. He makes my blood run hot, *oooh,* and my lashes curl at the sight of him. How could a woman ever walk away from a man like that?"

Hester looked at Nat, hating her la-de-da tone, shrewishly thinking: *I'm not telling you, you dumb witch. That's my secret.*

"Nat, I believe you're a natural at this type of work," Hester told her, "because you're already changing into the character suitable for this nasty job; you want Talon that bad. You really set your sights on Talon Clay, you'll get him." And then I'll pick up where you left off after you're dead. *"So . . .* did you make us something to eat?"

"Sure did. I'm a good cook and can build a neat campfire." Nat giggled. "Among other things."

Tossing aside a buttered roll she'd been trying to eat, Willow stared from her window, watching the town for anyone new. She wiped her mouth with a napkin. Especially that stranger, not the one with the black hair, not

72

Black Feather . . . the other one. What had happened to him, the man with the "plain Joe" looks? This was the second day she'd been here. Looking to the street below as a freight driver put on his brakes and climbed down to tie the mules, Willow did a double take, her gaze sliding back to the fellow in the brown vest. Ah . . .

There! There he was! The stranger she'd seen a few days back. He was looking for something. Or someone. Perhaps she was onto the wrong clue, yet, for some reason, she did not think so. Late in the afternoon Willow headed for the saloon once again, hoping this time to find some answers there.

Ned Thompkins stood at the bar as the young woman entered and, with the casualness of a cowpoke, ordered a whiskey. She was of medium height, face scrubbed clean without any make-up, not even lipstick. She was dressed in tight denim pants and a white cotton shirt. He thought she was striking even in her unfeminine attire. Then he spied the revolver she had tucked into a scuffed holster. Ned had a good idea she knew just how to use that gun, too.

They stood at the bar, boots hooked on the fat round rail, Willow trying to think of what to say first. Outside the sun was shining; inside it was still quiet at this time of day. Women didn't usually frequent saloons, unless they had something particular in mind.

Feeling tense, Willow sipped her drink, wondering just how to strike up a conversation with a stranger.

Ned Thompkins was a young cowpoke down on his luck, one who'd hooked up with outlaws to make some money. Years back, he had been a drifter, working at

73

different ranches, and then he had met Garnet Haywood as he wandered into a ghost town, thirsty, hungry, looking for a waterhole and possibly a can of beans. Garnet had sunk her claws into him and never let go; he did what she said and he got what he wanted: Her. Now, there was something achingly familiar about this young woman that reminded him of Garnet. He would do anything for Garnet, even though she was an older woman. What man wouldn't? She was sensuous, even if she was coarse and wicked. Garnet knew just how to seduce a man and get him to meet her demands and desires.

This one's got spirit, Ned thought. Even though she hadn't said much, just ordered a drink, he could tell how alert and healthy she was, sharp-witted and cautious, as if she was waiting for someone or something to happen. He wondered about the worried little frown between her brows.

The bartender quietly worked a white cloth in a glass until it was lickety-clean and squeakin'. Willow had no idea that Ned Thompkins was thinking the same thoughts about her . . . that she was waiting for someone or something to happen. They were just about to break the silence when a sudden stir at the swinging doors drew their attention.

"Heyyy, where's the brew, and maybe even some hot stuff to go with it?" The newcomer nudged someone on his way to the bar. "Get it, fella, *hot stuff!*" He guffawed at himself and headed toward the shimmering line of bottles lined up neatly against the mirror.

Willow and Ned Thompkins exchanged brief glances, then turned back to face the mirror.

The cowpoke stumbled up to the bar, bumping into Willow as she brought her drink up to her lips. Startled, she looked down as the liquid sloshed onto her neighbor's sleeve. Setting her glass down, Willow looked over at Ned. "Don't worry, I'll take care of this," she said, when she noted that her silent drinking companion was about to step in.

Ned's eyebrows rose an inch as he watched the proceedings.

"A bit clumsy there, ain't you?" Willow said to the drunk, waiting for an apology.

The cowboy looked at the young woman in a set of men's clothes and laughed. As he peered at her with glassy eyes, he patted her on the behind and leered while leaning back to get a better look, drawling in a deep slurred voice, "Looking for a little action ther', lady?" He said "lady" with a sneer on his lips, his arm like rubber as he drew a circle in the air.

Willow proceeded to bring the heel of her boot down on his foot so hard that the cowpoke howled in pain. Ned grinned as he jumped up and grabbed his foot with both hands and hopped around like a one-legged bird.

Ned chuckled softly. What a woman; she was just what Garnet was looking for. Not that simpleminded pair she had sent out to do a real woman's job. What was their names? Hester and Nat? *Nat?* Good name for the tall blond woman; looked just like a bug, she did. But for those pop-eyes, she was kind of sexy, in a stupid, silly sort of way. Garnet hadn't even seen Hester's partner Nat yet, but when she did, it was going to be *Adios idiot!*

Willow swung around and kicked the other leg out, sending the obnoxious drunk crashing to the floor. Then she came down with a boot, hard on his chest. Drawing her .44, she pointed it directly at his face. "Sure," she said. "I'm looking for action. How about you?"

With both hands flung out, the cowpoke stammered, "I dint mean anythin', really, lady," with a bit more respect in his voice this time.

Glaring at the downed man as she removed her boot from his chest, Willow snarled, "Get your sorry ass out of here, cowpoke." Willow was surprised at the roughness she heard in her own voice.

The randy young cowpoke hobbled out the swinging doors, glancing back once with a whipped dog look, then was gone. Holstering her revolver, Willow turned back to the bar, knowing the man beside her had watched her every move, taken in her every word. Maybe he would help her now; but first she had to get an idea of exactly what *his* game was.

Ned looked at her. "Very impressive. I guess you can take care of yourself."

"I—well, yes." Willow nodded, taking a bigger sip of whiskey than she'd planned on taking. She tried not to cough, but it burned her eyes, throat, stomach. Carelessly, she shrugged and turned aside to swallow. Holy sarsparilla! That was hot!

"Not to stick my nose into your business," Ned began, "but . . . would you be in need of some work?" He noted the look of sudden interest. "Seems you know how to use that gun pretty dang well." And I get the feeling you're desperate over some matter, Ned thought to himself.

Trying not to sound overly eager, Willow said with a casualness she didn't feel, "Depends on what the pay is, mister. The easier the work, the better." She narrowed her nut-brown eyes. "If you get my drift?"

Nodding, Ned Thompkins replied, "I think I do." He started to move away from the bar. "Why don't you come with me? Name's Ned."

"Yes, I heard the bartender say your name. Mine's . . . Will."

Ned chuckled. "Welcome, Will." Just first names, that was okay.

Could she trust him? She had to, because if her husband arrived, she would need to hide, to have someone to fall back on. If Talon caught up with her, he might just tie her to the bedpost . . . or have her wait in jail. Yup, Talon might be angry enough to do that to her. You had to be one step ahead of men nowadays.

Wiping down the already-shiny slab of varnished wood, the bartender shook his head as Ned Thompkins and the new hellcat in town walked out, heads together, already making plans for some mischief like cattle rustlings and robberies—make no mistake about that!

For the female of the species is more deadly
than the male.
—Kipling, *The Female of the Species*

Chapter Four

When Talon Clay arrived in Paradise Valley he heard
the gossip about the "hellcat" immediately, almost before sliding from his horse to tie him at the post. Beneath the dusty brim of his hat his face was stern and
hard. The townsfolk looked the tall man over, making
out strong thigh and bicep muscles rippling and bulging
through his clothes. Men in the West were nearly always from somewhere else. Yet, wherever they came
from, they brought with them an aura of their previous
experience, whatever it happened to be. Paradise Valley
had its drifters and gunfighters, and they knew enough
to know this lanky stranger for what he was: Ranger.

Talon Clay's scarred boots had just touched ground
when he heard the gossip coming from the old cowpokes tipped against the wall of the weathered building.
The sign read: Hotel Paradise. It creaked in a little
zephyr wind.

"Yeah, she really laid young Kinney low. Drunk he
was and tryin' to come on to her, smackin' her on the
rear—"

"He din't!" the other oldtimer disagreed. "That ain't

how I heard it tole. He kinda patted her behind and spilt her drink."

The Ranger heard the gossip but paid it no mind. He was glancing over his shoulder wondering what was keeping Sammy at the store where he'd gone to get a few items, saying he would catch up in a few minutes. Talon saw the clock in the lobby of the hotel, noting the time was almost noon as he stepped beneath the sign swinging above his head.

Fine white dust hung in a sifting cloud behind the wagon just passing, blanketing the sides of animals and buildings, dusting with a thin film the clothing of men and women, and all but hiding the sparse grass and sage at the edge of town. One man, with a lean, lantern-jawed face, spat on the ground at the corner of the building, his red-rimmed eyes staring down the dusty street into the limitless distance outside of town. The way *she* had gone, the female wearin' the nice, tight pants. Maybe, just maybe, this Ranger was lookin' for her.

The Ranger's nose was slightly aquiline, his cheekbones high, and his jaw strongly curved. At the time it was a hard face, lacking softness, even in the finely chiseled lips. The two men were not able to see the color of his eyes, narrowed against the glare and shadowed beneath the darkness of his hat. His hair was dark golden at the nape, and he wore it longer than most Rangers would have deemed proper. What they didn't know was that Talon hadn't even had time to stop for a hot nourishing meal, much less a haircut.

"The lady in the pants was lookin' for somethin', I'm sure . . . never saw such a pretty little thing in the clothing of a man."

80

"Yeah—she sure had nice yellow hair and a sweet look about her mouth, but she had steel in her eyes. Yup, she was up to somethin' all right, totin' a pistol and—"

Just as Talon was about to enter the relatively cooler hotel lobby, he stiffened at the words. Mechanically, he stepped aside, allowing a couple to precede him, nodded and tipped his hat, then faced the two gossipy men squarely.

With his mouth agape—because the Ranger had stepped so close, so suddenly—the first old fella looked up into striking grass-green eyes. "Did ya want somethin', Ranger?"

"Sure do," Talon said with ease, leaning an arm against the wall as he slouched toward the man. "About this little lady in pants—"

"The hellcat!" the second older man expostulated. "I knew it, I knew you'd be lookin' for that one. She done somethin' wrong, Ranger?"

"Not that I know of, old fella." Talon squinted his eyes into the dust and distance as he straightened away from the wall. "But you're right about one thing: She sounds like the woman I'm looking for."

The men nudged each other at the same time as the first oldtimer spoke up. "We don't know no more, do we, Abe?"

Shrewdly Talon looked the man in the eyes. "Do you, Abe?"

"Reckon not." He looked at his old friend right before a look of dawning light entered his red-rimmed eyes. "I know who you can go see, Ranger. Ask Big Louie. He's the bartender over at the Silver Spur saloon and he told us guys what happened."

"He's tough and he'll make someone talk," the first man said as the Ranger strode off in the direction of the Silver Spur. "Yeah," the other one said, "even if that someone don't want to."

"So, you don't want to say anything? Telling me to go to hell and go somewhere else to get my information?"

"I tell you, Ranger," Big Louie said disdainfully, emphasizing *Ranger,* revealing his dislike for lawmen, "I didn't see anything, no lady in pants, no medium-sized cowpoke down on his luck, and no drunken lad named Kinney. And I don't remember nothing, either."

"No?"

"No." Big Louie could see the Ranger tensing and he braced himself for what was to come.

Grabbing the bartender, Talon hauled him over the bar and stuck his Ranger-sized pistol under the arrogant Big Louie's chin.

A sardonic grin curled Talon's mouth upward. He snarled:

"Talk."

After a moment's thought and staring down that pistol's deep black bore, Big Louie remembered.

Later, in bed in his hotel room—Sammy asleep in a corner piled with blankets and fresh-smelling sheets—Talon laid his head on the pillow. They should have kept moving, out to the hills, but slow and steady wins the race, he'd heard, and he didn't want to burn out on beans and jerky and little rest. He and Sammy had gone to the restaurant and eaten a hot meal, then turned in early to be ready to ride out at the crack of dawn. He closed his eyes, remembering ... remembering ... one of the most vivid and sensual memories of his and Willow's wedding night ...

"Willow," he breathed against her cheek. "Sweet love, sweet love ... Aiyana."

She cried out, "Lakota! Oh ... please ... !"

"Now ... now, darling," he had told her, grasping her hips and, bringing her to the water again, he stood hip-deep and began to enter that first bit of her. He had discovered her passage to be small and tight, but he found her gratifyingly moist with honey. His massive length entered her body a little more, and then she gave a little gasping cry. "Oh ... please stop ... that hurts. No ... oh, no more!"

Breathing heavily, Talon tipped her hips upward and used his hand to rub his shaft against the sensitive, palpitating bud of womanhood. Finally, she had been ready, on fire for him. His abdomen clenched and he leaned forward with a powerful surge, tearing through the barrier. But he did not go deeply into her yet. He had heard cries of ecstasy coming from Willow, and then he began to thrust and wrench. When he pressed deeper he filled her completely, making her scream softly and pant. Willow's eyes rounded as the grinding force of his thrusts drove her deep into the grass. He climbed from the water, still joined with her, clutching her hips, covering her body with his full length but not crushing her.

In his dream the Ranger grew hard as he saw Willow's head begin to toss wildly. Then he could almost feel the sensation in his organ as her hips arched to meet every grinding thrust. She had grasped handfuls of grass and begun to sob ... no doubt from the same tension that was building so intensely in him. The pressure had built until he could stand it no longer. Surging pleasure ripped through him, almost tearing him apart ... he knew she was climbing with him ... waves of rapture had carried them higher, higher, the pressure building apace with the grinding sensation of pure lust. He drove home, putting all his power into the last surge that brought them to the pinnacle of ecstasy together, the shattering climax wrapping them in a cocoon of rapturous splendor.

Tenderly he drew her closer after it was all over and said the words she had always wanted to hear, "I love you, Aiyana. I love you." He had put his hand over his heart. "You are in here now and I'll never release you. No one has ever captured my heart and soul as you have this night. I know you are the most beautiful woman I have ever known. I must tell you this: there hasn't been another woman since the day we met."

Willow had looked away from him. "What is it?" he had asked, cupping her chin and forcing her to look back up at him. "Something is troubling you." She had looked shy all of a sudden, almost sad as she said: "I—I can't tell you ... it is really—nothing." She had looked as if she were about to cry and, when he'd asked if she loved him, she had rolled away. She didn't go far. Dragging her beneath him, he was *like a savage cat trapping her under his huge paws* ... this was what she had told him later. However, at the time, he said, "Something bothers you about me. Does it have to do with other women?" She had said nothing. "I am waiting, *impatiently,* Aiyana."

"You can wait all night then. I won't tell you." After these words, he had lowered his face, bringing it close to hers. She had turned her face aside and he had discovered the chance to nibble her earlobe, repeating his statement of impatience. He had heard her gasp when his tongue encircled her ear and then thrust itself inside. "Willow, Aiyana. Hear me; I have something to say to you. I care. I haven't had Hester for three years. Believe me, my pure sweet darling, she's the biggest slut around twenty counties and she comes pretty damn close to Gar—" Just then he had felt her freeze. He had almost said her mother's name . . . at that time he had not known Garnet was her mother . . . and when he'd discovered this he'd almost felt like killing her.

Talon shook himself alert from his daydream . . . *Jaysu*, he should be asleep, since they had to ride out early at the crack of dawn.

The next morning Willow was on her way to the ghost town with Ned Thompkins, but first he was planning to show up with her at the hideout which was a good two days from the ghost town. On the way along the dusty trail Ned filled Willow in on what to expect, failing to mention what a lecherous man Jake Tyler could be at times. He didn't want to frighten her right off the bat and have her run off. He needed her, because the boss lady liked cunning women outlaws to do her dirty work. Only thing was, lady outlaws were hard to find since most women wanted to stay home and raise a family.

After riding for a day and a half, with few stops in between for hard chunks of bread and sips of black bitter coffee and a carpet of green grass serving as a cushion for their tired backsides, a hideout disguised as a ranch down on its luck came into view, still a long distance away. Willow wondered if they would ever reach it.

Rising before dawn, they had come to the mountains shortly after first light. But first they had ridden through a tormented land of arroyos and sand dunes, and then they traveled west of the Pecos River. They rode across land that the Mescalero Apache had dwelled in and ridden upon for century-moons. Finally, when Willow thought she could ride no longer, they had reached the rugged foothills.

Willow's knees were quivering from gripping the horse's flanks as she looked below from a mauve and gray slant of hill. The mountain corridor emptied into a small, narrow canyon carved into the earth. On the way down her horse slid many times in the tortured mountains of sand and rock, bumping into desert brush, Spanish dagger, and catclaw.

"Are we in New Mexico?" Willow wanted to know, feeling as if they'd ridden into eternity.

"Just about, I do believe," Ned said, riding in front as he led her to the gray, broken-down structures below. When they were riding flat at last, Ned looked over his shoulder, watching the young woman come up alongside. "There's not much left of the ranch house—that burned pretty bad in a range war in '49. Rustlers began herding their stolen cattle into this little valley, and holed them up back there in the box canyon."

"When did it cease to be a home?" Willow asked as they neared the bunkhouses, and she could see five men coming together to stand before the long, low structure.

"That would have been in '50, right after the range war and the folks killed each other off, until there was only one half-breed by the name of Hank Rountree lived here. His father got the Indian woman pregnant and the product of their illicit affair was Hank. Everybody was killed off, even Hank's mother. It was a bloody war over land. Hank stayed on, got hitched with a pretty Indian woman called herself Summer Wind. Then big trouble arrived when some dance hall girl moved in on the big, handsome Hank when he went to town for supplies. It's a sad story, 'cause the family broke up after that."

No doubt, Willow thought, because the handsome Hank was a western rogue just like Talon Clay! "That is sad," was all Willow said. She watched as Ned swung a leg over the saddle horn and stepped to the ground. With the others looking on, she knew he dared not offer her help. She swayed a little but righted herself as she, too, stepped down. "Howdy," she said in greeting to the five dudes standing lax with thumbs hooked low in their pockets. When they said nothing she tried a mischievous grin, making two of them smile back at least.

"This here's the head dude, Mick Stone," Ned introduced Willow and Mick raised a dubious eyebrow. "Do you really think she can handle the job? Those other two the boss sent out ain't even come back yet. Probably won't ever show up with the kid, either."

Ned smiled at Willow who had hooked her thumbs in the same fashion, then frowned back to Mick, saying, "She handled herself in Paradise Valley real well. You should've seen—"

It suddenly hit Willow what the man named Stone

had said. "What child, uh, *kid* are you talking about?" Willow broke in, looking from one man to the other.

"Just a kid the boss wants delivered to her . . . that's all," Mick said, not catching the look of interest in the young woman's eyes.

Eureka! Willow thought she just might be on the right trail. Now they had clammed up, which led her to believe that "those other two" had kidnapped her son and she had to find out where that "somewhere" was that they had taken him. Maybe—her heart raced at the thought—just maybe Michael was not far from this old, gray ranch.

Lazily Stone searched the woman's face, trying to read her countenance and character; she was pretty, that was certain, but a little too skinny for his taste. "We're sure not going to call you Will. You're a woman. What's your real name?"

Saying nothing for several seconds, Willow finally blurted, "Willabelle!" Now, how would they take that?

Stone snorted. "We'll call you Belle. Okay with you?"

Willow said nothing.

"Let's mosey over to the bunkhouse. We got another dude we'd like you to meet." He winked to Ned. "You'll like Jake the Rake."

Entering the smoky bunkhouse with a clatter of boot heels, Willow smelled the greasy food cooking somewhere in the back; her stomach rumbled with hunger. Her brain started to pound with fatigue when she saw a lanky, narrow-faced man saunter over to them. Oh-oh, she thought, here comes trouble. Then her face softened in a relieved smile when the cook wandered from behind a dirty curtain. He looked fat and jolly and beamed when his smiling brown eyes took her in.

Stone started introducing her to the cook and the lanky outlaw. "This here's Jake Tyler, and the cook is Willie." He looked to Willow. "See why we'd of had a hard time if we called you Will?"

"Oh, of course. I mean—surely!" Oh shoot, she sounded just like her sister Tanya when she'd come back from school out East. Taking a deep breath and squaring her shoulders, Willow said in a slightly huskier voice, "Just call me Belle."

"Belle . . . shit," said Jake, moving away after giving her an evil sneer.

Willie leaned toward Willow, smiling adoringly, and then, giving her arm a gentle pinch he cooed. Frowning and nodding at Jake's back, like a warning to her, he moved back beyond the greasy curtain. Willow bit her lower lip, never having seen the likes of Willie. "He can't talk," Ned told her. "He's just letting you know he likes you. We've had other women here, lady outlaws, and Willie didn't care for them because they were . . . well, a lot different from you, that's all."

Willow didn't know about that. However, for certain, Jake Tyler had taken an instant dislike to her.

Realizing she couldn't back down now, Willow kept her mouth shut. She was too close to finding some clues. But the other men might think she was a coward, she argued with herself. She had to do something, because Jake was mean and cantankerous. Trouble was brewing. He wasn't about to accept the fact that she, another female, had come here to a man's world.

"Little bitch," Jake hissed as he looked Willow up and down. What she didn't know was that a dance hall girl, who resembled Willow, had promised to marry him and then run off with some other dude. That was years ago, but Jake still remembered her huge blue eyes and sluttishness.

"Let's all go outside now and cool off," Stone said, and Ned agreed, beginning to worry about Will . . . or Belle.

As they stepped to the yard in front of the bunkhouse, Jake shoved Willow to one side. "Now I don't have to spend the night with my favorite whore," he spat. "You're here and you'll do—more exciting than raiding and killing—"

"Wait a minute," Ned snarled at Jake. "We don't do no raidin' and killin'." In the next instant he looked down at Willow on the ground. "Why'd you have to go and do that for, Jake? What kinda devil's eatin' you?"

Willow had tripped on Jake's boot when he stuck his foot out as she walked by; she had fallen face forward into the dust. As it settled, she was on her feet, the leather thong unsnapped from her pistol's hammer as she stood facing Jake like a spitting hellcat.

"Look here, mister," Willow ground out. "I don't know you from Adam and frankly I don't care to know you . . . especially not in the way you meant! And I don't let a man put his hands on me or put me down no way." Ned was grinning, nodding his head, remembering the bar scene. "When push comes to shove, I'll be doing the shoving."

"Oh yeah?" Laughing deep in his throat, Jake backed up a few steps, putting him and "Belle" about eight feet apart. He tried taking a gauge on the young woman and would soon fall short on his reckoning. What the hell, he thought, and shrugged.

Without much thought to his own safety, Jake reached down for his gun, but never cleared his holster. With a speed that surprised Willow herself, she drew and fired her .44, sending the slug crashing through Jake's foot. He dropped instantly to his knees, a look of bewilderment on his face as he looked up into the astonished face of the new "lady outlaw."

There was the sound of another bullet, this one speeding much faster and coming from a greater distance, but no one knew this in the confusion. This time Jake toppled over sideways, seeming to bounce a few times on the ground until he suddenly lay still, his life's blood flowing into the dust.

Jake was dead.

Stone looked at Belle with wonder. "Holy mother, you *are* fast, young lady. With you we don't need him—" He nodded towards the body, adding "and maybe not a couple of others, either."

Willow holstered her gun, fighting to control her shaking hands and bewildered brain. Everything had happened so fast . . . and how and when did she fire that last bullet? She hadn't been aware of firing again. She had only been staring at the tip of the boot—and possibly part of a toe—she'd blown off. *Holy cow!* She had never killed a man—not even Carl Tucker, who deserved it—Carl, the man who had made her life a living hell. Carl had reversed the fates and killed himself trying to do evil to the Brandon family.

She felt sick and alone inside, but she had to do this. She had to find her son, no matter what she had to do.

There was a faint stirring in the tall weeds and grass at the end of the bunkhouse. Hank Rountree, the man with a bullet hole and feather in his hat, hunkered down and watched as the pretty blonde looked down in astonishment, thinking she'd shot the filthy-minded Jake herself. The others thought so, too, and Hank was not about to let them know the truth. Holstering his weapon—and the wicked knife in his other hand—Hank crouched low and ran back to his horse in the line of scrubby trees backing the bunkhouse.

Nat Lacey removed her hat and shook out her long yellow hair. Michael Angelo looked confused for a moment when he saw her and, thinking the woman must be his mother, he gave a hysterical cry of relief. When Nat turned, however, she did not look much like Willow Brandon. He screamed at this "lady" who had taken him from his mother and when she picked Michael up, he squirmed to be free.

"No! No! No!" he cried. "I don't like you! You are not Mommy!" He didn't like being held by strangers. "I want Mommy—go away, go away!"

"I can't very well do that, honey," Nat crooned, chucking him under the chin. Plopping him back onto the blanket, she narrowed her huge blue eyes. "Your daddy and I are going to be real good friends, pumpkin." Seeing that Hester was not in the vicinity of the campfire, Nat whispered to the boy, "I'm going to get you to him, honey, and he's going to be real grateful to me for saving you from that bitchy boss. With your mommy out of the way, we'll be a family, and after your daddy and I get hitched, I'm going to lock you up in your nice little bedroom so's your Daddy and I can have some fun."

"Mommy!" Michael yelled up at her. "I want

Mommy—and I want Jorge, too!" He blinked and began to stand up and face the woman glaring down at him.

"Who the hell is Jorge?"

"Jorge—" Michael shook his head—"Puppy!"

"Oh yes, honey, I'll get you a puppy if you want. Then you and the dog can entertain each other while your daddy and I are busy."

"No!" Michael persisted. "I want Jorge! Not you!" He frowned when he saw Hester coming from the creek to the camp. Michael was confused. Both women had yellow hair just like Mommy and looked like her, too, when they turned their backs to him. He blinked, remembering his "Auntie" Juanita, and Uncle Sammy. "I want Sammy and 'Nita! Not you!" He shook his finger at Hester and turned to Nat Lacey. "Not you!"

"Shut up, brat," Nat hissed down to Michael and, whirling about, bumped right into Hester Tucker. "What the hell . . . ?"

Hester's eyes glittered angrily. "I don't want you treating Mikey like that, hear?" Nat blinked and cocked her head. "I mean it, Nat, stay away from him. He doesn't like you. You're not nice to him."

The other blonde tossed her head. "He doesn't like you much better, Toots." Using her dance hall girl's dialect, Nat flounced over to her horse and mounted like a true cowboy. Her eyes narrowed darkly as she said with a snicker, "I'm getting real good at this 'lady outlaw' business and maybe someday soon a big handsome Ranger's going to come along and capture me. *Whooeee*—I'm ready!" she called as she kicked her horse into a run, skirting Spanish dagger and sagebrush, campfire junk rattling around in her saddlebags.

With a muttered curse, Hester shook her head. "Nat's

going to get captured all right," she said aloud, "but by the wrong man along the way somewheres. Someone's going to do that sluttish woman in—maybe that half-breed Hank'll do it—she really screwed him over good, jilted him she did." She cracked a smile as Michael squinted and stared up at her as if she was a squirrel in a tree.

Wrapping a squirming Michael in the blanket, Hester took him and mounted up, planning to ride to the ghost town a couple days away where the lady boss had her hideout. Hester didn't know how long she could keep this up. She wasn't used to caring for a child—the "accidents" he often had while riding too long, the washing up after him, feeding, coddling, soothing, it was all wearing on her nerves. That, and the constant bickering with Nat, was going to drive her plumb loco!

Bleakly she thought ahead to the time when she'd have to murder two women in cold blood. She shook her blond head. All this for a man . . . shoot, she'd always been in love with Talon Clay, even before Willow tossed her yellow head and gave him that come hither look. Her mama, Janice Ranae, knew it, too—always Talon Clay'd been her daughter's. This time, though, she was going to get him and he was going to remain hers.

The Ranger. Talon Clay. Lakota, half-breed. Her man. Worth the killing.

Wild Spirit, which art moving
   everywhere . . .
            —Percy Bysshe Shelley

Chapter Five

Shortly after sunrise—back at the rundown Rountree
ranch where the Green Mountain Gang was holed up—
Willow, or Belle, was rummaging in an old trunk.
Seated on the dusty floor, she pulled things out, tossing
useless junk over her shoulder, placing garments aside
that might come in handy.

Rising to her feet, Willow tucked her hair up inside
the sombrero and posed like a dangerous *hombre* before
the cracked mirror. "Ah, *Rinche;* Ranger, you would
like to fight with me, eh?" She swirled a serape across
her shoulder and opened one eye mysteriously above
the folds. The black pants she pulled on next were a bit
baggy here and there, but with a few tucks. . . . Ah, a
mask!

"Where did all this come from?" Willow wondered
aloud as she leapt to view her own reflection. "This
trunk holds secrets . . . I wonder whose eyes gazed from
this mask . . . what happened? . . . who got robbed, or
killed? . . ."

Then she screamed.

Forcing her voice to be calm as she turned slowly

around, her eyes darted into the corner where she'd seen someone . . . hadn't she? "Wh-Who's there?" A pair of eyes—dark ones—that was what she had seen in the mirror. "I—I know someone's there . . . I saw you in the mirror. Ha, you d-don't fool me."

Wiping the sweat from her brow, Willow plunked down onto the saggy cot, then screamed as a mouse ran out from beneath. "Ohhh," she moaned, pulling up her knees as she curled into a fetal position and lay down. But only for a moment. Then she was up and out the door, casting glances over her shoulder, her blond hair flying as she wondered if someone might be following.

Once outside, Willow realized she was still dressed in the outfit of a Mexican—or Spanish—outlaw. Shaking her head, she told herself, "No, no, no, I'm not going back in there." She found an old bench and sat down, her chin in her hands, as she began to think of her angel once again. "Michael . . . oh, baby . . . I have to find you." Sighing deeply and squaring her shoulders resolutely, she came to her feet, then looked down and realized the mask was still clutched tightly in her hand.

Ned found her way out in back shooting up some tin cans Willie had given her. "Gunsmoking?" he asked, ignoring her mysterious outfit.

Willow responded automatically to the kind voice. "No. But it *was.*" She looked down at the gun.

Ned laughed. "I mean 'gun smoking'? You know— target practice?"

"Oh—" Blowing on the tip of her pistol, she looked up at Ned. "So that's what you mean."

For a moment Ned studied the clothes and the mask she was just pulling down in place. "Meaning to put some bad guys away, Belle?"

"Say, how did you know it was me before I said anything?"

"I didn't. Honest to God. I was just being friendly."

"Mmm-hmm. To a total stranger?"

"No. You look familiar in that getup—" He chuckled. "Especially to another outlaw." Just having some fun, Ned tugged Willow's hat down gently over her brow. "Come, mysterious Willabelle, let's go get some grub. I cook a mean crock of beans and brew a cruel pot of black coffee. While we're eating, you can tell me what your real game is."

"Wha—?"

"Come on."

Hank Rountree lurked in the shadows of the torn curtains, watching the young woman in pants, seeing her gaze into the same mirror Summer Wind had detested. Many things that had been in the shadows in the back of his mind came to the fore. His Indian wife had gone to the gently rippling azure water to look at herself, gazed into the mountain pool that was all dried up now, just like his and Summer Wind's love. Hank was reminded of Natalie Lacey, the woman who had wanted to be called this stupid name "Nat." Hank's eyes grew sad. Nat Lacey had been the cause of his marriage break-up. His wife, Summer Wind, and he had two beautiful children together and Nat Lacey had come along when he had felt a little bored with life. He had gone into the dance hall where she'd worked. Being a half-breed had not been an easy path for him ... but he always got along. The first thing he'd noticed about Nat was her large blue eyes—too big, now that he seriously thought

97

about it, now that he'd come to his senses too late—and her cunning and artful way with men. He had been unaware at the time of how stupid and empty Nat really was ... she hid her failings under a veil of charm and flirtatiousness, using rouge and powder and sexy clothing. He had felt lust, all right, it had kicked him in the gut and brought him to his heels before the woman. She had laughed and batted her eyes lined with dark make-up.

Hank stared right through the young woman posing in the mirror as he continued to feel his sorrow. He had left his wife and children behind, abandoned them for a dream like summer smoke ... here in the morning ... gone in the afternoon. The small ranch was gone, too; Summer Wind could not take care of it without her man. He had no idea where his wife and children were and knew he might never see them again. Nat Lacey had up and left him then, just as he had abandoned his wife. What you do to others comes back to you, he thought. This was the full circle. Now he had to pay by living a life of crime and seeking a way to get his revenge on the wicked schemer—Natalie Lacey. Dear God, he had often prayed, help me get her before she ruined others as she'd done with him and his family ...

He had discovered God would not help him seek revenge. He would have to find his own way to do this because he did not believe—or could not bring himself to fully believe that vengeance was the Lord's, as white men did.

And Hank Rountree was out to get his own.

* * *

Talon and Sammy were just riding out of Paradise Valley, stopping often to question folks along the dusty road, asking about the boy, describing him. One woman, looking strangely suspicious, caught Sammy's eye. When he wheeled his horse to ride toward her, she began to run with a child in her arms.

"Talon, look there, that woman. That looks like Mikey with her! C'mon Ranger, let's go see!"

Casting frightened looks over her shoulder, the woman continued to run. Ranger! She had seen him coming . . . they had an air about them that scared her out of her wits. One time her husband, a white-haired miner, had tangled with Ranger Ashe Brandon. And he had lost. Now she was living with this man, an American with whom she had had this child.

The child was becoming heavy. Bending low to half-carry her son along, Calinda Vasquez glanced in frantic haste over her shoulder and hurried the boy inside the decent, white frame house. Slamming the door in the Ranger's face, Calinda called him a name in Spanish. "Don't you try to come in here. I have done nothing!" she yelled, keeping her son tucked behind her in case the Ranger came crashing through the door.

"Where's your husband, ma'am?" Talon questioned from the other side of the wood as the woman barred entry into her home.

"He is not here . . . at work. Go away, we have done nothing."

"I only want to have a word with you, ma'am."

"No! No! I have nothing to say to you! Go away, *Rinche!*"

Importantly, Sammy walked up to pound on the door. "Ma'am, this here's a Ranger out here. If you don't answer his summons and open the door, we're goin' to fetch the sheriff." He shrugged at Talon, hearing only silence on the other side of the wood. "Are you goin' to open the door, ma'am?"

"You come back when my husband is home!" Calinda Vasquez ordered through the crack in the door where she could see their shifting shadows. She heard the Ranger ask when that would be. "Next week."

Talon heard the boy begin to cry and his eyes shifted over to Sammy at once. "Does that sound like Michael?"

Again Sammy shrugged. "All kids sound the same to me when they're whinin', Ranger."

Serious and filled with an emotion Sammy couldn't read, Talon said, "I wouldn't know, Sammy—" He looked away. "I guess I haven't taken the time to notice what children sound like—" He spotted huge flowers growing at the corners of the house. How red they are, he thought, wondering if they smelled as good as they looked. He shook his head, getting back to his task. "Ma'am, you have to open this door or I'm afraid I'll have to enter by force."

"You will have to get the sheriff first, Ranger!" she shouted through the crack; the child kept whining.

"All right," Talon said in a stern and resolute voice, turning to face the street. "I'll do just that."

"Wait!"

The door swung open and there stood the woman with the fair-haired lad hugging her leg at one side. Talon looked at the boy, then at Sammy, belatedly reminding himself to watch the room beyond the woman for any furtive movements that might tell him she wasn't alone. "Well, Sammy?" he said, keeping his trained senses alert as he stared down at the boy who was looking up with round, inquisitive eyes.

"Nope. That ain't Michael Angelo. Mikey's got green eyes just like yours, Tal." He called the Ranger by the nickname he'd used when he himself was much younger.

While the woman kept staring at the Ranger, he tipped the brim of his hat forward and said, "I'm sorry, ma'am, but we had to check the boy out because—" What would he say now? Ah hell—"see, my son has been kidnapped."

Calinda's eyes were big and round. "You do not *know* your own son when you see him?" She clicked her tongue and shook her head. "How can this be?"

"Well—" he coughed. "I've never seen my son because I've been—" he thinned his lips—"busy."

"Santa Maria!" Calinda exclaimed. "Too busy to see your own son?"

Gaping at the dark-haired, dark-skinned woman, Sammy put in, "My sister, his wife, didn't let him see Mikey . . . cuz, see, she ran away with Mikey before he was borned—"

"Born, Sammy," the Ranger said, eager to get away since he felt like he was going to blush like a woman. "The word is *born.*"

Glaring at the Ranger, Calinda said, "You let your wife get away when she had a baby in the oven?" She clicked her tongue again. "My first husband would never do that." Her eyes roamed over the handsome Ranger. "But I never have a baby until I meet my next man, Nevada. He never tell me his last name and so my boy has the name Vasquez. See, he has fair hair like you, Ranger."

101

Talon Clay was beginning to feel uneasy with all this woman-talk ... yet Sammy appeared fascinated by the conversation. "Well, ma'am, I'll apologize for the trouble now and we'll be on my ... I mean, our way."

After digging into his pocket, Talon came up with a few pieces of hard candy and handed them to the woman. "For the boy."

Laughing, Calinda picked up her son. "Bless you. You find your son, Ranger—" She shook her finger at him. "And, ah! Do not let that woman of yours get away again!"

"Believe me," Talon said over his shoulder, "I won't."

Calinda watched them leave, the tall Texan and the handsome, freckle-faced lad. She smiled and closed her door, asking God to help the courageous *Rinche* and his runaway wife.

"Whew!" Sammy exclaimed after they had mounted up. "I didn't know these kind of things could happen to a Ranger." He laughed as he caught a piece of candy Talon had tossed to him. "Hey, peppermint!" He popped it into his mouth, looking like a gopher.

"They usually don't, Sammy, unless there's a missing child."

Sammy nodded. "I can understand that."

By dusk, they were riding out of town and heading for open country. Silent for a while, Sammy finally spoke up, mentioning Talon's brother Ashe. "He was a Ranger, too. Is he still one?"

"He's raising a family now. You know that."

"But they only got *one* kid!"

Nodding, Talon said, "Yeah. But they'll probably have more." Would he want to have more with Willow?

He told himself this wasn't the time to be wondering about that. He had his *first* child to find, and then, who could know beforehand what the future would bring?

"Is it true the Mexicans call the Rangers *Los Diablos Tejanos*, 'The Texas Devils'?"

"That's right, Sammy."

"Well then, how come that Mex lady back there didn't call *you* that?"

Talon laughed. "She probably did, at first, hundreds of times in her mind."

Sammy thought quietly for a time. He knew there was still a big mystery about Talon and his brother Ashe, one they would talk to no one about . . . Sammy wondered if Willow even knew about this darker side to Talon Clay's personality. It was there, just as it was with Ashe. They had secrets they weren't talking about.

After a meal of beans and jerky, that night, under the stars, Talon dreamed about what his son must look like. He awakened close to morning, with empty arms and tears hot beneath his lids . . . the child had not been his in the dream; no, the lad had belonged to the Mex woman. There was a twist in his gut. Would he even get to meet his son in this life? He was angry with Willow and tossed and turned until he awoke Sammy.

"What's the matter, Ranger? Havin' nightmares?"

"This bedroll is uncomfortable."

"Is that all? Yeah? Well . . . want to hear a story?"

"Sure. Why not." Talon sighed and bent an arm beneath his head as he looked up at the stars flickering out one by one; before morning there had been a diamond necklace scattered about on the black velvet of midnight.

"Do you want to hear the story about Nightwalker?"

Chuckling, Talon asked, "Who?"

"Willow told me all about the legendary Kiowa Sioux," Sammy said as he got up to stir the cold camp stones.

He had heard right, yet Talon Clay had stiffened at the mention of Nightwalker. Dark Horse. Almanzo. The man was called by many names. He was supposed to be his half-brother . . . he hadn't seen Almanzo for several years. He had married an Indian woman by the name of Kachina. Nightwalker—the name always caused chills to run along his spine, because it had been the real name of their father. Was Kijika Nightwalker still alive? Had he and his mother Martha really been lovers? Their Indian father was a recluse; either that, or he was deceased by now. All of a sudden he smelled coffee and, looking up, saw Sammy bending down to hand him his tin cup.

"What did Willow tell you about Nightwalker, Sam?"

"Want to hear all of it?"

"Sure." Talon leaned over on his elbow, sipping the cruel black brew. "Go ahead." He believed he knew this one already, but why not let the lad retell it, he asked himself. This was the story of his own ancestors.

"I'm gonna talk about the *Kwerharrehnuh,* the most arrogant and fierce tribe of the Comanches . . . but first I'll tell you about Nightwalker before we get into that one: His parents came out of the Black Hills of South Dakota. These were Kiowas and really and truly warlike. But before Nightwalker ever came along, his father met a beautiful girl who was daughter to the chief of the Dakota Sioux. She was called the Princess. After Nightwalker was born, his father's people—the first of the

104

Northern Kiowas—were harassed by the Sioux and they threatened to kill Nightwalker who was just a baby back then. The Princess was killed in a raid on their camp. Nightwalker's father took the baby with them, though his second wife was very jealous and she had her own children to think about."

"Is there more to this story?" Talon asked, getting sleepy again despite the hot, strong coffee.

"Yeah. Nightwalker's tribe was harassed by the Western Cheyenne and so the Kiowas began to move south. Then they started to live in the way of the Comanches and hunted bison on the Plains. With them were the Kiowa Apaches. Nightwalker's parents moved into Comanche country after a while."

"Then what?" Talon asked, smothering a yawn, having heard all this from the real source—his father . . . a brief accounting, at that, for Kijika was a man of few words. He had no idea if his Indian father was still alive; he'd not been back to the camp in years.

Sammy continued with the tale. "It was in Comanche country that his adoptive mother tried to do away with little Nightwalker. She took him into the High Plains hunting grounds. Luckily a Comanche war band was moving through and the chief of that tribe saw her. To take the place of a lost son, Pole Cat slew the woman and took the Kiowa Sioux for his own—"

"And Nightwalker was the first of many that followed." Talon twisted to face Sammy and he blinked at Talon's knowledge of the ending to his story. "Do you know that our friend and neighbor Almanzo has been called Nightwalker?"

"Yeah. I heard somethin' about that, and is Almanzo really your half-brother?"

"Yes. And his Indian name is Dark Horse. He married a beautiful Indian woman named Kachina in the same camp where Willow and I married."

"Is Dark Horse still with Kachina?"

"As far as I know, he is. Why?"

Sammy only shrugged, not wanting to say that before Talon and Almanzo rode off to join the Indians, Sammy had seen Tanya and Almanzo talking outside the house at Sundance. Talking was all right, but it was the way Almanzo was looking at his sister Tanya that *wasn't* all right 'cause Tanya was already married to Ashe Brandon!

"Sammy?" Talon peered up at the lad, and just then Sammy jumped up to empty his coffee grounds in the low campfire.

"How excitin'! I just love Indian stories, especially ones with some mystery to 'em."

"I like a mystery, too." And Talon had every intention of solving the one about his missing son.

"Willow's a mystery," Sammy said with a shrug, and when Talon gave no reaction, he added, "All women are a mystery to me."

Reaching over to ruffle the youngster's red hair—slowly darkening to a rich mahogany like his sister Tanya's—Talon asked, "All women, you say? Hey Sam, have you been visiting some of the 'big girls'?"

"Nope." Sammy's face turned serious as he shook his head vigorously. "Don't care for whores, never did."

Then, Talon thought to himself, you sure wouldn't have liked your own mother, Garnet Haywood!

"We got a couple more hours shut-eye, Sam. Let's get it before sunup."

Eyes closed again, Talon did not dream but his mind

traveled back in time to several years ago, actually more like five or six. . . . They called *him* Mustang Man. He was called this besides being called some bad words by competitive mustangers. Always he was seen with a raven-haired man riding beside him, one as bronzed as he: Dark Horse. Almanzo Rankin had long ago earned himself the reputation of having caught and handled more mustangs than any other man in Texas. Talon, White Indian, White Horse, Lakota, had joined Dark Horse and they became as brothers when, in truth, they actually were blood brothers.

White Horse earned himself the name when he'd captured the white stallion, "Beautiful One," also known as *Blanco* or Cloud. And the first time Willow had seen him riding in on the fresh-broke stallion, a long-bladed knife thumping against his buckskin-clad thigh, his chest naked and smooth and bronzed like an Indian's, his thick braid bleached white by the sun, she had fainted dead away. When she'd awakened, he had been staring down at her. Willow had been about to swoon again when he'd spoken her name, saying in a rich, deep tone, "Willow, sweet Pussywillow, why are you always lying flat on your back with your consciousness knocked clean out of you?"

"Is that you, Talon Clay? . . . It don't look like you . . . don't sound like you."

"It's me, darlin'."

She'd whispered, "You're beautiful." And he had carried her into the house. "You are the one who is beautiful," he murmured as he kicked the door open. His knee-high moccasins whispering across the carpet, he brought her to the couch in Ashe's cool study at the back of the house. She had asked him what he had said

107

and he had answered, "Nothing. Just rest." He went away, returning with a cool cloth.

"I was afraid you wouldn't come back," she had said. Lying there on the cool couch of Spanish leather, she had looked up at him, stretching out on her back. "You look so different, Talon . . . you even sound different."

He had found it to be a drastic mistake when he'd leaned closer to enable her to touch his cheek with her cool hand. He had compared her with other women: she was the blazing sun, the others merely candles. Then he had experienced the fiercest desire he'd ever known. He had been afraid to name the emotion for what it truly was. She had told him he looked just like an Indian. "How did your hair grow so long?" Her eyes slid from the braid to meet his gaze.

Narrowing to slits, his eyes had stared and taken in her sweet brown eyes. He didn't like the idea that the feel of her weakened him. He'd always been in control where women were concerned, but it had been a long time since he'd had a woman. This was the reason for the weakness, he'd warned himself. He had no idea what to do . . . he did not want another woman. Trying to smile and make light of the dangerous moment they were approaching, he had said, "I took a scalp." That was all, and she had smiled.

"A woman's hair . . . men don't have hair this long and fair. The whisper of the wind is in this hair." She had lifted his braid and brought it to rest against her softly flushed cheek, close to her ear. "I can hear the wind of your travels, the fleet hoof of your new white horse. You have already gone far and wide with this horse."

"Silly girl," he had said. "It's not a seashell you hold,

you know." Eyes sliding downward, he had watched her hand come to rest over the left side of his chest. "Now you hold my heart, Pussywillow." Their lips met in the slightest touch of a kiss. Fierce passion swept through him ... but he was not ready to acknowledge it yet. Willow said, "Please, Talon, just kiss me once?" Her breath came in quick panting gasps. "Just once ... and never again?"

What an idiot! He had told her, "I can't." *Can't.* And then she had begun to cry and he had been the cause of her heartbreak. All he'd done then was murmur a stupid endearment, shifted his weight so that he lay full length with her on the leather sofa ... her back against his pounding chest ... his body cupping hers.

Willow was lying in the bunk at the hideout, dreaming about a letter she was holding in her hands. Stepping toward a nearby lantern, she read the letter. It was addressed to Garnet's children: *Tanya; Willow Margaret; Samson* ... it was unfinished, the last word trailing into a squiggle. The letter vanished from her hands like puffs of smoke. Willow looked around. Now she was in the hidden room at Sundance, *her* room. She had discovered the secret room purely by chance one day when she'd been helping Tanya, when her sister had first come to clean for Ashe Brandon. While dusting the huge bookshelves in the library/office, she had lifted a peculiar-looking gold-etched book from its slot, reading the title: *Arabian Nights* ... she had heard these stories! She held the book and the spot where she was standing began to revolve. Suddenly she found herself inside a very dark, airless room and the words from *Arabian*

Nights came to her: 'Open Sesame,' the magic words spoken to open the door of the robbers' den in the story of Ali Baba!

Willow awoke in her bunk, hearing Ned snoring at the other side of the room. She sat up, leaning back against the wall, remembering the magical bookcase . . . to return to Ashe's office she had pressed a disc just inside the room. She also remembered discovering, the very first time, that the butt of a candle and the means to light it had been right beside her on a small oak table. After that, when she returned to the room filled with all Garnet's hidden stash, she had brought more candles for the following times she visited the magical bookcase . . . much later Ashe had discovered part of the Sundance legacy . . . an awful lot of money . . . *Brandon* money. Now she began to wonder if the Southern-style house had other such secret rooms . . . if there was more stash hidden somewhere . . . and if someone wanted to get to it!

Willow's eyes grew big in the dark. What if thieves who had knowledge of the room broke into Sundance while Ashe and Tanya were away? The house was guarded by drovers and mustangers, but someone could get in . . . especially now that so many men were joining the war, and Ashe and Tanya were in California. That would leave Sundance unguarded; there would *still* be Clem and a few others who would stay and guard. Yet, what if someone had a hostage!

Following a greasy breakfast of eggs fried in lard, fatback, and oily coffee, Willow felt the need to exercise to get rid of the bogged-down feeling the food gave her.

She checked on the horses, making sure hers got its fair share of hay and oats; she didn't want to be leaving with a sickly horse when the time came to mount up once again and ride out. She did a little snooping, too, walking casually around the rundown ranch, trying to eavesdrop on a barely audible conversation two dudes were having as they worked on a buckboard to make it even sturdier. Every time she tried to overhear, however, all conversation ceased until she walked or rode away again; then she could hear them resume in low voices. The men who rode guard around the ranch were even harder to get close to, since they were always on the move. And the men who worked putting up barbed wire fences on the ranch never talked at all, so it seemed. Maybe they did when she wasn't around.

It was three by the sun when a man by the name of Laredo rode in, and Willow heard the message he brought.

"The bitches just went through the pass; they got the kid with them." Laredo did not see the new "man" start as if to move in the direction he'd ridden from. He was talking about the "Lady Boss" out of one side of his mouth as he chewed on a cigarillo ... Willow's ears perked up. *Kid? Lady Boss?*

A woman.

A hostage. *Her child.*

It just didn't add up ... unless this Lady Boss used to work as cook or housekeeper at Sundance and wanted to get in there real bad, knowing there was another "hiding place" for the remainder of the money. But Ashe would have discovered that for himself by now, wouldn't he? She just didn't know and it made her feel jittery, angry, and helpless. And exactly as she had

111

thought following her revealing dream ... there was stash tucked away in the house somewhere, stuff she believed Ashe Brandon was not aware of. Journals? Money? Where would be a good place? She couldn't dwell on that now ... Laredo was still talking.

"Who're you?" Laredo looked Willow up and down. "Not another damn female in our gang."

Several of the others came out from inside. They were interested, and what Laredo was doing back after only two days out on the range especially caught their attention.

"I'm Will—" Willow shrugged saucily, watching the smoke spiral up from his gnawed cigarillo. "Or Belle ... whichever you like."

"You're pretty," Laredo conceded, biting down on an end of the smoke as if he'd bite it clean in half. "But you're too ... womanly for this job. Looks like you should be at home taking care of your kids."

"I only have—" Willow felt the red creeping up her neck—"me 'n' my trusty gun here. Yup, that's all."

"Got family?" Laredo asked, looking suspicious.

"I—uh—" She shrugged again, grinning impishly.

"What the hell—?" Laredo growled as Ned appeared at his side. "Who is she, anyway?" He tossed his cigarillo aside, spitting out a section of leaf that had stuck to his lips.

Ned laughed if off. "This here's Willabelle." He looked at her seriously, his eyes saying they still needed to talk about things. "I like to call her 'Willie.' Or 'Belle.'" His eyes twinkled, and he felt that kick in the gut again; every time she smiled like that she reminded him of someone.

Laredo growled, "Yeah, that first one's the name of

the cook; and I gotta go get some grub, come to think on it." He spit some tobacco juice again and Willow shuddered.

After he was gone, Willow giggled. "He, that Laredo, sure is skinny." She recalled bright red hair sticking out beneath either side of a strange blue cowboy hat. "And was that his stomach growling or his mouth?"

"Both," Ned muttered. "Don't let Laredo scare you. He barks and growls a lot but never bites." He walked along with Willow to the bunkhouse. "You got that far-away look in your eyes again, Belle." He stopped to look at her, noting the worry in her eyes.

"Willie—"

She laughed softly, her head to the side. "Don't you go starting to like me in a romantic way, Ned."

"You look so much like a woman I know. In fact, I think it's safe to tell you now: She's the Lady Boss."

"Who's the Lady Boss?"

"This woman who looks something like you."

Willow felt strange and cautious all of a sudden. "What is this woman's name?"

"Oh no, you don't. I ain't' goin' that far as to tell you her name. Not yet."

"Aww Ned, I thought you trusted me by now."

"I trusted you when I first laid eyes on you. All I said was, it's safe to tell you that the Lady Boss—"

"Looks like me." Willow gnawed her lower lip. "How much?" she asked, looking up and narrowing her eyes.

Ned stared down at the ground, kicked a few pebbles, frowned, then shot his gaze back at Willow. *"A lot."*

* * *

After sundown, as Willow sat at the long table alone long after mealtime was over, Ned walked in, scraped up a chair, and remarked, "What are you doin' there? Looks like whittling."

"That's right," Willow said, blowing on a "hand" she had carved out. "A man named Clem back on the ranch where I live . . ." Had she said too much? Feeling safe with Ned, she went on. "He showed me how to carve on wood."

"Whittling," Ned corrected, and she echoed, "Yes, whittling."

Tipping his head, Ned studied the piece of pale wood she was working. "That looks like a human you've been carving out."

She smiled. "It *is* a human I've been 'whittling' out." Willow blew on the piece again, holding it up for Ned to better see it. "It's going to be a boy. A little boy. See . . . this bag slung over his shoulder?" Ned looked at her with a nod. "He's lost."

"What's that on his face, under his eyes?"

"Tears."

"Oh." Ned hid his concern and got up to see about helping in the cookhouse. Besides, he needed coffee, what he used instead of liquor or other stimulants. He didn't like to get too emotional over anything— especially something as simple as a piece of wood.

In fact, there was the feeling that it was more complicated than that.

Keep thy tongue from evil, and thy lips
from speaking guile.
—Old Testament, *Psalms,* XXXIV, 13

Chapter Six

The ghost town was between nowhere and no place
and, like a ghost, "a shadowy semblance of its former
self," on the borderline of being dead or alive. Rawhide
was somnolent but still alive, with outlaws and gunslingers riding in and out like "night wraiths."

All supplies and foodstuffs came from a larger town
thirty miles north. Rawhide had its ghosts and most lawmen kept their distance; besides, she had her hidey-
holes in case there was a raid.

Tumbleweeds blew where no children played. Public
buildings lined both sides of the dusty, deserted street,
ornate arches along shady corridors decaying from the
many fires the town had sustained; there were long
cracks on the plastered walls of the stage depot where
bullet holes had damaged the structure.

Further out, where green lawns bordered by
flowerbeds once flourished, dry clumps of desert
grasses and sagebrush shared the courtyards with shriv-
eled corpses of trees and shrubs. The clapboard and
stone jailhouse west of the dance hall had once been a

convenient place to hold rowdies—when wild Rawhide had been alive and flourishing.

After a blaze in which a belligerent drunk had set fire to the dance hall, starting a chain reaction and burning all the town's wooden structures, Rawhide was rebuilt. Solidly lined again in '54 with wood-and-adobe buildings, this "newer" phase of the town's history was to be short-lived. The new town of Sweetwater had been born only thirty miles north and drained off the population of rowdy Rawhide, eventually leaving it an empty shell of weathered grays and murky browns beneath the blue horizon.

The little church had served Rawhide for many years, conveniently located at the edge of town where most of the humble abodes had once stood. Only a few of those homes remained standing, and the wind blew in the front door and out the back. Only the church and saloon had its human—and rodent—occupants. Inside the church a tiny filigreed organ had been stored in the corner and the woman who lived there—"hid out" was more like it—practiced on it only occasionally. Birds still nested in the walls, their holes noticeable from the outside.

A child cried in the back room of the church, a room that had served as office for the minister and his wife.

Ironically, out in back of the church there had been the largest saloon in the area, the ground floor having a bar on one side and a small dance hall on the other. Saturday nights saw wild times when cowboys, ranchers, and miners "blew her in." Windows with peeling green paint, beyond the balcony, could be seen upstairs . . . these had opened into rooms for "occupancy of short duration." Now the saloon served as a bunkhouse for outlaws, the Rawhide Gang. The Lady Boss kept these gunslingers on the "inside," the others "outside" at the Green Mountain hideout. When entering Rawhide—if anyone so dared—a guard would leap out from the entrance, demanding, "What's the password?" and if that answer was not "Open, Sesame!", no entrance was given.

A thin ribbon of a creek supplied water for Rawhide's gunslingers and lawbreakers as well as the graying blond woman who ran the whole show. You could almost hear the congregation singing "In the sweet bye and bye" . . . if it weren't for the woman's low, imperious voice at the moment punctuating the poignant atmosphere of the ghost town's house of worship. Her words were like cold rain falling on a hot campfire.

"Why, we can get rid of all the men," the Lady Boss was saying. "Sure, then there will be only us women." Her once-purring voice had hardened over the years, making her sound much like a dance hall madam. "Do you know, once the men left this town it was occupied only by women. Something to do with a war, men are always going off to war; maybe it was the Mexican War. Almost as exciting as the California gold rush." After she had left Sundance, there had been the gold rush. Oh, how she remembered those drunken parties and brawls . . .

Spawned by the California gold rush in '49, the Mariposa County town of Hornitos was without doubt the meanest, deadliest cutthroat community ever to mushroom in Mother Lode country. In a wild land noted for its lawlessness in the days of such as Joaquin Murietta, Three-Fingered Jack, Jim Weber, Tiburcio Vasquez, Black Bart, Charlie Jack, and a host of others, Hornitos was a haven for bandits, tinhorns, and cutthroats of every breed and description. They had all come often to "visit" Rawhide and "turn the ladies upside down." If Dodge City and Tombstone and Hornitos were tough, Rawhide was worse.

"Only us women," Garnet repeated. Women could have a good time without men—but for only so long, she believed.

Janice Ranae Tucker said, "I like the idea. But what about all your men? You aren't meaning to get rid of all them, are you?"

"Why, Lady Jane, not my men!" Garnet laughed in a husky whiskey voice. "I mean the Brandon men and all their macho friends like Almanzo and—" She waved a negligent hand in the air—"whoever all the others *might* be who step into our path."

Excited by the idea—excluding Talon Clay from Garnet's murders—Hester blurted, "What about Willow? And Tanya? What will you do with them once we combine Sundance and Saw Grass? They'll be in the way."

"Tanya?" Garnet asked of her eldest "daughter" as she swirled a sloshing drink of "Ginny Lemonade." "What about her?" She said nothing of Willow. And Sammy.

"Didn't you know?" Janice Ranae blinked her small beady eyes. "Tanya's married to Ashe. He calls her by his special name for her: Lady Red."

"Oh, shoot! That's great." Garnet shot a look at Nat Lacey, detesting her looks and not wanting her "special" men, like Ned Thompkins, getting a load of this blond tart with the saucy blue eyes and swinging breasts.

Nat Lacey just sat quietly, making her own devious plans for the future. All she had to do was pretend to act the dumb blonde on the outside, while no one had any idea how smart she really was. She was saving her brains and talent to snag Talon Clay Brandon, that rough, tough Ranger who made her heart do flip-flops, unlike dull, dark-eyed Indian Hank Rountree. Only problem was, she was afraid she'd never get to really have a "good time" with Talon Clay. Somehow she had a bad feeling about the Brandons, like a premonition that God could be looking out for their kind.

Hester Tucker was dreaming about the day she would at last have the handsome Ranger for her own; she had waited for Talon Clay Brandon almost all her life. She was going to be like a mad dog—sink her teeth in and never let go.

Janice Ranae was thinking about her own revenge she would one day get on the Brandons. One of them had killed her son, Carl, somehow or helped him meet his death in the caverns of Guadalupe Mountains. Tanya had shot Carl in the leg and poked him in the eye, saying she defended herself when he had tried to ravish her. Carl had ended up half-blind and walked with a limp. And where had been Talon Clay's loyalty? He and Carl had been outlaws together in the Wild Bunch, and Talon had turned Carl in, saying he had murdered a stagecoach driver. Well, she hadn't believed for a moment Carl did all that. Then the Brandons had said Carl took the alias *Randy Dalton,* kidnapped Ashe and Tanya's daughter, Sarah, along with Willow and took them away. Then Ashe and Talon Clay had trailed them into the Guadalupe Mountains. Janice didn't believe the story for one minute. Would her dear Carl do all that? Never. Those Brandons had it coming, and she would make sure they all got it real good this time. Sundance was going to be hers and Garnet's!

Janice Ranae went on speaking to Garnet. "And what about your son, Sammy? That sixteen-year-old'll kill anyone tries to harm those sisters of his."

"Sammy—" Garnet held a red fingernail up. "The youngest . . . my baby." She was thoughtful for a moment. "There's too damn many stones in the gears."

"More like rocks," Hester said with a giggle. She looked at Nat, and Nat giggled, too, then shrugged when the Lady Boss shot her a look of distaste and envy over the younger woman's firmer assets.

"Men—" Garnet snarled like a tigress—"I've done away with a few in my time. Now Sammy . . . I think I can get him to come around to Mama's side." In a chilling voice, eyeing Nat Lacey, she said, "Her—" She snorted dubiously. "That one can snatch up Talon Clay."

"What about Willow?" Hester was excited and eager to know what would happen to her adversary; Nat she could get rid of later, but Willow was another story altogether.

Dryly Garnet said, "Willow. Hmm—" Thoughtful and briefly tender, she almost appeared as lovely as her "daughter." "I'll send her away. Yes. I know just the man who'll take our little widow Willow away—for a while, anyway." She did not say the name Hank Rountree. The mysterious gunslinger had been hanging around on and off, doing odd jobs for her. Hank was a man with a past, a descendant of Mescalero Apaches, one who was searching for something or someone, and she didn't care *what* or *who* it was, as long as he didn't doublecross *her*.

Reluctantly, Janice Ranae brought up the eldest's name again. "Tanya."

Forcing her voice to be level, Garnet said, "Oh—Tanya. My beautiful redhead. I remember her most of all, always taking care of the other two when I was . . . never mind," she broke off. " 'Lady Red,' Ashe calls her?"

"Yeah." Janice Ranae bristled, unaware of her blatant jealousy and contempt for the beautiful redhead. "He has been known to call Tanya that. They're away in California just now, vacationing along the coast." Hester's Mama curled her lip as she went on, "There was this time I asked Tanya to loan me some money and she went to Ashe about it—"

"*Perhaps—*" Garnet broke into Janice Ranae's sentence, her feelings of superiority surfacing—"Yes, it might be a good idea if they *stayed* there. A way—" She tapped her chin. "There *must* be a way." Shrugging, she added, "It will come to me one of these days. Has to be soon, however."

"At times you really resemble Willow," Hester blurted, seeing her Mama's frown cut across to her. "Uhm, when you look a certain way," she said to Boss Lady Garnet.

"Do I?" Garnet's voice dropped huskily on the "I." "She's nothing like me, I'd wager. Willow . . . as I remember was a sweet child . . . a little mischievous at times. Oh, well. What am I doing . . . giving an account of my family album?"

Hester was curious. "Why did you ever leave Sundance? Everyone thought you was dead and buried."

"Did they now?" Garnet sashayed around the huge room where half the pews had been ripped out. Her

121

gaze skimmed over the silent Nat Lacey and stopped at Hester, right before the younger woman looked back up. "I was wanted by the law ... and that's why I high-tailed it out of Sundance. I knew Ashe Brandon had just become a Texas Ranger and I wanted out of there. I knew when he returned he'd be snooping around to pin something on me. You see, Ashe hated me something fierce. So did his younger brother, Talon Clay, by then. Ashe was out to get me." She wasn't about to reveal how she had taught Talon "the ropes" of lovemaking; she'd never been able to get to Ashe.

"Are you—" Janice Ranae almost jumped up and down for joy—"you're *still* Mrs. Brandon?"

"That's right. Pete Brandon and I never got a divorce. I went away to clear myself—" Her eyes rolled shiftily. "And I still carried the name Brandon. I'm still legal owner of Sundance ... I just have to find the damn papers— Among other things, a journal and money where I hid them in the house at Sundance. I'll remember soon and then I aim to take the kid with me as hostage and get into the house. And I have to do it while Ashe and Tanya are still away, if possible."

"Tell me something about Talon Clay," Hester said, tucking her feet beneath her on a cushioned pew, longing to hear details of Garnet's "tutoring" a younger Talon Clay.

"Let's get to work." With that, Garnet walked to the door, putting an abrupt end to the conversation.

At the door, Garnet met with one of her men just coming up to speak with her. "Boss, the boys up at Green Mountain hideout got a new woman for you—" He chuckled. "Another blonde to do your dirtiest jobs."

"Good," she whispered. "Get rid of this bothersome

Nat Lacey. I was going to use her to snag Talon Clay—the Ranger, by the way—but this woman with the big blue eyes just won't do."

"That bad?"

"Worse. Do what you want with her. She's got a nice body but she's empty upstairs. Wait a minute. On second thought, she might be acting the dumb blonde. Be careful of her, she's got something nasty and cunning on her mind. We've got the boy, the hostage in the back room of the church. Make sure you have the boys guard the back entrance real good. I don't want anyone snatching the kid as soon as we got him."

"Is it true the boy's your grandson?"

"I don't mean to discuss the boy, and I want my men discussing him even less."

"Have you seen him yet? He's a little tiger."

Garnet glared. "Did you hear what I just said?" Poking him in the chest, she added, "If you didn't, you'll find yourself sent out with the trash along with Nat Lacey."

"Sorry, Boss."

"Accepted, Winder. Just don't let me down. You've been a good man."

At Green Mountain hideout, Willow sighed as she looked at Ned Thompkins. "When am I going to meet the Lady Boss, Ned?" She dreaded what she knew he would say next.

"Soon, Belle. But first we have to pull a job. We're running low on some things."

"You mean you have to steal some cash in order to buy what you need here at the hideout?" Putting on the mask, she spied Ned through the slits and laughed. "Necessities, you mean ... otherwise we'll be living like, uh, real bandits."

"We're outlaws, Willow. *Outlaws* sounds better than *bandits*. Put your hair up in that hat real good so's no one can tell you're female."

Shrugging, Willow declared, "I don't see any difference in outlaws or bandits, Ned ... just words." She tossed aside the mask. "I'm getting real antsy to meet this Lady Boss."

"You will, you will." He laughed, retrieving the mask and handing it back to her. "Keep your pants on." He was worried about this young woman and what was going to happen to her once they hit the Trail; she seemed to know her stuff, though, and that made him worry less. But not a whole lot less.

Mentally and physically Willow had prepared herself for what was to come. She understood the chances she was taking. Still, she shook like a hanky in the wind as they waited for the wealthy King cousins, who were scheduled to pass through Comanche Gap on their way to Abilene. They would be riding in their own special King stagecoach, supposed to be carrying government money. Willow knew the consequences of stealing from the government. Yet, Ned had eased her mind a little when he said, "It's government money paid to the Kings. So, it's not actually the government's any longer—it's more like the army's."

"Why did the Kings get all this money from the government?"

"Sale of mustangs."

Mustangs. Mustang Men. Talon Clay and Almanzo Rankin. Almanzo—Nightwalker, Dark Horse. Despite

124

his heavy scowl, he was as good-looking as his Indian father Kijika with crisp, straight black hair and Indian-dark eyes framed by curly black lashes, and lean, predatory features. Willow reflected back to the happy days at Sundance, she and Tanya laughing and flirting as the drovers and mustangers brought in the wild horses from out on the range. She was snatched back to the present. "Which army?" Willow asked suddenly. Ned had never said just *exactly* who was paying the Kings for their special horses. She hated to steal from "horse people"; they were usually nice, easygoing folks.

"I suppose it has to do with the war, Willow. I don't really know. *Maybe* it's the army what's paying them."

Biting her lip, Willow said, "It's almost a sacrilege . . . stealing this money what's gone for good horseflesh. I don't know, Ned, this just doesn't sit right with me."

With a shrug, Ned looked away, saying over his shoulder as he saddled up, "It's a war, Belle, and the North and South are going to be fightin'. Experienced combat men in the army know that battles are won as often by good horseflesh as by reliable guns and men. The Kings afford an excellent pipeline to the best horses in the North since their relatives own not just these Texas breeding farms but even larger ones in Kansas and Oklahoma. They got more money and horses than they know what to do with."

Suddenly Willow wished she was back at Sundance; it would be a good time to breed horses and sell them. She wondered if Almanzo would realize this, leave Black Fox's camp, and return to Sundance. "I just don't like it, Ned."

He looked at her, knowing she would do what she

125

had to in order to survive. "War is war, Belle, and outlaws will always be outlaws."

Sure. And there was a private war going on right in Texas, she thought. Probably more than that.

"There's no time to linger; the other dudes are coming now. Saddle up, Belle."

Doing just that, Willow had second thoughts: I'll do anything to get my son back. Even rob good folk or shoot a man between the toes. But heaven knew that she did not want to commit murder. Never that again. Guess it's every man for himself—and every woman for *herself*.

The following morning, Willow's heart had calmed down a bit. By breakfast, her nerves were steel once again. During the holdup the day before, Stone's men had not hurt anyone or been hurt themselves, and she thanked God for that. One holdup followed another after that, and the days grew into weeks. She was nervous, restless, and frantic with worry to get to her son before something terrible happened, always knowing this was impossible as long as Ned didn't give the word that it was time to head to the ghost town.

Willow had to be very careful with her words, always afraid that someone would catch on when she asked questions about the "Boss Lady." One night she'd asked about "the boy" and Ned had given her a stern look, as if he had detected something and was wary that the others would catch on.

After they had finished eating around the campfire, Willow was just finishing washing the tin plates and cups when Ned came up to her. His voice was very soft and low. "You're the boy's mother, aren't you?" Willow stiffened but did not look at Ned. He watched her lift her eyes to the Texas moon, and he said, "I knew it. It's true, right?"

Her voice was soft. "Yes. I believe it's Michael Angelo the lady outlaws have brought to your boss. He vanished about the same time your women rode out . . . it was several days later I learned about the child this Lady Boss wanted. Can you tell me her name now?" She felt no answer forthcoming and shrugged. "Never mind, Ned. The name doesn't matter, I only want my son back. My husband is searching for Michael, too." She wouldn't say that Talon Clay was a Ranger . . . something told her to hold that back just as Ned was keeping quiet about the boss lady's identity. She was probably some woman who had been eager to adopt and hadn't been able to find a child.

But why her child? There had to be a reason . . .

Her mind drifted back to when Talon Clay had ridden into town, discovered at last his son was missing, then found the kidnapper to be a woman. "How many women took my son?"

"Two."

"Do you know their names?" Willow was eager to strangle them.

Ned paused. "No."

A lump growing in her throat, Willow asked, "What now, Ned?"

Mechanically he bent to toss a twig into the fire, all the while gazing straight into the hot flames. Finally he glanced up at her, then down again into the blaze. It crackled. "What will be, will be. All of us have our own road to travel. I won't stop you from doing what you have to, Belle." He had seen the sad, lonely look on her face as she had carved the little boy. "The others won't learn of this, but I have to tell you I'll protect the Boss Lady if anyone tries to harm her."

"I promise not to hurt her if possible, Ned. Just tell me what she plans to do with Michael. Why does she have to have him? Why my son?"

Ned blinked hard and came slowly to his feet, as if he'd just discovered something very important. "Lord God in heaven . . . you're from Sundance property."

Looking him straight in the eyes, she lowered her head slowly. "True, Ned." Her head came up then. "I haven't been there for a long time . . . over four years come June."

"The Brandons," Ned said with a hiss. "Are you a Brandon woman, married to one, I mean?"

"I—used to be." She prayed he didn't know Talon Clay was a Ranger. "My husband and I are . . . separated and we probably won't be getting back together."

"Well, at least that's something." He squinted at her as the flames reflected in his eyes. "Ashe Brandon still a Ranger?"

"No."

"Who're you married to?"

Willow swallowed. "Talon Clay Brandon. He's a . . . mustanger."

"Shoot. Talon's bride. No wonder you didn't want to rob horse folks."

"Yes." Willow nodded. "Why is the boss holding my son? Is he a hostage?"

"You're right smart, Belle." Heaving a deep sigh, Ned reached out and cupped her shoulder. "Tell you

128

what, lady outlaw, I'll help you get your son if you go along with my plans."

"What does she want him for?" Willow repeated. "She can't get Sundance; she has to have the deed to do that."

"I haven't gotten that far in my lady friend's plans, Belle. I'll tell you this . . . if this war gets going good, nothing is going to be sacred or worth much anymore, not anywhere."

"In our state it will be; Texans own Texas!" Willow lifted her chin. "I know there's killing along the borders, especially in Kansas, and Texas is fighting her own border war with the Mexicans."

"Yeah, and some of the Rangers have been relieved of border command and gone to Fort Brown with 'Old Rip'."

"Who is he?" she asked, becoming uneasy with Ned's knowledge of the Texas Rangers.

"John S. Ford." As soon as Ned said the name, Willow knew of whom he spoke.

"Oh, Rip Ford, the Ranger leader." She tried not to swallow too hard. Talon was one of Ford's Rangers, the Rio Grande Squadron; this much she knew.

"I know my Rangers," Ned said, making Willow blink in surprise. "I'd never tangle with one; respect 'em too much. The Rio Grande Squadron was made up mostly of seasoned frontiersmen," he went on. "Besides Nolan, 'Old Rangers' Dan Givens, John Ingram, and Voltaire Rountree were on hand, as were 'Chicken' Morris, who'd been Comanche hunting with Ford the previous winter, Corporal Milton Duty, Bennett Musgrave, A.C. Hill, and at least two hard specimens,

'Red' Thomas . . . I don't know the names of the rest."
Willow breathed a quick sigh of relief.

"Y-you like Texas Rangers then?" she asked, and
waited.

"Of course I do. Without them where would Texas
be?" Ned pressed his lips into a thin line. "Wish I'd
been one many times, but I . . . well, that's another
story."

"I . . . see. You wouldn't step in a Ranger's way if he
had a job to do . . . a very important job?"

"Never."

"Let's turn in, Ned," she said, stretching toward the
stars. "Tomorrow comes early."

For sleepless hours on end, Ned was in turmoil as he
lay in his bedroll that night. He was frustrated, wondering what to do about this lovely little spitfire who would
go to any lengths to get her son back. He guessed he
would, too, if the timing had been right . . . he'd lost a
beloved baby son years earlier because a beautiful
woman from the Texas Mexican border ran off and left
him brokenhearted; later he had discovered that Ria was
already married to a Mexican bandit and it was too late
for a father-son relationship by then. He would find
some way to help Belle without harming a hair on Boss
Lady's head.

The "Watering Hole" was one of those places that
made the western frontier what it was in '61. Wherever
there was money to spend, gambling joints could be
found. And some became fancy palaces of drinking and
gambling and whoring like the Watering Hole. This
place in Abilene was making money and lots of it.

Talon Clay knew a lot about gambling houses—and all that went with them—enough to know how much these "games" would be raking in and which sort of girls were the pick of the lot.

"Buenas dias, Rinche!" a man with slicked-back, greasy, dark hair greeted the observant Ranger as he walked through the door, spurs twirling and jingling. Talon Clay was trying to draw attention, since he needed to make contact with as many desperados and gunslingers as possible. These were the sort of men who liked flashy and noisy things, and they would speak to the lawman just for a laugh or a bit of horseplay.

The Ranger sauntered in and around tables, then came to a complete standstill, his heart pounding, his mouth dry. The painted lady, a young one, a whore when you came right down to it, was the spit and image of Willow. She stood across the room, daintier than most women, with a slender yet voluptuous body that made the pulse pound in Talon's throat. The blonde was dressed for sport, spending the evening walking among the tables of the gambling room. She was wearing a red-and silver-spangled gown, utterly different in style from the room. He looked away quickly when she caught him staring.

He moved to the back of the room, away from the blonde in the red dress; he could feel her searching gaze as if a string stretched between them, leading her to him. Felt it in his blood and loins. He wanted Willow. No other. No woman ever stirred him so deeply or made him realize so much about what he was missing in his lonely Ranger's life. True, it didn't have to be lonely . . . he could always have a woman. He looked at the bar-

131

tender, at the booze, at the woman in red, and walked away.

Sammy waited for him outside, out in the fresh night air. Texas air, big and wide as the sky ... all the buildings side by side, with their false fronts, long porches, high wood balconies with the blur of laughing faces leering down. Talon took big gulps of air to clear his mind of all the temptation he'd fallen prey to as a younger man and was trying to avoid tonight. A kid, that's all he'd been when he had first met Willow ... even eight years back, immature, never having known that she had been there when he had lived with their neighbors—the friggin' Tuckers—because Garnet was sleeping with his father. Forget it! Why did this come back to haunt him now?

"Damn Willow, you brought this on me." It was in her blood, in Garnet's; they would always lust for another man to take the place of the one they had jilted and left behind. No doubt Willow had found herself another outlaw to bed down with. She had loved him madly when he'd been lawless and whoring ... is that what she wanted? No; she had said that she didn't ... and it remained a mystery as to where she got that crock of lies about him cheating. "Where are you, Willow, and why the hell do you keep running from me?" He heard a giggle and looked up.

The woman in red stood above him on a balcony, blowing kisses from her dainty hand, laughing, eyes begging him to come to her. He probably didn't even have to pay ... that had happened to him more often than not. He got in free with the ladies of the night.

Sammy was frowning at the Ranger. "You know her,

Talon Clay?" He moved beneath the balcony and blinked. "Holy cow, she looks just like—"

"Shut up, Sammy." With the lad's shoulder hard in hand, he whirled on his boot and snarled, "Let's get the hell out of here!"

"But ain't that Will—?"

"No, Sammy. She's some man's entertainment for the night—and it ain't mine!"

After Abilene, Sammy and the Ranger parted. They had argued, Sammy saying he had to get back to Bountiful and check if Willow'd returned, the Ranger saying he had an idea Willow had headed west from Paradise Valley. Talon had withdrawn some funds from a mercantile firm in Abilene, having used the banking services provided several years back when he'd ridden in with the drovers from Sundance after having done an honest week's job with the dudes. Then it had been back to work with old Rip Ford along the Rio Grande. He didn't make much as a Ranger. He loved the work. At least, he used to.

Now all he could think of was rescuing his son and capturing his wayward wife.

The sixteen-year-old's face looked chiseled from granite when he and Talon had parted. "I'll find her, Ranger, make sure she's okay, and then I'll come lookin' for you. Together we'll go find Mikey."

"Whatever you think, Sam." Eyes dusty and tired, Talon leaned across his saddle, poking the brim of his black hat upward. "And whichever comes first."

"Yeah. Sure."

"Just don't go gettin' foolhardy, Sam."

133

Sammy tipped his hat upward, too. "I won't."

With a parting word, Sammy had asked, "Where you goin', Ranger?"

With a glance westward, Talon jerked his hat back into place. "To Black Fox's camp."

Not ten yoke of oxen
Have the power to draw us
Like a woman's hair.
—Longfellow, *The Saga of King Olaf*

Chapter Seven

Two weeks gone already. All around him it was quiet and green as he rode. Two weeks, his brain repeated. Talon Clay could hardly believe it: fourteen days since he'd ridden into Bountiful, talked to Willow briefly, touched her, wanting so much more. Now he wanted Michael, too, wanted to hold him, play and laugh. Oh, how he wanted to do that, since he hadn't felt like laughing or sharing good times in years.

Lordy, now he'd have to find his wife and capture her, bring her home if Sammy had no luck finding her back at Bountiful. He had a new worry. He would have to find someone to guard her at Sundance . . . and something was telling him to visit Black Fox's camp. He might find his answer there.

Days later, the Ranger was close to the camp. Briefly, he halted the big stallion, surrounded by sagebrush, prickly pear cactus, and Spanish dagger. The rocks were beginning to grow larger as he rode along one of the river tributaries. The unbroken expanse of bright green prairie spread out until it was lost in the hazy violet-blue distance. He came upon cool, clear water and drank thirstily, then continued over the mesquite glades. When day gave way to night the sky turned midnight black, and it was hard to tell where earth and heavens met. In the morning, as woodland began to fall away and Talon rode on, the mesquite valley reigned; by evening, a strawberry moonglow invaded, rising in the south.

Another morning, and he was riding the High Plains and then the steep rock walls loomed up ahead. It was almost noon when he reached the secret entrance, the crevice in the rock wall leading into the valley. Pausing at the cleft in the high wall, he gazed out over the uneven ripples of buffalo grass in the distance. Shrublike mesquite trees blew gray-green beneath the hot sun. To the West, cacti sprouted out of the sandy earth, their dangerously sharp thorns and growths pointing crazily in every direction. There was a certain type of plant, a cactus, that would cause a person to hallucinate if he ate a part of it.

Talon could smell the fragrance of wood smoke, heavier in the air than hours before, and he sucked in his breath as he emerged from the narrow rock canyon and looked down on the Indian camp below. His heart skipped in his chest as he wondered how Willow had felt when she rode downward from the cleft and beheld the beauteous sight. The smell of pine and earth and smoke titillated his senses. This is the place where he and Willow had become man and wife, he reminisced, as he rode the rough trail leading down into the camp, rugged and beautiful, so unreal in its isolation, wild as the towering mesa that bulged magnificently above it.

The rider had been recognized; the word traveled swiftly from tepee to tepee. The Kiowa, who numbered about sixteen hundred, embraced ten to twenty bands in all. Each one consisted of the occupants of twelve to fifty tepees. A new band came into existence when a leader, like Black Fox, separated from the parent group and left with a following of brothers and sisters, with their spouses and offspring. The Comanches were their allies, and some of the oddest names of those were Burnt Meat, Those-Who-Move-Often, and Man-Afraid-of-His-Horses.

Indians began to drift out from their tepees as they heard that Lakota/White Horse was coming. Little Coyote waved to him along with two bronze-skinned toddlers; he had a family now and he stood with his squaw, shoulder to shoulder. The Ranger greeted many friends and acquaintances, his gaze searching especially for a handsome couple by the names of Dark Horse and Kachina. He was eager to see them together again, Kachina with her night-blue eyes, she whose mother had been a white woman, her father chief of the Shoshone.

Ah, there he is. Talon saw him . . . and it looked as if Almanzo-Dark Horse was just in the process of getting ready to leave Black Fox's camp. Looking around, Talon did not see Kachina, thinking she must be inside the tepee.

Riding up to Almanzo and dismounting, Talon greeted his longtime friend as usual by making the sign for "Kiowa" in the language of the Plains tribes, holding his right hand close to his right cheek, the back of his hand down, fingers touching and slightly cupped while his hand moved in a rotary motion from the wrist.

"Son-of-Dark Horse," said Talon Clay.

"Named-Lakota," Dark Horse replied.

The dark-haired man laughed briefly as he went on. "I thought you were to use the shortened version of my

Indian name and I was to be known only as Dark Horse from now on, my brother." The laughter did not reach Dark Horse's eyes; Talon could see much sadness.

"What has happened?" Talon asked as he stepped closer to Dark Horse, who was fastening supplies onto his horse's back. "There's something—" He looked at Dark Horse's rigid back—"I can tell. Maybe you don't want to talk about it right—"

"She's gone, my friend. Kachina died in childbirth. Both—"

"Oh Lordy." Talon shook his head sadly, feeling his heart twist with compassion for his friend and brother. "I didn't know." She had been so beautiful and kind and loving . . . Willow would be grieved . . . they had meant to come and visit, but they never had, not since the last time Kachina and Dark Horse had come to Sundance over four years back. "What was it, boy or girl?" As soon as he asked this, he wished to God he'd kept his mouth shut.

"Boy." The child had been a son.

"Whew!" Talon swiped an arm across his brow, then clapped Dark Horse on the shoulder as they both bent together in mourning Kachina and the dead child for a few brief moments and then straightened with deep sighs. Talon only nodded as he stared at his Indian brother's profile.

"I have lost a son also," he said, then went on to explain as Dark Horse turned a look of concern his way, ready to ask about Willow. "He . . . Michael has been kidnapped, Almanzo." He called him by the name the Rankins had given him as a child.

"Kidnapped!" Almanzo snapped, his eyes blazing. "How could you allow this to happen?"

With a shrug and a deep sigh, Talon said, "I have never seen my son . . . Willow ran away when she discovered she was pregnant. She . . . we had words . . ." He ground his teeth together. "I lost myself in my job instead of going to fetch her back to Sundance. I know—" He looked at Almanzo—"I'm a friggin' idiot and deserve all the hell I'm going through now!"

"Don't let the others in camp hear all your cussing, my friend. They will ask questions, for if you recall, they never use swearwords."

"You're right, my brother. I'm just so . . . frustrated and ready to strangle the woman that snatched my kid away. If I catch up with her . . . whoever she is, I'll have to kick her stupid aa . . . butt up around her ears!"

"Hush!"

"Almanzo . . . will you ride with me?"

"Yes, my brother, I will come with you. For a time, and then I must find my own path."

"I have a job for you," Talon said, looking into Almanzo's deep, dark eyes sternly. "At first I will be with you for a time, and then later you will be on your own in this task."

"Good," Almanzo said. "I'll take the job, as I need something to get my mind off Kachina—" He sighed and looked to the summer sky, then back at Talon Clay.

"But you have no idea what the task is yet."

"No. I can tell it is something very serious and important just by looking into your eyes. You need this favor of me badly, otherwise you would not have sought me out. You want me to ride with you at once."

"Yes, I do. But first I have to find the one I want you to guard."

139

"Guard? Ah, Amigo, by the looks of your face it has to be a woman. Not just any woman—Willow."

"How did you guess?"

"How? She is the only woman who has ever given you trouble—and she is your wife." He laughed deeply, suddenly feeling less grieved by his friend's appearance in Black Fox's camp. "This is good news that you and she have finally come together, to have a son."

Had Almanzo forgotten already? "Yes?" he said, realizing Almanzo would get better as the days grew into weeks and months. "But the rest is not such good news. Come on, I'll tell you after we get some grub and rest and then ride out."

"Grub, huh?" Almanzo laughed at his half-brother's crude language. He shrugged, remembering he himself used to sound like a Tex Mex at times.

Under the star-splashed Texas sky they rode out of Black Fox's camp. Almanzo felt his heart breaking at a last glance over his shoulder to the green knob of hill where he'd laid his wife to rest in a Christian burial. His beautiful Kachina; one tear rolled down his cheek, off his chin, and onto his buckskin shirt. He looked straight ahead, feeling his blood begin to skip and flow again at the thought of new adventures. Kachina would have wanted him to face the sun each day and smile, even without her. Even so, there would never be another love for him like Kachina. There had been one other, and she, the flame-haired woman who had been his first true love—and not Ellita—the woman Tanya he'd only held in his arms when she'd been hurt; she, Lady Red, was married with another. And that man was Talon Clay's brother Ashe. Both Ashe and Talon had the same mother, Martha; she was gone from this earth now.

In the faint predawn light, Belle and the other mounted outlaws waited for the stage that would pull into Oak Creek, population seven hundred. They were well outside Oak Creek, however, and there was plenty of time before the stagecoach was due to come rumbling along the rocky, dusty road. She hadn't slept much the night before, and now her head nodded and her eyes slowly closed as she tried to catch forty winks.

She wasn't actually sleeping, just remembering past times before she and Talon had become a married couple. One day when the Tucker wagon had been going out of Sundance, taking Hester with it, she had watched until the wagon had become a mere dust cloud in the distance. Curiously, she had watched Talon with Hester and they appeared to have been arguing; then Hester had gone home. Willow had walked right up to Talon with a bright good-morning smile and asked him, "What would lovers have to argue about on such a beautiful day?" She was sighing with contentment on that lovely morning when suddenly Talon Clay whirled on her.

His eyes shone chillingly, his voice was scathing. "Don't you ever—" he'd been about to scold her when his eyes dropped to her shoulder with a frown. She had shouted "Ouch!" stepping back away from him. His grip loosened a little on her bruised shoulder until she cried, "Let go, Talon, it hurts." He peered at her closer, asking, "Why does that hurt there?" She felt miserable, afraid to tell Talon Clay that Carl Tucker had given her these bruises when he had tried to ravish her in the schoolhouse where she was a teacher; the children had been gone for the day.

"Let's have a look at that," he said. Swift as lightning, he shoved her sleeve upward, whistling and then frowning darkly. Suddenly his fingers had gentled, becoming soothing as he said, "Who done this to you, Willow? Tell me so I can go after the bastard and kill him!" Willow had swallowed hard, trying to think of something; it had to be a lie. She had told him she got it at school, and he had still looked at her with suspicion. He frowned, saying, "That looks like a man's—" Swiftly she cut him off, but he had learned of the other bruise Carl Tucker made on her tender flesh. Of course he *hadn't known* it was Carl who did the damage, and then she smiled brightly and charmingly up at him. "Oh Talon, I heard you got a pardon . . . that's wonderful."

When Talon had kept looking at her in his mesmerizing way, she brushed a hand before his eyes, "Wake up, Talon, and show me that horse; I'd like to see Dust Devil again." After seeming to come to a decision, he walked alongside her, his bare feet moving silently through the grass, like an Indian's. "The mustang moves like lightning," he warned her as he helped her mount the horse, "so be careful."

"I will," Willow said with a giggle. *"You* be careful, too . . . *you're* barefoot." When she began to move away from him, mounted on Dust Devil, Talon had shown admiration in his eyes . . . she hadn't known for which . . . the horse or her. His face looked flushed, then uncomfortable, and at last angry, watching her. She had wondered about this play of emotions.

142

She called something back to Talon and he had moved restlessly against the late summer sky. He looked aside, as if trying to control his emotions. She called to him again, "Look at me, Talon! I adore her and I think she loves me, too. Oh, I love riding her."

"Yeah, I would love to ride—" The rest she could not hear; he had said this under his breath. And then his voice was louder. "Guess I underfigured you, Pussywillow . . . you seat a horse pretty good for a woman." She had given her head an impudent toss, retorting "What do you mean—a *woman?* A woman can do anything a man can do—sometimes better!" And he had shouted agreeably, "You tell 'em, darlin'!" He spoke to Clem briefly, then shouted to her again, "Yeah. That's your horse now, little lady. I broke and trained her myself."

Willow pulled herself out of her reverie, feeling the spotted pony Magic move restively beneath her, and then the dust cloud was moving toward them. Pulling her mask in place, making sure her hair was tucked up good inside her hat, Willow tensed for the onslaught. Ned was suddenly at her side, reaching over to tuck one more strand of pale yellow hair up inside. "Better watch that," he said. "Most outlaws don't have long hair like that—not that squeaky clean nor that color."

The words came to Willow: *Why is your hair so long?* She had asked Talon Clay the first time she had been confronted with those striking green eyes. *Your hair is close to my own hair color . . .*

"Let's get 'em!" Laredo shouted.

"Yah!" Willow called, giving her mount a swift jab in the flanks.

As they thundered across the range, Willow had the haunting, troubling thought once again: Was this what it had been like for Talon Clay when he had been an outlaw? It was crazy, like running against the wind, feeling as if you belonged nowhere, to no one. Lonely. And sad. This was the outlaw's life and she didn't want to have to put up with it much longer, because the strain of the past weeks had taken its toll, her delicate features drawn and pale and her brown eyes dull with fatigue. Too, her nerves were on the edge of collapse and she would find herself crying over trivialities. Like now. Tears sprang to her eyes for no good reason.

As Willow stepped off the wooden boardwalk and into the dusty street, she stiffened and her pulse began to beat erratically. Someone had been following her—she could see his dark shadow again, moving out from between two storefronts.

The deep voice behind her was a shock.

"Ah, *desperada,* we meet again. So, where have you been keeping yourself, hmm?"

Almanzo Rankin!

Whirling to face the dark-visaged, handsome man, Willow's face bleached beneath the rim of her large sombrero. She licked her lips, softly asking, "What did you say? I'm afraid I don't know you, hombre." Her eyes scanned the area; in the past wherever Almanzo showed up, Talon Clay wasn't far behind. "You better move along, make room for me to pass, stand back, or somethin'."

The tall man with eyes like black glitters of obsidian drawled, "I do not think so. You and I have an appointment to keep, *desperada;* he has been searching, and now he is waiting for you." When she seemed about to

144

bolt, Almanzo warned, "Do not try it. We have seen the 'WANTED' posters and the artist's likeness could not be better; in fact, they are almost perfect. And no one could mistake you for someone else with hair *that* yellow." He leaned closer, deeply purring, "Get out now, *desperada*, before you find there is no way but a life behind bars. You will soon be recognized. We will make it easy for you, if you come quietly and do not alert the townsfolk or the others in your bunch."

She could make out a second figure lurking in the shadows of an overhang across the street, and her hand automatically went to the gunbelt slung low across her hips. "Reach for the sky, hombre!" Willow's voice was as low as her gunbelt. "I don't want no trouble, no shootin', 'less I have to."

"Tsk, tsk, Willow, you do not make a very good bad-man," Almanzo said, shaking his head and lifting his arms only slightly. "You leave me no other choice but to see that you are arrested."

"For what?" Willow snapped, keeping the silent figure across the way in her peripheral vision. Almanzo was ruining her plans; soon the others would know what was happening, and they would make a run for it, see-ing that she had been recognized by this dark-eyed man. "Are you a lawman now?" When Almanzo shook his head, she peered back at him. "Please go!" she hissed. "If you know what has happened, and that man across the way is who I think he is, then take him with you and leave me alone!" She was so close; she would soon have Michael if she was left to her own plans. . . . Oh, no!

Ned Thompkins had just come out of the General Store across the way . . . not forty feet from where the

145

silent stranger wearing a long serape draped over his shoulders was standing. Ned saw her with the tall man and frowned: Belle was just tucking something away; she looked angry and defeated. Was this her husband? No, he couldn't be sure . . . he'd thought the gossip was that the Brandon men were fair-haired with eyes that ran to hazel or green. This man with Belle had a face that was all angles and planes, a cruelly handsome visage beneath the shadow of his hat brim. His eyes were black, it seemed . . .

"Ned," Belle said in a low voice. Then she jerked her head, meaning for him to get the men and go! He understood, as his eyes shifted to the dark man, up the street, down the street, over to the fellow at his . . . left. The adam's apple in his throat worked as he swallowed. Could he be mistaken? Or was this the fierce *bandito*, Desert Hawk? What did they want with Belle? Ned's eyes sought Belle's, his look asking if she would be all right, and she nodded again, more strongly this time.

On passing Belle and the dark stranger as he cut across the street at an angle, Ned gave a curt nod, catching the look in Belle's eyes that said *Get the hell out of town and fast!*

Squaring her shoulders and planting her feet, Willow hissed, "Get the heck out of here, Almanzo! I'm riding out and catching up with that bunch—and I don't want you stopping me!" Her eyes grew round and she gasped then as the stranger stepped out from the shadows, coming to pause in the light of the sun at the edge of the boardwalk. She could see the bandoliers that crisscrossed his chest, the pistolas slung low on lean hips. "Who is he?" she asked of the dangerous-looking dude across the way. When Almanzo remained silent, she asked, "Did the Ranger send you and this . . . this desperado out to get me?"

The *mustachio* above Almanzo's full-lipped mouth twitched. Was he about to smile? Why didn't he say anything? She was beginning to feel uneasy with the stranger staring at her so boldly, ice in his eyes. What color were they? Beneath the brim of the sombrero—larger than hers—she could not make out the eye color. Too, he was keeping his head down, in order to slant the brim to his advantage, to conceal his identity as much as possible. Idiot! With hat tipped down, he was being so very obvious every time a person walked by, as if . . . he didn't want to be recognized. He must be . . .

Swiftly, Willow's eyes flew to Almanzo's face. "No, don't tell me . . . you have become an outlaw, too? Am I right, Almanzo? Hey, why don't you and your mysterious dude come and join *our* bunch?" Willow pursed her lips in disapproval. "Tsk, tsk, and you lied to me, saying I'd get arrested if I didn't come along. Who is your friend, Almanzo? Is he someone special I should know about? Hmm, I've seen that, um, guise on a 'WANTED' poster, too."

"*Si.* He is the Desert Hawk."

Willow laughed. "The fierce one, wanted in over twenty Texas counties? The desperado who can shoot the fleas off a running dog? Pshaw, you're funning me."

"I do not fun now."

"I don't believe you. By the way, Dark Horse, where is Kachina? Who is she with? Why are you with this . . . what's wrong? Why are you looking at me like that? You look as if you've seen a—"

"Kachina is in the spirit world now; her flesh is no

longer among us. She passed on giving birth to our first and only son."

Now Willow was not laughing. Her face was white and she was frowning . . . her frown going deeper at the somber-visaged desperado who was leading two horses over to them—Lordy! one of those horses was Talon's Cloud!

Mounting up, Willow put the soft spurs to Magic's sides and rode out of town. Looking over her shoulder, she saw that they were gaining, and she rode harder, but their horses were faster than hers. Almanzo caught up with her while the one in the concealing serape dropped back and hung behind.

"What is he doing with Talon's horse?" she asked Almanzo, knowing she could trust him, and yet wondering why he had taken up with the bad fellow.

"Cloud's offspring threw a shoe and Talon was searching frantically for you. He could not search with such a horse, and so Desert Hawk loaned him his black and when the shoeing was done, Desert Hawk still had Talon's horse. We have not seen Talon and have no idea when he will return." Almanzo arched his dark eyebrows. "You look as if you do not believe my story. Why is that?"

"You don't lie very well, Almanzo. Sometimes I used to think you were a saint. Even with Kachina in the Indian camp . . . you were very proper, always kind and gentle. I'm sorry. I should not have said the name of Kachina."

"It is not bad that you do. Kachina would have wanted me to say her name. I can do it now, little one; you see, I have let her go." He smiled warmly, adding,

148

"It is true about the horse throwing a shoe—" He did not add which other part was true, however.

"Yes, that might be the case; I will try to believe you, Almanzo." Willow nodded, tossing a glance over her shoulder to see the other man trailing quietly and solemnly. "But something else does not fit."

Almanzo shrugged, making a little joke, "It could not be the shoe on the horse."

"Go ahead," she said with a sniff, "keep your secret. I'll soon find out. I always did in the past when you and the Ranger played tricks on me."

"He wasn't a Ranger at that time," Almanzo reminded Willow.

An hour after sunset, they were camped beside a creek emblazoned with rays of pinkish-gold and shimmering red. After a casual glance at Willow, the mysterious *bandito* hardly looked her way; yet, he seemed to be aware of her every move, as if he watched her covertly from the corner of his shifty eyes. She, too, did not have to look at him in order to be very aware of his presence and his movements. She had asked Almanzo where they were going and what they wanted with her. His answers were always indirect, meandering around every subject she brought up. As they sat around the campfire that evening, Willow had a feeling this was going to be another such conversation.

"Almanzo," she began, chewing a bite of buffalo jerky, "you still have not told me what all this mystery is about. Could you please enlighten me just a little. I'd like to get back to my new friends."

"And get yourself thrown in jail." He frowned

blackly. "Or hung by a noose. You are playing with fire, Willow Hayes Brandon."

"Hm? That's nothing unusual, Almanzo, except this time I'm going to see that I get what I want, what belongs to me, and that is my son, Michael Angelo. He is my child, no one else's. He belongs with his mama as he has for four years." She nodded, trying not to look in the direction of the Desert Hawk; he gave her the creeps. But she could tell he was hanging onto every word she spoke. "I aim to take Michael back with me to Bountiful. We've made a home there with Juanita, and that's where we're going to stay. No one on God's earth is going to keep my son away from me, because I'll kill if I have to."

"I believe you would, Mrs. Brandon." Almanzo detected a stiffening in Willow's spine. "You do not like being called that?"

"No, I don't, especially because I'm angry with Talon Clay for not taking me with—"

"What else?"

Willow did not intend to discuss her relationship with Talon, not with the dark stranger overhearing every word. "Doesn't he ever say anything? All I've heard from him is a few mumbled syllables and deep grunts . . . Oh Lord, I'm *really* sorry, stranger—" she said to the silent figure on the other side of the fire—"I really don't mean to be so bold and nasty. You're probably a very nice . . . desperado, it's just that I really have to get to that ghost town." She jabbed a stick into the fire, resting her chin on her forearms. "I'm worried sick about Michael."

"What ghost town?"

The deep voice across from Willow was as shocking

150

as Almanzo's had been the first time she'd heard it. She looked up. Why did his voice sound so muffled? And why did he always hide his face in deep shadows? What else was he hiding? Maybe some real bad scars, terribly ugly? She decided not to be rude again—that way she might be able to get away as they slept, because he would think she trusted that he would release her by morning light. But she didn't trust any man anymore. She thought about this for a moment. On some hazy level she knew he wouldn't let her go, not tomorrow, not the next day. She wondered what he had in mind for her.

"I asked you: What ghost town?"

With a shrug, Willow answered, "I have no idea. All I know is that the Lady Boss's ... dudes called it ... 'the ghost town'." Wait a darn minute, Willow warned herself as her gaze slid to Almanzo. What did her neighbor from past times know about this Desert Hawk fellow? And what was Almanzo doing away from Black Fox's camp? True, Kachina was gone ... still, why would Almanzo wish to leave? To try again with Tanya, because her sister and Ashe didn't always get along? No, she told herself. Almanzo had been away from Sundance for five years, and Tanya and Ashe had been happily wed all that time ... but for a few arguments now and then.

"What is troubling you, *desperada?*" Desert Hawk asked in that deep, flat voice that sent chills up and down Willow's spine.

She quickly averted her gaze from his tight brown breeches. ... Was that a knife she saw gleaming at his side? Willow bit her lip, wishing now that she had remembered to bring her own Toledo steel knife along,

151

but she'd been in a very big hurry when she had left Bountiful.

The chills running along her spine were beginning to feel like *thrills* to Willow, thrills she was powerless to control; the man's voice was exciting to her somehow. It felt almost familiar being here, and that was beginning to trouble her almost as much as those beckoning eyes she could not see, eyes that were observing and inspecting her, all the while, closely, as if analyzing ... Willow's eyes rounded. Dear God, as if he knew *her,* too!

Later, the camp was quiet as Willow lay asleep—at long last—for she had planned to feign sleep and then slip away to find Ned and the others. Weariness won, however, and she knew finding the other outlaws would be like searching for a needle in a haystack—in the dark.

The eyes of Desert Hawk rested on the sleeping form of his beloved. He had removed his sombrero and his longer blond hair made a striking contrast with his sparkling green eyes, darker brows, and tanned skin.

Holding a cup of hot coffee, Almanzo slipped down beside his amigo and sighed. "She sleeps at last."

"Did you tell her anything?" the low-voiced man asked, his gaze intent on a slim arm peeking out from the blanket.

"Just a tiny white lie. It is true Desert Hawk lent you his horse, at first, and then his clothes for your mission." Almanzo finally grinned, his teeth very white in his dark face. "Do you think you will get back your favorite pistol?"

"I'd better." The Ranger tossed back the serape and handled his other .44, adding, "I need them both to make a matching pair—a Ranger should never be without both his trusty weapons. What did you say Desert Hawk's real name is?"

"Ah—that would be Hank Rountree. He's an angry dude; he was doublecrossed by a deceitful woman."

"She ran out on him, huh?" Talon Clay clicked his tongue when Almanzo gave his answer. "Wonder if she had a good reason. Do you know?"

"His first woman, his wife, Summer Wind—yes, she did have one, but not the second woman. Hank ran off with some yellow-haired dance hall girl and his wife Summer Wind did not wait around. She left Rountree . . . now it's a hideout for desperados . . . and Hank went crazy when he returned shamefaced and found his wife and two children absent. Hank searched every place he could think of but he did not find them. This man rides like the wind and he is very fierce—"

"I wouldn't know about being fierce," Talon drawled in his deep voice. The cords in his neck stood out as he twisted to look at his friend. "He looked kind of tame to me . . . he's after someone, though; I can see *that* in his eyes. As if he's got unfinished business to take care of."

Almanzo nodded as Talon went back to watching Willow. "Yes. I believe it has to do with the dance hall girl who left him high and dry."

"Willow did that to me. I believe someone told her a crock of lies and she took it seriously and ran off to other parts, pregnant to boot. I've got her back now and

I mean to keep her, even if I have to lock her up at Sundance until I get the boy back."

"Just as you imprisoned her at Black Fox's camp when you slyly made her become your wife."

"Yup."

"I will leave you now." Almanzo leapt to his feet, lithe as a cat.

Talon bent a leg, looking up at his friend, ready to rise with him. "What do you mean?"

Lifting his saddle blanket, Almanzo went to toss it gently on his mount's back. "Catch up with me near the San Antonio-Nacogdoches road. I will be there waiting, or else I will go on to Sundance and check on things while Ashe and Tanya are away." He tipped the old dusty hat he wore. "Adios, amigo." He winked. "And have a good time with the little spitfire."

In mock fear, the Ranger gripped his pistol as if for protection from a fierce foe. *"Be Jaysus,* don't leave me alone with that one ... she will rip me to pieces!"

With a chuckle, Almanzo said, "You deserve it, amigo, for abandoning her."

Talon frowned, dropping the humorous act. "What do you mean?" His look was hard as he rolled to his feet.

"Ranger," Almanzo sniffed disdainfully, looking his friend and brother up and down his lean length, "you call yourself a lawman? This is good only for you. But what about your wife? Perhaps she did not wish for you to be this sort of man. You have always left her alone to go do what 'a man must do'." Again, Almanzo snorted. "Are you a man? Or a mouse? Do you protect your woman or not?"

"Come on," Talon growled, jerking his head toward the larger clearing on the other side of the bushes. "You want to fight with your fists instead of your mouth, big dude?"

Talon walked and Almanzo followed.

Suddenly Almanzo spun about, catching the lighter-haired man off guard, growling, "I cannot wait to beat some sense into your head!" His fist flew and landed on Talon's jaw with a dull thud; then he danced up and down, sideways, as Talon got his own fists into position.

The fight went on and on, fists flying, heads jerking, and chins snapping back. It was like old times when they used to go to dances and frequent the saloons. The men battered each other until they lay on the ground, sopping wet, bruised, and laughing low but hysterically. Almanzo stood at last, running over to his horse, leaping up and mounting like the graceful Indian he was. With hands on lean hips, Talon watched Almanzo prepare to leave.

White teeth flashed in the dark beyond the fire. "Give Willow a big kiss for me in the morning!" He rode away with a bloodcurdling whoop as Talon stood hunching his shoulders, afraid that Willow would wake suddenly and scream when she beheld his bruised and battered face.

Checking the camp out, Talon discovered Willow was still asleep. This was good; he could get some things done. Walking beyond the firelight, he bent at the stream that ran behind the line of scrub pines and washed his face, wincing at the ache in his jaw.

Willow slept on, unaware of the "surprise" creeping up on her.

O, what a tangled web we weave,
When first we practice to deceive!
—Walter Scott, *Marmion, VI*

Chapter Eight

There was a reddish glow all around her, garnetlike clouds of sunset with purple streaks invading. But it was not that time of day; it was night. Willow was dreaming that someone was rubbing her back . . . it felt so very wonderful; she hoped he wouldn't halt his sensuous movements and go away.

What!

Instantly Willow came awake and could make out the long shape in the dark of the moon. The clouds slipped over the luminous ball in the sky and the figure was draped in mystery. The campfire had burned low; she could see *him*.

The fierce outlaw!

Rising to sit on her legs, Willow shouted, "What are you doing? Don't touch me!"

"I'm just trying to make you relax, *desperada*. You are about as tense as nestlings ready to fly the first time."

"What?" What was this talk of flying birds? "Relax?" she said aloud. "I was sleeping . . . how would you know?" His touch had bothered her and she could still feel the wonderful tingles it had provoked. Her mind was full of Talon Clay—her husband. But this was not he, no, this was the fierce desperado. "How—?" she repeated.

"How would I know you are tense?" The man shrugged. "I could feel it."

"B-but you weren't lying next to me . . . *were you?*"

He laughed. "Of course not." Then again, he wouldn't tell her the truth at this time, and what she didn't know wouldn't hurt. "I thought it might do you some good to get . . . uh, rubbed."

"What will do me even better is if you leave your paws off me and . . . don't ever touch me again. I'm a married woman," she said sharply, acting on pure bravado with this ominous character. That would keep him away, wouldn't it? He wouldn't touch her anymore, would he? "Who do you think you are that you can touch any woman and . . . and rub her back while she's asleep?"

"Not just any woman, *desperada.*"

His voice, there was something about it that nagged at Willow. She tried seeing his face, but it was impossible with the swaying branches of the scrub pine and cottonwoods blurring his expression. What did he have in mind? "Why do you talk so low? And what are you trying to hide, crouched in that striped serape, with your . . . Lordy, you've still got your hat on. Isn't that a little strange to be wearing your sombrero at this time of night?"

"I wear a hat any time, night or day, rain or shine. What does it matter."

"What I meant was, why are you not sleeping?"

"Maybe I'm not tired. And when I sleep, little Belle, I wear my hat over my face."

"Oh." Willow looked around. "Where is Almanzo?" She shivered, hoping he was not far away; she wouldn't like to be spending the rest of the night with this dangerous stranger.

"Almanzo went on ahead."

"At night?"

"Yup."

"What? Say that again—*Yup.*" He sounded very familiar ... almost like ... no, it couldn't be. Or, *could it be Talon Clay hiding in that desperado's outfit?*

"Yeah," he drawled instead, his voice lower than before, sensuous, startling to Willow who'd been without a man for over four years. "Almanzo thought he'd give us some time alone together."

"Oh? And why would I want to spend time alone with a desperado?"

"Because you're one yourself?"

He had her there. "I see."

"Desperada," he said in that same low, sensuous drawl, drawing it out.

A cold shiver trickled down Willow's spine. "I'm not really a lady outlaw. You see, Mr. Hawk—" she emphasized the name—"I'm searching for my lost ... or kidnapped son, Michael Angelo." Why was he looking at her so intensely? She could feel more than see the bold gaze beneath the lowered brim of the dark sombrero.

"Is that so?"

Still lying on his side, he reached out to cup her chin and then, with a swift movement that startled her, he crouched before her, on his haunches, too close for comfort.

159

Willow was uneasy. "Are you a killer, mister?"

"No," he answered, seated on the ground Indian-style.

Suddenly Willow doubled up her fists and aimed them both at his arrogant and handsome face. The sombrero went flying and the man's legs scissored out from beneath his buttocks.

"You little spitfire! What do you think you're doing?" Forestalling the attack easily, catching both of her wrists in his big hands he pressed her backward until she lay prone in the young spring grass, looking up at him in amazement for the swiftness of his guard. "Ah . . . *desperada,*" he murmured against her cheek.

"Off! Get off, Talon Clay!" she screeched. "You cheated! You always cheat!"

An ominous gleam filled his eyes. "What do you think you did, running away from your husband a second time, wayward wife. Hmm?"

Slow and gentle, Talon brought her hands down to the soft and fragrant earth, but he didn't release his hold on her wrists. He whispered her name and Willow felt his hard length stretch out upon her, though the crushing sensation she had expected did not come. His lips came to hers, tasting, rubbing, moving, the roughness of his unshaven chin heightening her sensitivity to his touch. Willow's entire body quivered with the torrent of needs that had been unleashed by this one action, and she moaned as Talon Clay's kiss deepened, became demanding. His tongue prodded her lips to part and when they did, he explored her freely and fiercely and she found her own tongue fencing with his.

When the kiss came to an end, Willow pulled back to look into his face. She gazed up at him, seeing the moonlight frame his head like a hazy nimbus, capturing his hair with a silver fire, his face shadowed and filled with secrets.

"Take your clothes off, Pussywillow. I want to see you and touch you and make love to you."

"In that order?" she questioned, one eyebrow arched.

"Unless you want to reverse the order."

Inwardly intimidated, Willow held her ground and lashed out at him. "We are separated, Talon Clay, lest you forget."

The skin was taut at the edges of his bruised lips. "Shoot. Separated by what? Two or three feet of ground?"

"I won't take my clothes off for you, Talon Clay. You are like a stranger to me. Besides, it has been a long time since anyone looked upon me in the buff, much less a man. I'd feel *uncomfortable.*"

"I'm familiar with your nudity, Pussywillow. As your husband, I've seen you several times, have learned the upward thrust of your small, firm breasts, the smallness of your waist, and the way your shapely little hips were made to receive a man . . . not just any man." He knew her cheeks flamed hotly but he pressed on, "In the past, I'd thought we'd not fit together, that I would hurt you. But now I'm certain no other woman fits me as well, and no other man could fill you as I and still give you comfort and ease and fulfillment." He chuckled sensuously, "Like an old glove."

"You would know about a woman fitting you well: you've had enough of them!" A strangled sob escaped her and she covered her face with one hand. He was immediately before her, grasping her hand and pulling it from her face.

161

"Look at me, Willow."

"Why?" She sniffed and looked up. "It's been too long for me, Talon Clay. I'm afraid of what will happen to my . . . independence."

"Well—" he stared at her intently—"we might as well get unhitched then. Hell with everything, right? You go your way, I go mine." He blinked at her as if she weren't real. "What happens if I find Mikey first? Do I get to keep our son?"

"Michael," she corrected. "No, you don't get to keep him. He's mine."

His jaw appeared to be hewn of granite. "Correction. *Ours.*"

Willow moved closer and peered at him. "I can see your face better now that you've removed your sombrero. Turn this way. Now that." She gasped. "What happened to your face? It's all purple and . . . *bruised!*"

Pulling a wry face, Talon explained, "Almanzo and I had a little fun getting our frustrations out a while before I woke you."

"Does it hurt?" Touching a fingertip to an especially dark purple bruise, Willow felt him flinch away from her. "I'm sorry; I should not have touched—" her voice slowed—"you."

"I'd rather you did touch me, Willow. I haven't known a woman's touch in the last four years."

"Oh-ho! You expect me to believe *that?*"

"Believe what you will, woman. I've told you the truth."

Willow looked aside in irritation. Had Hester Tucker been lying to her about Talon being her lover? She had also said that she was not the only woman he was making love to.

Talon was studying her and she reddened profusely beneath his perusal. Responding to the intensity of his stare, Willow shivered and wondered what would happen next, now that they were alone, sharing the same frustrations and fears for their child's safety.

"Even though I've never met my child, I love him, Willow. I feel him now, know he's alive. I want him as badly as I want you."

Willow's heart seemed to stop. "In what way, shape, and form do you want me, Ranger?"

"Whatever I do from now on, believe me, Willow, I want to share it with you. Every way. Every shape. Every form. *Because I love you.*"

"Oh, really?" Willow gave her long yellow hair a toss. "I can share your coffee and your grub and maybe the earth beneath the Texas stars, but I can hardly ride out with you, Ranger, nor be at your side when you battle with Mexican bandits, nor when you—" Biting her lower lip, she stared aside and frowned with bitter frustration.

He stared at her hard. "Leave off, Willow. I know you were going to say, *When you hop in the sack with your next conquest,* right?"

"Does it matter what I think, or say, or do?" she asked, sending a well-aimed shaft of anger through him.

He felt compelled to force a different response from her. "Yes. It matters much to me. Remember, *I* wasn't the one to walk out on *you.* Damn and tarnation, woman, you did the walking."

"Before I forget," she began, "what were you doing dressed as a desperado? Explain that one, Talon Clay."

"I met up with a few of the Comanche mustangers I used to know. Fellow by the name of Hank Rountree was with them. Never met him before. Almanzo Rankin knew him—" He shrugged—"I gathered, from the Indian camp of Black Fox."

"What has this Hank Rountree to do with the fierce Desert Hawk?"

"They're one and the same."

Willow laughed softly. "Hank the Hawk?"

"There goes your schoolteacher's logic again. Tsk, tsk, Willow, the children back in Bountiful must really miss their teacher."

"We, or *you*, are getting off the track here, Ranger. We were discussing this Desert Hawk and how you came to impersonate him." Her eyes lit up to golden brown. "Oh, let me guess: You were trying to get into the Green Mountain hideout, too?"

"Close. I couldn't very well get near any outlaw gang while dressed in Ranger's attire, now could I?"

She remembered how handsome and commanding he'd appeared in his tight black Ranger's pants and shirt that stretched across wide shoulders, Western hat, and army issue boots, black and polished. He'd worn his Texas star pinned to his shirt, winking out importantly from the edge of his buckskin vest. She shivered as she thought how it would feel if he made love to her just now.

"And so you kept your outlaw identity to fool me?"

"Yup."

Talon was feeling desire, too. He could hardly remember a time when he did not want Willow Margaret, but there'd been varying degrees of the emotion, because at first meeting he had almost been afraid of her great brown pussywillow eyes searching his soul and his innermost thoughts. Before they had finally gotten together he had tried steering clear of her, since he had no hankering to be tied down by any woman, least of all Garnet Haywood's daughter!

"Do you want to make love, or what?" Talon Clay threw at her suddenly. He saw that her velvet brown eyes had gold fires in them. Now he felt stupid for having blurted that like a dunce; he couldn't take it back, though. He meant every word, and so he waited.

"What?" Willow gasped. Had she heard correctly? Of course she had. She wasn't dreaming, though at the moment she wished that was all she was doing. "You are plumb crazy, you know that."

"And you really are something else, Pussywillow." Talon's eyes twinkled. "Sure enough."

"Talon, you big flirt." What was he thinking to do next, Willow asked herself, feeling her nerves shiver—wracked by those beautiful green eyes eating up every move she made.

He touched her shoulder briefly, sending a shudder coursing through her and she relaxed in his arms. "You can walk right back into my arms, Willow, and I won't blink a lash if you want to stay." He smiled. "Don't be afraid."

Willow frowned as his smile widened, then suddenly she felt his arms begin to fall away from her and she reached up around his neck to keep from falling into the dust at his feet; it was a place she vowed never to be.

Would he have her back? She thought of Michael and all she loved back at Sundance. And home, if only they could both go there together with their son.

"Oh babe, we have to get some things straightened out between us," he said softly, his lips close to hers once again. His arms hadn't left her completely, and now they tightened just before she swayed to the ground. "Wife—" He looked down at her. "You're almighty tempting."

Willow could feel his body next to hers; the sensation was so heady that she unconsciously tried molding herself even closer to him. He held her pressed against the muscular length of his body, and his mouth found hers without hesitation as she looked up at him in surprise. Her soft, parted lips fitted perfectly against the hard, finely chiseled curves of his as he pulled her to his chest and helped her rise to stand with him.

"You have haunted me for years, wife." He kissed her as though he could not get enough of her.

It never changed, did it? Willow wondered helplessly as she felt that same breathlessness and sudden twist in her stomach whenever he was near. Lips, warm and sensuous, moved against hers, his arm around her waist bending her slightly backward, bringing her hips more firmly against his. Her world became one of feeling and reaction as her body responded to Talon's touch. Willow knew she was lost, and it frightened her, because she didn't want to give herself again, not unless she knew there was love between them and it was going to last this time.

The kiss deepened, his tongue touching hers intimately, and Talon Clay sighed, loving the feel of Pussywillow.

Willow's senses were so filled with his scent, she felt as if she were drowning in him, and she couldn't draw a breath of her own. Willow's breath had become Talon Clay's.

All of a sudden he felt her pulling—none too gently—his hair, which was tied back with a thong. She was trying to lift his mouth from hers. Her slender body fought against his, but her actions only served to meld them closer, and he couldn't control the tightening in his loins. When she tensed, he knew she felt his masculinity hard against her. Talon winced when she gave the pony-tail another painful yank, refusing to lessen the pressure. She nipped at his mouth and, slowly, he allowed his mouth to lift from hers.

Willow was breathing heavily, her dark brown eyes staring up at him victoriously, then widening a bit when she saw the corner of his lips twitch slightly as he grinned. Before Willow could draw her breath to protest, he began to lower his mouth to hers once again. He ignored the pain as she continued to grip the braid. It was as if she sought to control him. Holding her attention, Talon's hand moved from her waist, dropping lower over the soft material of her pants until he found the curve he sought.

Willow gasped.

He had lightly pinched her buttock in retribution, her indrawn breath and surprised look of indignation causing him to laugh aloud with the joy of having Willow in his arms again. "Remember, sweet Pussywillow, I always like to come out the winner in this game."

She shot back, "So do I."

His nostrils flared slightly as he remembered her passionate response to his lovemaking years back. Willow was not indifferent to him; if he believed that, he would have nothing of her to claim as his own. He wanted more than the physical union between them. He wanted her heart. And he wanted her to come to him willingly.

Talon stared down into eyes that by day put to shame the velvet brown of the pussywillows that grew near the gorgeous green swamps. She was leaning toward him now. Her heady scent floated around him and he was drawn closer to the lips parting in such sweet appeal. She was inviting him, he suddenly thought. Touching her silken hair as he tipped her head back against his shoulder, ever so slowly this time, his lips lowered to hers. The pressure deepened.

Willow felt his hand moving beneath the curve of her breast, his fingers sliding around the firm roundness, the fine linen of her shirt of little protection against the heat of his hand. Talon felt Willow's trembling body become pliant in his arms as he pulled her against him. His arms enfolded her waist as he began to turn her around to hold her closer still, one hand sliding upward to cup the back of her neck. His arm left her waist, then his hand was moving along her hip. He came to rest on her buttocks, where he lightly fondled the soft curves beneath the fabric of her pants.

Moving her hand to his cheek, Willow allowed the swell of her breasts to come in contact with the nakedness of his chest where his shirt parted in a vee. She felt him shudder and his hand left the nape of her neck to discover the buttons of her shirt. Lightly touching her lips, his tongue licked them, his teeth nibbling against the soft inner flesh. She opened wider to allow him to touch her tongue and the kiss deepened as his tongue slid against hers; they were joined together by the intimate contact of moist soft flesh to moist hard flesh.

"I've been waiting a long time for this to happen again," he said, his words soft against her ear.

"Yes," Willow said, her voice barely above a whisper.

"I never had a chance to dance with you at Rankin's party; you were very beautiful that night. In fact, I'd never laid eyes on such a gorgeous woman. I wanted you the first day I saw you in Sundance yard. But you were beyond me," he said, his voice roughening as he recollected the frustration of knowing she was too virginal for the wicked likes of him. "You are even more gorgeous tonight, not a girlish creature anymore, but a real woman. And now you're mine."

"Yours?"

"Yup. We *are* still husband and wife, Willow Brandon," he said slowly, savoring the name as his lips touched the gentle curve of neck revealed by a bright, cameo moon. His hands traveled from her waist, along her back, and in a minute she felt her shirt fall slightly. Next, the fastenings at her waist gave way and her clothing was pulled down and left on the ground as she was lifted free of the tangle of material.

They were bathed in the pool of moonlight, the lamp of night casting a silver glow over them. His hands slid along her arms, his mouth trailing his touch. Willow found herself shivering as she felt his lips on the soft flesh. He pressed a kiss into her palm, moving along each finger. Suddenly her smallclothes landed in a heap around her ankles, her pantalettes having slid downward around her stockinged feet. She felt the coolness of the night air against her hot, flushed skin. Then his eyes burned her as they moved over her, before he pulled her into his arms. Now his kiss was hard, demanding. His hands roved over her intimately as his mouth opened against hers, forcing her lips apart as his knee forced her thighs apart. She could feel the hardness of him pressing against her as his tongue continued to circle hers.

He picked her up, holding her close as he gazed intently into her face. His lips sought hers, and he tasted deeply of them before placing her on the blanket of leaves. Talon stood before her, slowly disrobing, his eyes never leaving her flushed face. Willow watched the moonlit god standing naked before her. His broad shoulders and muscular chest tapered down to the narrow waist, hips, and flat belly he'd always had. His manhood was erect, and Willow felt the stirrings of a wilder desire deep within her as she watched him bend, his thighs long and sinewy with muscle.

Neither could say a word; they were too caught up in this spellbinding moment. He came to kneel beside her, leaving a trail of fire across her stomach as he touched her, then she gasped when she felt his fingers probing gently between her thighs. He moved deeper as he sought the sensuous core of her. Seeking a fuller satisfaction from the contact, Willow moved against his hand and felt the sensations begin, moving through her in waves of delight, filling the aching emptiness inside her.

Moving lower, his hands against the trembling of her thighs, his fingers then held her apart. Willow felt the roughness of his hard cheek against her inner thigh, the soft warmth of his tongue penetrating her. He moved inside her, his hands holding her hips against him. She writhed against him, coming close to bittersweet pain as the feelings traveled through her like silken coils. She was almost crying out with pleasure and felt she would soon swoon from the erotic ecstasy he was creating. She reached out, clasping his shoulders, then his golden hair as she pressed against him.

Rising above her, he knelt between her thighs, spreading them, catching his breath when he felt her fingers brushing with a feathery touch over the flatness of his belly, moving downward. She touched him, feeling him softly as she held his manhood in her small hand. Her fingers slid along its length as he throbbed hard and pulsing in the softness of her hand as she aroused him with her woman's touch.

With a deep groan, he lifted her. Her thighs went around his hips with an instinctive knowledge as she fitted herself to him. The physical joining with her robbed him of his breath as they became one, moved as one. The soft warmth of her surrounded him, holding him sheathed deep within her. He felt her muscles pulling him deeper and felt her swelling around him, increasing his pleasure. She stared up into her lover's face; it was like a mask of bronze. His eyes shone a bright silvery green in the moonlight.

They ignited like wildfire. They melted together from the heat of their coupling. Her hips moved rhythmically with his as he began slowly. As he thrust deeper and deeper, over and over, she felt the world tipping around her. Gradually he increased his rhythm, the pulsating movement building apace until it was unbearable and difficult to endure a moment longer.

Willow exploded several times before he did, as he held himself poised to watch the enraptured expression on her face. He prolonged the intense pleasure and clung by a thread until he could bear the tightly coiled, aching sensations no longer. With a final, powerful surge he poured himself deep within her.

He took her again before dawn. Or was it the other way around? he was to wonder later.

Chuckling provocatively in Talon's ear, Willow

played, tugging and teasing him into a new rigidity as she tempted him to carry on. And he did just that, his narrow hips moving against her.

"Oh, you sweet Pussywillow, offer your sweet womanly secrets to me once again." He groaned against the slim column of her neck and the magnificent heat blossomed in her again and sang throughout her veins, nerves, muscles, tendons, and most secret places. "Willow, wider . . . ah, that's it."

"Love me, Ranger Brandon, love me this night and forever!"

"Oh?" He stared deeply into her eyes, adding in a hushed voice, "I'll remember you said that."

Willow's mouth fashioned a little "O" as he moved against her, bold and aggressive, hungry and heavy.

When he came into her this time, he plunged so deeply, filling her with a new burning ache so that she yielded completely to the wondrous pleasure that was near bittersweet pain. Thrusting to the hilt, he made his way like a young stallion as her thighs lifted to urge him deeper. Sometimes he almost left her completely, but stayed her hips within his loving grasp. Willow was so enthralled by her freshly-found womanhood that she cried out for the sweetness and joy of it.

Soaring on wings of passion, Willow and the Ranger climbed high hills, dipped in and out of golden valleys, and then, at last, mounted the highest mountain of pleasure, man joined to woman, as they exploded in joyful bliss.

She will come back to me now, Talon thought, holding her coupled to him, feeling her breast thumping hard against his. Someday he would have her total love, but for now he would keep her happy and satisfied out of her body's need for his. He had employed seduction, making her once again erotically aware of her body. Soon she might be with child again—maybe not this time, but some day, some time. She could never leave him then and *he* could never leave her and two children.

With her woman's instinct, Willow knew she would never love another man as she loved Talon Clay, never know such sweet fury and satisfaction. Ranger Brandon was the only one who could give this to her; the knowledge filled her with anguish. He never stayed long, and he had caused her to retaliate and run away.

Willow sat up, but it was some time before she could bring herself to look up into that handsome face; there was humor written on his features in the soft encroachment of pearly dawn light.

"Now, let's get those matters straightened out, here and now."

Yawning wide, Willow said, "Can't it wait till morning?" She laid her head on her blanket roll. "I'm so . . . sleepy."

Shaking her shoulder, Talon said, "I'm afraid not. Come morning—" he looked up at the sky—"and that's not far off, I have to know what you're going to do."

"I'm going with you to search for Michael."

"No. It's far too dangerous. You've already gotten yourself known as Belle, the *desperada,* and what good will you be to Michael if you're sitting in a jail cell when I bring him home?"

Willow frowned. "I want to find Michael. I was so close, the outlaws were going to bring me to the ghost town. That's where he is, Talon—at that Lady Boss's hideout!"

"How can you be so sure it's the same child?"

173

"He, this child they spoke of at the Green Mountain hideout, is our own because Michael disappeared at about the same time, give or take a few days. That's too much of a coincidence to be forgetting that they ever mentioned 'the boy they were taking to the boss'."

"All right, we'll check it out," Talon said, up and moving to make coffee.

"Who's 'we'?" she asked, watching him toss grounds into a tiny, battered tin pot.

"Almanzo and myself," he lied, because Almanzo was going to be guarding *her* if she didn't go home and be a good girl. "We'll return you to Sundance, where you'll stay put and wait for us to bring the boy back home."

"But, that's not Michael's home now. His home is with Juanita, Jorge, and myself back at Bountiful!"

With a hard look in her direction, Talon asked, "Are you going to be difficult?" He handed her a chunk of hard bread and a cup of steaming coffee.

"Of course." She chewed the bread and gulped. "Haven't I always been?"

"True." He thought for a moment, then seemed to capitulate, "All right, you can come along." He stood and walked over to his saddle, not looking at her. The sky was lightening and the stars had faded one by one. "But first we have to go and meet Almanzo."

"Good." She shook out her hair and finger-brushed it. "I thought you'd see things my way."

Talon did not look back.

Early in the morning Talon and Willow raced across the sloping grasslands, their horses splashing through a wide stream that meandered across the fertile plain and brought life to the hills and valleys. Their destination was the southwestern end of the valley, where hills cut through low and lush, then climbed to pass through bumpy cactus fields and rolling tumbleweeds. They followed a narrow trail through dark green foliage sweeping down from a stand of fir and spruce trees, almost touching the ground and dusting the trail before them. Midmorning they rested and watered their horses by a crystalline stream.

Sitting on the soft bank, the sunshine filtering down through shadowy branches rising high above her head, Willow stretched out lazily, the warmth soaking into her bones; she was warming her chilled body from the coolness of the ground the night before. She watched as Talon Clay rummaged in his saddlebags and gave her the gift he'd kept for a moment like this: a beautiful mirror set with a tortoiseshell frame and handle. The gift was a perfect match to the comb-and-brush set he'd given her years ago, a gift to seal their love.

"A mirror of our love."

They looked at their reflections.

"Thank you, Talon. It's beautiful and I'll cherish it forever and ever."

"I thought you'd like it. A feminine gift for a feminine woman. You should be at home where you belong, not traipsing over the country in search of—" He bit off his words.

"Yes, Talon. You are right. I've changed my mind; you and Almanzo go to search for our son. I will stay—" She looked up at him meekly.

"You will?" he asked, knowing she had to yield a lot to give up her stubbornness.

"At home," she stressed.

"At home," he echoed and nodded.

Willow turned away from him at once so he could not read her face.

"Good," he said. "Then it's settled."

So he *thought*.

There is a Reaper whose name is
    Death,
    And, with his sickle keen,
He reaps the bearded grain at a
    breath,
And the flowers that grow
    between.
    —Henry Wadsworth Longfellow

Chapter Nine

As Willow and Talon rounded the last bend in the road, Sundance property spread wide before them, and she saw Almanzo Rankin sitting his black horse some distance off. The homecoming lent a strange enchantment to the moment and, putting Magic to a gallop, Willow rode toward the lane swiftly, her hair blowing in the wind. Suddenly, rounding the big oak tree, she stopped and caught her breath, as if she had been running.

The wide, magnificent sweep of Sundance lay before her, green and splendid in the early morning sun. Over the grassland here and there cattle grazed with beautiful horses, belly deep in the tall grass. Bushes, trees, and flowers were all brilliant and lush. She could almost hear the mustangers riding, singing, and yelling to cattle and horses. Caught up in the sight and sound, reliving it in her senses as if it were as real as yesterday: The mustangs would be caught and brought in, causing a thunderous commotion. Sometimes a horse would panic and rear, but the mustangers and drovers always brought them under control and kept them from milling which could be very dangerous to horse and rider. To Willow, this homecoming was overpowering; it was breath-stealing. Home! *Home!* Her heart shouted with joy.

Sundance—rolling hills and level grasslands, gorgeous sun-mottled wooded areas and tiny valleys. This was the glorious spread of the Brandon men; they protected their family and property. This was the place for their . . . children. Suddenly Willow's eyes misted over and the homecoming was not so wonderful. Her heart wrenched painfully when she thought of her beloved child, he who should be with her now to share this glorious moment. There had been many moments as she'd held Michael when her thoughts had strayed to Sundance and how wonderful it would be to come here, to her old home, with him, and walk the. . . . Dear Lord, this was where she had become pregnant with Michael . . . listened to Hester Tucker whisper all those lies about Talon Clay. Hester had never given up trying to steal Talon from her, not even after they'd been man and wife for several years. Hester had not been able to believe that Talon finally belonged to Willow Hayes. She had left Talon all because of Hester's lies. She wasn't fat, she had never been fat, only a little chubby when she'd carried Michael Angelo.

She was married to a Brandon man, strong, resourceful, energetic, virile men Ashe and Talon Clay were, too. She couldn't wait to do all the things she wanted to do here at Sundance. Sad but true, she wouldn't be staying here. She had to find her baby . . . and then she'd think from there; she was never going to lose hope that she would find him.

She turned in her saddle at the sound of horses' hooves. The Ranger rode up beside her, his face glowing. "Magnificent, isn't it?" He knew what she was feeling; it always happened to him when he returned after being absent from Sundance for more than six months.

Almanzo rode up, too. "It is good to be home, eh amigo? Willow?"

"Oh yes, Almanzo!" She looked at the handsome man who had made his dwelling place Black Fox's camp for the past five years. He and Kachina had made one visit, and that was right before Willow found herself pregnant. Almanzo's gaze met hers, and he knew the sadness and hopelessness she was feeling, since he'd lost a son, too. And not only a child, but a wife also. Willow and Talon had a chance to find their child; he would never have a chance with his beloved family again, for they were gone from this earth.

Talon chuckled, leaning across his saddle. "I know what you two must be thinking. Hmm. Almanzo? You can't wait to feast your eyes on Willow's gorgeous sister, Tanya. Willow, you can't wait to burst into the door of the little house, and then—" His words slowed for what he'd say next—"You will want to go to Le Petit Sundance . . . where we lived before you, uh, went away."

"Why is it so hard for you to say, Talon?" Willow turned on her horse to look at him. She was grateful that Almanzo had seen fit to ride on up ahead just now. It would give her a chance to speak to Talon before heading for the house.

Talon's eyes narrowed. "Why was it so easy for you to leave here?"

"I might as well get this out into the open now." Taking a deep breath, she went on. "Hester told me all those stories. That you were sleeping with her and other women. That you said I had become fat and lazy, and you could find better company in a pig pen. But were they truly lies, Ranger?"

Talon had been staring straight ahead at the magnificent house glowing like a pink diamond as the sun cast its glorious rays over it. At her words, his head had turned quickly, sharply. "Well, Mrs. Ranger—what do you think? Did you believe Hester? You must have, otherwise you wouldn't have been gone with the wind as you were by morning light. It didn't take much for you to pack and get out of here, either." God knew that first night had been a miserable and lonely one for him. He had no idea she had left Sundance for good, instead believing she had gone over to the "big" house to stay with Tanya until their argument had blown over. With time, he thought, she would come around and return to their own slightly smaller house.

"You never even came looking for me," Willow shot over her shoulder as she nudged her horse along the slight incline leading to the little house above the creek. Sundance property contained three dwelling places besides the bunkhouses for the hands and Clem. . . . Dear Lord, was old Clem still alive? He had been as old as the hills when she had ridden out! "Why did you *let* me go, Talon Clay?"

Following her, frowning over the fact that their little reconciliation had been of such short duration, Talon rode beside her to the front porch of the little house. They sat their horses, neither making a move to dismount. "Why did I let you go?" he mused. "I had no idea you had lit out for good, just thinking maybe you'd gone to stay with your sister."

"You never bothered to check? Did it mean so little that you woke in the morning to find your wife gone?"

Talon took a deep breath and released it with a hiss. "Gone? You had more than left Sundance, Willow. You deserted the hell out of me."

"Don't make sense, what you just said, and you are mean sometimes, Talon Clay."

"I don't give a damn, Miss Schoolteacher. And life is hard and mean sometimes, Willow."

"I have nothing more to say," Willow snapped as she dismounted and tied Magic up to the hitching rail.

"That's it, huh?" Talon snorted. "Just like *ole* times, Willow, with you walking away before the conversation really gets heated up. I'd like to have it out with you real good one of these days—"

"Of course," she broke in, "then we could resort to fisticuffs!"

"There you go, Miss Fancypants." He ogled her behind as she walked to the porch. "Oooweee! You got the prettiest ass in all of Texas!"

Willow whirled. "Just as usual, you've got lust on your pea-size brain, Talon Clay. Don't you ever get exhausted thinking about sex all day long?"

"Not when my thoughts are about you, Pussywillow!" He followed behind her, did a skip and a jump over the rail, grabbed her from around the waist, and spun her into his arms. "I'm going to kiss the hell out of you, Willow Brandon. And just you try and stop me, you little spitfire!"

"Talon! *No!*"

With hard fists, Willow pounded on Talon's shoulders as he kissed her with such lusty force it took her breath away. When he finally released her, she staggered back with as much grace as a newborn colt, to bump her hip against the old washtub stand and, righting herself, she blurted, "Don't *ever* kiss me again!" Swiping the back of her hand across her mouth, she continued in exasperation, adding for good measure, "Not ever!" She calmed down a bit. "You could have . . . *asked* me nicely."

"Oh?" Talon queried with crisp humor while she stood glowering up at him. "Dainty, well-bred Miss Schoolteacher needs a man to go down on his knees and kiss her hand . . . like Harlyn Sawyer did for you?"

"Don't mention . . . that man."

"Yeah, how about that, Willow? You lied about marrying that fancy, dimwitted dude."

"How dare you speak of the dead like that?"

"You just did."

"You tortured Mr. Sawyer at the Indian camp. That was a terrible thing to do."

"If you remember correctly, our Mr. Sawyer was a devious schemer, working along with Carl Tucker, alias Randy Dalton. That bastard would have made your life hell if you had run off with him," he roared at her.

"I did run off with him, if you recall!" Willow shot right back. "He . . . I don't want to talk about him."

With a nod of his head, Talon replied, "Touché, and I don't want to talk about Hester 'The Slut' Tucker or your equally amoral mother, Garnet Haywood."

For some reason, Talon mentioning that name gave her a strange feeling. Suddenly she asked, "Where is my mother buried?"

"What?" Talon stared at her as if she'd lost her mind. "You never visited her grave, so why ask now? What's the deal, Willow? Why do you want to delve into the past? Let it lie."

She tossed her head like a snarling tigress, loosening strands of hair that fell like yellow sun rays around her face. Her brown eyes smoldered. "I want to see that grave!"

"*Jesu,* don't you want to see your sister Tanya first? Let her know you just rode in? And how about Clem? He's an old man, you know, and he'll worry and wonder."

"I believe Almanzo will do that; we don't have to see him or her until later." After a moment she spun about to face him. "Wait a minute! I thought you said Tanya and Ashe were vacationing in California."

"With all this talk of war and border conflicts I'd think they would have returned by now." Nonchalantly, he shrugged as he walked alongside her, removing the sombrero to slap it against his thigh. He hoped Hank Rountree would keep his promise and meet Almanzo at the crossroads later; he wanted and needed his Ranger clothes. As for arresting the "Desert Hawk," well . . . he combined his thoughts and gave voice to them: "We'll see, as you said. Later."

"Where's the grave?" Willow was excited now. Suddenly it was very important that she visit the burial site and behold the grave marker, and know for certain that Garnet "Haywood" Brandon, née Hayes, was *really buried* there!

"I have another idea, something that will fit in much better with our plans," Garnet said to Janice Ranae Tucker, who was all ears as she leaned forward. "Why don't we have Willow Brandon captured and brought here? Of course, leaving the Brandon brothers a clue as to where she was taken . . ."

"What good'll that do?" Janice countered. "And who'll do the job?"

"What *good?*" Garnet asked, stroking the tawny-haired child's fingers where he was sleeping curled up beside Hester on the lumpy brocade sofa next to her. She didn't look at Janice, but she wondered how the woman could be so stupid. Once again she explained, "Once Willow's here, the men will come looking for her . . . and then we can nab them."

Hester's eyes were wide. "You'll kill them?"

"No, I won't kill them," she lied with a husky laugh. "We'll just have them put on a ship and taken to a far-away island somewhere. I know just the sea captain who will do the job, too." Hmmm, perhaps that *was* a better plan than having Ashe and Talon Clay disposed of. And again, there could always be a fatal "accident" once the captain brought them to the island paradise.

"Who?" Janice repeated. "Who you going to get to kidnap Willow?"

"Why, Hank Rountree, that's who."

In the makeshift kitchen area where Nat Lacey had been preparing tortillas, there was a slight stiffening of her rounded shoulders. Eyes huge, she came around the curtain, saying, "No, no, not him."

"Oh?" Garnet's eyebrow shot up with interest. "And why not? Do you happen to know Hank Rountree?"

"Y-Yes!" Nat recovered from the shock of having heard her former lover's name. "Don't you know that he is the fierce desperado Desert Wind?"

Garnet laughed, then sipped her gin and lemonade slowly. "Is that right?" So, she thought, this must be the dance hall gal that Hank had taken up with. Maybe she wouldn't get rid of Nat after all. This might prove to be very interesting. A favor for a favor. She produces the two-legged prey he'd been hunting, and he, Hank, brings Willow Brandon here. Naturally she'd have to hide Nat Lacey for a time, to make certain Hank did his job thoroughly. Not that he wasn't to be trusted—so far he had proven trustworthy, but one never knew when his "kind" would turn on you and do a double cross. Then again, she could always get rid of Lacey herself—and then take and use her name to keep an even lower profile!

"You won't have to be here when he comes to speak with me," Garnet told Nat. "In fact, you can take a little trip with Winder and some of the boys to go fetch some supplies."

All Nat wanted to know was when she would see Talon Clay again, in order to get to know him. "What about the other plan?" Nat asked. "I was supposed to catch the Ranger and seduce him, if you recall."

"I recall!" Garnet exploded. She shot to her feet, spilling her drink. "Damn and tarnation . . . clean it up," she ordered Nat. "And then get me another drink!"

Nat obeyed and feigned meekness, making her own cunning plans for this Willow Brandon once she returned with the boys and got some time alone with the Ranger's *supposedly* pretty wife. She exchanged glances with the other blond woman, a bit younger than herself. Hester, too, was making plans. This time, nothing or nobody was going to stand in her path. She would fill Willow's head with all kinds of lies, just as Nat Lacey had done with Hank's wife, Summer Wind!

Wearing a cotton nightgown, Tanya sat in the colorful brocade chair near the window, where she could look out onto the lane to see . . . what could there be to see and wait for? Ashe would not be returning to Sundance, not today, not tomorrow, not ever.

Ashe Brandon was dead.

At first she had been numb with shock when the men returned from the deep-sea fishing trip to say that Ashe Brandon had drowned. Ashe had been strong, intelligent, resourceful, a true-blue Ranger. He had been in his late thirties, his biceps and forearms heavy with muscle, his shoulders large, his stomach flat and solid as Talon Clay's, his legs columns of strength. He had been lean and still as mean as when he'd been a Texas Ranger. His shoulders had had the strength of years of living in the open, fighting Mexicans and Indians, working, rebuilding Sundance. Yet he had drowned.

Now she was in her late twenties, a widow with one daughter to raise by herself. Sarah was eight years old and she felt the same grief as did her mother, Tanya.

"Mother?" Sarah walked in, her red hair more coppery than Tanya's. "What are you doing sitting by the window again? This isn't good for you—Miss Pekoe said." Her voice was sweet and soft, her mouth a pretty cupid's bow. "I wish you'd get dressed and come downstairs. We could bake a cake or a pie. We could make Daddy's favorite—" Sarah left off saying pecan pie.

"Come here, Sarah." Tanya held out her arms and Sarah rushed to her mother. Stroking the silken hair, Tanya laid her cheek on the top of Sarah's head. "Do you remember the little puppy you played with at the

Turners' in California?" As her daughter nodded, Tanya went on. "Would you like it if we picked up a puppy for you just like that one?"

Turning her face up to Tanya's, Sarah said, "No, Mother. I don't want a puppy. Not now. I just want you to get well and be happy. Daddy's gone and nothing's going to bring him back." She gulped. "He drowned."

Tanya sighed. "You're right, darling. I have to revive myself for you and for Sundance."

"Oh!" Sarah bounced away from her mother. "*Guess* who's here?!"

For a moment Tanya's heart skipped a beat as she thought of Ashe . . . would she ever realize that he was really gone? "Now, who is this you are all excited about? Don't tell me one of your favorite cowpokes has returned?"

"No! It's much better than that!"

Finally willing herself to move and sit straighter, Tanya looked her daughter in the eyes, excited ones they were, and her own steadily got rounder. "Willow." It was almost a whisper.

"Yes!" Sarah jumped to her feet. "She and Talon Clay and Almanzo Rankin!"

Almanzo. The name whispered in Tanya's heart like a broken melody from the past. There had been a time when Almanzo had been attracted to her, but she had just married Ashe back then, and Almanzo had conducted himself as a true gentleman. Suddenly Tanya frowned as her nervous fingers stilled over her knees. "Has he brought his lovely wife Kachina?"

"No, Mother, he's all alone. Leastways, I think so. I don't remember Kachina, but I do remember you talking about how pretty and sweet she was." Reaching out,

Sarah began tugging at Tanya's hand, her winsome eyes and mouth begging. "Come on, Mama, let's go see Willow and Talon Clay. We'll go outside and find them . . . it will be so much fun!"

"They are there, Mama! Up on the little hill!"

Tanya tilted her head. Visiting the Brandon cemetery? Willow and Talon Clay hadn't done this in the past . . . what in the world could bring them there? And why, she wondered briefly, even before they had come to visit her at the main house? They must have heard the terrible news and decided to ease into it.

Even now, Tanya's heart gave a twist of sadness as she walked with Sarah, her entire being crying out for the loss of a husband and wonderful friend.

Sensing something and looking over his shoulder, Talon saw Tanya and Sarah coming up the low rise of the hill. They would want some time alone, he thought, deciding to go and find Almanzo; they had to make plans as to how Almanzo was going to manage the difficult task of keeping Willow here while he rode out to meet Sammy to resume the search for Michael Angelo.

While Willow bent at the gravesite, pushing tall wildflowers and weeds aside in order to read the name carved horizontally on the wooden cross, Talon left her side and walked to meet Tanya and Sarah. Engrossed in her troubled thoughts, Willow didn't even know that Talon had walked away.

As Talon neared Tanya he detected something amiss. It was there in her eyes, a profound sadness and mauve shadows beneath her lids, making the redhead appear hauntingly beautiful. In fact, Talon had never seen

Tanya look so attractive; she wore a faded dress, a ribbon trailing negligently in her barely-combed hair. He looked slowly down and then back up. She was like a barefoot princess, tired and world-weary.

"Tanya." He moved forward to hug her lightly. It had not been all that long since he had last seen her, maybe seven months, and yet he could detect the drastic change and aura of melancholy. Turning to Sarah, Talon hugged her, then looked at Tanya again as he straightened away from the girl. "What is it, Tanya?" Talon swallowed hard as he looked behind her for Ashe. "Where is my brother?"

Touching Sarah's head, Tanya said, "Why don't you run on ahead, Sarah, and tell Willow, uhm, 'hello.' Will you do that, sweetheart?"

Snatching up a wildflower and breaking it carefully, Sarah looked up at Uncle Talon and then her mother, knowing she was going to tell Daddy's brother the sad news. "All right, Mama." Sarah walked away, slowly, glancing over her shoulder once, twice . . .

Tanya pressed her lips together as the tears threatened to come. "Talon—" She sucked in a deep breath. "Your brother is—" Again she pressed her lips and jerked her head to look away from him.

"Dead." Talon finished for her. Then he asked in a tear-choked voice, "How?"

"Fishing off the coast . . . an accident." She gulped, looked down, and then up at the blur of Sarah and Willow up ahead.

Slowly, like an old man, Talon nodded and walked away.

Tanya stood still for long moments, gazing over Brandon land, a lonely feeling washing through her as

189

she wondered if she would ever, ever be whole again. "Time," Miss Pekoe had said as she stroked Tanya's back, "it's gonna take time, you know. You jest gotta go on livin', Missa Brandon. Ashe woulda wanted you to do jest that, honey bunch."

Heaving a deep sigh and fortifying her emotions with a prayer, Tanya clutched her pale mauve skirt and put one foot in front of the other; it was the best she could do for now.

Feeling a change of presence beside her, Willow turned her head slowly, a chill moving along her spine. She gasped when she saw not Talon Clay but a much smaller person. Willow had never known how tall her mother had been, but this girl, this lovely slip of a thing, had given her a start. And she was happy to see she wasn't really a ghost.

"Hello," Sarah said, looking up at a woman who was a little smaller than her mother, but not much. "You're my Auntie Willow. I remember you a *little* bit, but then you went away, Mama said."

Willow was whirled back in time. Sarah getting her first tooth. Sarah crying when she and Willow had been kidnapped by Carl Tucker. Sarah's first birthday ... Christmas ... second birthday ... third ... and almost fourth. The memories of sweet baby Sarah stopped there.

"Sweet Sarah!" Willow cried, enfolding the pretty girl in her arms. "How lovely you've come to be, Sarah Brandon."

"And you, too!" Sarah exclaimed. Then she frowned lightly. "How come you're wearing pants, Auntie Willow, and carrying that funny looking hat?" She wrinkled her freckled nose. "And Uncle Talon, he's got funny clothes on, too!" Sarah remembered Talon well, since the Ranger had only been gone a little over six months. "Where'd these clothes come from anyway?"

Pushing a blond wave out of her eye, Willow licked her lips and began. "That's a long story, Sarah. I'll tell it to you sometime."

"Gosh, you will, really?" Sarah's eyes misted over. "Mama doesn't tell me many stories lately. Auntie Willow—" Sarah swallowed. "Mama's really sad." Then she blurted, "Because Daddy's dead!"

A wave of dizziness rippled over Willow, settling in her extremities and almost making her faint. She blinked at Sarah. "Ashe—? Dead?" This was hardly believable, since Ashe had always been so vital, so alive, so strong, handsome, indestructible!

"Yup." Sarah nodded fast and hard. "Daddy's gone to heaven to be with *his* mama and daddy. That's what Miss Pekoe and Clem says all the time." She tossed a look over her shoulder. "Here comes Mama." Her voice fell to a whisper. "Be nice to her, Auntie Willow. Maybe you can help her be happy again."

Being the intelligent child she was, Sarah wandered over to the huge cottonwood and whistled softly to the birds up in the tree. It wasn't long before she was climbing and then shimmying along the first fat limb that reached ever upward into the cool shadows of the tree.

Willow whirled and at once Tanya was in her arms. Sobs wracked the redhead's frame and tears wetted Willow's Western shirt. Tanya muttered, "Sarah . . . she . . . told you?"

191

"Yes, Sis, she told me." Willow patted and rubbed her sister's back as they continued to hold each other. "Ashe is gone, Sis, but not his spirit. I felt him when I was up here." She wouldn't say that what she felt was only a memory, and that, come to think of it now, it was hardly believable that Ashe Brandon, so vital and strong, could really be dead. Maybe he had survived, but she wasn't going to say this and give her sister false hope. "We'll keep him alive by remembering him always and . . . wait a minute, Sis. Have you let him go?"

"I know what you mean, Willow." Tanya sniffed delicately. "It's too early to let Ashe go; I must grieve for him first. Miss Pekoe said to do this and then let him go."

"Oh, I see." Willow felt all choked up. "I guess I'll have to do that if I find out that my baby didn't survive the kidnapping."

For the first time, Tanya noticed Willow's unusual clothes. "You had a *baby?*" Tanya was confused. "When did all this happen? Why are you wearing those strange clothes? Are you back to stay with Talon Clay? He was so worried about you, and yet so angry that you had run off after a 'simple little argument,' he called it. He did check with all the Ranger stations and no one had discovered a body fitting your description. He was so stubborn, though, when . . . Ashe—" She gulped— "tried to get him to go searching for you."

"Tanya." Willow was alarmed at her sister's rambling. "I sent you a letter, don't you remember?" This was not the time to bring that up! "Oh, maybe Juanita forgot to bring it to the mail coach that day just as it was leaving . . . she's always forgetting things." Willow missed Juanita terribly. As an afterthought, she said almost to herself, "I hope Sammy and Juanita are all right."

"Willow, I think we're both tired and need a week to rest and talk."

Her brown eyes gone huge and suddenly disturbed. Willow blurted, "I don't have a week to spare, Tanya. Michael has been kidnapped. Didn't you hear me?"

Taking Willow's hand, Tanya led her away from the grave with the barely readable name scrawled on the tilted cross. "We do have to talk. You will need to rest and get some ... different clothes before you go in search of your son."

Willow stopped walking, bringing Tanya to a halt with her. "Sis, you must keep a secret for me. You can't tell Talon Clay, and not Almanzo either."

"I promise."

"Talon brought me here and I have a feeling Almanzo is going to try and *keep* me here. You know what I mean?" Willow saw her sister's nod. "I have to get away before Almanzo locks me up somewhere and throws away the key."

"He wouldn't!" Tanya gasped. "That's awful! Why would Talon and Almanzo want to do that?"

"Talon doesn't want me getting in the way, Sis. He is afraid I'll get killed trying to get Michael back. But I have to try ... I won't be able to sleep or eat or anything if I don't get back to that gang of outlaws and have Ned take me to the ghost town where the Boss Lady—"

"Willow, please, I feel weak from all this crazy talk. Let's go inside, get coffee and sandwiches, rest a bit and

193

then resume this conversation." Tanya sighed deeply. "I have a feeling it's going to get even crazier."

Tanya didn't know the *half* of it!

As sundown fell across the landscape, the shifting shadows moved like restless ghosts through Rawhide. One could almost hear the tinkling of an old piano and the laughter of "scarlets" down the street. In the old church, a woman's shadow could be seen to pace the hallowed walls, stopping occasionally, and then resuming the restive pacing. Suddenly the troubled woman halted and rested her hand on a pew.

"Mrs. Tucker!" Garnet suddenly hollered, clenching the bench and whirling when a sleepy woman entered from belowstairs. "I've got it!" Swiftly she ran to the cabinet where she kept her supply of gin and poured herself a liberal amount, then faced the woman whose hair stuck out in all directions. "We're moving our operation to Saw Grass, and from there we'll make our plans."

Janice Ranae blinked as if she couldn't believe what her partner in crime had just told her. *Ordered,* was more like it, since the woman seemed to lead everyone around by the nose and always get what she demanded. "That's too close to Sundance," Janice Ranae argued. "It won't be long before the hands at Sundance discover that we've moved in."

Sipping her drink slowly, Garnet turned, planning to manipulate the other. "We'll keep a low profile, and they will think that you have returned home with Hester, that's all."

"Where will you hide the boy?" Janice Ranae's faded

194

blue eyes went in the direction where the child was kept beneath the wide stairs. "And yourself, where will you be all this time?"

"We'll take a wagon to Saw Grass and the boy will be hidden under blankets . . . and we'll have the hands pile hay around the perimeter. I'll be disguised and will be riding with my men. We're too far away from Sundance to get our devious task accomplished. This way, they'll never believe their enemy is hiding right next door." Garnet thought for a moment, then asked, "How far *is* Sundance from Saw Grass?"

Janice Ranae, too, thought for a moment, calculating. "The northern border of Sundance butts up to my property and I'd say . . . hmmm—" The woman scratched her head, causing her hair to stick out even more on top.

"How far?" When Janice Ranae continued to look dumbfounded, Garnet asked, "Saints preserve us! How the hell long did it take to get from Saw Grass to Sundance?"

"About half an hour's ride, less on good days."

Garnet shook her head. She was beginning to believe Janice Ranae was tottering on the edge of senility. "What the blazes are *good* days?" she questioned fiercely.

"You know, sunny days. Pretty days. Misty days take longer, 'course depending on what time of day you're going there." She gave Garnet a sidelong stare and saw the Boss Lady's impatience. "As the crow flies, on horseback, it'd take about . . . well, a lot less than half an hour. Quarter of an hour, yeah, I'd think. 'Course, I never rode a horse over there . . . always took the wagon." Janice frowned at Garnet. "Don't you remember? I used to come visit you when you married Pete

195

Brandon. That was before your first husband ever come along with Tanya, Willow, and Sammy. Rob must've followed you there all the way from California."

"Right. Too bad I told Rob where *I* was living in that letter I sent him. It took a couple months to get there, and by that time I was already married to Pete Brandon. Now Talon Clay, that there boy sure knew how to pleasure a woman." Tossing her head, she added, "Then again, I'm the woman who taught that lover boy everything he knew, and whew! did Talon Clay catch on fast. Wish he hadn't gone to live with you over at Saw Grass. Think his own father sent him to your place. That fair-haired Ranger hates me now, I'd wager. I never did get to Ashe Brandon, but I know I gave him plenty to think about on nights when a man's lonesome and his urges strike like a rattlesnake in the dark."

Shaking her messy head, Janice Ranae remarked, "You sure have led a lusty life, Garnet Haywood. Wish I could've been as bold as you. Shoot, I didn't care about no man after my husband was killed. Sex don't excite me. Now, land! That excites me and I can't sleep nights thinking about coveting Sundance. It's always been on my mind to get that property in my clutches. My son Carl wanted it, too, and now he's gone I'm goin' to fulfill his wishes."

"Well, my friend, we'll get *our* wish one day soon, won't we?"

"Yup, you're right there. One day Sundance and Saw Grass will be joined together, just as it always ought to have been."

"Janice Ranae—" Garnet said, getting up for another slosh of spirits—"I believe this is going to turn out to be a bigger and better war between the Tuckers and the Brandons."

"Don't forget *Garnet,* too."

"Oh, I won't."

Adjusting her blouse that was rumpled from her son sleeping against her, Willow smiled in poignant remembrance of happier days. Her lips were softly blurred with a tender smile as she gazed out the window of the stagecoach. The rising sun was sending its swordlike rays across the Texas hill country, striking up ahead on the flatter land that lay before them, stretching ever onward to their destination. Where was she going? She still did not know. All she knew was she was with her son and that was what mattered. The vast prairie stretched off into clumps of cottonwood and sprawling ranches sprang up in the distance. Whose ranches, she wondered, feeling so lonesome . . . for what? Who? Her son was here with her. The new sun splashed color on the dew-encrusted grass at the edge of the road and God and Nature decked the land in a hundred shades of summer green and gold. All sorts of beautiful pastel wildflowers fluttered softly against the horizon. All different, all magnificent. Even the weeds added their own special color and shape to God's wonderful world.

"Mommy? Are we almost there?" Michael asked sleepily, turning from one side to the other, re-tucking his short legs against his mother's lap. "I can't wait to see Daddy. What does he look like?"

She gazed down at her beloved child. "Soon, Michael. Soon you will meet your daddy."

When Willow looked down again there was no child

on her lap. She was alone . . . and she was slowly awaking. Staring up at the ceiling in the night, Willow felt the tears come. *Dear God, my arms are so empty.* She was alone in the little house. Talon was somewhere else, no doubt getting ready to hit the trail again.

So empty. *Dear God, Michael, where are you?*

The fields fall southward, abrupt and broken,
   To the low last edge of the long lone land.
If a step should sound or a word be spoken,
   Would a ghost not rise at the strange
      guest's hand?
                    —Algernon Charles Swinburne

Chapter Ten

Slowly-creeping dawn lit the Texas landscape, inch by slow inch, across the rolling hills and grasslands. Morning mists that moved like restless ghosts across the terrain began to lift as the sun burned them away. Willow awoke feeling refreshed and eager to face the day; she could not remember when she had slept as well. Had she dreamed? She could hardly remember any of it. There was only one thing that would not let her hum a carefree tune as she walked from the little house to the main dwelling: the absence of her beloved child.

Soon she would be leaving Sundance to go in search of Michael again. First she had to make plans and prepare her clothing and camping items; she knew Talon Clay was riding out today to resume the search. He had to meet the man called Desert Hawk and then go on to see if Sammy was still in Bountiful waiting to hear from him. Or her. Whoever got there first, she thought with a sly grin.

For now, Willow walked the halls cautiously to search out her hiding place for the things she would take with her. Downstairs she could hear Miss Pekoe humming a melancholy spiritual as she worked in the small kitchen. There was also a chuckhouse out back for the many hands Sundance had acquired in her absence. There only used to be about ten—now she believed Tanya said there were twenty or thirty at times. The war could change that number, too.

Looking down from the windows, Willow could see the hands tending to their chores, and out back further, more bunkhouses had been added as Sundance property had grown; she had heard Clem say they even called it Sundance Spread or Brandon's Ranch oftentimes now and had their own special "S" brand for their cattle. Clem was getting very old but he still got around on bandy legs and creaking limbs.

Under a full moon the Brandon ranch had been gorgeous the night before as Willow had gazed out the window wondering if Talon would come to her. He had not. She hadn't seen Talon Clay since he had left her standing at the gravesite and Tanya and Sarah had come along, making her forget that Talon had been there, too. Her mind was occupied with the grave and why it was so hard to read the marker there where Garnet Hayes-Brandon was supposed to be buried.

Sarah had awakened and was coming along the hall just then, and when she saw Willow she called out a cheery "Hi!" and skipped down the stairs on her way outside. The child was intelligent and knew when an adult had things on his or her mind and wanted to be left alone; she had already detected that virtue in Sarah Brandon.

In a room down the hall Tanya was seated in a huge loveseat she and Ashe used to occupy on romantic nights following a candlelit dinner prepared by Miss Pekoe. "That black woman is the best thing that happened to us, Tanya," he had told her after Miss Pekoe had been with them for a year. "Besides you," Ashe had added, following his declaration of appreciation for the black housekeeper. Tanya was never sorry, and Miss Pekoe never got in her way. Tanya loved the slim black woman who loved her and Ashe and Sarah right back. Miss Pekoe had been mourning Ashe's death ever since Tanya's return the week before, placing flowers on the hill near an unmarked grave, but still she kept cheerful for everyone else in the house; she was a boon to everyone's morale.

Tanya was daydreaming . . . it had been so long ago but actually only a little over eight years . . . when she was a younger woman missing Ashe, the man she had fallen in love with when she'd only been on the verge of her teens. "I'll come back, missy, when you're all grown up"—Ashe had laughed in that easy way of his—"and you better be waiting." She had waited and waited, and when she least expected him Ashe had shown up near the little house and snatched the rifle from her unsuspecting fingers. She had been in an "all-fired hurry"—as Willow had called it—to bushwhack the Rangers and run them off Sundance property.

At present, Tanya kept on recollecting as she rolled her head on the back of the sofa to gaze at nothing in particular out the window.

The Ranger had stared right into her eyes, saying, "You weren't planning on using this rifle on us?" meaning himself and the other Rangers accompanying him. Still holding her pa's old rifle, his eyes had slid to Willow. Later Ashe had told her he had ridden with Captain John Hays and had faced Comanche braves, dodged Indian arrows, faced Mexican spears, been tried and tested in various ways he could not even count. Yet he had been totally at a loss as to what to say or do with "these two kitten-eyed females staring him down," he had told her. Thinking Willow would be the first one to speak up, he'd questioned her, *"Was* she going to bushwhack us?"

To turn aside his smooth but fierce interrogation, Tanya had said the first thing that came to mind, "Are you hungry?" With a deep chuckle, Ashe had lowered his head. With the bore of his rifle, he poked his hat up so that a strip of lighter skin showed on his handsome forehead . . . Tanya took the time to look him over: wide, relaxed shoulders, buckskin-covered chest, snug khaki trousers, and long-boned fingers that rubbed lightly the butt of the rifle he held close to his thigh.

This is where you belong, Ashe Brandon, here, here at Sundance, not off killing wild Indians or Mexican bandits—or chasing women, she had wanted to scream at him.

Now, years later, she wanted to scream at him again, for dying and leaving her lonelier and more broken-hearted than ever!

"Sis?" The past melted away as Tanya heard a voice.

Tanya looked up as Willow stood in the open doorway, wearing one of her old dresses, a blue calico with white crocheted collar. Actually, it was a dress Willow had made for herself before she had run away from Talon Clay—the first time!

"Come in, Willow." Tanya lowered her legs to make room for her sister. "I've been thinking about you . . . actually, that was awhile ago, but now—"

"Now, Sis?" Willow thought she knew. She had felt

the same way Tanya looked—knew it for looking into a mirror—because she had experienced the same when she'd been pining for her lost child. "What were you daydreaming about now?" she repeated when Tanya still wore that faraway look.

"At the moment I was dreaming about Ashe." Tanya sighed, pressing the material of her dressing gown into a deep fold. "Truthfully, I was recollecting the time when I pined away for Ashe Brandon to come back to Sundance. I could almost hear his voice, Willow. It was so real it was almost like yesterday." She made a sound much like a tiny creature in pain.

"Oh, Sis, I know just what you're feeling because I've known the same, when Mikey, or Angelo—that's what my housekeeper calls my son—when he was kidnapped I thought the world had come to an end."

"Willow . . . dear, sweet Willow." Tanya hauled her sister into her arms and they held each other, cheeks pressed to shoulders, palms rubbing backs, tears threatening to spill. Tanya was the first to break away, brushing a tear from the corner of Willow's eye. "Here I am thinking about myself, when you have a cross to bear yourself." She smiled and tilted her head, red hair spilling over one shoulder. "What was Mikey like? Do you mind if I, too, call him that?"

In answer, Willow began, "Mikey was a beautiful child . . . *oh Lord!* I mean *is* a beautiful child!" Understanding, Tanya nodded as Willow went on. "He is what every woman would want in a son," she chuckled, "even if he is only four years old! No one could ever be angry with him, no matter how much trouble he gets into. He and Jorge get into mischief and Juanita has to clean it up, always, and—"

203

"Willow, who is Jorge?" Tanya pictured a huge man—perhaps this Juanita's husband—playing with little Mikey.

"Big dog." Willow nodded as she held a hand several feet from the floor, feeling a little choked up, praying that one day soon she'd have her son and Jorge and Juanita back together where they belonged. "Jorge is a very large, long-haired dog and he's Mikey's best friend. Wherever Mikey goes, Jorge is not far behind."

"Where is Jorge now?" Tanya asked in a voice soft as silk.

"He is back at Bountiful with Juanita."

"Oh my!" Tanya clapped her hands together. "Your letters, I almost forgot. You *did* mention something about the big dog, when you had first gotten him as a puppy."

"Actually, Jorge is Juanita's dog. But we take it for granted that he belongs to Mikey. We were a very happy family ... and it's strange, Sis, but immediately after Mikey was kidnapped Talon Clay shows up in Bountiful and was real suspicious, thinking we were hiding Mikey from him."

"You don't say!" Tanya was losing herself and her grief in Willow's problems. "When will you be leaving us?" she asked, realizing that the "us" did not include Ashe anymore.

"I will—*listen,* someone is calling from the bottom of the stairs." Willow got up to go to the hallway. "Be right down," she shouted to the person below. Returning to Tanya, she said, "Oh Lord, it was Almanzo. Talon Clay's getting ready to ride out and he wants to say good-bye."

When Willow just stood there, not making a move to

go downstairs, Tanya asked, "Willow, what is it? Aren't you going to send Talon Clay off with best wishes for finding your son?"

"I'm going, too, Tanya. But, I'm going to be riding out alone with no one but you and I aware of it."

"When?"

"Soon. I know where to look. The only problem is, I don't want Talon Clay beating me to the Green Mountain gang. He'll wreck my plans if he gets there first and questions them about my riding with them."

"You rode with outlaws?" Tanya almost shot up from the loveseat. When her sister only nodded with a brooding look, Tanya said, "That sounds very dangerous, Willow. You won't be going to search for them and ride out with them again, will you?"

"Yes, I will. I have to in order to find out where Mikey was taken. I'm certain it was Mikey that they took to the ghost town where this Boss Lady is holding him captive. It has something to do with Sundance, I'm almost positive. I even talked to Ned about it—he's one of the Boss Lady's favorite gunslingers—and he is pretty sure it's the same boy, too. He was even agreeing to help, when I met up with Almanzo and—" Here she chuckled—"the Desert Hawk ... who, by the way, Talon Clay was pretending to be, trying to get to the outlaw gang himself. He had to make friends with this Desert Hawk in order to borrow his clothes and such. I don't know about Desert Hawk; he could be a threat to my plans. I'm not sure just what he's after, but I overheard Almanzo and Talon Clay discussing a dance hall girl. He's looking for her and he seems to have the idea that I'll lead him to her. At least, this is what my intuition tells me. I even think he shot a man dead, when everyone thought *I* killed a man named Jake."

"Still reading people's thoughts and determining what is going to happen in the near future?" Tanya asked her sister.

"Yes. It really bothers me sometimes. Yet, in a way it's good because I know for certain that Mikey is still alive and well. I can feel him." She wouldn't tell Tanya that when she'd been up to their dead mother's grave-site, she'd felt the same, as if Garnet still lived and breathed her evil.

"Willow!"

"Who is that shouting your name like a big bear?"

With a giggle, Willow said, "Don't you recognize Almanzo's voice?" When Tanya nodded slowly, Willow explained, "Almanzo's a lot calmer than he used to be. There seems to be more to his personality than just stern looks and clipped sentences. Still—" she sighed—"he guards me like a hawk, and as soon as Talon's gone, I believe I'll never be let out of Almanzo's and the guards' sights."

Tanya laughed. "Ever the schoolteacher, aren't you, dear sister?" She was still chuckling softly when Willow reached down to give her sister another hug, then she stood back.

Tanya began to rise from the sofa, but Willow pressed a hand to her shoulder. "No, you rest a while longer. I'll go say good-bye to Talon Clay and get Miss Pekoe to fix you a special Texas-size breakfast. How does hotcakes with lots of gooey syrup, steaming coffee, and fresh strawberries sound?" Before Tanya could answer, she added, "I do hope there are strawberries this season?"

"Yes, there are. Almost a constant supply spring and summer and even in the fall. We have wild strawberries . . . they're growing on the rise from the creek and they are the most delicious!"

"Yes, Strawberry Creek. I remember." Almost five years ago she and Talon had made love there and eaten strawberries afterward, gotten the juice on their mouths and chins. And when their lips were all red and tasty, they had made love with wild abandon again. She flushed, thinking they should have named Mikey "Wild Strawberry" instead of Michael Angelo!

That had been the glorious day they had made their baby.

The smell of bacon and coffee still hung in the air wafting out to the porch in back as Willow stepped up. Breathing deeply of the glorious flowers as she hung her arms over the side-railing for a moment, her hands dangling loosely over the edge, she looked out over everything that was familiar to her, achingly so. She straightened and walked into the kitchen of Le Petit Sundance to find Talon Clay waiting for her. A tender longing filled her as she entered.

"Just washing up my breakfast dishes here. Hungry?" He didn't look at her as he worked the indoor pump and sloshed some water around. "There's some vittles left over there in the frying pan, if you want some."

"No, I just came to say good-bye and wish you well in finding our son." Shoot. Why did she feel so tongue-tied all of a sudden? After a moment she spun around and blurted, "Talon—you don't even know what Mikey looks like! How are you going to *recognize* him when and if he's right before your eyes?"

Wiping a dish with a rag, Talon said over his shoulder, "I got a pretty good idea and description from both you and the sheriff of Bountiful as to what my own son looks like. Juanita even tossed in her own version of the story."

Willow blinked, *"What* story?"

"How Mikey got kidnapped. What do you think?" Whipping the drying cloth aside, Talon turned and walked directly to her, taking her in his arms and kissing her lustily and hungrily. Pulling back, he growled, "I want you, woman." His hands slipped around in back to cup her buttocks and yank her closer.

"Demanding rogue, aren't you?" Willow let him pull her to him until she could feel every rise and fall of his virile manliness. "Now I suppose you think you're going to lure me into our old bedroom, hm?"

"Aren't you going to give me something to take with me? More than words, Willow, I need your love and reassurance that you'll be waiting for me when I return. Who knows, I might get killed trying to rescue our son."

She nodded. "With or without Mikey, you want me here waiting for you." Sliding from his embrace, Willow walked to the window to stare out toward the lane leading out to the road. She sniffed, loud enough for him to hear. "I won't be able to stand it if you don't come back with Mikey. Life won't be the same, things will have changed drastically." In worried misery she continued to stare and pray. "You don't know what it's like to love your own child, Talon. You didn't see him after he was born. You didn't hold him, play with him, feed him, tuck him in at night."

"No, I didn't!" Talon exploded in anger. He walked over and spun her to face him. "Why do you think I didn't—or couldn't—let's put it that way. Wasn't it you who took that privilege from me? You ran away, Willow, not the other way around."

"I thought you were dallying with Hester! She made me believe as much and . . . and now I don't know what to believe, because I saw you and Hester talking together outside, and it looked like pretty secret talk to me."

Grabbing her chin and yanking her back to look at him when she began to stare out the window again, Talon gazed deeply into her eyes. "I don't want any woman as much as I want you, Willow. I could've gone to bed with a hundred women since you left me high and dry, Hester Tucker included, but I never did. Not even when I was in Abilene here awhile ago with Sammy. The whore there looked just like you and she was beckoning me to come share a bed with her."

Willow frowned up at him. "Did you?"

"Don't look so fierce, Pussywillow." His gaze lingered on her slightly parted lips, where they curved upward at the corners, delicately proportioned and with an underlip full and soft. Shaking his head with the lusty thoughts in it, he went on, "I said, I *could* have. But I did not. Either you believe me, or—" He let go of her chin and dropped his hand to his side in a helpless gesture. "This is getting to me just as much as you, you know. I feel frustrated, too, knowing my son is out there somewhere and I can't get to him. That's what's got us up in the air, you know."

"Right. And you couldn't even find your own *wife* when she took off, and haul her back. Rather, you didn't even *try* finding her!"

Snatching up her hand and pressing it to his thigh, Talon looked at the yellow wave across her forehead, wanting to kiss her there and everywhere else besides. "You didn't want to be found, not right away. I knew it. I felt it. So I went and did my own thing, true. Can you fault me for that?"

"Following in your brother's shoes—or boots." Willow suddenly gasped. "Oh, Talon, I plumb forgot! Your brother Ashe . . . how awful." She fell forward against his chest, hugging him as strongly as she could. "Oh, I'm sorry, you must feel very lonely and sad, just like I did and still do after Mikey was stolen away."

He smiled against her temple. "Yes, I'm lonely and sad. Why do you think I want to take my gorgeous wife to bed?"

Willow felt nervous; even more unsettling was the full evidence of his sex beneath the tight pants he wore.

Willow looked around the bedroom, at familiar surroundings, like the bed, still with its carving on the headboard, the declaration of Talon Clay's love for Willow Margaret, carved there forever; she hoped in her heart this would be so and prayed fervently for their lost love-child.

Her eyes slid to the right. The comb and brush set were missing; she'd taken that set with her when she'd run away to Bountiful. Now she had the gorgeous mirror, but she would leave it behind; it wouldn't get broken in her wild ride then, since she meant to trek all the way to the town on the other side of Paradise Valley. Once there, she'd find out where the Green Mountain outlaws had gone. She was sure the gossips would fill her in on that score.

Talon Clay came up behind her. "What are you thinking?" he whispered against her hair, slowly sliding her dress away from her shoulders.

"How everything still looks the same. Only the comb and brush set is missing. Almost all my clothes and knickknacks are here, excepting a few items of clothing still packed away over at the little house."

"Hmm," he murmured against the soft flesh of her neck, a golden tan where the wind had lifted her hair and left the kiss of the sun on her skin. "Tell me something about the little house, teacher. Maybe a poem or something like that? You know, you always used to quote stuff from those little brown and purple books you carried around on moonlit nights."

"Uhmm, yes." She recollected those enchanted evenings when she'd read him poetry and then they would fall asleep in each other's arms on the floor amidst pillows, at the fireside, with the moon peeking through the curtains. "I have one, by Percy Bysshe Shelley: *O wild West Wind, thou breath of Autumn's being, Thou, from whose unseen presence the leaves dead . . . Are driven, like ghosts from an enchanter fleeing . . .*" She wrenched around to look into the sparkling green eyes. "Are the ghosts that haunted you gone now, Talon?"

Heaving a deep sigh, Talon moved against her, as if restless and worried, kissing and holding her forehead. Then he spoke. "I feel her again, Willow." He gulped, pressing harder upon her. "Garnet. She's back to haunt us. Either that, or she's preparing to move in on us with her restless spirit. Why won't she leave us alone!"

"Oh Lord!" Willow pushed away and looked up at

him as shock waves rolled over her. "I felt her, too. Did you feel it up at the gravesite?" He looked around the bedroom, clenched his teeth, and nodded fiercely. Willow breathed, "Oh . . . Jesus, what does it mean? Talon? *Talon!* Is she buried there—or not?"

"Damn it, Willow, I can't be sure!" Talon jerked his shirt back on, leaving it unbuttoned as he faced her. "Why did she have to come between us again? What the hell *is* she? For God's sake! Won't she ever let go? What do we have to do to get rid of the woman's hold on Sundance?"

Pressing her lips together, Willow answered, "I don't want to make love right now."

"I beg your pardon, ma'am." His voice was cool. Tossing her a glare, Talon began buttoning up his shirt as fast as he could. "Don't you think I know it? Hell, I don't either. I wouldn't make love if you begged me!"

"Talon." Willow looked at him in serious consternation and swallowed. "Talon. She's a devil-woman and she has always been out to destroy us. What if she even—? Could she have something to do with Mikey's disappearance . . . do you think, just possibly?"

"Hey, don't say that." Talon sat on a hard chair to pull his boots back on. "You give me the shivers when you talk like that!"

"I mean . . . supernaturally." Another word from one of her high-brow books, Talon thought. She shrugged to lighten the dark mood. "A curse . . . aha! The curse of Sundance!"

"Shoot, woman! Be serious."

She tossed her head, giving her long blond hair a shake. "I am. You said just as much a few moments ago yourself. I'm not saying anything much different than what you wondered out loud, having to do with Garnet and her hold on Sundance."

Talon shook his head, hoping to clear it. "We better go see Pastor Cuthbert."

"Is he still around?" Willow asked, remembering the dear old pastor who had opened a schoolhouse especially for her to teach impoverished children.

"Sure is. Maybe he's got some answers to our daffy riddle."

"Right, Talon. And he's sure going to think *we're* 'daft' if we go visit him and tell him this insane ghost story."

"No. I think his library had some books in it about this ... what'd you call it?—supernatural stuff? Yeah. Ghosts and the like. Yeah," he repeated. Looking down at the floor, Talon suddenly snapped up to stare her in the eyes. "Have you seen her ghost yet?"

"Now you're giving *me* the shivers, Talon Clay!" Nibbling on her lower lip, she nodded fiercely. "Over at Brandon's cemetery. I saw her. Only she wasn't wearing a filmy dress like in that dream Tanya had of her. Now ... don't laugh." Talon said he wouldn't and she went on, "She was wearing a cowboy hat and there were spurs on her *boots!*"

"She wasn't a lady Ranger, was she?" Talon asked, taking to laughing, to lighten the serious mood.

"No. She was a—" Willow laughed softly, yet almost hysterically—"a lady outlaw!"

Grabbing Willow by the hand, Talon yelled, "Then let's run not walk to the preacher! This could be very serious," he mused, the fine lines around his eyes crinkling when he smiled.

"Why, Talon," Willow shouted, still feeling crazy and

213

untamed and breathless as they ran out the door, "Are we getting hitched all over again?"

"That's not a bad idea, Pussywillow . . . we might do that, too, while we're getting this spooky riddle solved."

"But what about letting the others in on this strange thing that's happening to us? They might like to know there's a curse on Sundance. Look—Ashe drowns and Mikey is kidnapped. Don't they deserve to know we've been seeing ghosts? Almanzo might even have some ideas . . . he's been living at Black Fox's camp; Indians deal with spirits every day, right?"

"Heck with everyone else! It's just you and me now, darlin'! We got a ghost to get rid of and a baby to find!"

Willow tugged at Talon until he was forced to stop half way to the barn where the horses were kept. Looking into his eyes, she excitedly begged, "Does this mean I'm riding out with you to search for Mikey?" A cowboy Willow had never seen rambled by, tipped his hat, and all she could manage was a tight smile for the man. "Well?" she repeated after the cowboy walked across the greensward.

Talon's stare trailed the man until he vanished around the chuckhouse. "I'm afraid not, darlin'. You're still staying put and I'm still riding out. But first, we're going to get us some answers to lay your fears to rest a little bit regarding this ghost story."

"All right, Talon." Willow followed him inside where he saddled Shadow and Sally, fresh-broke mustangs from last year's accumulation. She helped him with the bridles, saying meekly, "I guess I'll just have to stay behind then . . . with all the ghosts." She sniffed.

"Just one, Willow. Just one."

Meekly. But that didn't mean a *promise*.

214

Pastor Cuthbert was not in residence. He had left a note for all his friends and parishioners with his house-keeper. "I'm sorry, but da good pastor iss gone for da suumertime and von't be back until vintertime," Mrs. Emily Vandanecker said. "Vat did you vant him for?"

"Uh," the puzzled Ranger stammered as he fumbled for an explanation, then came up with, "We'll catch him in the wintertime, Mrs. Van, uh, Ecker."

"Nooo, it iss Vandanecker, young man. Villow knows," she said, nodding at Willow. "You vant cafe before you ride avay to your home? I have not visited vit Villow for a long time. You stay?"

"I'm sorry, Emily, but we really do have to get back to Sundance. You see, we—" Willow jerked. "Ouch."

"Vat is it?" Emily asked. "Vas it one of dose awful ants vat bit you?"

"No, Emily, it was more like a big rat."

"Oh nooo, you did not—" She laughed then. "Ooooh, I see, your hoosband vants to get back home for someting vat ve vill not mention, ya?"

Taking a deep breath, Willow blurted, "Emily, our son has been kidnapped. If you see or hear of anyone having done this awful deed or if you have any idea who the culprits might be, you let us know immediately." Willow nodded. "All right?"

"Oh, my Gott!" Emily placed her hand over her chest, looking as if she were scared out of her wits. "Vat you must do now is make up dose posters vat show da face uff your little boy. You do dat right avay now!" She shooed them with her hands. "Go! You find him dat vay vit da picture before it's too late!" Emily nodded until the door was finally closed all the way.

Walking to where they had hitched the horses' reins to the long rail, Talon and Willow exchanged looks, and she was the first to speak up. "Why didn't you do that, Ranger?" When he said nothing, she went on, "I wonder if Sheriff Somers thought to do that?"

With his hand resting languidly over a lean hip, Talon looked right and then left, then back at her. "I wonder if Mrs. Talon Clay Brandon had enough smarts to give the Sheriff of Bountiful a drawing of her son that he could circulate? Did you think to do that yourself, dear lady rogue?"

"Rogue? What the heck's *that* supposed to mean?"

"You should know. *You're* the teacher, lady."

"I know what *rogue* means, Mr. Ranger. But in my case . . ."

"Rogue?" Talon hunched his shoulders. "Same as outlaw." He nodded once, twice. "And when this is all over I'm going to arrest you and put you in jail for aiding and abetting outlaws."

Willow could only gape as Talon mounted up and rode away from her. She shouted after him, *"You know why I fell into them outlaws, Talon Clay!"*

"Yeah. But no one else knows."

She yelled, "Your threats don't mean a hill of beans, Talon Clay Brandon!"

She could hear his devious chuckle drifting back to her as she mounted in a huff, reined her horse and rode slowly after him, muttering, "One of these days, I'm going to show that man who's really the boss!" And then she scoffed, "Ghosts of a terrifying nature?—*huh!* I don't believe in them. There ain't any, if you ask me."

Long, long be my heart with such memories fill'd!
Like the vase in which roses have once been distill'd:
You may break, you may shatter the vase if you will,
But the scent of the roses will hang round it still.
        —Thomas Moore, *Farewell! But Whenever* ...

Chapter Eleven

"He tricked me!" Willow's anger was riding high. She stared at Tanya's gold locket, suspended from a fine chain, the only jewelry adorning her plain daydress of summer muslin. Willow, too, was dressed in a simple calico of orange and green; her collar was peach crochet. "He has ridden out already. Oh, as soon as I turn my back, he sneaks off—that no-good drifting Ranger!"

Tanya allowed a distraught Willow to get her emotional outburst over with, then spoke. "I thought you gave him a 'sweet' farewell. What happened?"

"Oh ... we just started talking about all kinds of jiggery and pokery." Willow plopped into a wingback chair near one of the open French windows. "Just ghosts." Laying her head back, she stared up at the ceiling, its ornate plasterwork rising high, as startling white as the first time she'd seen it ... what? Eight, nine years ago?

"Ghosts, Willow?" Tanya felt a shiver along her spine as she clutched the mahogany arm of her silk-upholstered chair; it was one of several pieces Ashe had

217

acquired over the years. "I hope you and he did not discuss the woman who used to live here . . . our mother."

"She's Sundance's biggest ghost!" Willow exclaimed. "Maybe there's others like lovely Martha and Pete and Rob, but Garnet, *whew!* She's the busiest one!"

"But . . . we all put her to rest years ago, Willow. The curse she had on Ashe and Talon Clay has been broken. From the moment Ashe let Garnet's memory go, he began to live and enjoy life once again." She felt stronger saying his name, and did not feel like crying or mourning so deeply that she could not function; Ashe would have wanted her to be strong and glad for yet another sunrise, and their gift of Sarah.

"I know that, Sis. It seems she is haunting us again. I am beginning to wonder if she's really dead. This ghost is so alive and troublesome *it's* almost real!"

Tanya's eyes flickered as she recollected a past when she had been angered at Ashe's accusations that she was as deceitful as her mother had been: "You don't have to gawk at me like that. I'm not leaving you, Brandon; you're too good a man for that. Besides, I kind of like you when you're sober and much calmer than you are now. I'll just take the room next door, *her* room, and wait until you come to your senses. I know there's a man in you somewhere, Ashe, one that will chase that frightened little boy out of you and drive that cursed ghost from this house!" Tanya remembered she had stood her ground like a spitting tigress before a ferocious lion! "You're plagued by the ghost of my mother. That's too bad. Wake up, Ashe, or tomorrow will be too late and you *will* find me gone with the morning sun."

To Willow she said, "You know, dear sister, I used to suspect that the man I had loved and married was a little

218

crazy. He had me really frightened at times, like when he pulled out his Colt and shot that vase apart in my hands. He could have blown my hands off—" She smiled painfully—"If he'd been less accurate in his aim. Ashe was a perfect shot. It bothered me when he didn't believe I was telling the truth. Discovering that Garnet was my mother was quite a shock—and he'd just made me his wife! I used to ask myself where the trust was that was supposed to go hand and hand with marriage. It was crazy, but I even thought he had married me to get even with a ghost! I was not a quitter, though. I loved Ashe and knew he loved me. I finally decided he had a very serious problem concerning my mother and I promised one day to resolve it."

Willow had been listening closely, and now she had a question to put to Tanya. "What is a ghost really, Tanya?"

"Just like I'd thought back then and still do: A ghost is nothing but a strong memory, the aura a deceased person might have left behind. I remember telling Garnet, 'Go away. Ashe is my husband; he belongs to me, the living'."

"I wish we had talked more about this back then, Sis, then maybe we could deal with this better than we are now. I don't mean you. I mean Talon and myself. We have this mutual feeling that Garnet's ghost had something to do with the disappearance of Mikey and that she has some influence over this woman who's Boss Lady at that ghost town. Who knows, maybe she got into that woman's body somehow and is inhabiting her."

"Now that is ridiculous! I've never heard of such a thing," Tanya scoffed. "Garnet is dead, she's buried right on Sundance property; how could she have had

Mikey stolen from you or even be influencing this woman as you say?"

Willow's eyes narrowed. "*Is* Garnet truly dead, Tanya?"

Late Saturday night Sammy arrived at Sundance. He rode in, dusty and weary, stumbled to the bunkhouse, and fell into bed. In the middle of the night, old Clem slipped in there and carefully and quietly removed Sammy's boots, then covered the lad with a thin blanket. When Clem turned, he gave a start.

"Almanzo, dagblasted, you sure gave this old heart a giddyup." Clem's flesh sagged and his grizzled head was now pure white. "What you doin' up so late fer, young man?"

"Just checking up on things, old man." He knew Clem didn't mind, because he often called himself that. "I might ask you what keeps *you* awake and walking from bunkhouse to bunkhouse."

"Well, I—" Clem seemed to forget what he had been doing, up and awake after midnight. He looked around and then grinned. "I heard Sammy here ridin' in. I knowed it was Sammy 'cause his hair stands out like a moonlit-carrot at night." He chuckled. "Ever seen that yourself?"

"I cannot say I have, old man. Now you must go back to bed and let me take care of things that make noise in the night."

"Huh?" Clem had been slowly walking to the door, when he turned back to Almanzo. "You always prowl at night, young feller? You do? What's the matter? Can't sleep, eh? Woman keepin' you awake and hankerin'?"

He nodded to himself. "That's what it is. Hear tell Tanya's lonely, too. She'll be doin' better once Ashe comes back home. Damn Rangers, never could keep at home where they belong—'taint natural nohow. 'Tweren't back then; ain't now. Man's place was . . . is at home." He scratched his head. "Woman's place is . . . well, home too, cookin' and ranchin'."

Everyone was used to Clem's lapses of memory, Almanzo told himself as he stepped outside with the old man. Clem's hair was liberally streaked with silver under the Texas moon. His walk was slow and burdensome, soon to be fatiguing if he remained on his feet too long. One thing Clem said had bothered him. About Tanya, the woman Almanzo loved and had never forgotten. He had even told his woman Kachina about his feelings for Tanya; Kachina had understood this with a tender and compassionate heart. She loved Almanzo so much that when she had met Tanya years ago at Sundance Kachina had found room in her heart for Tanya also.

And now Tanya was lonesome for her husband. This troubled Almanzo.

Suddenly the old man turned. "Have you been up to see Tanya yet, young man?" Clem could not see Almanzo's eyes; even by day they were as black as a moonless night.

Almanzo answered. "Not yet. I have been in the house when Tanya remained upstairs. We have not said 'Hello' and I would keep it this way until Tanya is strong enough to speak with me."

Clem squinted one eye, whispering, "You keepin' a lookout for that little gal of Tal's? Hmm? Well, that's good, 'Manzo. Tal told me if I saw her sneakin' away

I was to tell you and you'd make sure she'd, she'd—" Clem shook his white head. "What was I goin' to say? 'Tweren't about li'l Willow, were it?"

"Yes, old man. I have been watching that my lovely prisoner does not escape. This is why I am awake tonight, my old friend, not because I long for a woman's embrace. Soon I will take my rest. Another guard will take my place."

"I'll do it, 'Manzo!"

Patting the old man's head, Almanzo carefully went on to explain. "We have several changes of the guard already. I shall let you know if we need your assistance." He smiled while Clem smacked his lips, seeming satisfied. "I have an idea. You can watch for her tomorrow morning, but you should get your sleep in order to be awake early."

"Good idea, Nightwalker." He used the legendary name of Almanzo's Indian father. Nightwalker—Kijika. One who had been friendly with Clem when Kijika used to sneak onto Sundance property to get a look at his love, Martha Brandon, but that was a long time ago. "I'll be up bright and early sittin'. in my chair outside. No need to worry, young'un, Old Clem'll make sure she don't get away!"

"Let me go!" Willow's cornsilk hair hung in a golden curtain over her face; the tip of her nose and her sparking eyes peeked through. "I said, Get your stinkin' hands off me, *dudes!* You, too, Almanzo! I'm going after my boy and no man's stopping me!"

Clem stood by, chuckling while lifting and lowering his bushy eyebrows. "Hold her down, boys, she ain't goin' nowheres, Tal said so. We's to keep 'er here!" He hadn't had this much fun since Talon Clay and his outlaw buddies hid some loot under a loose board in the bunkhouse. "Don't hurt her none, Frank. Jesse, get your boot off her butt, I tol' you!"

At once Jesse and Frank listened to the old man whose word was law around Sundance. Willow spun around, putting her back to Almanzo as she tried to escape. Almanzo lifted Willow around the waist, gently but firmly pinning her arms down against her sides as she kicked backwards and hissed like a wildcat. "Calm down, *desperada*," he whispered into her ear; then in a louder voice, "You are a God-fearing woman, Willow, and what your husband says goes. You believe this, do you not?"

"Sure—but *he's* not God!" She squinted with the sun in her eyes.

Almanzo chuckled warmly. "Rangers are pretty close to Texas gods."

"Right, but no man is going to put the fear of God in me; only my Creator can do that. Now, let me go before I kick the heck out of your shins, Almanzo!"

"Do you believe what the Bible says, Willow?"

She looked up into those dark eyes and through the strands of her hair she could see the cheekbones set high in his face. She had never seen his straight black hair so tousled and she almost laughed that she could be the cause of this large, dangerous man's dishevelment. As she thought this, he released one hand to run it through his hair to keep it from his eyes. At last she said, "Yes—I believe what the Good Book says. *Why?*"

"It says in there that a woman should be subject to her husband's wishes—"

223

"We aren't talking about lovemaking, mister!"

Ignoring her outburst, Almanzo went on, "And his wish is that you stay here."

"But I'm not obeying him and so you should not interfere—doesn't the Bible say to mind your own business?"

Willow glanced over at the back door to the big house and grinned. Tanya was standing there. Now Almanzo Rankin would find out who was boss here, man or woman!

Her mouth agape, Tanya stared at Almanzo as he held her sister prisoner in his arms. She saw the other ranch hands, looking as though they, too, were preparing to attack Willow if she moved an inch. What had she done to deserve such bad treatment? She would have really been alarmed had she not spotted Clem standing nearby, chuckling and slapping his knees as if he enjoyed the scene immensely. She was not going to stand by while her little sister was being mauled for no good reason!

"Almanzo!" Tanya picked up her skirts, coming at full speed across the greensward. "Let go of my sister! What do you think you are doing?" Relieved to see that the ranch hands had shrunk back at her warning, she surged forward, making Almanzo's back her target. "Let loose of Willow, I say!"

Almanzo stared into Tanya's hot blue eyes, feeling his body shiver at seeing her so suddenly and without any warning. She was beautiful still. Her skin was dewy and her hair a fiery, shining red. She made his blood stir, as she had so many times before. Suddenly the sun shone more brightly for him and his heart was beating like a happy drum. She had finally come outside to face him—like a spitting tigress!

MORE PASSION AND ADVENTURE AWAIT... YOUR TRIP TO A BIG ADVENTUROUS WORLD BEGINS WHEN YOU ACCEPT YOUR FIRST 4 NOVELS ABSOLUTELY *FREE* (AN $18.00 VALUE)

Accept your Free gift and start to experience more of the passion and adventure you like in a historical romance novel. Each Zebra novel is filled with proud men, spirited women and tempestuous love that you'll remember long after you turn the last page.

Zebra Historical Romances are the finest novels of their kind. They are written by authors who really know how to weave tales of romance and adventure in the historical settings you love. You'll feel like you've actually gone back in time with the thrilling stories that each Zebra novel offers.

GET YOUR FREE GIFT WITH THE START OF YOUR HOME SUBSCRIPTION

Our readers tell us that these books sell out very fast in book stores and often they miss the newest titles. So Zebra has made arrangements for you to receive the four newest novels published each month.

You'll be guaranteed that you'll never miss a title, and home delivery is so convenient. And to show you just how easy it is to get Zebra Historical Romances, we'll send you your first 4 books absolutely FREE! Our gift to you just for trying our home subscription service.

BIG SAVINGS AND FREE HOME DELIVERY

Each month, you'll receive the four newest titles as soon as they are published. You'll probably receive them even before the bookstores do. What's more, you may preview these exciting novels free for 10 days. If you like them as much as we think you will, just pay the low preferred subscriber's price of just $3.75 each. *You'll save $3.00 each month off the publisher's price.* AND, your savings are even greater because there are never any shipping, handling or other hidden charges—FREE Home Delivery. Of course you can return any shipment within 10 days for full credit, no questions asked. There is no minimum number of books you must buy.

4 FREE BOOKS

TO GET YOUR 4 FREE BOOKS WORTH $18.00 — MAIL IN THE FREE BOOK CERTIFICATE T O D A Y

Fill in the Free Book Certificate below, and we'll send your FREE BOOKS to you as soon as we receive it.

If the certificate is missing below, write to: Zebra Home Subscription Service, Inc., P.O. Box 5214, 120 Brighton Road, Clifton, New Jersey 07015-5214.

FREE BOOK CERTIFICATE

4 FREE BOOKS

ZEBRA HOME SUBSCRIPTION SERVICE, INC.

YES! Please start my subscription to Zebra Historical Romances and send me my first 4 books absolutely FREE. I understand that each month I may preview four new Zebra Historical Romances free for 10 days. If I'm not satisfied with them, I may return the four books within 10 days and owe nothing. Otherwise, I will pay the low preferred subscriber's price of just $3.75 each; a total of $15.00, *a savings off the publisher's price of $3.00.* I may return any shipment and I may cancel this subscription at any time. There is no obligation to buy any shipment and there are no shipping, handling or other hidden charges. Regardless of what I decide, the four free books are mine to keep.

NAME _____

ADDRESS _____ APT _____

CITY _____ STATE ____ ZIP _____

TELEPHONE ( ) _____

SIGNATURE _____ (if under 18, parent or guardian must sign)

Terms, offer and prices subject to change without notice. Subscription subject to acceptance by Zebra Books. Zebra Books reserves the right to reject any order or cancel any subscription.

ZB0793

GET
FOUR
FREE
BOOKS
(AN $18.00 VALUE)

AFFIX
STAMP
HERE

Then Tanya came to a halt. The black eyes were watching her like a hawk does its prey. His aquiline nose was as she remembered, his taut cheekbones just as high. Blue-black hair glistening in the sun. Tall and muscled. All man. Tanya's heart was beating so hard and fast she felt she might choke; her voice was breathless and emerging with difficulty.

"Almanzo, please."

Why did he have to be so tall and handsome!

"I'm sorry, *querida,* but I must restrain Willow on Talon Clay's orders. You would not wish to see your sister hurt, would you? No," he said when she automatically shook her head, "I did not think so."

He had called her *Sweetheart!* Tanya's voice was almost a whisper. "What will you do, tie her up?"

He bent his black, glistening head. "If that is what it takes, then that is what I must do." His voice was breathless. He did not wonder why, however, for he had always loved Tanya Brandon. He had almost been glad upon discovery that his bride-to-be, Ellita Tomas, had been sleeping with another prior to their wedding years ago. And then the blow, that Ashe Brandon had taken Tanya to wife on the very eve of his engagement . . . and *broken* engagement.

Coming closer, Tanya ran her hand the length of Willow's unbound hair. "Willow. Listen. It will be much too dangerous for you to follow Talon in the search for Michael."

"I want to finish what I started with the Green Mountain gang." She did not see Jesse Campbell sidle closer to listen. "I have to get to them."

"I have told Talon about them," Almanzo revealed. "He is going to find them now. First he will go to the

225

station and enlist the help of a fellow Ranger—" His eyes shifted to Tanya, who stood listening raptly. "Perhaps more than one Ranger. You would only be in the way and could come to harm yourself. If you get hurt, what good could a weak and crippled mother serve her young son? She might even get herself killed. The Rangers know just what to do to get him back without losing any men."

Willow began to whimper and relax in Almanzo's strong but gentle grip. "I have to try . . . doesn't anyone see?"

"I see!"

Everyone in the circle around Willow and Almanzo turned in amazement to see little Sarah holding a rifle pointed directly at Almanzo's side!

Close to the sun in lonely lands.
 —Alfred, Lord Tennyson

Chapter Twelve

"Let Willow go," Sarah ordered in a crisp voice, full of command and not a bit shaky. "Move away, Mama. Willow, you, too. I'm keeping this rifle on Almanzo right now. I want him to let Auntie Willow go so she can find her baby." She nodded. "Mikey."

Tanya looked in horror at her daughter holding the rifle aimed directly at Almanzo's head. Sarah was wearing the soft pink dress she'd finished sewing for her just that morning; she looked pretty enough for a party. Clem grinned and chuckled, looking nervously from one person to the next. Almanzo stood wary and alert to any sudden movement from the child. Fortunately the rifle did not have a hair-trigger. In fact, Almanzo knew the gun; it was one of Pete Brandon's old weapons and the mechanism was hard to pull and release a shot. He wasn't even sure the rifle was loaded, or if the girl even knew how to load one.

However, Almanzo was taking no chances.

"Sarah," Tanya tried in a quavery voice. "We're having blackberry cobbler this afternoon, after fried chicken and biscuits. I even feel like helping in the kitchen.

Miss Pekoe works so hard, as does Flap Jack for the hands. Would you like to help me prepare this special treat for everyone?"

Sarah blinked; she was wearing a poke bonnet with a projecting front brim, crocheted lace adorning the edges. The girl had been so worried about her mother staying in her rooms upstairs, wandering around as if there really wasn't anything to live for anymore. She drifted in and out of depressed moods and nothing seemed to make her smile for very long. She was angry at all men, especially her daddy, for dying and leaving them with all these problems. And now Willow had her own problems to take care of—she had a baby named Mikey and someone had gone and stolen it from her. Sarah had been happy a few days ago, but suddenly everyone seemed too busy for her—and she missed her daddy so much!

Sarah dropped the rifle and ran to her mother's waiting arms. Tears were wetting her face and Tany brushed them away, hushing her and pressing her ow flushed face to her daughter's. Pulling back, Tanya said, "I'm proud of you, Sarah. You did the right thing by dropping the rifle. We don't want anyone getting hurt, do we?"

"Uh-uh." With a wet face pink from emotion, Sarah looked up and placed both hands on her mother's shoulders. "Could we make chicken curry with rice instead, Mother?"

"Yes, darling, and we'll even make some lace cookies with sugar sprinkled on top."

Sarah's eyes shifted to the left, where someone had hitched the reins of the pinto to the corral; Breeze was saddle-less with only an Indian blanket thrown over her back, but no one seemed to notice this or anything else that was taking place as one moved stealthily while Sarah was the center of attention.

Almanzo came to stand before mother and child. Sarah looked up, seeing Almanzo's head haloed by the summer sun. "You're not mad at me, are you, Almanzo?" she asked, touching the tip of a long, tan finger.

"Never, *querida*," he said to Sarah while his eyes were all for Tanya. "You are much too pretty for anyone to stay angry with you."

Grasping her hand gently, Almanzo tugged her to her feet while Tanya stared with round blue eyes wondering what the handsome man was up to. His voice had troubled her. It was smooth, soft and cultured, each word spoken with the eloquence of a well-educated Spanish gentleman. At times she wondered how he could be half-savage and still look as if he belonged out on the range tending cattle as well as at ease in a lady's parlor. She had never been in that room alone with Almanzo; Ashe had always been there, too. He had fit right in. She had always been careful around Almanzo, since he did things to her mind and body when she was close to him. Ashe had been the one she wanted to spend the rest of her life with. He had been more comfortable to be with, while Almanzo stirred something in her that was wild and passionate, and she had trouble looking into those dark eyes.

Deeply affected by her presence, Almanzo couldn't help staring at Tanya Brandon; this fiery redhead stirred his blood.

The hands were beginning to drift away and Clem, too, was returning to his bunkhouse that had been refurbished especially for him. Clem had all the conveniences and enjoyed them. Almanzo stiffened, and almost at the same time, so did all the men; Clem, Tanya, and Sarah, too.

Relaxing quickly, Sarah was smiling from ear to ear beneath the sun-stopping brim of her bonnet.

Willow had escaped on the pinto horse Breeze!

Riding hard and fast, Willow could hear a horse pounding after her before it reached the sound-deadening carpet of fallen leaves. She thanked God for Sarah; first, the child had inadvertently created a diversion in order for her aunt to escape and then she had kept silent as the deed was in progress. Willow slipped easily into the woods she knew so well and spurred Breeze on until she could hear her pursuer's horse no longer.

"Good girl," Willow said, resting the horse, patting the silken black mane, stroking the white, brown, and black face. "You're a beauty. You must be an offspring of my own blooded horses Dust Devil or Istas. I think I'll keep you. You like me, girl, I can tell. You ran for me as if you were pulling for me all the while. Well, let's get going as long as you're rested. We have a long way to go. First, we have to sneak around to the back of the little house where I hid my things. Ready girl, let's go!"

Silently Almanzo rode through the woods, crossing Strawberry Creek, then going to the other side to enter the northern stands of trees. Willow was not about. How had she escaped him so easily? She had been like sand running through his hands, she and the pinto, he thought as he checked the little house, riding around the perimeter. Almanzo chuckled to himself. "What kind of Indian am I supposed to be? She is more Indian than I in this chase!"

Concealed behind the huge cottonwood that had been her favorite haunt when she'd lived at the little house, Willow watched Almanzo circle the house and come around to pause at the front porch. She almost giggled; he looked so puzzled. She would wager that no fleet-ahorse Indian had ever given him such a merry chase!

"Come on, girl. Let's be gone from this place. Almanzo is going back to the main house. His back is turned. Now is the time to light out before he decides to pick up the search further."

Breeze stretched her strong legs out and ran for the road; they would follow it for half a day, rest by a creek, Willow would eat a little lunch while Breeze munched some wild, sweet grass, then they'd continue through the cooler night until they were riding westward to their destination.

"We'll make it, girl." She patted the silky mane. "You and I were meant for each other. I'm sure glad I discovered you. What a strong beauty you are! We'll go far together with the Texas wind in our hair and you'll help me rescue my angel—that is, if Talon Clay doesn't reach Mikey before us!"

Breeze whinnied at the wonderful freedom of the chase and ran at an angle for the road. Willow's hair flew behind her with the wind. Her two saddlebags thumped and patted Breeze gently on the sides. They

231

were one with the wind, Willow and her new horse. Yes, Breeze was hers and hers alone from now on. *Just let anyone try and take her from me!* Willow thought possessively of the beautiful Breeze as they flew across the land and kicked up particles like bits of powdered gold dust behind them.

Puzzled and still shaking his head, Almanzo returned to the house. Tanya was waiting outside for him, while Sarah remained in the bake-house with Miss Pekoe finishing up with the lace sugar cookies. The larger kitchen, reserved for baking, had five windows to let out the hot air, all across from each other and open the entire time the ovens were going. It was attached to the house by a walkway that kept the bake-house separate from the main house, thereby keeping the living room, parlor, dining room, and various other rooms from heating up. Especially on a hot summer day like this one.

"Did you find her?" Tanya asked anxiously, standing on tiptoe to see behind the huge black Almanzo rode. "Oh, I see that you did not."

"She slipped away on that swift pinto like the wind," Almanzo explained, trying not to be too affected by the flushed, pretty sight of Tanya wearing a white apron spotted with flour dust. He had seen her this way many times . . . before he'd gone away to Black Fox's camp. Tanya loved to be in the kitchen, and he would love to be there with her; he loved to cook, too. "If you ever need any help in the kitchen, I'd be glad to oblige," he said. After she had nodded absently, Almanzo added, "Willow has a mind of her own and it seems no man is going to tell that woman what to do."

232

"She's always been a bit on the willful side." Wiping away some flour that had begun to tickle her face, Tanya spoke in a voice that was softer and lower. "If only I could be a little bit like Willow, more independent, like I used to be before Ashe—" Tanya bit off her words.

"I believe you're angry," Almanzo offered, coming smoothly down from his mount and standing still while his hands worked to loop the reins over the hitching post.

Tanya nodded reluctantly. Her eyes were narrowing and her heart was beating faster . . .

Wrapped in a translucent lavender mist, evening was stealing in. Thin shreds of foggy clouds lay over the grounds, some swirling above the galleries of the house. It was a sight Tanya would never forget. But forget she must, someday . . .

A phantom wind, sweet with the fragrance of hay and bluebonnets, rustled the cottonwoods and post oaks; it stirred up a gauzy mist of low-lying fog.

Memories came flooding back to Tanya; the beauty of their joining, hers and Ashe's.

Through the low-hanging mist, the horse and rider neared . . . it was long ago, and Almanzo stood beside her as he had then as Ashe rode in. "Finally he comes," Almanzo had said. "Yes," she had answered softly, "finally." Almanzo had stepped up on the porch to join her, asking, "You have missed him, *senora?*" And she had snapped, "Of course, what kind of question is that?" He told her he had wondered, that was all.

She had told Almanzo that he had better leave, since Ashe was a very jealous man. About to step from the porch, Almanzo had returned to Tanya's side, and he had told her he was not a fool. If her husband noted his haste to leave her side now that he was coming closer, then *that,* Almanzo had informed her, *would* look suspicious. She had seen the wisdom in his decision, for he could not just step down and go out to meet Ashe, and could not suddenly go back the way he had come in the first place; it was more plausible to stop and talk to her a moment before walking on to the bunkhouses.

Tanya had remembered that her heart fell when a scowling Ashe walked right by with his horse, only nodding and tipping his dusty hat as if they were mere strangers on the street of a Texas town. Ashe had taken his horse out back and Tanya had watched him for as long as she could make out his ramrod-stiff back.

"You and your husband are not getting along, *senora?*" And then he had told her he was sorry, to please forgive his trespass, it was none of his business. And then, "But if you wish to talk about it?"

Her own answer had been very crisp and forward: "Would you like to discuss how you came to live with the Rankins instead of the Kiowas?" And he had only answered with, "Ah, you are so right, *senora.*" To him, and to her, his question had been a trespass.

Now, on this summer day much like the one back then, with the gauzy mists gathering, Tanya turned to Almanzo. He had been watching her staring down the road as if she'd seen someone coming along it. But no one had come.

"Do you remember that night, Almanzo?"

Tanya surprised him a little and he said, "Yes. I know the night of which you speak. We had talked about . . . things . . . and prison."

"Prison?" Tanya looked up. "Oh yes, you had said

you lived in New Orleans and that you had not always lived in Texas. Is this so?"

"Yes, *senora*. Do you recall what I said?"

"You said—" Tanya thought back and then smiled tenderly and reminiscently. "You said that you had drawn your knife for a good reason, and still you had been sent to prison. You had used your knife on a man who had been trying to beat and rape a girl—of eight or nine perhaps—you could not be sure. The girl did not recover her faculties for an entire year, and you were kept locked up in jail until she could speak. If she had not helped you . . . you might have perished in that prison. And then—I cannot remember the rest. Tell me, Almanzo." She was enjoying this talk immensely, forgetting her own grief, getting away from the hot kitchen.

"The conditions in that Louisiana prison were not fit for a dog; many were already dying from a swamp fever." Almanzo was recalling their conversation of that night eight or nine years ago. "There had been death all around me." Almanzo nodded. "Then your husband stepped from the shadows. You had wondered how long Ashe had been standing there listening to our conversation."

"Spying on us?"

"That is what you thought." Almanzo began to grow warm; this was almost too pleasurable with Tanya—and very dangerous. "He had said 'Long enough, my dear. You look pale, and I think you are thinner. Are you tired?' "

Tanya gasped. "You remember all that?"

"Of course. I see it all and hear it in my mind, as if it were yesterday." He would not tell her that all their conversations were written in his heart as well as his mind. "You left us both standing there, slamming the door as you went inside the house. Ashe had been quiet for a time and then he had turned to me. He was very angry and asked me what the hell I was? I still do not understand that question, but I left him there alone. I believe your husband was a lonely, disturbed man back then."

"Oh, Almanzo, you don't know the half of it."

"No? What was the matter, *senora?*"

Before turning to re-enter the walkway into the bakehouse, Tanya said over her shoulder, "Why, Almanzo, didn't you ever know about the Sundance ghost?"

Almanzo was left staring blankly at the spot she had just vacated.

The sun was sinking behind a stand of massive cottonwoods, setting their wide spreading branches ablaze, making them appear like one giant, burning Mosesbush. Ranger Talon Clay had ridden for two days, with several rests in between. He had gone all up and down the Nueces, Pecos, and Devil's rivers; that is, he had divided his last search and this one amongst the rivers, coming to the conclusion that Willow's "ghost town" must be further to the west. He had run into mating wild mustangs, cow thieves, horse thieves, rattlesnakes, barbed wire and "picketwire," and a lot of other unmentionables. He had been a hunter of bad Mexicans, riding far and wide to bring 'em down while taking a Mexican whip in the back. He traveled the dark and unknown of that borderland between Nueces and the Rio Grande, where for generations Texans and Mexicans killed and raided so viciously that it made the Indian troubles of the region seem insignificant.

With a pang of nostalgia, Talon remembered some of the stories his brother used to tell when he was a Ranger back in the fifties. One day back then, when Ashe had ridden with Captain Callahan, some of his men surprised a gang of Mexican horse thieves in a thicket on York's Creek near Seguin. They killed three or four of them; the others got away through the brush. The next morning while attempting to track down some of the escaped Mexicans, Callahan's Rangers came upon a Mexican who was wounded in the leg. He made signs that he wanted to surrender. Callahan rode near and asked him if he wanted to go to Seguin. The Mexican replied that he did. "All right," said the captain, "get on behind me." The Mexican, having bound his leg with a large silk handkerchief, began hopping towards Callahan's horse. The Ranger captain drew his pistol and shot him dead.

Talon had argued with his brother Ashe that this was cruel and brutal. Ashe had told him a few years back that those had been desperate times, and it was death to all horse thieves when caught. "Texans have suffered terrible things at the hands of Mexicans. The Alamo and Goliad were still fresh in their minds."

"Brother," Talon had said to Ashe, "did you ever shoot Mexican soldiers taken in battle?" His brother had replied in the negative, but told of another time some of Callahan's Rangers captured two Mexican horse thieves and brought them to Seguin.

"What happened to them?" Talon wondered out loud, hating to hear the rest.

"We turned them over to Callahan himself for judgment," Ashe had said and Talon moaned. "Callahan immediately ordered them shot, and led the way to a stand of live oak trees out from town."

Ashe went on, telling how the two condemned men were given picks and shovels and ordered to dig their own graves. One of the Mexicans was an old man, and he dug away in an unconcerned manner, "taking particular pains" to make a good grave. The other Mexican was young; he wept, protested his innocence, and was so nervous he could hardly work. The captain explained that there was no convenient jail and that therefore the execution would have to be expedited. Finally, when the graves were finished, Callahan's men drew lots to see who would have to do the shooting.

"Some of us didn't want to take part," Ashe said. "At the signal the guns all fired except one." Ashe nodded that it was his gun that did not fire. "Both Mexicans fell over at the discharge. The old man was killed dead, but the young one was breathing freely when they came up to where the Mexicans lay; the younger looked up."

"What happened then?" Talon had asked anxiously.

" 'Brandon'," Callahan said, turning to Ashe, " 'being as your gun misfired, you can finish this fellow.' "

Talon watched as Ashe hung his head to finish the story. "The Ranger thus addressed, without a word, primed his rifle and, stepping back a few paces, took quick aim and fired, the ball striking the Mexican in the head and killing him instantly."

"Shoot, Ashe," Talon remembered saying, "I don't think I could ever be that kind of Ranger—no way."

"Maybe you won't have to kill many men," Ashe had said and walked away. His brother was like that, never giving more to a conversation than he thought was necessary.

Talon remembered the years following that conversation, years that found him becoming a Ranger himself. He was as tough and mean as the others, but he was not cruel and unmerciful. He had had his run-ins with Mexicans just as Ashe had. During the fifties and sixties Mexicans were doing a great deal of freighting in Texas. As the Mexicans freighted for less than their American competitors, business interests protected them. The year of '59 found in command of the Department of Texas one of various bullheaded and pea-brained United States Army officers that have bungled affairs on the Texas borders—General D. E. Twiggs. In March of that year he declared: "There is not, nor ever has been, any danger of the Mexicans crossing onto our side of the river to plunder or disturb its inhabitants, and the outcry on that river for troops is solely to have an expenditure of the public money." He had already ordered Fort Brown, in Brownsville; Ringgold Barracks, of Rio Grande City; and Fort McIntosh, of Eagle Pass, abandoned; he was expecting to patrol the road between San Antonio and Eagle Pass, most of it infested by Comanches, with a few companies of infantry! Fortunately, early in March, 1860, he was relieved from command in Texas by Colonel Robert E. Lee—and then a year later the Civil War had broken out. Talon could see it now: the Texas border was becoming a border matter that concerned nobody but the people on it!

Talon recalled that Cortina remained in possession of Fort Brown only a few days. Then he retired to his mother's ranch, which he set about fortifying, meanwhile beginning the issue of a series of proclamations in the tone of a righteous liberator. "Our purpose had been," he said, "to punish the infamous villainy of our enemies. They have banded together ... to pursue and rob us for no other reason except that we are by birth Mexicans. ... An organized society of Mexicans in the state of Texas will untiringly devote itself to the extermination of their tyrants until its philanthropic purpose of bettering the condition of the unfortunate Mexicans who reside here shall have been attained."

As soon as Cortina got out of sight, the citizens of Brownsville organized a guard. Their cries for help were frantic. The governor of Texas sent Captain W. G. Tobin and Captain John S. Ford—"Old Rip"—with the Rangers to clear the country. At the same time General Twiggs, although declaring the reports concerning Cortina to be "mostly false," dispatched Major S. P. Heintzelman, with about one hundred and fifty troops, to occupy Fort Brown and patrol the border. Talon liked Heintzelman; he proved to have horse sense—a rare quality for a United States officer in Texas.

Combining forces, the soldiers and Rangers dislodged Cortina from the San Jose and then for months chased him up and over the Rio Grande. Talon would never forget that chase last year; he had been so busy with the Rangers he'd almost forgotten he had a wife somewhere. By June of '60—Talon had been with Heintzelman when he'd made his report—fifteen Americans and eighty friendly Mexicans had been killed, while Cortina had lost one hundred and fifty-one men. Before he was driven across the Rio Grande Cortina sacked Rio Grande City. Talon had never seen anything like it! The whole country from Brownsville to Rio Grande City and back to the Arroyo Colorado had been laid waste.

Tex-Mex citizens had been driven out, their horses and cattle driven across the Rio Grande into Mexico, and there sold; a cow with a calf by her side for a dollar, for example. Many of the Mexican ranch houses that Cortina left because they belonged to his friends were burned by the Texans.

Riding along Cross Creek, Talon thought of Cortina. That was one Mexican who was not finished yet . . . he would no doubt become someone very high in the Mexican army. He hoped he would not have to deal with or cross paths with that one again.

That night, sleeping under the Texas stars and Texas moon, Talon Clay dreamed a most disturbing, recurrent dream of the past. . . . He had taken a handful of Hester Tucker's bodice and shaken her, rattling her teeth. "Stupid *puta!*" he snarled. "Don't ever come here to Sundance again spreading your gossip. They're lies, and I don't want to hear 'em!" He had shoved her backward, so hard she almost fell. "Where did you ever hear so many lies?"

He had been quickly bored with her silly gossip. It was morning and he had pulled the glimmering length of his hair over his shoulder and proceeded to braid it, as if she was not still standing there watching. She sure had stared, her mouth agape, at such an uncommon, unmasculine task. "All of a sudden you don't remember who told you, is that it?" he drawled. Hester had rocked back and forth as if comforting herself. "Ma told me. She knows everything about everybody. Your pa was a half-breed and his name was Hunter-of-the Horses. So there!"

"Oh, bull!"

Suddenly, Talon sat up, clamping a hand over his

knee. "Garnet ... Garnet ... don't ever say her name around me—ever ... and don't come whoring around Sundance again! You do, and I'll round up a passel of guys ... guys that'll pump you over really good ... hear?" Talon stared down at his knee, then blinked until he came fully awake. He heard Willow as if it was yesterday: "What would lovers have to argue about on such a beautiful day?"

Now, shaking his head to clear it, Talon brought his knee up and rested his forearm across it. "Willow, Willow, whatever made you think Hester and I were lovers? Damn, that whoring female never interested me in the least. It's you, Pussywillow, you I want. You kept coming after me until I caught you. Sweet Willow, dearest angel, you always knew what was best for me. You knew you'd heal my broken heart. Now I've done something to hurt you. Didn't I pay enough attention to you when we were first married? I thought I did; took you for granted, I guess. I wanted to come after you, but I thought you'd left me for good. You weren't hurt, I knew that, otherwise I would have felt it. Now I feel like our love is lost, just like our son Michael. Lordy, but I want to see that boy, hold him, laugh with him, let him know who his daddy is." Talon chuckled. "Shoot, I even want to take you and him to that Pastor Cuthbert's church. You used to go alone, but if we ever get back together as a family, you'll never go one Sunday without me."

Lying back on his bedroll, Talon continued to smile. "I'm goin' to win you back, Sweet Pussywillow. Just you wait and see."

We're going to be a family.

Nearby in the bushes, Hank Rountree peered out,

242

wondering what the fair-haired Ranger was doing talking to himself in the middle of the night. His campfire was burning low, near embers now. What was wrong with him? Is he touched in the head? Rountree asked himself. He is said to be one of Black Fox's people; if this is so, he will recognize the sound of a bird that I make.

Hank Rountree, alias Desert Hawk, cupped his hands around his mouth and whistled low—not the cry of a desert hawk, but the sound of the desert owl.

Suddenly alert, Talon sat up and looked around, reaching cautiously for his gun. Flinching, he blinked, recalling the sound of the owl, the call his friends usually made when "coming in peace."

"Who is there?" Talon asked in Kiowa. "Friend or foe? You must be friend, for you know the sound my people and my friends make when they come in peace."

The Indian stood up. *"Hou!"* He said the Lakota word for agreement. "It is I: Desert Hawk," Hank Rountree said. "I come in peace, this is so. We will talk at this time—" His chuckle was deep, warm. "And you will give me back my clothes."

Talon did not swear, but he wanted to. "I have forgotten them."

Desert Hawk came into the eerie shadow of emberlight. "Then you must go back for them."

With a groan, Talon sprang to his feet, already gathering his bedroll as he stood. "I'll have a hard time of it. You see, my wife Willow, whom the Indians call Aiyana, will give me a big fight if I return now."

Desert Hawk tipped his head. "I know what they call your wife, but I need those clothes for what I must do."

"I tell you, Hawk, I'll have to argue with my wife if

243

I return to Sundance. She's wild when she's crossed . . . like a strong, obstinate wind that goes where it will."

"You have crossed her?"

"Oh, you wouldn't believe me if I told you."

Desert Hawk nodded and smiled knowingly; his wife's image and her charming ways would always be with him, like a keepsake of lovely memories. "My wife Summer Wind was like that," Hawk said, feeling sadness flutter in his heart. "She was beautiful and strong and willful."

"Oh?" Talon said as he assembled the fixings for coffee. "Sit down and tell me all about Summer Wind. Then you can ride with me back to Sundance."

"First I will tell you: I have killed a man for your wife. They called her Belle at the Rountree ranch where the banditos have a hideout. Some call them the Green Mountain gang. I know you have lost a son and that your wife searches for him. She had much trouble with one man and I shot him dead when she only shot him in the foot." Hawk heard the Ranger chuckle.

"We must speak, Desert Hawk. Tell me, who is it you are after?"

"I believe the same that you are after. They took your child and I have gathered enough information to believe the female kidnapper is the same that killed my marriage."

"Well, then—" Talon Clay shrugged—"why don't you just go there yourself? You know where they have taken my son, so let's have it: Do you know how to get there or not?"

Silent for so long that Talon thought he was finished speaking, Hawk surprised him when he said, "You and I, we will go there together—to this ghost town I have traced her to. I will get the woman I seek and you will get your son."

"The woman you seek will recognize you, Hawk."

The clever Indian laughed huskily. "Not if I am garbed as a priest. She will not even see my face."

"Lordy!" Talon slapped his lean thigh. "That would have been a good disguise to use on Willow. She found me out in your clothes, Hawk. Wait a minute. If you're going as a priest, why do you need your desperado outfit?"

His smile was slow. "I need that to keep up my image—along the way. You could say my clothes keep others at a distance."

Talon smiled at Hawk's cowboy outfit; he didn't look very dangerous. In fact, he almost appeared down and out. Talon stared at the ground for a time and then frowned in mild puzzlement. "Why is it we get along so well? You seem familiar. Your face, there's something about it. It's as if I've seen it before; or part of it, which is an unusual thing to say, I realize."

"I am Kachina's twin brother."

"Whew!" Talon almost spilled the coffee on himself. "Wait till Willow hears this. Almanzo must know."

"He does. This is how we came to be friends at Black Fox's camp. Kachina thought I had perished when our tribe fought another. She was taken away and used by the half-breeds." Hank Rountree spat on the ground. "I am not like those who disgrace the Indian nation. I would not touch a woman if she did not want my touch. But I will kill those who have done harm to my family, even a woman; I am still that savage."

"You won't kill the dance hall girl. You might give her lots of hell, but you won't end her life."

"You don't know me very well, Ranger. There are

many faces I own. I have been called dangerous to meet in the dark. This is true. Mrs. Lacey found this out when I carved up an evil friend of hers."

"Mrs. Lacey? The dance hall girl? Ah," Talon said after an affirmative nod from Hawk. "You won't always be this way, wanting to kill all the bad folks you come across; I say let God sort 'em out and deal with 'em. Come to live with us at Sundance when all this is over. We could use another hand and the pay is good. I won't even arrest you for all your crimes."

"I cannot. I will remain wild as long as I cannot have my Summer Wind and my two young children back. I have prayed to my Creator and He does not send them back to me; I believe they are lost to me forever. I cannot go to live among others."

The Ranger regarded the Indian outlaw thoughtfully. "We'll see about that. I'm bound and determined to get my son back and, Hawk? You should be just as stubborn about getting your family back. You see, I not only have to find my son, I have to win back my wife, too!"

Desert Hawk nodded. Then he handed the Ranger his hat. He had decided not to go into the ghost town as a priest. Something else was going to happen, but he did not know what it could be—just yet.

He had a strong feeling that the outlaws were going to make it a little bit easier for him to do what he had to do. The task would be difficult and would require much patience and care. He might not have to seek revenge on Nat Lacey all by himself. That woman was going to find her own violent end and perhaps he wouldn't have to work too hard to help her along.

God will not look you over for medals, degrees or diplomas, but for scars.

—Elbert Hubbard, Epigrams

Chapter Thirteen

There was only the lonely echoing of the wind as a dagger of sun struck the ground through a gray edifice where, beneath, not a soul walked the streets of Rawhide. The cry of a child was heard no more, nor was the sound of men, few though they might have been this last time the town was sparsely occupied. Whatever claim man had once had upon it had yielded to the sun, the wind, and the blown sand. Tumbleweeds detached themselves from corners of buildings, chased one another, and blew along the deserted streets once again, with no one to kick them aside. Dirt and debris swirled into angry spirals, creating dust devils. No women. No men. No children. And the cry of a mourning dove went unanswered.

There was only one human who sat his horse on a knob of hill overlooking the town. You can almost hear the voices from up here, he thought, like the wailing of the wind across prairie grasses. He saw a double row of false-fronted buildings facing a dusty street into which the bunchgrass and sagebrush blew. It had become a by-way for an occasional rabbit or coyote, or the rattlers that had taken refuge in the foundations of Rawhide. The town had been destroyed by a fire—maybe more than once, for he had seen charred ruins in several sections—with varying strengths of burned odor. And the town was not all that old, yet the fires had made it seem very old. Rawhide was a forgotten place, slowly giving itself back to the land from which it had come. It had lived wildly, desperately, and had died hard in a flurry of gunshots and smoke.

Wiping the dust from his eyes, Sammy held a piece of Mikey's clothing. He looked around once again, down at the desolation and the church he had painstakingly searched, turned his long-legged buckskin toward the old wagon trail, then rode off in a southeastern direction. Toward Bountiful, and then he would head to Sundance. He had a feeling Talon Clay had already found her, and he would find his sister there at Sundance. He rode away, not looking back over his shoulder, not even one time.

Rawhide had once again lived up to its name: ghost town.

Days later, Sammy rode into Bountiful. There was still light in the sky, and the crimson along the westward hills was just fading, leaving the higher clouds still flushed and pink above them. He stopped at a saloon to drink a sarsparilla and hear the latest gossip before he made his way to Willow's house. He had a strong feeling he wouldn't find Willow there, but Juanita would tell him what she'd heard, if anything. Little groups of overweight men clustered in the saloon, engaged in a conversation which they were at pains to keep private.

They were talking out of the side of their mouths and behind hands, like gossipy women at a church social. Sammy's gaze was met with sullen, defiant stares and he couldn't understand it. He overheard several of them discussing a woman in low tones.

A woman can be hell for a man, Sammy thought. Or heaven, he guessed, but he had no way of knowing that just yet.

Sammy heard the men talk louder. "There's gonna be trouble, I tell ya, Louie." And another: "Already there's gossip about the schoolteacher and her Ranger lover. Their kid got kidnapped and she went out looking for him."

Sammy swung his head to the other side of the room and heard more: "Yer right, Jamey. That Tex-Mex woman Juanita has that house to herself with only a big dog for company. The wife's sister, Mary Lou, lives on the next lot and she says all that tan-skinned woman does is looks up and down the street every day, lookin' like she's prayin'."

"Yeah, well, she probably is, Ed." He chuckled. "Wonder what else that pretty skirt's lookin' and prayin' fer." His words were met with guffaws and Sammy steamed, listening to them gossip about Juanita and his sister like that. "That young'un over there, I seen him goin' to the schoolteacher's house lots of times."

They kept jawin' and Sammy kept drinking his sarsaparilla, listening to all he could; maybe one of them would slip and tell him something he needed to know. He would just bide his time and sit here sippin' while they kept up the gossip.

Billy Debb said, "Maybe he's toodlin' with that Tex-Mex housekeeper." The fat, balding storekeeper belched

249

and drank some more beer, peering from the corners of his bloodshot blue eyes over at the tall boy sitting alone at a table. "Heard tell the schoolteacher was seen in the next town wearin' pants and totin' pistols, drinkin' at a bar and lookin' for some work." He winked. "Not solicitin'—but outlawin'!"

Every time Sammy looked in their direction, the town's male gossipers were looking somewhere else; but Sammy could feel their eyes on him soon as he looked down at his sarsaparilla in feigned preoccupation. Then the male chatter would pick up once again. Sammy had a feeling he was in for a few discoveries and some remarks that might give him all the leads he needed. Then he'd head for Juanita's and get the rest of the story.

"First the kid disappears," Joe Dustin said, pretending he was whispering but making sure the tall boy heard every word. Joe's dark eyes flicked about suspiciously as he spoke; yet he wore a niggardly smile. "Then the Ranger up and comes along. Oh, before that happened, the schoolteacher, Willow Brandon, leaves all the kids hangin' at school while she runs off with that yellow-haired boy over there. They goes to the house at the end of the street and there's a bunch of commotion there. Hah! Then the Ranger rides into town and pops in at Willow's place and makes himself real comfortable. Sheriff's deputy fills us townsfolk in: Seems that was the *Ranger's* kid what got stolen—now listen to this!—by a strange woman ridin' in and scoopin' up Willow's tot and whiskin' him away somewheres."

"Naw. You got it wrong, Joe," Tom Tooley, the town's expert on every issue said, coming to his feet. He was the heaviest man in the room; he weighed over

250

two-fifty. "You're right about Willow being the Ranger's woman and the kid being their bastard child—"

Suddenly the attention was taken away from Tom Tooley.

Fuming, Sammy stood up, squaring his shoulders like his two Ranger brothers-in-law. "Holy jumpin' Josie! What a bunch of gobbledygook! All you dudes got it wrong. Willow Brandon is my God-fearin' sister and Talon Clay Brandon happens to be her husband. Talon's a Texas Ranger, so was my other brother-in-law, Ashe Brandon; he's an ex-Ranger now." He heard whispers of respect, regard, and recognition being passed around the room like silver cookies on a wooden platter. "Another thing, I ain't foolin' around with Juanita; she's a good friend of Willow's and mine. She's Willow's housekeeper and babysitter. Besides, she's too old for me; she's in her twenties and I ain't hit 'em yet. And another thing: if Talon Clay Brandon heard you callin' his son a bastard child, I just believe he'd hang each of you guys up by your family jewels!"

With that ringing real good in their gossip-lovin' ears, Sammy walked out of the saloon, leaving the doors swinging behind him and the words "I didn't know . . . I didn't either . . ." trailing him out the door.

Billy Deb said, "Now if that don't put goosebumps on your goosebumps!"

"Juanita!" Sammy called into the house. "Where are you?" Before he could take one more step, a huge fluffy lump hurtled towards him and knocked him over; Sammy had a mouth full of fur and big Jorge pinning

251

him down when he looked up to see someone standing there. "Oh, hello, Juanita."

"Sammy, Sammy! Where have you been?" Juanita threw her hands in the air. "Where has everybody been? I am so worried, you could not know. First Angelo is taken away, and now Margarita does not return. Where is she? Why does she not come back home? Has she gone back to live with her husband, the *Rinche*—Ranger?"

"Margarita?" Sammy blinked over the fuzzy bulk of Jorge. "Oh, I forgot. That's what you call Willow. I guess she got duded up and went out chasin' outlaws. Or chasin' with 'em, I can't figure which one the town drunks was jawin' about."

Hands on her slim hips, Juanita asked, "Why do you always drop your 'g's'? You do not do this all the time Juanita has known you. Only sometimes you do this. What is wrong with you, little *gringo?*"

"Aw, Juanita, you know I do that when I'm especially nervous or excited about something."

"You are right." Juanita exhaled on a huff. "You do do that. Sit down, I will make you something to eat and you tell Juanita all you have learned. Come, come, into my kitchen."

"Get off, Jorge." Sammy finally helped the giant fur ball off his lap. "What are you feeding this dog, Juanita? He gets bigger all the time."

"He eats special food I make for him." She chuckled. "I call his food *Jorge's dog food.* I mix many good things together for him. *Now!* You sit and talk. I will cook and listen."

"All right. I'll tell you about the ghost town and the piece of clothing I found. I don't know much about Willow Margaret yet. I met up briefly with Talon Clay again. He went with Almanzo and some other dude and that's the last I saw of him—*them.*"

"You just keep talking, Sammy." Juanita mixed batter with a furious stroke. "I know what you are going to say after you eat and we talk: I have to ride out now, Juanita. It is always the same for you. You have what the Americans call 'wandering lust'. *Jes,* that is what you have." She put her hands on her hips. "What are you laughing about to yourself?"

Sammy could hardly stop laughing, but he did, finally. *"Wanderlust,* Juanita. Whew! You're really funny sometimes."

"Oh?" She gave the batter one more smack with the wooden spoon, then looked him in the freckled face. "When you talk you sound funny to me, too. You say things as if it will take all day to get them out, like you drag a sack of words behind you. You mumble, too, like you have a mouthful of beans. You grin? *You do!* You sound so funny, Sammy Hayes."

"Aw, Juanita," he drawled, giving her name the Mexican inflection, just like she sounded, only his was a deeper voice. "Say 'yes'."

"Jes."

Sammy hooted and tipped back his chair. He stopped smiling, however, when Juanita reached into a bowl and began tossing huge "doggie biscuits" at him; one clunked him on the head, he grabbed it up, took a bite, saying, "Hmmm, not bad for dog food."

Grabbing the biscuit, Juanita tossed it to Jorge, pulled up a chair and sat square before him, her arms folded. "Be good. Talk. No more play. Serious talk."

Sammy laughed. "Okay, Injun Nita!"

Willow was dressed like a lady outlaw again. She kept riding through the night as if driven by a force greater than her own will. She became aware of how frightened she felt. It came over her all of a sudden, and she clung, trembling, to Breeze's back. After a while, when she had prayed for strength from above, she felt better, less lonely and afraid. The stars came out and the big pinto moved on steadily, seeming in no hurry to stop for the night. A light wind swooped across the land, and several times Willow almost fell asleep, but the horse plodded on. The trail turned slightly north, then still farther north, but Willow was only half awake, and scarcely noticed. Emerging from a stand of trees she came into a valley of long purple shadows, midnight black streams, and scattered clumps of mesquite and sage.

Suddenly, Breeze came to a halt.

Willow opened her eyes wide. The pinto, ears up, was staring ahead and seemed to be scenting the air. Willow sat up tall and peered past Breeze's head; there, some distance off, right down on the ground, was a light. Red and glowing, it was . . .

A fire! *Campfire!*

Breeze hung back, reluctant to go on. Willow rode cautiously down the slight slope, then started when somewhere ahead a horse whinnied and there was the flurry of movement near the fire. She walked the horse a little closer; she could see one saddle, two pack saddles, and a coffeepot on the fire. Oh Lord, there was a smell of bacon and beans; even beans smelled good just then. She had forgotten to take along enough food, and she was very hungry.

"Set right still," a low voice said, "or I'm likely to fire. Now you just walk that there horse right up to the fire an' let's have a look at you."

Willow tried to speak, but her throat was tight. She walked Breeze forward, and suddenly she heard the undisguised voice say, "Heck, it's *you*—Willow!"

Daylight arrived with a little chill, but soon the sun would warm even the chilliest hands and toes. The camp lay on the banks of a small stream; there were clumps of willow, a few cottonwoods, and on the irregular slopes of the hill the wild mustangs grazed in thick stands.

"Horses!" Willow was up, tossing off her blanket and rolling to her feet. "Look at them all, Sammy. Where did so many horses come from?"

Sammy shrugged, stuffing things into his pack. "They're probably being chased by horse hunters to be used in this crazy war between the north and south."

Willow, cheerful and feeling optimistic, rose from her blankets and bedroll, smelling the strong black coffee Sammy had brewed. "That sure was a good supper last night, little brother. How did you learn to cook like that?"

With a grin, Sammy turned to face Willow. "Why, sis, you and Tanya taught me. Recollect it was you always bribin' me. You'd always ask me to do your work so's you could go for a walk. I knowed you went to spy on Hester Tucker and Talon Clay."

"Oh, Sammy! What do you know about that?" Willow had stopped braiding her hair to frown at her brother. "And it's not 'knowed.' It's *knew.*"

"Sis," he said with a sigh, "you know I'll never get my words just right. I've got a problem with that and sometimes I want to say a word in front of another instead of behind, where it belongs. But sometimes I catch myself."

"You just sound like a cowpoke, Sammy, or a dude from the hills." She chuckled. "And your drawl sounds very 'Texas,' Sammy. Don't worry. You're doing just fine."

"But, sis, if I want to be a Texas Ranger I'm gonna sound kind of stupid, ain't I?"

Willow poked her face in front of his, and with a smile, corrected him. *"Aren't I?—or, Don't you think?"*

Nodding, Sammy went back to fixing breakfast. "Sis, where you going now? I told you last night about the piece of Mikey's clothing I found."

"My plans are still the same, Sammy. I'm going back to Sundance. I have a feeling our culprit is going to send us a message very soon; I believe this has something to do with them using Mikey as a hostage and with Sundance property. Remember, I told you last night—we'll stop in Bountiful and ask Juanita if she would like to come along; we'll lock and board up the house and head out."

"Right, sis. Sounds good to me. I think Juanita would love to come to Sundance." His reddish brown eyebrows formed a frown. "What about Jorge?"

Tapping her chin, Willow thought for a moment, then said abruptly, "Let's get there first, Sammy." She had tears in her eyes and turned away, hoping and praying she was doing the right thing by giving up the chase and returning to Sundance to wait for a message. Maybe all the outlaws wanted was money.

"Willow?"

"Yes, Sammy?"

Following her lead, Sammy tossed out his coffee grounds. Hands on slim hips, the handle of his cup looped over a finger, he said after another hesitation, "What if those outlaws don't know you're going to Sundance? What if they come looking for you in Bountiful?"

Willow shrugged and sniffed. "What would I have in Bountiful that they'd want? Jorge? Juanita? The simple house on a mere two lots? That's not much house or land. No, Sammy. Their war is not with me. I've figured this out at last. Their contest, or hers, is with the Brandons."

"Mikey's a Brandon."

"Of course. Why do you think they stole him? He's a Brandon, worth something as a hostage. The only things I'm wondering about are, How did they know a Brandon child was in Bountiful? Did they know Talon and I were separated? What do they want? Do they think just because this war has started they can get more? Only thing is, they have to deal with the . . . Brandon . . . men." She gulped and turned pale.

"What's wrong, sis?" Sammy felt alarm slamming through his slim frame. "It ain't . . . it couldn't be. Oh, Lordy. I know Talon Clay's all right. I saw him just last week. It must be something else, like—is it about Ashe, sis?"

"Oh Jesus, here we are trying to make light of everything and our world is falling apart. Mikey has been kidnapped. Ashe is—" Feeling miserable, she looked at her brother—"He's . . . dead, Sammy. He drowned in a fishing accident. Debris from the shattered craft returned and there was nothing more."

"I don't believe it." The young man shook his auburn head. "Nope. Not Ashe. He's the Ranger I always looked up to. He was bigger than . . . Lord, words can't tell. It seemed like nothin' could hurt Ashe." Sammy's moist eyes flew wider. "Tanya . . . I plumb forgot about her. How's she takin' it? Is she holdin' up?"

"Just barely. Matters are a bit confusing and taxing at Sundance these days. Sarah seems bewildered; she even held a rifle on Almanzo so he'd let me go. Talon Clay put me under Almanzo's protection after he rode out. He was my guard, I should say."

"Really, sis, you a captive? Almanzo must've needed to be protected from you!"

"Not so. Sarah took matters into hand, though, and gave me a push towards escaping Almanzo and the ranch hands. There are some new faces I've never seen at Sundance. Much can happen in the space of four and a half years. Two dudes, one called Jesse Campbell, another named Frank . . . I don't know what his last name is."

"Yup," Sammy said. "I remember when they come to Sundance, let's see, shoot, not longer ago than three months it was, maybe less. They seem like pretty nice dudes, though." Sammy shook his head, wiping away the moisture at his eyes. "I'm sure gonna miss Ashe; he was like a brother to me. A big brother when I needed one after Pa died."

"You remember Pa." She waited for him to nod. "How about Ma?" Her brown eyes narrowed. She waited.

"From all the talk at Sundance I do know her name was Garnet. Come to think of it, I heard one of them new dudes talking about her."

"Oh? What did they say?"

"I couldn't hear 'em real well because the cattle were bawlin' and we were ridin' fence that day. They did say her name, though. At least, it sounded like that's the name they mentioned. It'll come to me one day, what they were sayin' about her." Sammy placed his saddle blanket on his horse, then paused. "I think there's going to be some trouble at Sundance soon, sis. I can feel it in the wind. A lot of it has to do with Mikey's disappearance, too. I think this is only the beginning of a big war."

"Like the one between the north and south, Sammy. Only on a smaller scale. That war has just begun, too. I wonder what the future will hold for all of us in Texas."

"I don't know, sis. But it's kind of scary to think about it."

"All we can do is return to Sundance and see what happens. We'll be patient, Sammy, and God will be on our side. He's our strength and He will renew it over and over, come what might."

"Yeah. But what if God is on the other side, too? What then, sis?"

Willow wrinkled her delicate nose. "God ain't on nobody's side whose gone and kidnapped a child and plans to use him in . . . *whatever* kind of war this might turn out to be!" Feeling her heart beat in such a flutter of anxiety, Willow decided out loud, "We will return to Sundance and then go to Bountiful for Juanita and Jorge later on. Maybe you can do that, little brother."

259

A chuckle came from Sammy. "You know what, sis?"

"No. What?"

"You just said 'ain't' and 'nobody.' You should've said: God isn't on anybody's side whose gone and kidnapped a child and plans—"

"Okay, okay. That's very good, Sammy. See—you can be a Ranger some day and use all the big proper words just like they do." She swallowed, trying not to think of Ashe.

"Yeah. But by the time this war's over, there probably won't be any need for Rangers. They're already thinnin' out and the *big* soldiers, the military men, will be comin' in."

Willow shook her head. "I don't think so, Sammy. Texas was declared out of the Union on March *two;* she was placed on record as having seceded before Lincoln's inauguration on the *fourth.*"

"There's already a couple thousand U.S. soldiers along the Rio Grande, on the western frontier, and more at the Eighth Military Department headquarters in San Antonio."

Willow's face swung away from her horse and her eyes sought Sammy as he cinched his saddle. "How do you know that?"

"Talon Clay told me. He was with McCulloch when the Committee of Public Safety issued commissions as colonels of cavalry to Ford, Henry McCulloch and Ben McCulloch with orders to get the federal troops to surrender, along with the installations and property."

"It's called *capitulation,* Sammy."

"Whew! That's a big word to learn and remember. Anyway, Ben McCulloch was supposed to go to San Antonio right away to support—forcefully, of course—

the state commissioners' demands on General Twiggs for the surrender of the headquarters property and personnel. Henry McCulloch was going to occupy the western forts, and Ford was supposed to be in command of the Rio Grande posts."

"Sammy," Willow cut in graciously. "We really got to be riding, little brother. Tell me more about it on the way. I want to hear all about Ford and the Rio Grande and—" she laughed lightly—"General *Twiggs*. Where's he from, anyway?" she asked, mounting Breeze and bending to pat the silky mane.

"Twiggs? He's Georgia-born and a known secession sympathizer."

"Sammy, are you sure Talon Clay was all right when you saw him?"

"Yup. And like I told you, he's looking for Mikey and he might just find him afore anyone else does."

"Before, Sammy, the word is *before."*

"Okay, okay, sis. Let's ride out *before* it gets too late!"

Saw Grass was the name of the Tucker spread. Their land was not as extensive as Brandon's spread, Sundance Property, and this was one of the reasons the Tuckers had always coveted Sundance: it was bigger and better. Janice Ranae sat looking out the window of her greasy kitchen, staring longingly toward the border where Tucker land met Brandon land; she couldn't see the fence line. But she could imagine where the line was drawn and she sat with her chin in one hand, the other clutching the hem of a ragged curtain as she longed for the day when the two ranches could be combined. It had not worked with Carl, her son, when he had tried to get Talon Clay to reveal where the Brandon treasure was hid. Part of the money had been concealed in the house—she had learned that much—but where the remainder was hidden along with the deed, she had no idea. It could be anywhere on Sundance property. Over the years, Carl had done some digging over there, careful not to get himself caught; there had been a pretty woman looked a lot like Garnet, maybe related, maybe not. Carl said he had spied on the journal the woman had written in—her name was Margaret. One day years later Tanya had come along the road where their property ran alongside and Carl had worn an ugly burlap sack over his head. She had to confess—if only to herself—that her son had meant to do Ashe in so that he could marry Tanya and take over Sundance. They had been foiled again, this time by Tanya herself and Talon Clay.

Janice could go on and on thinking about their sometimes-secret war with the Brandons, but it got her nowhere. Romantic fools, she thought, that's what those Brandon men were. If only her daughter Hester had been able to latch onto Talon Clay, they might've had a chance to worm into the Brandon house and work from there. This way, they were always on the outside looking in. Now she had the sharp and cunning Garnet Haywood here to help her, and things just might start to happen, Janice thought with a bittersweet half-smile as she sipped her hot coffee, wishing there was sugar; maybe Garnet would send Winder or one of his men to get her some.

While the cloud-covered sun rose behind Saw Grass, warming the mists slightly, Janice Ranae, Hester, Garnet, and Winder shared a breakfast of salt pork and eggs. With a sharp eye, Garnet looked at her gunslinger, ever watchful lest a hint of deception creep in and taint him or any of the others against her. She would stand for no trickery. The task before them had to be carried out, at all costs, and no man was to be spared if he didn't do his job right.

"Where'd you hide my grandson?" Garnet asked Winder, staring at him for a moment with narrowed eyes.

"We—" Winder started to tell the Boss Lady, then thought he should tell her in private—just to be on the safe side. "Don't you think we should talk about this later, Garnet?"

"Winder! I told you not to call me Garnet. Call me Nat Lacey. In fact, I prefer Natalie. Nat sounds too much like a bug or a male person. I'm neither." She winked at Winder. "What news do you have for me? You rode in late last night and we didn't get to talk much."

"I'll tell you about the kid later. For now—is it all right if I talk about the kid's mother?"

"Of course!" She slammed her palm down on Janice Ranae's knee, making the frumpy woman jump. "We're all family here, isn't that right, Janice?"

"Uh, yes, of course. We're all family. I just hope you can help join Saw Grass to Sundance."

"Help!" Garnet exclaimed. "I can do more than help. Me, Winder, and the boys, we can do it all, and you won't hardly have to lift a finger, Janice Ranae Tucker. We might have to use Hester—we aren't sure about that yet. So many of our plans have changed that we've moved our lair to your place." She cooed, "And we're

so close to our main objective, I can hardly believe it. They won't even know we're hiding out here. We'll just lie low and do the dirty work at night while everyone sleeps over there at Sundance. They'll never know where the trouble's coming from."

Janice Ranae frowned and Garnet asked, "You have a problem with something?"

The owner of Saw Grass looked out the window, then up at Winder who'd gone to stand behind Lady Boss, then back at Garnet. "I'd just like to know where the child comes in. What do you have in mind for him now that we've moved your gang here to Saw Grass? Your man has hidden the boy and the hiding place remains a secret. This is my spread and I'd like to know what's going on; I might not like some of your plans."

"Why, Janice Ranae." Garnet tipped back in her chair, leaning her face against Winder's arm in an affectionate gesture. "We're all in this together, I said. We won't make a move that you won't be in on. I might be devious—" She chuckled warmly. "But not against my good friends. Winder—" she patted his arm—"would you go out and check on the men and see how they're doing getting set up in that nice big barn out there? See if they need anything and pick a few to steal us some supplies later, in the dark, away from the merchants in bigger towns. Try to make it look like the border Mexicans are up here doing some of their dirty work. It will be easy, with so many ranch owners getting worried about the war. You know the reckless pranks of Mexican and Texan politics. Our so-called friendly relations with the Mexican frontier are fast dying away."

"What is it, Garnet?" Janice Ranae asked. "What do you want to tell me in private?" She knew it was woman-talk, because Garnet had excused the men before in order to talk privately with Janice Ranae, and sometimes Hester was included.

Garnet was looking at Hester, trying to decide something. "I guess she can stay. Hester should hear this, too." She might need the younger woman to throw a chink in the works again, just in case Willow and Talon Clay got too close and planned to live happily ever after on Sundance property. She wanted to get them all out, and didn't know how she was going to manage that just yet.

After Winder had left, Garnet revealed in a whisperlike voice that she was wanted for the murder of her own brother, the real reason she fled California first and then Sundance.

Garnet harbored one other secret, one that *no one* could learn about! This was about the Hayes offspring: she was in actuality their aunt! Margaret Hayes had been their true mother! Garnet commended herself for pulling a fast one with that letter, making the Ashe brothers believe she was the mother of the Hayes children. Now she had to keep them believing she was their mother: Tanya. Willow Margaret. Sammy. If worse came to worst, she could always play on their sympathies with lies and trickery in order to get a piece—if not all—of Sundance for herself. Tuckers be damned, if nothing turned out as she plotted and schemed. That would be her last resort.

Winder popped into the kitchen just then, announcing, "Ned Thompkins is back. He just learned something I believe you'll want to hear."

"Wait, Winder, before you return to the boys. Is it good news?" Garnet asked, seeing that excited light in his eyes. "It must be. Well, let's hear it. I can't wait for Ned to come in."

"Ashe Brandon's dead!"

Garnet had to sit down. "Now—that *is* good news. One down—and we didn't even have to lift a finger. That leaves Tanya as joint owner with Talon Clay and Willow."

"The couple got their own place, but it's still on Sundance property. Talon built a house for him and Willow some years back and they haven't been living in it together for over four years. 'Course, you know they been separated. Heard some more gossip in Bastrop just yesterday. Guess the news about Ashe Brandon, his family, and Sundance travels fast." He stared hard at Janice Ranae. "How come you didn't tell us you had two men working and spying over at Sundance?"

"Well, I plumb forgot. What's wrong with that?" Janice Ranae glared at Winder. "You didn't trust *me* enough to tell where the boy has been taken or what the plans for him might be. I want to know what's going on. This happens to be my spread. I always kept it up and got money wherever I could to keep from losing it. It might not look like much but it's all us Tuckers got left. Carl's gone, dead by the hands of them sonofabitchin' Brandon men. They was always one step ahead of us and I'm not going to be letting them get the best of us forever. I believe it was a Brandon who stole this land from my pa and I aim to get back what's supposed to be mine, even if a Brandon man won Sundance property from my relative in a card game; I still think that game was rigged somehow."

Garnet was looking at Janice with hooded eyes. "She's right, Winder. This is *her* spread." Her eyes

266

looked hard and there was a guileful glint in them. "She should know what's going on. Everything."

"Let's talk about that now," Winder said, looking first at Hester and then Garnet. "All right with you, Lady Boss?" After Garnet gave him the go-ahead, Winder told the woman and her daughter where Michael Brandon was hid—and what their plans were.

When he was finished he smiled at his boss. "What do you think of my plans, *Natalie?*"

"Great, Winder. We keep the boy for our last step. With Ashe dead and gone forever, Talon Clay out searching for his son . . . when can we begin to rustle us some Sundance cattle?"

The house of every one is to him his castle and fortress, as well as for his defence against injury and violence, as for his repose.

—Sir Edward Coke, *Semayne's Case*

Chapter Fourteen

In the small hours of the morning, Sammy and Willow rode in, dusty and trail-weary. It was still dark outside, with the moon and stars yet to fade, when Willow sought her bed. *Her old bed.* She didn't want to disturb anyone in the main house, so she let herself into the little house and fell across the mattress. She was so tired her brain was spinning and her limbs felt like lead. Sammy had pushed them the last twenty-five miles, and she felt as if she'd been dragged through a peep-hole and kicked over a high fence.

"Where you gonna sleep, Sammy?" Willow asked.

"It don't make no nevermind to me," Sammy groaned, just as trail-weary himself.

Willow dreamed of tumbleweeds blowing through a ghost town. She saw herself and Talon Clay in a mirror, a beautiful tortoiseshell mirror, a gift. He was brushing her hair, and the comb was clutched in her right hand. His fingers were long, his hands tan. Then the mirror began to crack and she was crying. She tried placing the jagged pieces back together, without success. There was a beautiful boy playing with a huge dog and a pretty

Tex-Mex woman hanging clothes out to dry. It was a sunny day where one could enjoy the scent and the feel of earth. Then the picture faded and another replaced it. She was going back in time again. This time she was "dreaming a dream."

She was a golden-haired woman and she had flirting blue eyes. But those eyes were not flirting at the moment; they were scowling and scolding as she stepped into Willow's vision. The woman was ordering Tanya, the red-haired girl in braids, to stay in the house with her little sister and baby brother. This only whetted the older girl's curiosity and, when the woman went into the back yard of the clapboard house, the nine-year-old could not restrain herself. Tanya thought Willow was sleeping; Willow was not, only Sammy was. Following her older sister as she went to peer out the window, Willow saw what Tanya saw that night. In the moonlight, in the overgrown weedy garden, their eyes found the golden-haired woman. Her mother was not angry now. Her mother? Was this her mother? Willow could hear Tanya's breathing quicken as she took in the couple partially obscured by the shadows of the tallest bushes. Again Willow wondered: is this my mother, Garnet? She kept staring, as had Tanya. The woman—standing on tiptoe—writhed scandalously against the stranger . . . a man who was not Tanya's and Willow's father, but another man she had never seen before . . . and who was this woman? Was she really Garnet, their *mother?*

Then Willow had another dream. This time it was a horrible nightmare. She was following Tanya again. Her sister was running on bare feet, her red braids swinging about her head as she searched this way and that. She carried her baby brother in one arm while pulling Willow along with her other hand. "Mother!" she cried. "Where are you ... *Mother!*" Willow added her own small cry in the anguished search. Their skirts became muddied and clung wetly to their legs, and Willow knew Tanya couldn't carry Sammy much longer. Even so, they ran on and on, searching for their parent. "Mother ... don't leave us!" Tanya cried. "Come back." And Willow added her own pleading voice to Tanya's. "We need you ... Mother!"

Willow crashed into the woman they had been chasing. Her blond hair swirled about her face and her scarlet dress fluttered in the wind as she turned to face them. "I am not your mother," she kept saying, while she laughed and laughed and laughed. Willow felt the tears sting her eyes. "Who is our mother? Where is she? Why do we think you are Mother?"

Garnet kept laughing. "You will never know ... never, never know, because your mother can't talk!" She smirked. "You are a pitiful little girl. Didn't Margaret ever teach you anything?"

"Who are you? Who are you?" Willow cried over and over. "I want my mother! *Mother ...*"

"Willow, wake up!"

Willow came slowly awake. Not as abruptly as she should have, considering that there was a man in her old room in the little house, and it was night, very dark, very late.

The dream faded, leaving a flat, dull memory.

"Willow, it's me. Talon."

"Oh, Talon!" She hugged him around the neck. "When did you ride in?" Willow stared at his face silvered by moonlight stealing into the curtained bedroom. "I had a bad dream."

271

"Oh, I know, darlin'. I just got in. I knew you were having a bad dream 'cause I heard you crying for your mother. She's gone, Willow, and we have to give up her ghost."

"Hold me, Talon." When he crawled into the bed, Willow wrapped her arms about him and placed her face against his throat. "I had a dream—or nightmare—that Garnet was not my mother."

"That's not a nightmare, darlin'. That would be the greatest gift to learn that you and Tanya are not Garnet's children—Sammy, too."

"Oh, Talon. What if she was not our mother? Where could our real mother be? Is she dead or alive? Was she good? Or bad like Garnet? In my dream Garnet kept laughing and saying 'I am not your mother. You will never know your mother, because she can't talk.' " Willow gripped Talon's strong forearm. "Does this mean our real mother is dead?"

"It was only a dream, Willow. You can't go by a dream, even though it was often done in the Bible and in ancient Egypt."

She looked up at his handsome, rugged face in the night's deep shadows and pale moonlight. "You've been reading my books while I've been away. I never heard you mention the Bible."

"Yup. It was real interesting, what it says in there about romance. The Song of Solomon, that's a good one."

"That's about the celebration of love between a man and a woman: Solomon and the Shulamite shepherd girl." She was silent for a moment, then asked the question she was dreading to ask. "Did you find out anything about Michael?"

"No." He looked sad. "How about you?"

"What?" How could he know that she had not stayed put on Sundance as he had ordered.

"I know you got away. I was ambushed by Almanzo while riding in tonight. He told me all about you and that you returned safe and sound—with Sammy. You must not have been gone very long."

"No, I wasn't. Sammy found the town of Rawhide and discovered a piece of Mikey's clothing. Once more the ghost town lives up to its name. Now we have no more leads as to where our son might have been taken." Tears smarted against her lids. "What are we going to do, Talon? I might never see Michael alive again." A sob wrenched from her and Talon held her closer.

"Think how I got to be feelin', darlin', when I never saw my son in the first place." He stroked her cheek, throat, upper chest. "Tell me the story of Solomon and the shepherd girl, my love."

Willow began slowly, "It is also called the 'Song of Songs.' They're a collection of poems, in the form of songs. They portray the deep and pure love of "two" who are now looking back over memories of their relationship. The poor Shulamite girl had worked in the country in a vineyard owned by King Solomon. Upon visiting the vineyard, Solomon and the Shulamite girl fell in love. He took her to his palace in Jerusalem to be his wife. The lyrics that follow cover almost every area of their mutual feelings, like admiration for each other's physical attributes, their marriage, sexuality, desires, and joys."

"And," he finished, "the problems of separation and jealousy arise but are quickly resolved by emphasizing their original true love." He kissed Willow's cheek as her lashes created purple fan shadows beneath her eyes. "The 'Song' tells about the qualities of a pure love and ingredients for a successful marriage. This kind of relationship has to have total honesty, unselfishness, and *unconditional* support."

Sleepily Willow mumbled, "In other words, what the story is saying is: The couple fall in love; they are united in marriage; they face painful struggles; they reunite and grow in their love. Uhmmm, how . . . nice . . . if only . . ."

"It can be that way," Talon said gently, stroking Willow's back as she fell asleep in his arms. "Oh yes, sweet Pussywillow, it can be. If only . . . we . . . give it . . . our best . . . shot."

Now Talon slept, too.

Awakened in the middle of the night, Willow rolled over and her arm flopped over onto Talon Clay's middle. She squeaked in fright, then recalled that he had come in after she had fallen asleep. She had had a bad dream, and they had talked. Now he was asleep—but not for long.

Willow made another little squeal, this time as Talon's hand came up and snatched hers, pressing her palm flat to his groin area. "I captured a little white dove, what do you know," he said, bringing her hand up to kiss the back of it, his tongue tickling between forefinger and middle finger. He heard her murmur contentedly and he smiled. "I could kiss you in other places that would feel even better, if you like."

"Is that a question, Talon Clay? Or do you just want to know if I'd *like* it?"

Rolling over, he came to face her, his hand resting on her elbow, two fingers stroking her inner arm. "A question."

"Hmmm. I might consider it. Just where would you like to kiss me, Ranger?" Willow asked with a purr, feeling his knee sliding up between her bare thighs and rubbing.

"Everywhere," Talon Clay said, kissing the tip of her ear. "And when I'm done, you can kiss me where I like."

Following the sexual banter, Willow asked, "Where could that be?"

"Well—my lips could do for starters."

Let him kiss me with the kisses of his mouth; for thy love *is* better than wine.

—Song of Solomon, *Ch. 1;*

Chapter Fifteen

Victory with Willow once more, Talon Clay thought as she threw her arms around him and gave him back passion for passion, as her entire body began to move sensuously.

Restlessly, she pressed her lips to his, trembling, desperate to get even closer to her husband. Heavenly, that's what it was to be in Talon's arms again—and for the second gratifying time since they had been separated.

Paradise, that's what it was to be in Willow's heart again, Talon Clay thought, hoping and praying this would continue, and that they'd find their child and live happily ever after. Was it too much to wish for, they both wondered as they shared this time together, one of few they had known since becoming man and wife.

He kissed her back, and the lovemaking that had always been magic between them began. Tantalizingly, she moved and felt the full evidence of his sex beneath his tight black pants. Suddenly she stiffened.

"Are you afraid of something, Willow love?" Talon

asked, his breathing ragged. "It's not the dream again, is it?"

"No. I don't feel right, though. I know what it is—I hear a strange horse." Willow pulled away.

Talon snatched her back down to his embrace. "It *is* another horse, Hank's horse."

"Hank? Who is *he?*" Willow shivered, having the feeling they were being spied on through the window.

"He's the real Desert Hawk. Don't be so jumpy and worried. Hank is most likely sleeping already. He won't stay long, maybe a few days at most, then he'll ride out."

"Hank Rountree; Desert Hawk." Willow nodded. "That man has been following me, Talon. I mean *was* following. Does he have a feather in his hat, with a bullet hole in it?"

Laughing, Talon said, "Yup. That's just one of his outfits, darlin'. He wears several. Now, stop worryin' about other folks and get back down here where you belong."

"In your arms, no doubt." Willow settled closer in a huff. "I've lost the mood, Talon."

"I'll revive it. Remember when you used to follow me all around Sundance? I wouldn't even look at you sometimes because I knew what I'd feel, and I didn't want to scare you away. You were like a shy doe. Actually, I guess I did want to scare you off, 'cause you were gettin' under my skin and I wanted to steer clear of your charms; you were like a seductive little temptress."

"You are not without your own special kind of charm. Look at the way Hester chased you for years. Where is that woman, by the way."

Shrugging, Talon said, "Who cares? Come here, sweet darlin'. Pick up where you were kissin' me and I was kissin' you back. I want to make up for lost time, again, and again, and again. Over and over and over!"

"Talon!" Willow squealed when he licked her ear and blew in it.

"Let's get serious, Pussywillow."

"I know what that means, when you call me *that*. You've got one thing and one thing only on your mind!" She wanted to have love and lust on her mind, too, but at intimate physical times like these she missed Michael and worried about him and it was hard to relax and make love. She had her memories. But the memories always faded into sadness, because she couldn't hold Mikey in her arms, could only remember.

"Darlin'," Talon Clay murmured. "Let me kiss away those tears, hold you against my heart, and make you forget the loss of our beloved angel—for only a time."

"Oh yes, Talon, we made him together and we should be agreeing with each other on ... everything." Like searching for Mikey together! she wanted to shout. For a short-lived moment, she felt deep, instinctive fear course through her, "vital" fear that they would not find their child alive.

There was a vulnerability about Talon Clay that even his unyielding strength could not hide at moments like this, and Willow reached out to touch his bronzed cheek, saw the hard curve of his mouth soften beneath her fingertips. In the moonlight streaming into the little house, they faced each other for a long moment, a hundred words and declarations of love passing silently between them.

But actions, in the next hour, proved their love for

279

each other, as his lips tasted again of hers, his arms enfolding her. Lifting his mouth, he said, "Do you know how much I love you? From the moment I saw you I wanted you. I loved everything about you, even your eyes when they were a bittersweet brown and flinging arrows at me. I want to possess you. I want you to be mine."

"Oh, Talon. I love you, too. I was tormented when I left Sundance, thinking I was leaving you to Hester. Not only did I take something within me from you, I'd hoped you would never forget me, would follow me to the ends of the earth. But you did not. As time passed, this only made me love and cherish you more. You never forgot me, it's obvious, and you allowed me to leave in order to find myself."

He grinned, kissed her, and stroked her chin. "Did I do that?" he asked, looking into her eyes deeply.

"You sure did, even if unthinkingly. It was in your heart to let me go. Now I know you could never love Hester Tucker. She's not your type of woman."

"But *you* most definitely are. Why do you think I took you captive and forced you to marry me at Black Fox's camp?" he growled impatiently, grasping her shoulders and putting her beneath him.

"I don't know. Tell me. *Show* me."

First one of his hands and then the other enveloped her head in a gentle, protective gesture and his lips played on hers softly. Willow's hands moved to his shoulders and she liked the feel of his bare skin under her palms. Bare skin! When had he taken his shirt off?

She didn't have time to think about it, for just then he was helping her do the same, removing the clothes she had ridden in and had gone to sleep in. "Lordy, woman, you are so warm, so sweet," he said against her throat. He was eager, as all of his weight seemed to settle in his groin.

"You are soft breath, strong hands, you warm, vigorous man," she murmured back.

Gently, he moved her head to one side and his kiss deepened as she allowed him to take her mouth fiercely and passionately. "Open for me, Willow. Let me give you my tongue."

Opening her mouth, she felt the thrust of his tongue, which began to move like the motions of lovemaking. He entered, withdrew, entered again. Everything was feeling and emotion, and she felt the heat begin, burning, grinding.

He sighed against her lips. "Ah, much better."

She was his now and Willow sighed when his mouth continued to take full possession of hers, ending their conversation. She wrapped her arms about his neck as his tongue swept in and out of her mouth and his hand moved beneath her knees. He shifted with her, brought her closer, with her back to his chest; then he dipped his head over her shoulder. With his tongue, he stroked her bare skin, lapped her firm breasts, rubbing the nipples into hard buds with his fingertips along with the moisture as she moved restlessly, moaning, licking, and nibbling his forearm.

His grip was determined, hard, but gentle. His hand slid down into the heat between her thighs and he stroked the embers until she was fire-hot. She was wet, ready for him, as his other arm held her around the waist and she tried to turn around.

"What are you doing, Talon?" As she studied him, his

lashes lowered, then lifted as his eyes opened, green eyes as deep and languid as pools.

"You talk too much . . . stay, Willow."

"Is this another one of your *positions* you learned from those dance—"

"Hush. No talk about the whores."

"The—!"

"I said *Hush.*" The velvet tip of him touched her. "This is just you and I, Pussy—" With one powerful thrust he felt himself reaching deeper into her tight sheath—*"Willow!"*

He groaned as she opened under him, took him in, held him, until he was in to the hilt. He wanted her ability to make him forget, to see her as something strong and secure and right in his life; he wanted things to be the way they were between them right after he married her. He felt a curl of pleasure then as she opened and closed around him.

"Oh my . . . so hard," she purred, reaching down to cup the heaviness between his legs, pulling his velvet jewels against her womanly form, her huge eyes sparkling in the dim light.

He growled, "And you . . . so soft."

As Willow moved with him she felt the power a woman could wield over a man, and she loved every minute, since she had chased Talon for so many months until he had turned around and met her halfway. "Who had been the most afraid back then?" Willow asked now between gasps as she continued to knead that velvet-soft part of him.

"Both. It's always been you, in my heart . . . my dreams," he groaned. Then, "Easy love, we've gotta slow down," he added with forced patience.

"Every time only gets better, Talon."

One full tawny eyebrow arched as his strokes almost stopped completely. "Glad to hear that, ma'am," Talon said with a hoarse chuckle and a thready sigh. "Now, please be quiet so I can finish making love to you."

She told herself she was obeying simply because it felt so wonderful to be with him again, his glorious flesh warm, dark, invading, and she knew he would make love to her again and again this night. Talk could come later.

Kissing the fragrant hollow between her neck and shoulder, Talon pulled almost all the way out to prolong the sweet agony. As he bent over her, his hair fell over his shoulders, having grown Indian-long again as in the past—framing his face in the pale fingers of moonlight. Willow felt as if it was daytime. Tiny suns exploded inside her. Glorious sights filtered in and out of her mind, lifting her senses to a higher plane. She was climbing hills and mountains, laughing, feeling the stimulating air and warm sunshine, thinking she couldn't remember ever being so happy.

"Talon," she whispered, "Talon, keep loving me."

"Always," he murmured, kissing her on the back of her neck. "Willow . . . how I have waited."

He drove into her again and again, until he was lost in the sweet, wet tightness of her; it was the ultimate victory to feel her arch her back, like she used to, meeting him with the undulating rhythm of her slim hips, forcing him to penetrate deeply as she sucked him back into her. Her hands moved to his hair and pulled his face to hers, urgently, like a warm kitten. Gently he pushed her onto her stomach, then rolled her over, this time facing him. She knew what he wanted. She drew her knees up, clutched Talon's hips and when she did, he re-entered her. She locked her legs about him as he increased his speed.

When he knew he was about to come, he rasped, his face tight and strained, "Oh God, *no!*"

Her fists clenched on the sheets and she cried out, "It's all right . . . Talon, *Talon* . . . I'm ready to *go!!*"

Still he clung to that tiny thread of sanity, to await her as chivalry dictated, then heard it in her voice as she cried out again, stiffened, as if waiting for the ultimate and then, with one blinding flash, her release was melding and exploding with his.

Their climax was magnificent. He withdrew and pulled her into his arms. "Are you still alive?" he asked when his breath was again his own.

"Yes," she said with a feathery laugh. Her fingertips caressed his warm chest.

"Do you want more, love?"

"Well . . . I might." She laughed again. "Later."

"Do you have something to eat? I'm starved."

"No. You'll have to wait."

"I can think of other things to satisfy my great big hunger."

"You're a pig!" Willow giggled.

"Only a glutton for you." He looked into her moonlit, doll-like features. Then he moved to kiss her already-bruised mouth.

Another hour passed, and then they closed their eyes, tucked in the bed together, her body cupped to his like a curved spoon. They had a whole lifetime of touching, caressing, and loving to make up for, Talon Clay thought as he fell asleep with his woman. Yup. *Talon's woman.*

Sometime in the middle of the night Willow felt chilled, got up to put on a nightgown, and spread another blanket over them both before she crawled back in. Then she felt the need to get up again, making her way in the dark of the moon to the water closet in back. On her return to the bedroom, she heard a noise at the side of the house, and went to the window to lift it carefully and peek out. The noise was not as near as she'd first thought, but more in the trees that flanked the yard. She closed the window, walked through the main room, and slowly opened the screen door.

Slipping outside, Willow made her way around the side of the house on bare feet, her night vision growing better by the second. She held the hem of her nightgown off the ground so it would not get dirty. Looking this way and that, trying to peer into the trees, she again heard the strange sound . . . like chanting.

It was so sad, she thought. Like a man singing and crying softly at the same time. It was a man, that much she knew. Hank Rountree—Desert Hawk. She swallowed hard, clutching the folds of her nightgown, glancing over her shoulders to see if someone had crept up behind her. She couldn't see anyone in the trees; maybe he was beyond them.

Slowly she crept toward the bunch of tall trees, slipped inside the small wooded area, then walked cautiously through until she was nearing the other side. Her pa had started a junkyard of sorts and ever since, the ranch hands had hauled useless items to this spot. Her eyes widened, for there at the edge of the junkpile sat the dark man, Indian fashion, knees bent out, buttocks

285

on the ground, his face turned toward a small fire he'd built right there before him. His face was a rich dark umber in the firelight.

He was moaning. Or was he chanting? Then her heart went out to him. He seemed very sad, lonely, heartbroken, and she suddenly wished there was something she could do to end his melancholy and distress. She stepped closer, at the side of a scrubby pine. Maybe he was in pain.

Just then a hand touched her shoulder and she jerked. But she did not cry out, and the Indian was not alerted. She stared at the lanky Jesse Campbell as he shifted and leaned forward. She was watchful and aware of his every movement, hoping he was not going to try and "capture" her back for Almanzo, possibly unaware Talon Clay had ridden in and everything was all right, so he needn't bother.

"What is it, Jesse?" They called the ranch hands by their first names and had always been in the habit of doing this at Sundance, so this was not saying anything unexpected. "You made me jump a little."

"Sorry, Mrs. Brandon. But I saw the fire and thought I'd come and check it out."

"It's all right, Jesse. The man sitting there—" Willow waved a hand—"doing whatever he's doing, is perfectly harmless. In fact, Talon rode in a few hours back and this is a friend of his he's brought along. Nothing to fret about, Jesse."

"Knowed Talon Clay was back, Missus, but I didn't know anything about this here Injun having a chantin' party right in the back yard of the little house."

"It's not really in the *back yard*, as you can see. It's quite a ways from the little house—several hundred feet, in fact, and down in a dip. He's not bothering anyone, Jesse, so you can go back to what you were doing." Why did she get the feeling that Jesse was spying on her *and* the Indian? There was something here that didn't sit well with her. Jesse made her feel uneasy, as if he was up to something she should know about. Her curiosity was getting the best of her.

"Sorry, ma'am. I'll just mosey on to the chuckhouse and get myself a midnight bite to eat."

"Wait, Jesse." Willow watched the slow and wary motions as the relatively new ranch hand turned back to face her. "You have more than one question on your mind, not just concerning this Indian. What are they?"

"My questions, ma'am?"

"Yes—that's what I asked." Suddenly she realized her naked body must be visible with the reddish-orange glow just behind her nightgown. She would not have been made aware of this, but for the fact that Jesse was staring her up and down, slowly, and as if clear *through* her. "Something caught your eye, wrangler?"

"I just have to say that you're awfully pretty, Mrs. Brandon." He cleared his throat noisily. "I just wonder what you're doing out here spying on the Injun when your husband's snorin' in yonder house."

Suddenly irate, Willow snapped crisply, "That's none of your business. Also, we're going to have to run a check on you and your past *activities,* wrangler."

Jesse looked a bit contrite and embarrassed over his blunder. "Excuse me, ma'am, for meddling. I didn't mean to. What I really meant to say was, you should be careful coming out here by yourself when your husband's sleeping and—"

"No need to explain, Jesse. I understood fully the

first time. I've ridden the dusty roads of Texas all by my lonesome the past two weeks; there's no call for you to go worrying about me. This woman can take right good care of herself, thank you. You can go to your midnight meal now and leave me to my own inspection. I can take care of myself around Indians; after all, I lived among them for a whole summer. They don't frighten me, nor does any man. Good night, Jesse."

"Good night, Mrs. Brandon."

As he vanished within the trees, Willow watched him go, wondering about the stress he had put on *Mrs. Brandon*. She received the next shock of the evening—an even bigger one—when she turned and found a pair of the blackest eyes she'd ever seen staring into her face. He was right there, big as a bear, half naked. Oh no, was she going to eat the words she'd spoken to Jesse Campbell?

Willow is always fainting, Talon used to say. It was a trick she had used on Ashe Brandon, but only once. Thereafter, around Talon Clay, the fainting was genuine.

It was this time, too.

After she had fainted, Willow was again flung back in time, and she reflected on the dream she was having. She was coming back to Sundance again, after being at the Indian camp. The first thought that came into her head when the uppermost roof balustrade of Sundance house came into view was *Home,* and it was so good to be there. A warm sensation was growing in her chest. This was home to her. Freedom from harm. Freedom from danger. This was where she had laughed and played, cried and sung, made wishes and prayed, grown from little girl to young woman. And this was where she had fallen in love. As she turned her horse into the long drive to the house, autumn winds swept before her as if clearing the way to make a welcoming path. A small dust devil swirled across the lane before her. It was all so familiar and dear to her, and she felt choked up somehow. Excitement grew in her as she drew ever closer to the house, and another emotion tugged at her when she heard a baby's delightful screech. Baby Sarah ... *or was it Michael?*

Michael ... Mikey ... where are you? She couldn't find him in her dream. There was only Sarah, Tanya, Harlyn Sawyer. ... What was he doing in her dream? There, over there was Miss Pekoe, popping her turbaned head out the door. "Why, if'n it ain't Miz Willow!" She grinned. "If dis doan beat all git out! Miz Willow's done come home! There's gonna be some good ol' times at sweet ol' Sundance ta-night ... yessuh—" She performed a little jig and then looked at Willow. "What's wrong, honey chile? You doan looks like you use to. Where'd you come from this time? My, my, you musta been gone long time. You looks older now."

Michael ... where's my baby? I can't be home, back at Sundance without my *baby?*

Baby ... baby ... baby ...

"What are you saying? This sounds like 'baby', these words. Wake up. You have fainted. I should not have frightened you like this. I will go get Talon Clay and he will know what to do."

Willow opened her eyes with a low moan. "Who are you? Why are you here?" Then she remembered the dark eyes of the Indian before she'd fainted dead away. "I'm not afraid of you, so you can just stop looking at

289

me with those nasty eyes. I told you: you don't scare me."

"I am not trying to frighten you, Talon's Woman."

"Why did you make those sounds as you sat before the fire? It was like you were in mourning for someone. Have you lost someone, fierce Desert Hawk?"

"I have lost *three*. My beloved wife and my two beautiful children. They are gone from me because of an evil yellow-haired woman, Natalie. You are like her. But now that I see you up close, you are not much like her. You are of a sweeter nature, as my wife Summer Wind was."

"Was?" Willow sat up, seeing that he hunkered before her. "What happened to Summer Wind? Did she pass on to the afterlife?"

"I know you have lived in Black Fox's camp. You know of our people. They are a mixed breed at his camp. They are not all good Indians. Some are, but not all. Just like in your people, there are some rotten fruits we must cast aside."

"Where is Summer Wind?" Now Willow was remembering some of what Talon had told her about Desert Hawk. She wanted to test him, to see if he would deceive her and tell lies. "How is it that you are not with her? You were crying and chanting for them before the fire, were you not?"

"Summer Wind has gone away with our children, Little Hawk and Morning Wind. I will not tell you their names that are not Indian, this will not matter. I was with the evil white-hair-woman and sinned with her. I am not with her because I broke my love's heart and she has run away. I may never see her or my children again."

"Yes, this is the story—or part of it—that my husband Talon Clay has told me." She knew how to talk to Indians so they could understand her. "I feel very bad for you, Desert Hawk. Would you like me to call you Hank or—" she almost giggled—"Hawk?"

"What you would like best," he said. "I am not that bad. I only kill when one or more would slay the innocent and take what is theirs. They covet and this is bad."

"But Our Lord said vengeance is His and Thou shalt not kill, Hawk, and we must remember those two things." She grew even more serious as she sprang to her feet, dusting the dirt from her hands. "Bad people have stolen my son—Talon's and my son—and I have gone to look for them so I might get back my child. I don't know what I'd do if I had to kill someone to get Michael back."

"You wouldn't think twice, Talon's Woman. You would do it and there would be no one to ask questions later."

"What if a woman was holding onto my son?" she asked Hawk, tilting her head, her hair looking silver in the moon's ray. "I have heard that a woman kidnapped Mikey."

"A woman can be a bad human, too. I have learned the hard way that sometimes a woman's heart is more evil than a man's."

"Lordy," Willow said, putting a hand to her forehead, not wanting to think of Eve in the Garden of Eden; then she frowned. "I must be loco, standing out here in the middle of the night—or morning—talking like this. You must forgive me, Hawk, for intruding on your prayers and grieving time, but sometimes I get carried away and go investigating; I can't help it, this is my nature. I will

291

leave you to your peace and quiet—" she waved a hand in the dark moonlight—"and I better get back to bed before Talon finds me gone and thinks I ran off again!"

"I have enjoyed talking to you, Talon's Woman."

"Me, too—to *you*." Then Willow turned back to Hawk. "Why do you call me Talon's Woman?"

"Why? Because that is what you are. You should never forget it."

"I am my own woman, too, Hawk. And I never forget *that*. Good night—for what's left of it."

As she walked through the trees in the purple hush of coming dawn, her steps silent as a kitten's, Hawk renewed the deep respect he'd once had for women. Feeling a greater peace and joy, he smiled as he went back to his prayers, somehow knowing this time that his entreaties would find elevated and honorable strength; he might find Summer Wind and his children, some day, just perhaps. He frowned then, wondering how much of it he must leave up to the Creator.

Dawn painted the earth as the cry of a hawk and the beats of wings echoed in the hush. Hawk was gone.

Two more weeks passed. Sammy came and went. One evening, beneath the Texas moon, he rode in, accompanied by another horse tugging a buckboard. On the shiny black seat of the open carriage sat a woman and a huge dog. She cried *"Hola!"* and the horse came to a halt gratefully, tired, hungry, and hanging its head.

Sammy twisted his mouth as if he'd bitten into a sour apple. "Hush, Juanita, you want to wake the dead? The horse is dead tired—you didn't have to rip 'er head off."

"I wish to make noise, Samuel. I feel ghosts walking

here and I want them to know I am not afraid of them. You must do this right away to show them who is boss."

"Ghosts?" Sammy asked with a chuckle. "That's hooey, Juanita. Sundance ain't got no ghosts. They're all sleepin', buried over yonder cemetery."

Juanita clutched her shawl and Jorge barked softly as he blinked at Sammy with fuzzy lashes. Hugging the dog's neck with one arm, Juanita said, "Sundance has secrets, Samuel."

Now Juanita had Sammy's attention. "Sundance secrets? Yeah, you could say the old place has lots of those."

"Secrets and ghosts," Juanita said with a determined shiver as she jumped down off the buckboard seat, Jorge leaping off beside her. The dog went bounding off toward the creek. "Jorge! Come back!"

"He's just lookin' the place over, Juanita. He'll come back after he's sniffed it out and done important things what need doin'."

"Dang and tarnation, what's all the fuss out here?" Old Clem came hobbling out from the bunkhouse, blinking when he took in Juanita and her silver hoop earrings flashing in the semi-dark. "Who's this here woman, Sammy? Ain't she a mite, ah, *old* for you, boy?"

Sammy chuckled. "Juanita is my friend, Clem. Willow was living with her, don't you remember? Willow's son Mikey was kidnapped and Talon Clay and Willow have been searching for him."

"Oh . . . yeah." Clem said after scratching his head for a second. He peered at Juanita again, noting how pretty the Tex-Mex woman was, how shiny her hair, how perfect her teeth when she flashed a friendly smile to the old man. "Quarters in the second bunkhouse are free. You can bring your things in there, ah, Juanita is it?" He waited for her *"Si"* and, as he began to walk toward the second bunkhouse, he talked to Juanita over his shoulder as she followed. "I must be hearing things." He chuckled warmly. "Thought I heard a dog bark. Last dog we had here passed on years and years ago; Shep was my pal, he's gone now. I sure do miss him."

Juanita said, "You did hear a dog, old man. He ran to do his business in the bushes. Jorge loves Mikey most of all and has been very sad because the boy is gone. They were best friends."

"Mikey?" Clem asked, standing at the open door to the bunkhouse. "Do I know him?" He smacked his lips and saw Sammy approaching with a few travel bags.

"Mikey; Michael. He is Willow and Talon Clay's son, Clem, don't you remember?" Sammy was immediately sorry for questioning the old man; sometimes Clem couldn't remember things as he got older. "It'll come back to you, it always does." He explained this to Juanita as they followed Clem inside, and she turned to him when the elderly man was busy making some light in the huge room.

"I know, Samuel. You do not have to explain this to Juanita. *Jes*, I know what you mean. My grandparents were this way before they passed away; sometimes they forgot what was going on, names of people, places, and then suddenly it would come to them. Sometimes they would wonder why *I* was so confused about what they had been talking about once *they* came out of their haze."

"Haze?" Sammy asked, blinking and wondering about that word.

"*Jes*. When their mind is in the cloud, and then they are all right after they pass through it. The cloud is very dark and this is very hard and confusing for the old ones."

"Oh," Sammy said. "I see what you mean. Kinda like being looped on corn likker."

Coming closer to them, Clem stepped out of the circle of light. "I remember who Mikey is, Sammy boy."

Sammy gulped, looking to Juanita for help; she just shrugged. "How could you know Michael Angelo, Clem? You ain't never seen him. He's just a little over four years. Willow has been gone all that time; now she's back, of course, but without Mikey." He was going to humor the old man, he thought. "You must have had a dream you saw Mikey, Clem," Sammy added with a chuckle.

"Oh." Clem looked a little disappointed and hung his head to think on this a bit. Suddenly his fuzzy eyebrows shot up along with the widening of his poor eyes. "I knowed what it was now: Someone was talking about the lad. They said they knowed where he was hiding." He nodded as vigorously as old age would allow. "Yup. Someone's hidin' Mikey."

"Who?" Sammy asked excitedly. Then, when Clem began to frown and fret, Sammy decided to make it sound less serious. "Where is Mikey hiding?"

Agitatedly, Clem's mouth twitched and he looked down at the floorboards, then up into the waiting faces of Sammy and Juanita. "I can't remember," he said with a shrug and walked away.

* * *

Hidden at the side of the bunkhouse, Jesse Campbell chewed his lower lip as he listened to the conversation on the other side of the wall. There were some chinks in the wallboards and he could hear everything that was being said. His hand rested on the butt of his gun, slung low at his hip, yet ready to be whipped out in a flash in case he heard his name mentioned. Either that, or he'd have to make a run for it, and run *fast*.

Jesse relaxed as he heard the old man say, "I can't remember," then he detected Clem's slow footfalls as he returned to his bunkhouse.

The gunslinger hired as broncbuster to Sundance hunkered down as he listened to Sammy Hayes and the pretty Tex-Mex woman he'd seen briefly outlined in the moonlight. She was a delicious morsel, Jesse was thinking to himself, and he'd like to get him some. But not now. He had matters that needed tending. Things were getting a little too hot for him around Sundance. Willow and Talon Clay had stayed put for two weeks, as if they were waiting for word to come in about their son Mikey. Jesse knew where the kid was hidden, and he had cussed himself out a hundred times or more this night when he'd heard the old man jawin' about things he shouldn't even know about. He cussed *himself* out, 'cause he should have been more quiet and wary in case someone overheard what he had been telling his buddy Frank about the kid.

To make matters even worse, that Injun dude him and Willow Brandon had been discussing two weeks before, Hawk, with the sneaky ways and dark knowin' eyes, building his little campfire every night out in the junkyard, that one gave him the total *creeps*. It was too bad everyone on Sundance seemed to be getting in on the action about the lost kid, even his boss, Almanzo. That Injun-Spic gave him a bad feeling, too, and he didn't like taking orders from someone so arrogant and unapproachable. That redhead Tanya Brandon could ask him anything and the huge man Almanzo would do anything for her. He'd even bring down the stars from the heavens if she asked, Jesse thought with a snort of contempt. He wasn't jealous, not a bit, not when a man had an Injun name like Dark Horse. That was really dumb, he thought, to name a man after an animal, but then, all Injuns were dumb and dimwitted. But for this one and the other, he revised his thoughts. A man called Horse and a man called Hawk. How revoltin'.

He better keep it cool for a while, he thought to himself, and keep a watch on the old man and what he was blabberin'. It wouldn't be hard for Clem to have an "accident" at his advanced age. He would have to also watch out for Almanzo and that big Injun, Hawk; they were being awful curious and suspicious lately. What to do about Clem, he wondered. Ah, leave him be . . .

Still, the man had said too much.

Much too much.

That night Willow cried herself to sleep again. Nothing could help, not anything Talon did, not anything anyone did. Tanya and Almanzo had teamed up; he had been helping Tanya grieve with less torment over Ashe, but Talon couldn't seem to do anything about Willow's misery. She wouldn't even allow Talon to touch her, even briefly, because this set her to suddenly cry-

297

ing. Talon began to worry that Willow might be pregnant.

He sat with chin in hands that night. That's all they would need right now. They hadn't even found their first baby, and now they might have another. He lifted his face. Maybe she wasn't pregnant, just worried sick over Michael.

He hoped so. Something had to be done. It was time to resume the search; he'd waited long enough for the kidnappers to send a message.

However, the very next morning, that's just what happened. The note was addressed to Talon Clay and Willow Brandon, and after they had read it together in the rising sun, at Le Petit Sundance, Willow slammed some pots around and then sat down to cry some more.

She stopped then, as Talon softly glared. She could see that Talon Clay was holding his temper. Then it broke and the flood came: His anger; her tears.

Before storming out the door, Talon called over his shoulder, "We're going to have the Doc take a look at you, woman!"

"No!" she shouted after him.

"Yes!"

"I don't need the *Doc!*"

"Yes you do—you're pregnant!"

"No—I'm not!" She blinked at the ray of sun. Could she be? Oh, dear Lord, that would be just terrible. Wouldn't it?

Talon had left her alone, going out to do some broncbusting before he drove himself crazy; he needed time to meditate on the note's message, too. He'd left it behind and Willow took it up where he'd thrown it on the table, reading:

If you want to see your son alive, start getting rid of some of the people at Sundance. There are too many. Don't you know the war needs men?

Willow blew her red nose. The note didn't make any sense, none at all! Oh ... my ... *God.* Quickly, she dried her eyes and jumped up out of the chair, running toward the door.

"Talon!" she hollered as she ran down the stairs, picking up her skirts. "Talon, don't you know what this means?" She didn't care if he could hear what she was yelling just yet, she just kept crying out, "Talon, Talon!" He didn't realize what this meant! "Mikey's *alive!*"

My wind is turned to bitter north
That was so soft a south before ...
　　　—A.H. Clough, *Poem (1841)*

Chapter Sixteen

In the parlor of Sundance, the group of four were talking about the War between the States. Talon Clay, Almanzo, Willow, and Tanya. Sarah was off playing with big Jorge, following the dog into mischief and forbidden corners he was usually in the habit of snooping into with his large, wet nose. It was one of the nights in the week they came together to discuss what was happening at Sundance, what they were going to do about the note Willow and Talon had received, and address the problem of having had some cattle and a few choice horses stolen; it was as if the animals had disappeared from the face of the earth. Talon Clay and Almanzo had gone to visit the Tuckers, but as usual, Janice Ranae and her daughter Hester didn't have much to say about anyone else's problems, just their own and how their ranch hands were doing, the weather, and the war. Talon was surprised that not even a cup of coffee or a drink of water was offered; Tuckers must be down and out again, he'd thought as he rode away with Almanzo.

They were in the deep summer days and some nights were hot and sticky. Juanita was in the kitchen with

Miss Pekoe, the smaller room set off from the house by a screened walkway. It was too hot to cook or bake in the old kitchen.

To settle nerves after discussing what to do about "dismissing" some of Sundance's people, or just pretending to for their enemy's sake, was the main topic for over an hour; they were back on relatively safer ground with talk of the war.

"Pockets of Northern immigrants in north Texas resist allegiance to the Confederacy," Talon was saying, "and the Germans living in the hill country above the Balcones Scarp do not rally to the Stars and Bars. In communities like Fredericksburg and San Antonio, social pressure works the opposite way, because a majority tend toward neutrality. The Mexicans, now there again a majority take no part in Anglo-American politics whatsoever. They regard the war as a 'gringo affair' and keep out of it."

"Sammy was telling me," Willow began, "that efforts by Union officers to stir up rebellion along the Rio Grande failed. He said because of the remoteness of the areas of Mexican population from the rest of the state, Mexicans are mostly left to themselves." She liked discussing the war; it kept her mind off her worries about her beloved son. Too, it relieved some of the tension over the fact that they had an enemy who was very near. They had their own war here at Sundance, on a smaller scale. She had begun to think of the possibility of there being a spy on Sundance property.

"Several thousand men who could not or would not support the Confederacy *did* leave the state," Tanya remarked, relating what she'd read in Pastor Cuthbert's bulletin. "Most of these congregated across the border in Mexico, where U.S. consuls helped some return to the United States and recruiting officers enlisted others in the U.S. Army. Some men simply hid out or "laid low." Both slackers and those who joined the Union armies are generally thought of as traitors throughout Texas."

With two fingers Talon rubbed the new mustache he was growing, using his forefinger and thumb. "A few state troops were dispatched to take over the abandoned Federal forts in the West and on the Rio Grande. The western counties up against the Indian danger were instructed to organize companies of minutemen."

"What else did Governor Clark do?" Almanzo asked, having been in Black Fox's camp while Talon was riding with the Rangers at the beginning of the year gathering information, obtaining a firsthand view of the blossoming war.

Talon went on, "Clark further ordered that all arms and ammunition in the hands of private merchants be surrendered to the state, but very little was ever turned in. A canvass of firearms in private hands was also ordered, but this proved something of a disaster: only forty-thousand weapons, mostly out-of-date, were reported. Few Texans were willing to list their firearms because they feared they'd be confiscated, in due time. Guns've always been one thing the self-sufficient frontiersmen can't make themselves. Texas depends on Europe and the North for firearms."

"So, how many men are joining?" Willow asked Talon Clay, afraid to hear the answer, to discover that he might be one of them someday. He never wanted out of a good fight, and he might just go, once they recovered their child; if not, he would do it in the name of patriotism. She knew her husband well.

Having discovered just a few days ago that his wife was pregnant, Talon decided to be cautious about what he said. He didn't want her losing this child, as she had lost the first one by miscarriage and the second through none of her or his fault. Lost! Heck, no. He would find his son—he was sure of that, and he might have to kill a few people to get him back. This was war, their own private war, and he was ready. For now, he would discuss the topic she wanted to hear about.

"Frank Lubbock is beating the drums of patriotism in Texas. He issued a proclamation urging all able-bodied Texans to enlist. He'll be coming to Sweetwater Springs and Wood Creek to raise the flag and hold a rally." He saw his wife's worried expression before she looked away. "Yup, he'll be stopping at all the scattered, dusty towns. Richmond has asked for companies of infantry, 'For service in Virginia, the enlistment to be for the period of the war.' These Texans will be called Hood's Brigade."

"Oh Lordy," Willow said, wiping the moisture from her brow. "If you go, Sammy will, too." She had him to worry about, besides all the others.

Tanya and Almanzo looked at each other, waiting to hear what Talon would say. Willow's beautiful, earthy sister was sitting on the edge of her chair. Almanzo tried not to smile, but it was hard with everyone else looking so unsettled and intense. Especially Tanya. She was so beautiful, he thought, displaying her many animated emotions with such lovely charm, that oftentimes he longed to grab her, embrace her, and kiss her. But he had not touched the radiant redhead, even though he loved her and always had.

Willow was still wondering what Talon Clay was going to say. She looked up at him and he clenched his jaw, looking ready to explode.

"I'm not going anywhere, Texas tradition or not, until I find my son." Talon got up from where he was sitting and slammed out the front door, leaving the bang echoing through the house like a loud gunshot.

"Well," Willow said, "that's good to hear."

"He's just a little tense," Tanya said, smiling across to Willow. "Talon wants to go search for Michael some more; and he wants to stay, and wait. He wants to seek out our enemy; and again, he wants to stay and wait for further word."

Almanzo leaned forward, putting his elbows on his long knees. He was a quiet man, but when he had something important to say, he said it. "I believe there might be a spy here on Sundance. Couldn't tell you who, though. The ranch hands have grown to number close to twenty-five. That is many men to deal with. In defiance to that note you and Talon received—" He nodded at Willow. "He plans to hire more men before summer's out."

"I think there's a spy, too!" Willow had waited for Almanzo to finish speaking. "I couldn't say who, either. I've been gone from Sundance for close to five years and I haven't gotten to know the men all that well. There's quite a few new ones, and only a few that have stayed on."

"Some have left to join the Southern cause. One was very young, only twenty. I believe some more will leave Sundance when this Lubbock comes into Sweetwater

Springs and Wood Creek. He has received official calls for several men for the Confederacy. I believe he will return to recruit many thousands more."

Tanya stopped staring at Almanzo's hands, his long fingers, his bronze skin. She was feeling a bit warmer than usual, and she began to cool herself more briskly with the colorful bit of fan she was holding. "The tradition in Texas observes that young men should join the colors—in any crisis. Ashe—" she stopped fanning and looked down—"Ashe believed that boys below eighteen and even men above sixty could fight in any kind of war or task set before them. You are never too old or too young to give your strength and might."

Almanzo agreed, up to a point. "I would go and join the planters and professionals, and the men from countinghouse and factory, the half-breeds and the whites . . . if I did not have the more important task at this moment in defending the lives on this ranch. A child is missing. Tanya has just lost her man. Willow is in a delicate condition; she has lost a son and is going to have another baby. Talon is beside himself—" He chuckled—"He is not pregnant, but he has a heavy load to bear also. Will he be called to serve with the heroic Rangers? Will he find his son before time runs out? Will—"

"Wait," Willow stopped him. "What did you mean by that last question? What does anything doing with our son have to do with time?"

"Oh—" Tanya began with a small gasp—"maybe you shouldn't."

Deeply and intensely, Almanzo stared into Tanya's eyes, noting her flushed cheeks, her moist lips, her hands twisting a handkerchief in her lap. "And maybe I should," he said. He saw Tanya's head drop, her lips press together, and her slow, imperceptible nod. "There is a time when everything must come to an end." He knew Tanya realized this, having lost her beloved Ashe. "I am not saying your son will not be found. He *could* be, and we all pray that he *will* be, and soon. There is the chance you will never see Michael Angelo alive again. Things can happen quickly and cruelly at times. In this case, time crawls like a thirsty man across the desert, one who cannot find his way." He saw Willow pull in a deep breath and square her shoulders; there was the slightest quivering of her pink mouth. "And time runs out in everything, Willow, Aiyana," he said her Indian name. "Even in the hourglass the sand does not stand still."

With tears in her eyes, Willow looked at Tanya, and believed she knew what Almanzo was trying to tell her. Only time would tell. If time was to be against them, then time could be the Great Healer also. However, this could take years, and she knew it.

It was a hauntingly beautiful summer night. Almanzo and Tanya stood out on the gallery, and she turned to him as he was staring at the round Texas moon. "We have spoken of our hearts, our losses, our wants, and our sorrowing. You haven't said much of what you feel, Almanzo."

Still facing the moon, Almanzo said in a quiet voice, "You must know what I feel. What I have always felt." His black lashes swept up and down. "I love you."

"Please, Almanzo."

"Please?" He still did not look at her.

"Don't say that to me now." Tanya's shoulders lifted

slightly and lowered. "Mourning takes a long time." She smiled at the word. "At least, it seems to."

"I can help you to get over his death, Tanya. You must allow me to. If you want this." The tips of his fingers swept across the back of her hand resting on the railing. "I have wanted you since the day your blue eyes and red hair swirled into my vision. I had no idea such a beautiful, charming woman existed so near my own home. I would have stolen you from Ashe had I known you resided at the little house on Sundance property. He was already in your heart by then."

"Ashe was in my heart when I was a girl of fourteen, Almanzo. He was a man's man, and a Ranger . . . like General Ethan Allen Hitchcock had said: *Hays's Rangers have come, their appearance never to be forgotten. Not any sort of uniforms, but well mounted and doubly well armed: each man has one or two Colt's revolvers besides ordinary pistols, a sword, and every man a rifle. . . . The Mexicans are terribly afraid of them."* She nodded with intense emotions smoldering in her blue eyes. "He was a Texas Ranger, through and through."

"And I have read the Sketches of Giddings."

"What does it say?" Tanya wanted to know, realizing that Almanzo was coming near to making her cry like a baby.

It was in Almanzo's plan to drive Tanya into his arms; he knew what would do so. He began: ". . . The character of the Texas Ranger is now well known by both friend and foe. As a mounted soldier he has had no counterpart in any age or country. Neither Cavalier nor Cossack, Mameluke nor Moss-trooper are like him; and yet, in some respects, he resembles them all. Chivalrous, bold, and impetuous in action, he is yet wary and calculating, always impatient of restraint, and sometimes unscrupulous and unmerciful. He is ununiformed, and undrilled, and performs his active duties thoroughly, but with little regard to order or system. He is an excellent rider and a dead shot. His arms are a rifle, Colt's revolving pistol, and a knife." Almanzo looked out of the corners of his eyes to see Tanya's shoulders lifting and falling in a slow, mournful dance; her hands were over her face.

And she was crying.

Pulling Tanya into his arms, against his chest, with her cheek resting there, Almanzo felt as if he'd come home to his heart at last. He was sure Kachina must be smiling down from paradise.

"My beloved," Almanzo said softly.

Sniffing, Tanya stopped crying and they stood together, simply enjoying each other, hearing their hearts. Quiet. Peaceful.

In her summer splendor Sundance was shining in the afternoon sun. Tanya sat in a lavender gown of Victoria lawn, and Almanzo had just come from the range to share lemonade and sandwiches with her; she had invited him to join her when he was halfway through with his work, for lunch, and dinner if he liked. She had been enjoying the *parterre*—an ornamental arrangement of flower beds of different shapes and sizes; Ashe had brought a gardener from Austin, and he had created beauty on the grounds of Sundance, but he was long gone.

Before they began to eat, Miss Pekoe popped around the corner, her turbaned head bobbing. "Ah knew dat good-lookin' 'Manzo was out here jes' waitin' fo' me ta bring out some soda-and-buttermilk biscuits. They's warm from de oben an' here's some peach preserves to go along with dem. You go ahead an' eats what you wants first. That there lemonade is ice cold. Ah brought it up from de well myself." She flapped her apron after she'd set down the added fare. "Ah gots ta git back to dem raisin pies Ah'm makin' fo' supper."

"Thank you, Samantha."

"Oh shucks, Miz Brandon. Ah done never should've told ya my name. Ah doan like it all dat much."

"It's a beautiful name, Miss Pekoe," Almanzo said, smoothing things over. "Do you mind if we use it more often?"

"Well—" she seemed to be debating this in her mind, then she blurted—"Jes' as long as you don' go an' use it too much. Ah doan want you to wear it out!" She laughed on her way back to her favorite place—the kitchen.

After quietly sharing the light fare, Almanzo brought up subjects Tanya didn't know he even knew about.

"What do you know of this Hester Tucker, your nearest neighbor whose property flanks yours?"

Tanya was astonished. "You don't know her?"

"I know *of* her; her brother's name was Carl. He tried to murder Ashe and tried to hurt you . . . this was before he passed on to the afterlife by his own hand, doing evil to the folks of Sundance. The younger woman is a mystery. This week I passed her in the town of Wood Creek. There was a darkness in her eyes that boded a black heart and soul."

"Hester," Tanya began to explain. "Her parents and older siblings had taught her greed, hate, jealousy. There was another male in the family, but he was murdered because of his thieving ways. I believe a distant neighbor gunned him down after his many attempts at stealing what was not his. I also had something happen with Janice Ranae—" Tanya shrugged it off. "It had to do with money. Ashe and I argued because of her devious and greedy ways."

Almanzo leaned back, letting his long legs fall open. "The whole family is that way, I believe. I never had much time for the Tuckers." He straightened again. "Now they interest me."

Tanya felt her heart thump heavily. He must be interested in Hester Tucker . . . many men had been over the years. There had been some jealousy over Talon Clay and Willow. "Hester has always wanted Talon Clay," Tanya said aloud, smoothing a lavender fold of her dress. "Willow has had to keep an eye out for Hester. I believe Hester might be the reason Willow ran away from Sundance while she was carrying Michael Angelo. Hester spread lies about her and Talon Clay."

Almanzo said facetiously, "Nice people."

"You say that with sarcasm," Tanya came back with a laugh. Her gaze joined with Almanzo's and once again she felt that magnetic pull. But she knew she didn't know Almanzo that well after all, even though she thought she had in the past. She was seeing different aspects to his personality, and what she noted and perceived was very good. He was charming, funny, cheery, loving . . . *and she must not go on,* she thought.

"What happened to Martha Brandon?"

Again Tanya was surprised. "Martha," she began. "I can only tell you what Ashe has told me. Would you like to hear?" Almanzo nodded. "All right. Ashe remembered as a child that his mother had been captured by Comanche Indians, enslaved, then returned only to die not long after. They had used her to secure the liberation of a Comanche boy. I believe ... yes, Martha was first captured by her Kiowa lover. I'm not sure how the story goes exactly, but Talon Clay is the product of that savage union." Biting her lip, she paused. Almanzo had flinched at the word "savage." "I'm sorry. You don't like the word ... well, I won't say it again. Ashe used that word a lot."

"Ashe was sometimes mean to you." Almanzo's dark eyes appeared darker yet. "I did not like this one thing in him. There was something about him from the first that said, he treads lightly where women were concerned. He was cautious, afraid of being hurt by you. He even had a taint of hatred running in him. I have had a long talk with Talon Clay. I hope you do not mind. There are many secrets and ghosts here on Sundance property. I would like to know about them, in case anyone tries to hurt you."

"Secrets?" She had the feeling Almanzo had more knowledge than he was letting on.

"Both. Ghosts can be closet skeletons also. This is what is hidden in the past of relatives and friends. Tell me more about the past, Tanya, about Sundance."

Tanya nodded. "Pete had remarried, almost before Martha's grave was cold. He married Garnet Haywood ... the woman had come all the way from Monterey in California when she heard one of the biggest Texas ranches was advertising for a special cook. It was a lie on Garnet's part, of course; she was not a "special" cook. I don't know exactly what her game or real name was ... maybe she was just looking for her children.

"Ashe remembered Garnet coming up to the house, after having fed the ranch hands—and it wasn't particularly good cooking—he had thought she was too pretty, a silly gold-haired woman with blue eyes who flirted with his father. Ashe came to hate Garnet Haywood. There was something strange about her—like she was keeping a secret all the time. More than one, in fact. Ashe said she was several years younger than Martha. Ashe couldn't stand her moving into the main house, so he moved his belongings back to one of the bunkhouses that were vacant at that time. His little brother tagged along, but Garnet always came to fetch Talon Clay back to the house. Ashe came to learn ranching quite well by living with the hands, working hard side by side with them all day long. Then, it seemed while Ashe was looking the other way his little brother went to live with the Tuckers."

Suddenly Almanzo asked, "What was Garnet doing all this time?"

"She always *complained* of being sick—" Tanya kept it to herself that she had discovered a lost page from Garnet's journal—"She *pretended* to be sick. Pete, Ashe and Talon's father, said she couldn't be that ill every day and he couldn't take care of the wild little boy Talon Clay; he wasn't really all that 'little', the woman wrote." Here Almanzo let her "slip" go by and listened to the rest. "He didn't have to worry about Ashe, because he wasn't interested in Garnet as Talon had been."

"There was some trouble between Pete Brandon and the Tuckers?"

"Yes, Almanzo, there certainly was. Their land borders Sundance property. It seems there had always been a border-war going on. The Tuckers coveted Sundance, even said at one time they had proof that Sundance was part of Saw Grass. They could never prove this, of course. I presume there's supposed to be papers of some sort, like a deed, hidden somewhere; I don't know if they meant hidden at Sundance or Saw Grass."

"What happened to Garnet? You said she was ill?"

"She died all of a sudden and Pete Brandon became a gruff man, older than his years, always riding the range alone. Then Pete died. Ashe went away . . . but first *we,* the Hayes, came to live on Sundance property. The big house was vacant then."

"Garnet was your mother."

It was said so softly that Tanya wasn't sure he had said it. But she knew it was so. "Yes, Garnet was my mother. Willow favored Garnet in looks more than I. Garnet was blond, as Willow is. Rob, my father, had reddish hair, as Sammy and I do."

Almanzo had a thought, asking, "Garnet was no relation to Martha?"

"Of course not. My mother was not related to anyone residing on Sundance at that time. My father followed her there, only to find that she had passed on already. We stayed on, Rob, Sammy, Willow, and myself. Both Ashe and Talon Clay went away and the halls of Sundance stood empty. There was only old Clem, myself, Sammy, and Willow. We hardly had enough to eat some days and few clothes to wear."

Taking her hands and smoothing the soft skin, Almanzo lifted her fingers and left a tender kiss here and there. "If I had known I would have come to you like a knight in shining armor and saved you and your little family." When he smiled just then Tanya thought he looked just like a dark, handsome knight. "I had no idea there was a princess so near."

"You're very gallant," Tanya said, pulling her hands

slowly from his. She smiled. "Your men are waiting."
She studied his profile as he turned to look at Frank and
Jesse. "They look like it's important. Someday soon I
will ride out to take a look at those fences you've been
putting up."

"I would like to ride with you, Senora Brandon."

"And I would like to have you."

His eyes were very dark, very intense as he said,
"Would you?"

"Yes, I—I would like that very much."

Almanzo wondered if she was aware of the tantaliz-
ing slip she had made.

Both were distracted just then by a dark-eyed woman
wearing a colorful print dress; Frank and Jesse stared
hard at the new woman at Sundance as if trying to figure out what she was doing here.

"Buenos dias," Juanita said cheerfully as she walked
briskly by, a basket loaded with wet wash in her arms.
She smiled and headed toward the clothesline out back.

Tanya blinked. "Who is *that?* She is very pretty."

Almanzo stood, reaching for his cowboy hat. "Yes,
she is. But she does not wear the stars from the skies in
her eyes."

Tanya blushed and Juanita looked over her shoulder
and grinned. The redhead decided to follow her and find
out who she was and what she was doing on Sundance
property. It was not that she was suspicious and jealous;
she just wanted to know why she hadn't been informed
of a strange woman's presence.

That was all.

* * *

315

Willow smiled, leaving Tanya and Juanita discussing the best way to make tortillas and hot sauce to go with their supper; of course, Juanita was the expert on that.

She had walked over to the clothesline after seeing Tanya making her way there to talk to Juanita. Tanya laughed softly and smiled upon realizing that this was the woman her sister had lived with in Bountiful. Juanita had taken care of Michael while Willow taught school there. The house had been boarded up in their absence and Willow hadn't decided whether to sell it or move back there if things didn't work out with Talon Clay.

Willow had no idea that her presence in the tackroom at that moment was going to create an argument, but as soon as she entered she felt the tension in Talon Clay. She knew right then that she should turn around and go the other way, but she was a woman, and she was curious.

"Are you going to join the fight?"

Talon was trying to fix some straps and buckles and he snapped over his shoulder without looking at her, "What fight are you talking about?"

"What do you think?" she snapped right back. "The war. What else?" She knew it was time to leave, but she didn't do it.

"Oh that. Are we going to discuss my "ambition" again, Miss Pussywillow?"

"I'm *so* sorry. I see you're working hard on fixing that harness. I should not have bothered the 'king' at his work. Good afternoon. I'll see you later. I, too, have things to do."

"Willow!" Talon shouted, straightening from his task.

"Where are you going? You can keep me company, you know."

She tossed her blond hair. "I'd rather keep company with a grizzly. Have supper at the chuckhouse; I'm too pooped to cook."

"You can't be tired. You just got up an hour ago," Talon said, picking up the harness again. "Don't you ever get enough sleep?"

"Don't you ever get enough in the bedroom?"

"Hell—you used to love it. And you still do—you're just not admitting it. What's wrong with you again, Willow? What do you think I'm doing now—fooling around with Juanita?"

"Oh, you already knew. I saw you looking at her yesterday. You're always looking at other women. It's one of the main reasons I left you, and you know it."

With a hand on one slim hip, Talon asked, "What's the other?"

Brushing back a wave of lemony hair, Willow stood in a shaft of sunlight, wondering why they always seemed to come back to this same conversation. Maybe she could trap him and see what he really had been up to after she had run out on him. She couldn't seem to stop herself.

"The same thing. Women."

"Oh shoot! That again?" Talon tossed the harness onto the floor, then bent to pick it back up and in the process, the long end of leather snapped at Willow's arm. "Oh, no," he said, seeing the look on her face. "Now you're going to say I did that on purpose."

"Well?" she cried hotly. "Didn't you? This is exactly the way you acted when you were dallying with Hester

317

Tucker right after I got pregnant that first time and you thought I was frumpy."

"I wasn't dallying with that woman. You know I can't stand her. Willow, how many times are we going to have this same discussion about all the women I'm supposed to be after—either that, or they're after me. Whichever. You never make sense on that subject."

"You told me to steer clear of you because of all the other women in your life—"

He didn't let her finish. "That was a year before we ever got married!"

"There you go—snapping at me again." Willow pouted, kicking hay with the toe of her tan boot. To alleviate her suspicions, she put another question to him. "What were you and Juanita talking about yesterday? And what's this about Almanzo saying Hester's back?"

"What do you mean Hester's back? I didn't even know the bitch was gone."

"She's back and I'll bet it won't be long before she'll be sniffing around Sundance. I don't have to guess what for; I already know."

"If she comes here I'll shoot her. How would you like that? Then would you believe there's nothing between that woman and myself?" He saw that she did not respond. "As for Juanita, I was just asking her some questions about Mikey."

"Michael." Willow corrected. "And you could have asked me the questions. After all, I'm his mother and know more about him than Juanita does."

Jorge barked just then, bounding into the barn to stop and lick Willow's hand, then Talon's. The shaggy tail hit Talon in the face and he yelled at the dog. Grabbing Jorge around the neck and bending down to hug the big mutt, Willow looked at Talon as if he were part of the "stuff" on the floor in the horse stall.

"You're mean, Talon Clay. I should have realized this long ago, then I would have never married you. But you were always tempting me to chase after you."

"Oh Jaysus. Are you going to walk out on me again?" He took a step closer. "I swear I'll hog-tie you, woman. You won't go anywhere without my say-so."

"*Oh!*" Willow stood. Jorge barked and sat next to her. "You can't talk to me like that, Talon Clay Brandon."

"I sure in hell can, Willow Margaret Brandon. You're my wife and I'm going to start treating you like you haven't got a lick of sense in your head and you need watching after. Because you do."

"I'm not going to stand in here and debate with you, because you always seem to get the best of me. You're a blasted Texas Ranger just like your brother Ashe was. I'm sorry," she apologized immediately, "I don't want to say anything bad about the dead. But Ashe wasn't always nice, you know. He had a head on him the size of a rain barrel, and you think you have to be just like your big brother and toss your weight around."

Talon grasped her arm and Jorge barked again. Willow squealed but he continued to hold her. "I don't take kindly to you talking about my brother like that, Willow. What's wrong with you? I know you miss Mikey and you're scared to death for him, and we got this note that we can't understand . . . everything is getting out of hand. This talk of ghosts and Sundance skeletons has spread, too. Do you have something to do with that, Willow? The ranch hands are talking about getting out. Miss Pekoe is very superstitious and now she's talking about Ashe's ghost! For God's sake, everybody's talking about the Sundance secret, whatever the heck that is! They're even including Mikey in all this hooey. You better be careful, 'cause you're raising ghosts you shouldn't be raising. Forget Garnet, Willow, forget my stepmother and your mother. She's trying to separate us again."

Willow's jaw dropped. "Again? What do you mean by that?" She nodded then. "Oh, I see. Garnet did get in our way again. You think I'm just like her, so you got to go play around and find your other women first. Then if I drop you for another man, you'll have one waiting—"

"Stop it, Willow!" Talon shook her and Jorge growled. "You sound real stupid, you know that?"

"No!" Willow shouted. "I don't!"

"You're a jealous and suspicious woman, and I'm afraid you're going to be something like Garnet if you don't watch it. Her tainted blood is in you, Willow Margaret. What the hell were her parents like anyway?"

"My grandparents on her side?" she said, watching him nod. "I never knew them. I hardly knew *her*, you know that. Let *go* of my arm, Talon. You're digging your fingers in too hard."

Dropping her arm, Talon stood back, but he didn't glare as he felt like doing. He just felt sad that it had to be this way; there was always something troubling their relationship. His ambition. Her suspicions. That made an unlikely pair, and mostly lies, too, in the name of "other women"—like Hester Tucker. Why did they always have to bother him? It was the yellow-haired bitches; he couldn't get away from them. Not since Garnet.

He didn't want to get away from Willow, though. He loved *her*. Probably too much. He moved toward her and stared hard at an upflung arm. "I'd never hit you, Willow. Even though I'd love to take you over my knee sometimes. Is that what you're afraid of? I would not hit a woman with child." He took another step. "Not any woman."

Willow backed up a few steps, taking Jorge with her. "I just don't think we're ever going to get back together, Talon."

He looked down at the harness, not at her. "You don't know *us* very well then. It's already started, Willow." He looked at her standing in the door like a pretty statue. "And there's no turning back."

If a step should sound
or a word be spoken,
Would a ghost not rise
at the strange guests' hand?
—*Algernon Charles Swinburne*

Chapter Seventeen

Willow was walking in the wildly wooded backyard
of Le Petit, the house on the "eastern seven hundred" of
Sundance property, the place Talon had built for them to
live in after they were married. It was also the place
where she'd left her husband wondering where in the
world she had gone off to, when she fled to Bountiful.

She continued to walk away from the immediate area
surrounding the house, staring up at the dove-white
clouds, walking backwards for a few moments as she
looked at the house basking in morning's first glorious
rays. Outside, the wooden porches and railings typified
the exuberant carving that characterized the carpentry of
the early nineteenth century. Inside, architectural details
included pine floorboards, paneled doors shipped from
New Orleans, and brick fireplaces. All in all, Le Petit
Sundance was a mix of the old and the new. There was
a windmill and a running creek nearby—Strawberry
Creek—and Willow loved to come here when she
wanted to walk and just think, or take her lunch out to
eat on a fallen log.

She had a lot to think about just now. She had left

Talon ... and she could hardly believe she'd actually done that.

Had Talon really been worried about her? Maybe he only followed up on that note because he thought he had to. Rangers were good at etiquette and they knew how to treat the ladies, but they were not very good at being family men. The truth of the matter was, she hadn't wanted Talon Clay to become a Texas Ranger. He had been gone all the time and that had caused her to wonder if he loved his job so well *only* because there were always admiring women. Even though the Rangers wore no uniform, they were spotted a mile away. They had an air about them, an air of virility and danger, and it drew women like flies.

"I gotta stop being so jealous," Willow told herself.

"Who you talkin' to, Missus Brandon?"

"Oh *Lord!* You!"

It was Jesse again, and Willow wondered what he was doing out here back of Le Petit, when he should be working with the hands over at Sundance. There was fence repair; also, they were adding a large room with a fireplace onto the bunkhouse, and a sitting room for weary wranglers. And they were rounding up more horses they would eventually sell to the Army—and Jesse, she had learned, was also a broncbuster.

"Don't you have some horses to bust, Mr. Campbell?" Willow looked up at him—he was tall and skinny, but good-looking—and she tilted her head to study him. Her hands were stuffed down into the deep pockets of her patterned skirt of pink, yellow, green, which she was wearing with a white blouse. "What's your interest over here at Le Petit? Why have you come along again while I'm out for a walk?" She fired questions at him to alleviate her nervousness. "You should be working, shouldn't you?"

"Well—" Jesse looked embarrassed. "I don't know how to ask you this. You see, I, uh, I got a problem."

"You have a problem?" Willow nodded her head, wishing she'd brought her Toledo steel blade with her, or her gun. She was suspicious and wary nowadays; she'd become more so since Mikey had been stolen— and since the "note." She had the strangest feeling that Jesse had been watching her. Taking her hands out of her pockets, she went on. "If your problem has to do with work on Sundance, you'll have to see Almanzo or Talon Clay. If your problem has to do with *me* in some way ... I don't know—" She shrugged. "Then you'll just have to move on, because I have my own problems and I don't need a dude trailing me around." Her head tilted again. *"Comprende?"*

Jesse laughed. "How did you know I've got some Tex-Mex blood?" When she didn't say anything, he pressed on. "I know you're giving me a cold shoulder, but I don't care, ma'am. You see, well—" he laughed as if embarrassed. "I find myself fallin' in love with an angel. Oh now, don't go thinking it's yourself. It ain't ... it's that dark-haired Tex-Mex lady who's come to Sundance, Juanita. I can't keep my eyes off of her. She's the most beautiful *senorita* I ever saw in all my born days ... her dark eyes ... her creamy skin ... her, ah, her *gorgeous shape."*

Now Jesse had Willow's interest. "You love Juanita?" She didn't know if this was bad or good. Juanita was special to her and she did not wish her friend to become involved with the wrong dude. After Jesse nodded fervently, Willow took a moment to think. "What do you want me to do?" she asked, watching him closely.

Jesse scratched beneath his brown cowboy hat, near his sweaty hairline. He dropped his hand and looked at Willow with "cow eyes" and appeared to be blushing. "I would like you to talk to her, tell her that I would like to get to know her better."

Willow shrugged lightly. "Why don't you tell Juanita yourself?" Her eyes narrowed. "How do you know Juanita is not married or in love with someone else?"

Jesse's eyes widened for a moment. "I can always tell. She is like the Madonna. She has no husband and I think she has no boyfriend. I think she's looking for one. I could be that one."

Jesse grinned and Willow became even more suspicious. Was it her imagination, or did the inflection in Jesse's voice change? Maybe it only seemed to, because Jesse was embarrassed and a man in love. Or was he? What was his game? Were his feelings genuine? She guessed they could be. Talon had said she was being overly suspicious lately, and she had no idea why. It was something that she had no control over. Or, she thought with resentment, maybe Talon was trying to drive her away from him. He'd always seemed to do that, ever since the first time she had chased him when he had been an outlaw with the Wild Bunch and she had warned him that the Rangers were out looking for him. He had been wild and uncontrollable. She had loved him without reservation; he could do no wrong in her eyes.

Why couldn't she love Talon Clay that way now? What had happened to change things? Maybe there was something besides Michael's disappearance bothering her ... what could it be? She had a feeling that she would know very soon and that would be the beginning of the end of her problems.

"Have you been listening to what I've been saying, ma'am?" Jesse had kept walking as he talked, and he stopped to look at her. "I don't think you've heard a word. What do you think? Could I be the one Juanita's looking for?"

"I didn't know Juanita was looking for anyone, Jesse." She watched as he slumped down onto a long log. "I didn't mean to be so blunt, Jesse, but I doubt if Juanita is interested. All she can think of is finding Mikey—romance must be the farthest thing from her mind!"

He looked up at her with a dumb look on his face. "Who's Mikey?"

"Oh, you must know. Everyone is talking about my son around here. He was kidnapped. Remember, I told you?" She shook her head. "Maybe I didn't, I don't know. I've been very confused since Michael disappeared. A woman took him." A woman! Suddenly it all seemed to make sense. *A jealous woman!* One who wanted her husband, of course. Women were always chasing Talon ... his looks ... his legacy.

Ashe, he's the one with the legacy. You weren't left out, Talon. There's a safe hidden in the house somewhere, in a room no one ever saw. Your pa hid it damn good. Told no one, he did. He just told me he had it hid there, that's all. You find that safe before your brother and it's yours, boy, and the deed will be too.

Suddenly Willow felt faint. She had to sit down and hang her head between her knees. She swallowed tightly. Where had she heard those words? Where did they come from? Who had said them? Rob? Pete? Clem? The words had been spoken not exactly as she thought them; her mind had left out the correct articulation. But they had been there, in her brain, and that's what counted.

The Sundance mystery was thickening, she thought.

"Well, ma'am, what do you think?" Jesse asked, rising from the log. "I can see you got other things on your mind just now. I'll leave you and get back to my work. Good day, ma'am." Jesse tipped his hat and was gone.

Glad that Jesse had left her alone, Willow took the time to glance around, then suddenly realized they had walked farther out back than she was aware of. Or had he led her here purposely, she wondered as she stood up to return to Le Petit. I'll think more on this later, she thought, because suddenly I feel quite tired.

With her back turned to the clearing, Willow felt the hair standing up straight on her back. She knew if she turned back to the clearing she'd see someone there, watching her, waiting.

Slowly, cautiously, again wishing she'd brought her knife, Willow turned. A woman was there, standing with her hands in the pockets of a brown leather jacket with fringe. Maybe it was buckskin, she couldn't tell. She was dressed much like the wranglers of Sundance, or the way she herself dressed on the trail. The woman didn't seem to pose any harm ... then again, Willow asked herself what the strange woman could be doing here. Then she thought she knew.

"You've brought another message, haven't you?" Willow looked to the right, left, and in back of the woman; there was no one else. "Is it about my son? If not, who are you and what are you doing here?"

The older woman with a sprinkling of gray in her blond hair tipped her head; she wore a cowboy hat and it shaded the features Willow knew could be womanly or hard. It seemed she was both, as she tipped her head up even more, so Willow could see the pale green of her eyes. Or was it blue? Seemed to be a mixture of both.

"I might be," was all she said. "You ask me those questions, miss, but aren't you going to even ask my name?" She shook her head. "I'm sorry. You have a son, so you must be a missus then."

"I am." Willow felt threatened; she wished Jesse were back. This woman looked slightly familiar and the fact that she'd never actually seen her around was beginning to give her the willies. "What's your name then, if you're in such an all-fired hurry to give it to me?" Willow had a sudden thought. Was this woman a ghost? She swallowed tightly. You can't see ghosts, can you?

The woman laughed, but stayed right where she was. "You look as if you've seen a ghost." Her chin dropped. "Oh, I hit the nail on the head, didn't I? You're much prettier than I thought you'd be."

Curious and cautious, Willow asked, "What's your name? What are you doing here?"

"My, my, you're full of questions, aren't you? Well. Let's start with my name: Nat Lacey. And you are—? Ah! You must be Willow Hayes . . . I'm sorry! Willow *Brandon*. Correct?"

Willow stiffened. "You better hightail it out of here, lady. I don't know what you're doing here, but if you don't leave quickly, I'll call the hands and they'll come runnin'."

"Talk like a true country Texan when you're nervous, don't you?" She planted her hands on her hips. "I'm sorry, I'm really being quite rude, aren't I? This is your land, true; well, half of it is yours anyway, and I should practice more etiquette, right?"

Like an angry cat, Willow hissed, "You sure do talk a lot about land, Lady Lacey." Suddenly she remembered something: *Lady Boss. The Boss Lady. You'll see her soon. I think your boy's up there.* The ghost town lady. Ned Thompkins's words. "Do you have my son?" Willow blurted.

Garnet pressed her lips together, then said, "I might have. Saints preserve us! I'll bet you think I'm the Boss Lady. Hell no, child, I'm the woman who kidnapped your son. Just doing a job, that's all, a 'lady outlaw,' they call me." She didn't walk closer to Willow as she chuckled and smiled in a friendly way. "If there is such a thing as a *lady* in this sort of business."

Willow's eyes narrowed. "What do you want, Nat Lacey?"

Unladylike, Garnet snorted. "That should be worded differently, shouldn't it?" As Willow spun quickly to see if someone was there behind her, Garnet looked at the silky golden knot at the nape of the younger woman's neck. Envy and resentment began to eat at her; once she had looked just like this lovely woman but time and bitterness had taken its toll on her features and her allure. "You should be asking me: What do you have for me, Nat Lacey?"

"If you have my son, please give him to me. Then I'll give you what you want." She looked at the hard chin and mouth of the woman. "Don't tell me you want my

330

husband." When the other said nothing, Willow said, "Well?"

"I might."

"You what?"

The older woman laughed. "What would I want with a *boy* like him?"

Boy? For some reason that word carried an ominous and haunting tone . . . it was as if . . . no, it couldn't be.

Willow slapped her forehead. "Oh shoot. I know what you want."

"Yeah? You do?"

"Of course. With war coming and all, you think it'll be so easy. You want to steal the deed to Sundance. Or your boss does."

"How very perceptive, little lady." Garnet continued to keep her distance. "Actually, it belongs to her. Oh, I see you wondering about *that* statement. Don't wonder and fret too hard. It's true."

"That could not be possible. Sundance belongs to the Brandon brothers." Even as she was saying this, Willow let it slip, meaning to find out how much this woman knew about Ashe and Talon Clay. "Of course, Tanya and I are married to the Brandon brothers, so one of us inherits in the event one of them should perish."

"Ah, but one already has expired. You didn't think I knew that, did you? Or, you might have been testing me. You are smart and clever, Willow Brandon. Or should I say Mrs. Brandon, if you are happily married?"

"That is none of your business, Lacey—or whatever you said your name was!" Willow stuck her arm straight out. "I think you should be leaving now!"

"Tsk, tsk. Without you ever knowing if your son is

331

alive or dead?" The hat tipped forward, then up. "You said I could have anything if I handed your son over."

"Yes!" Willow said, her mind ticking with a ruse to trick the woman once her son was back in her arms. "Anything."

The voice was hard and demanding, "You get me the deed to Sundance and you'll get your kid. No tricks, either. First the deed. Then your son."

Willow swallowed tightly, muttering, "How in the heck am I going to manage this," almost as if to herself. "I love Sundance but I love my son more than any land. You are very cruel; this is the only home we know."

"It was the only home—" Garnet almost slipped and said *I knew.* "My boss used to live here, you see."

"Tell me who? I know everyone who has lived here in the last twenty years."

"It was further back than that," Garnet lied. "There was a woman who used to be married to a Brandon man. I see you are trying to think back to the Brandon line. Actually, Sundance was won in a card game and that woman who married the Brandon—I don't know his first name—*her* father had owned it and lost it in that card game. The woman's granddaughter wants her mother's home back."

"I've heard something about that, but not about the woman's daughter," Willow said, wondering if this had just been a story. "You *are* trying to confuse me, Nat Lacey. I am going back to the house and think about this. I believe you're telling me that your boss is the former owner's granddaughter, am I correct?"

"Yes."

"Even so, a card game is just that. What was won must have been won fair and square."

"I don't know about that. There's talk that the Brandon man cheated." The woman looked into the woods for a moment, then back at Willow. "Do you know anything about one of the Brandon men being an outlaw at one time?"

Willow paled. Talon had been an outlaw. Ashe had got him pardoned by the governor. What could this be all about?

Garnet went on. "You nodded, so that must mean 'yes.' Oh, I see it does by the look in your eyes. You look worried. You should be. You see, he—"

"Why don't you just say his name!" Willow snapped. "You and I both know his name is Talon Clay. Go ahead, tell me what you know; I'd like to hear this."

"Talon Clay, all right—he stole some things that were never recovered—"

Willow was furious. "You don't have to blackmail me, Miss Lacey. You have my child, that's all I want. You can keep the bad things Talon Clay did to yourself—that's all in the past. He's a good man now, and he's a Texas Ranger."

The woman in the fringed jacket turned to leave, putting in one last jab. "All the more reason he wouldn't like his superiors to find out how much he stole and how many innocent folks he killed."

You lie! Willow's mind screamed.

"Don't try to have anyone follow me," Garnet said. "If you do, your boy might not live to see the next sunrise. Don't tell anyone what we've discussed, either. I'll meet you here again in two days, same time."

After the woman had gone, Willow thought to herself with her quick and clever mind as she walked from a spindrift of shade: Two days, huh? That woman must not live very far away then. I wonder if she has anything to do with the Tuckers, and if she, this Nat Lacey, could be staying there.

She aimed to find out—on her own. Too, she had to be very careful where she stepped and proceed with caution. Lives were at stake here, especially Mikey's.

She walked for hours and it was time for supper when she finally emerged from the woods on the other side of Strawberry Creek.

And then she saw them, *Oh no, not again* . . . Talon Clay with Hester Tucker.

There was the smell of strong perfume in the air, and Talon whirled on his boots to see Hester Tucker.

Hester knew if she could get Talon Clay to look at her, maybe he would listen to what she had to say; then things could go easier for her when she reported back to Mama and Garnet . . . oops, Nat Lacey. Nat Lacey. Nat Lacey. Garnet didn't want to be called by her own name, because she didn't want to get the law sniffing around her skirts in these here parts. She had said it had something to do with the law tracking her here after she had left California. Garnet had had to fake her own death, paying the "special" doctor to say she'd died of influenza when she'd been living at Sundance.

Sometimes Hester wondered if Garnet's crime had been so serious . . . like murder? She thought the woman was capable of murdering someone. But who? Is that what she had been running away from in California? Had she murdered a man? A woman? Friend? Relative? Hester wouldn't doubt Garnet would kill a relative if that person doublecrossed her or stole something she wanted.

Hester didn't have time to think on it now because she had sneaked up on Talon Clay—just like she used to—and she could tell he was sniffing the French perfume in the air; Garnet had let her borrow some of her expensive fragrance. Hester felt sexy and confident that she might be able to snare Talon Clay this time. She might just get Talon for her own man the rest of her life. She had to be good, though, and convincing.

"Talon! Howdy—nice day, ain't . . . isn't it?" Damn and tarnation! She had to go and sound just like Mama. She had been away from New Orleans for too long, and should have gone back to visit her cousin to regain some of the charm that that city had rubbed off on her. She even forgot some of the proper words she used to know. Garnet said that could easily happen and had tried to help her be more seductive.

"What are you doing here, Hester?" Talon Clay kept working on the fence, not looking at her again after he'd seen her sashaying toward him, her perfume wafting in the air. "My wife will strangle me if she sees you here."

Hester laughed, trying to sound enchanting, like Willow. "Why would she strangle you? I'm the one who come over." Came, dummy, came, she reminded herself fiercely.

"Try to explain that to Willow."

Oh yes, this is going very good, Hester thought. "Talon, it appears you're lonesome." I'm sounding better all the time, Hester thought smugly. "Doesn't your wife ever spend time with you? You're so much nicer than you used to be . . . gosh, I'd love to spend time with you."

"You never do stop, do you?"

Hester pouted. "What does that mean? Oh, I never stop trying to make you love me? That's true. I'll be honest." Just like Willow, honest to the end, Hester thought. "I've always loved you, Talon Clay." She shrugged. "I know, you're going to say, *So has Willow.* Why did she come back? Where did she go? I heard she had a baby. Is that true?"

"Lordy, Hester. Why don't you go ask my wife all these questions; have some tea or coffee with her." Talon kept working as if she wasn't even there.

Hands on her generous hips, Hester made a long, loud hoot. "Visit Willow? She hates my guts. Everyone around these parts knows that. She'd sooner stick a knife in my belly than sit down to tea with me."

"You had a nice long visit with her before she ran off, didn't you?" Talon Clay looked over his shoulder, wanting to see her as she answered.

Hester appeared flustered as she thought this over for a few seconds; she took too long in answering. "Sure did, we had a nice little talk." Suppose Willow had told him just what that conversation had consisted of; she had to be careful again. "I was really jealous, you know. I might have said some things that were little white lies. She didn't run away because of what I said, did she? Oh Lordy, I—"

"What do you think?" Talon walked to the next section of fence without waiting for her. "You gotta be careful what you tell Willow; she just might believe you. Especially if you tell her anything about me. When it comes to other women, she just doesn't trust me."

Hester looked up at a pretty bird singing in a tree; she tweeted back and Talon Clay turned to smile at her.

Hester's heart went crazy. "I'd be real trusting, Talon Clay. Anything you said would be law. I'd even believe you if you told me you went to church last Sunday."

"I did."

"You what?" Hester hooted. "Why Talon Clay, don't tell me you've become a church-going man."

"No, Hester, not yet anyway." He looked very serious. "My son has been kidnapped and I went there to pray that he is returned safely. He means very much to me. He looked at her meaningfully. "So does my wife."

Laying a hand lightly on Talon's sleeve, Hester murmured, "I'm real sorry to hear that, about your son. At least you were a family before he was kidnapped. You'll always hold him in your memory. You can't forget that."

Wondering about her game, Talon Clay decided to play along. "No, Hester, I can never forget the good times we had together. Mikey is very special and I'm sure the good Lord is going to bring him back to us."

"Oh yes, I'm sure." Hester turned, then hurried to the horse where she'd left it tied. She raced the beast all the way home, jumped off, and ran into the house.

"What the heck's wrong with you, Hester Tucker?" Janice Ranae blasted her daughter with these words as she flung open the oven door on a pan of doughy dessert. With an oven cloth in each hand, she planted her hands on her generous hips. "You must've gone over to talk with Talon Clay, just like Gar ... Nat Lacey ordered you to."

"Sure did." Hester walked back and forth, then around the kitchen table three times before she spoke again. "He's on to me already. I tested him and he

337

played along with me instead of telling me anything Garnet—"

"Wrong name!" Garnet yelled as she came from the back room, brushing off her jacket. "Nat Lacey, as we agreed. Garnet's deceased again." She laughed as she made herself a strong drink from her liquor supply. "So is Nat Lacey—" she went on with lowered voice—"if the boys did their job well."

How did I forget so easily, Hester wondered. Couldn't I remember that Winder had Nat Lacey taken care of? That woman was *no more*. Hester shuddered at the thought of murder. That was one thing she could never resort to.

"I'm going over to see Michael," Hester said, miffed that Garnet had yelled at her.

Boss Lady's eyes narrowed. "Just be sure to use the words we agreed on to get in to the line shack. Here, too, at night."

"Open Sesame!" Hester yelled. "I remember."

After Hester had left, Garnet sat down just as Janice Ranae was removing the gooey treats from the oven. She sipped her drink slowly, shuddered, then spoke to the woman who only cooked fattening foods. "Better talk to Hester. She's getting a little too defiant. If she isn't careful, she's going to wreck all our plans. I don't tolerate no nonsense. We could get into a lot of trouble if we don't watch out." She snatched one of the hot, dripping biscuits from the tray. "Is this all you know how to cook?"

Janice Ranae narrowed her pale blue eyes at the dangerous woman. "I don't like to cook. Take it or leave it. This is the only kind of food agrees with my stomach. Dainty vegetable dishes ain't my cup of tea. Now, if you'd like to get us some meat, like steak, I'll cook that."

"We just might have steaks, my friend. A few of the boys are going to slaughter that young'un they wrestled out of the Sundance herd. Nice tender meat. I could use some good red meat."

The frumpy owner of Saw Grass looked worried. "We better be careful. Talon and that Almanzo Rankin already been over here snoopin'. Won't be long they'll begin to sniff the real culprits." Like rats, she thought of Winder and the gunslingers. Big, bad rats.

"I already talked to the boys. It's all been taken care of. Don't worry." Garnet bit into a crunchy, sugary biscuit and grimaced. "Nothing to worry about," she repeated, sipping her strong drink after shoving the trashy food aside. Meat, that's what she needed, juicy red meat.

Janice Ranae slammed the flatiron onto the wax cloth at the corner of the ironing board. She looked out the window, her back to Garnet. Janice Ranae wasn't smiling this time as she fingered the collar of an old shirt that used to belong to her son, Carl. Then she began ironing her dead son's shirt methodically, as if Carl would walk in the door any moment and whoop, *"I got the best of the Brandons, Ma, I sure did!"*

But Carl would never speak or yell again. He was as dead as the empty space in Janice Ranae's ice-cold heart.

Later that evening, Garnet took Winder aside and spoke to him where no one could hear. "We've got to get rid of Janice Ranae and her daughter, Winder. They're going to mess everything up for us. The fewer people around, the better. Oh, of course, I don't mean you and the boys. We're a different story; we stay, we win. But we've got to do something about the Tuckers. Hester's still got the hots for Talon Clay and she's gonna screw up all the plans we already made. We have to get her and her Ma away from here. Any suggestions?"

"Sure," Winder said. "Just send them to New Orleans to see their cousin Fleurette—and what's her other cousin's name?"

"André. And it's not Floretty, Winder. Say Fleurette."

"Yeah, André and Fleurette. Tell the Tuckers we'll have it all set up by the time they get back off their vacation. You'll share Sundance with them once we get the two properties together. There won't be any borders, no fences. Like you said, Sundance and Saw Grass will be one huge ranch."

"Tell the Tuckers to sell a few things and send them on their way, Winder."

"Right. We'll get to it right away. There won't be any Tuckers here come next Monday."

"Good," Garnet said, tossing off her drink. "Then we can really get down to work. Hester went over to see the kid—" she laughed—"the Sundance kid. I'm going over to see how that brat's doing, too."

Winder watched her slam out the screen door. There had been a sneakin' suspicion from the first day he laid eyes on the "Sundance kid" that the boy wasn't her grandson—and now he was certain. He was beginning to suspect foul play out in California before Garnet came to Sundance the first time, or after. Garnet had mentioned a woman named Margaret, and once when she'd been drinking heavily with him and Ned

Thompkins, Garnet had laughed, saying that Margaret used to be her sister.

Those three words: *Used to be.*

He wondered what had happened to Margaret. Was she the real parent to the Hayes offspring ... Willow, Tanya, and Sammy? Was Garnet their aunt? Could be, Winder was beginning to think. He'd know one day, or he'd die finding out.

I went, and knelt, and scooped my hand
As if to drink, into the brook,
And a faint figure seemed to stand
Above me, with the bygone look.
—*Hardy, "On a Midsummer Eve"*

Chapter Eighteen

Talon Clay had been scraping paint all morning with Sammy, up early, even before the morning light had begun its glorious advance. Now, busy wielding the paintbrush, Talon was painting the gallery posts that supported the hipped roof—pale mauve over white this time. He paused in the lavender shadows for a moment, staring at the heavy, paneled front door; he reflected on the time when Le Petit had been nearing completion. He and his brother Ashe had hung that front door together. "It's going to be a very happy place," Kachina had said, and Willow had repeated the words to him later with a joyous laugh. Now the beautiful Indian woman was in heaven and Talon Clay wondered about those momentous words.

Yesterday he had been working on fences nearby and Hester Tucker had come over for her visit. And yesterday he and Willow had argued about Hester's visit, and why, of course, that would not be something new! Willow must have seen him just as he had been looking up at Hester and smiling as she mimicked the bird. Oh Lordy! The real reason he had smiled was because he'd known Hester had been up to something and was just waiting for her to practice her trickery, like a witch. Long ago when he'd been a mere boy he had asked a minister about witches. The man had informed him that there was no difference between a "white witch" and a "black witch," a "good witch" or a "bad witch." He had asked him, "Did you ever hear of a Jesus witch?" and Talon had shook his head "no," and the minister said, "You never will, either. A witch is a witch, any way you look at it, boy. Watch out for them."

Was Hester a witch? Talon often wondered, because Willow called Hester that often enough!

Wearing a grin, Talon wiped it off the moment he saw Willow heading his way. He dropped his paintbrush. Something was wrong. Willow didn't look very well . . . she appeared to be ready to faint!

"Willow!" Talon rushed toward her, preparing to catch her. He should not have argued with her so hotly the night before, he thought as he ran toward her and saw hay and chaff in her hair. "Damn you, Willow— you been working in the horse barn again." He cupped the silky golden knot at the nape of her neck. "I told you to take it easy. You didn't look so well yesterday." He went on to curse Hester Tucker under his breath; that woman always started trouble between him and Willow!

"Talon . . . I don't feel so good." She clutched the blousey shirt she wore over a pair of tight pants. "My stomach hurts real bad . . . and my head is whirling. Do you think . . . oh no, I hope I don't lose another one. Talon! Everything's turning black!"

* * *

344

The next morning Willow awoke to the sun streaming in through the curtains in Tanya's bedroom. Holding her hand to her head as she tried sitting up, Willow didn't make it, but fell back to the pillow, her hands shaking, her forehead breaking out in a sweat. What's wrong with me, she wondered, staring up at the high ceiling. And what was she doing in Tanya's bedroom, lying in Tanya's bed? Oh God, have I lost . . . the baby?

"I seem to be real good at that," Willow muttered as she rolled her head to see who was standing in the shadowy corner of the room, having just gotten out of the chair to stand there, looking so lost. "Talon? What happened? You look like you just woke up. Did you sleep in the chair? Where is everybody?"

With a small, shaky laugh Talon walked over to the bed. "You must have woke up feeling awful energetic to be firing questions at me like you are. How *do* you feel?" He stood looking down at her, admiring her cornsilk hair as it spread out on the pillow like a golden fan above her head. "You look better than you did yesterday morning."

"Yesterday!" Willow slapped her forehead. "I been sleeping that . . . *long?*" Her voice trailed off in whispery pensiveness.

"Yup. You sure have. You —" He looked down at his hands that were clasped together tightly.

"I lost the baby. I know. I seem to be good at that. First I miscarry our first one, then I lose the second one by kidnapping, now I again miscarry the third baby." She stared up at him with a sad look. "Do you suppose God just doesn't want me to have any more babies to love?"

Talon went down on one knee, grasping her hand and

345

pressing his lips to her white fingers. "Oh, sweet Pussy-willow, don't be saying anything like that. Of course God wants you to have babies. We'll have lots of them if you like. But you gotta keep 'em in the oven until hatching time." He kissed her hand again and pressed it to his cheek. "I love you, darlin'. While you were out of it I formed a private posse. They're out searching for Mikey even now. We're not going to give up until we have him back—or know what happened to him. We gotta get serious about this now, Willow, *real* serious, and search until we feel like dropping. We been just standing around, waiting for notes to come, while our son is out there somewhere waiting for us to rescue him."

"I've got to get up, Talon." Willow tried to rise but the dizziness hit her again. "Oh Lord, I never felt so weak. That doctor must have given me some medicine; at first I thought I'd dreamed taking some off a spoon. Talon, did the doctor say if the baby—" She couldn't finish and her gaze trailed off to stare at the copy of *Arabian Nights* on Tanya's table.

"He couldn't tell if it was a boy or girl; it was much too early."

Willow moaned and rolled over. "Hush, Talon. This talk is just making me more lost and depressed. Would you leave now? I just want to sleep." *And come tomorrow I'm going to be out there looking for that woman who's got my baby!* She won't be blackmailing anyone here at Sundance, no way.

"What's wrong, Willow?" Talon's green eyes narrowed, looking like jewels. "Why do you look like you have a secret?"

Because I do, silly. But she wasn't going to tell Talon

346

Clay about Nat Lacey and get her boy murdered. Uh-uh. This was woman's work—not Ranger's!

A soft morning wind gently tossed the leaves of the trees and the sky was a smoky pink behind the blackness, as light showed in the east and slowly crept toward the heavens where a pale blue was just beginning to show itself and erase the dark.

The soft-blowing breeze stirred the slightly-shorter strands of hair at Willow's forehead, where she had cut them the day before to keep them from falling into her eyes. This gave her face an even younger look as she hurried, wearing a white, peach, and cinnamon-striped dress, her long braid bouncing in back as she walked. She was trying to get to the back of the property, of Le Petit, before anyone saw her going there.

She had missed meeting Nat Lacey, but it couldn't be helped. Two weeks gone. She had recovered from the ordeal of losing her baby, and now she suddenly felt much stronger, more confident, ready to meet what came her way. Determined to get her child back, she walked swiftly, knowing that there was no hindrance or obstacle strong enough to keep her from her goal.

It was time to fight. Her strength was renewed, and she would not get weary or faint this time.

Talon Clay had left the house earlier to form the search party and ride out with them. The night before this glorious morning had been wonderful; she and Talon had slept close together, their hearts and spirits had touched, not only their flesh. This, too, might have given her the added strength, because togetherness and love was the answer to everything, she believed, and should have practiced when she left Talon years ago. True, they had had their arguments, but they were both tense and worried. The only thing she wasn't doing right was not letting Talon in on her secret. She could trust him, true, but the question was: Could she trust this Nat Lacey in anything? About as far as she could throw her! And that would not be far.

"Over here, *psst!*"

Whirling to face the line of trees on the other side of the creek, Willow's heart picked up its beat. She felt faint and prayed for strength. Keep being strong, Willow, she begged herself. Don't let this sudden surprise weaken you. Oh dear Lord, but she wanted to run to him! To hold him! Her baby—!

"How does he look?" Lacey, under her lowered hat brim, peeked up while she held Mikey by the shoulders as he stared across the creek. He was holding something in his hand; it looked like a sugary treat. "He's been well taken care of," the woman added with a crooked smile. "You can see that for yourself."

Mikey dropped the treat and flung his hand toward the other side of the creek where Willow stood. "Mommy! There she is—*that's* my Mommy! You got Jorge with you, Mommy? I don't see him. Is he comin', too? I want to play with him."

The sun was just peeking through the trees, creating a glorious blaze across the creek, with her beloved angel standing there like a golden child, his green eyes eager as they searched for his best friend, Jorge. "No, darling, Jorge is not coming." Oh, dear Lord, where is the big mutt? She prayed he would not come along right now, barking and setting off an alarm. Too, she hoped that Talon and the others were far away. She had spotted the gun in a deep pocket of Nat Lacey's sweater. "Can I—?" Willow looked up at the woman who had anticipated the question and was shaking her head.

"No. I'm afraid you can't." She looked down at the golden head of the little boy. "Some other day. First you have to bring me what I want. Have you brought something? You didn't meet me here the last two weeks. For some reason, I knew you would not. Then again, I had the same feeling, this time with the certainty that you would make it today. This is why I brought the Sundance child."

Willow didn't let Michael out of her sight; she wanted to stare at him and memorize everything about him. Almost three months had passed since she had learned of his kidnapping; even in that short space he appeared a tiny bit older. "I couldn't," Willow said, wildly clutching a fold in her striped dress, happy now that she had worn it, now that her beloved child was here to see her. "I was very sick . . . in bed and could not get up."

Of course, "Nat Lacey" knew all this, all about Willow's miscarriage, since Jesse had reported all to her. Patting Michael's head, she said, "Now that I've whetted your appetite, Willow Brandon, you be sure to bring me something next time. It's in that house somewhere and you better find it."

"What do you want? Sundance money? The deed?" Willow shook her head, the blond braid dusting her shoulders. "It would be impossible to give you the deed. I wouldn't know where to look, in the first place. You and your friend—whoever the woman is who makes claim to Sundance—are greedy. Talon Clay would *never* allow you and your friends to live here, no matter what claim you make."

"But, you see, I've already told you: Sundance was won in a card game. Don't *you* also think it's a sin to gamble with needed money? Ah, I see you're thinking *that* over. My friend, my boss—"

Willow interrupted. "What name does your 'boss' go by?"

"I told you before," a soft male voice nearby said. "You really don't need to know that . . . *Belle.*"

With a soft gasp, Willow turned to see Ned Thompkins standing in the shadow of a leafy cottonwood tree. Willow's eyes narrowed and shifted back and forth, looking for others who might be hidden. Ah, there was another one, dressed in dark clothes, standing under another tree, and another, and yet another, over there. The rising sun was beginning to reveal them and they were melting back into the deeper shadows of the misty hills. Ned tipped his hat and vanished behind the big tree; Willow's eyes went back to Lacey and her child.

They, too, were gone.

Was it her imagination, or was it the lingering whisper of a longing child that had said, soft as down: " *'Bye, Mommy. See you later.*"

On her way into the back door of Le Petit, Willow spun about as she heard barking and laughing. Running up to the house were Sarah and Jorge, the girl's hand resting on the dog's huge head, Jorge barking in little nips of greeting, Sarah giggling as if her sides would split.

"Aunty Willow!" She stopped to take a breath, then

rolled her eyes as Jorge sat right beside her; he was still whining. "Jorge has been driving me crazy! He's been running all over and I've been trying to keep up with him. Gosh, Willow, he jumped into the creek, in the deepest part of Strawberry Creek. Oh, don't look so scared, Aunty, I didn't jump in with him. He's acting mighty strange, though, and I almost thought it was like he was trying to find something." Sarah paused to run her arm across her brow. "Whew!" She patted Jorge on the head again. "I better lock him up in the barn, otherwise he's going to run out on the road and get hit by a wagon or something."

Biting her lip for a moment, Willow stood there trying to still her shaking limbs and quivering nerves. "Sarah," she said, quickly coming down the few stairs she'd gone up, "I think that's a very good idea. We wouldn't want Jorge to get run over by someone driving crazy—"

"Yeah! Like those new dudes over at Saw Grass who come riding by here like they're being chased or something."

"New . . . men?" Willow stared at Sarah's freckle-dusted face. "How many new men have you seen? You were out by the road?"

"Geez, Aunty, you're asking a lot of questions. Is something the matter? Okay, I'll tell you. But I don't see why it's so important. Be quiet, Jorge, stop that whining." Sarah took another breath. "Oh, here comes Uncle Talon. I've got to tell him about Jorge . . . what's the matter, did you say something?"

"Don't tell Uncle Talon about Jorge. Let's keep it a secret," she added, smiling, "between you and me.

We'll take care of Jorge ourselves. And Sarah, *wait* . . . before you go."

"Yes, Aunty?" Sarah blinked up at her pretty relative and said in a whisper, "I won't tell Uncle Talon about Jorge acting so crazy."

Willow saw Talon coming closer, almost within earshot. She quickly said, "Sarah . . . I have an idea. Wait for me at the house. Tell your mother I have a great idea for making dresses out of that pretty material she brought back from California. Don't go outside again, please, Sarah, just wait for me. I'll keep Jorge here and take care of him myself." When the girl started to walk back to the main house, Willow called out, "Be careful!"

Cocking her head curiously, but keeping their "secret," Sarah called back, "I will!"

Walking up to Willow, Talon asked, "What was that all about? Making clothes?" He peered at her closely. "I'm happy to hear you're planning to make something for yourself."

"Yes—I am." Willow started to walk away. "I'll see you later, for supper."

"Whoa!" Talon grabbed for her arm. "Wait just a darn minute. Where do you think you're going in such an all-fired hurry?" When she didn't answer him, he tugged on her hair, forcing her to look up at him.

Oh no, she had to keep him from reading her mood and finding out what she'd done that morning and who she'd seen!

He bussed her cheek and rubbed her nose, then flattened it as he pressed kisses over her mouth voraciously. "I came home for some 'lunch,' if you get my meaning," he said as his lips left hers.

"Again, Talon?" They had just made love the night before. "I'm hungry," she said, trying to break away. "Listen. And Jorge's barking—he's hungry, too."

"No, love. Jorge can wait. Stay, Jorge! And you won't starve. I've been working hard searching the area, combing it inch by inch for clues to where our 'messenger' went, and questioning those new wranglers over at Saw Grass."

"Oh yes, them!" She followed Talon as he walked into the house to wash up. "I meant to ask you who they are and what they do at Saw Grass. That's where they work, isn't it?" Staring at the muscles showing through his shirt, she gulped and asked, *"Messenger? We've had another one?"*

"Of course." He stayed by the sink and didn't turn to her. "You know the messenger I'm talking about."

"Hester?"

Tossing the drying cloth aside, he turned to stare at her, his head tipped. "Hester? She didn't leave any message. But she was questioning me awfully hard, come to think of it. I'm talking about the message we received while you were indisposed, in bed, you know?"

"I don't know . . . Talon. Really." She stared blankly.

Talon waved a hand in front of her eyes. "Come on, don't tell me you haven't an idea of what I'm talking about. I told you about the note—oh, shoot—you were just driftin' off to sleep. I suppose you don't remember."

"No." She frowned. "I already said I don't. Are you keeping something from me, Talon Clay? What did the message say?" Now she really was curious, especially since she had met Nat Lacey twice. *Why a message?* Hadn't they discussed what she wanted? Or what her boss wanted, to be exact, whoever that could be; she was beginning to think there wasn't any other woman but Nat Lacey. "Can I see it?"

"I gave it to Sheriff Becker. Said practically the same thing. He's going to try and match the handwriting up with some of these new dudes who signed up with him for a cattle drive. A few of them looked mighty suspicious, Bernie was saying. He wants to check them out, and one of them might even be a bounty hunter who committed some crimes up in Austin."

"A bounty hunter? That's strange. I never did trust Bernie Becker. He has shifty eyes and I don't like the way he looks at me, as if I'm a piece of trash under his boots. That wife of his acts the same way, snooty, and just sticks her nose in the air when I shop at the mercantile. She reminds me of Janice Ranae and Hester, just like they used to be so snobby when Tanya and I went shopping over in Sweetwater Springs. They were always gossiping—"

"Willow, I don't want to jaw around about the Tuckers and the Beckers right now. We're just wasting time."

"Well?" She raised her tawny eyebrows. "What in the world *do* you want to do?"

For answer, he kissed her mouth, filling her with his tongue and then withdrawing in a delectable rhythm that set up the more intimate pattern that would soon follow.

Before they could even reach the bedroom, Willow was wrapping herself around him, in the entryway where they stood, as she coiled one leg about his thigh. Tightening her grip, she pulled him upward again, her back against some articles of clothing where they hung down from hooks on the wall.

"My God, but you're sexy," Talon breathed against her throat. His body was wonderfully male, lean and

354

hard as he pinned her gently, pushing himself slowly, rhythmically into her heat.

She still had her clothes on as he threw his off in a flash, and then went to work on peeling hers away slowly, inch by inch, and soon he was deep inside her. Her body squeezed him tightly. Willow gasped as he gently filled her, then sank her nails into Talon's shoulders while he gripped her and lifted her into his thrusts.

The dappled light of morning reached in through the kitchen into the hall and played on their movements. His thick blond mustache tickled her a few times in their lovemaking and she cried out his name with joy, clutching at him as he lifted her higher and higher. Then her whole body shuddered as they exploded together.

"I feel drained," Talon murmured, smiling like the happy man he was.

Willow's eyes twinkled. "Yet *renewed?*"

"Oh yes, always that with you."

With you, he had said. Willow wondered about that. But only briefly. She had many things to do.

The sun was a misty ball hovering above the trees as Willow and Talon dressed hurriedly and went their separate ways. Recalling the events of the morning by the creek, Willow had wanted to please Talon. She had needed to desperately, knowing that now that he was satisfied he would go on his way whistling a bawdy Texas tune and she would not see him until suppertime.

She hurried to Tanya's house, taking the shortcut over the creek, getting the hem of her dress wet.

Bursting into the kitchen, Willow was met by two pairs of eyes, dark ones, Jasse's and Miss Pekoe's. Willow had almost forgotten about Jasse, the black girl who had bloomed into quite a beauty. There were no slaves at Sundance, and Jasse had been fortunate to have been sold to Ashe Brandon on the auction blocks. When Ashe had given the shocked woman her freedom, Jasse had a choice as to whether she wanted to be left to fend for herself or come to live and work at Sundance. She had chosen a life at Sundance and had worshipped the ground Ashe Brandon walked on. Jasse, like Miss Pekoe, preferred to address the folks they worked for in a respectful fashion, but it was done more as a symbol of gratitude than anything else.

"Hello, Jasse; Miss Pekoe," Willow said, grabbing a peach tart and hurrying out the door into the hall.

"She's like the wind—you hardly see her when she passes by," Jasse said in her delightful French Creole accent, her grammar cultured and precise. Jasse had belonged to a white woman, Carolinian by birth, who had come as a bride to live in New Orleans and had thought nothing of giving Jasse a sound beating once in a while—just for good measure—to keep the black girl "in line."

"Willow wind," Miss Pekoe said, laughing. "Or breeze, just like that hawse she adopted. That hawse's name is Breeze, too."

"Hawse?" Jasse queried. "Don't you mean 'horse,' Samantha?"

"You hush, hear?" Miss Pekoe brandished her rolling pin with a hearty chuckle.

"Yes'm." Jasse replied playfully. Her plum-black eyes twinkled merrily. Her mind was lightning-fast. "What do you think of that President Lincoln?"

"Oh, Ah likes Abraham a lot. Yessir. He be tryin' to

free de slaves. But we is awready free here at Sundance, Jasse. We always got a home an' dere be nobody gonna harm us. Everybody here be good to us, yes'm"

Jasse rolled out some more dough for tarts. "I know this is true. We don't have to worry. I feel sorry for those blacks who do." She sighed. "If only there was something we could do to help those in bondage. All men should be free, Samantha. It was terrible to live with that white woman who used to beat me all the time. I used to pray to Jesus that she wouldn't hit me when I did something she thought was not right. I thank God for men like Ashe Brandon—" Jasse brushed a tear aside. "I will miss him, but he has gone to be with Jesus, this I know."

"Ah knows, honey, Ah knows." She patted Jasse on the back. "Whilst we work tell me agin how Ashe came to find you dere in N' Awlins."

As Jasse was relating the happy occasion of seven years ago, Miss Pekoe began reflecting on all the trouble at Sundance. Willow had returned, bless her heart, but with her reappearance had come problems. Now they searched for that lost babe. There was something about a note warning Talon Clay to get rid of some of the people at Sundance. That didn't make much sense. Now, suddenly, their peace might be shattered. She looked at Jasse. How happy they had been, working side by side, taking care of the beautiful Tanya's clothes and house, and making food for her and the others, like Talon Clay. She prayed to God that nothing would happen to him, because he was what kept the ranch going, he was the "new" man now who had to make sure no one came in and took Sundance over. With the War Between the States going on, there was going to be more trouble than just Jayhawkers, proslavery men and spies, Abolitionists bringing in people from the Northern States, and bushwhackers creeping around the back woods. No sir, it ain't gonna be safe nowhere!

In the sewing room where Willow had urged Tanya and Sarah to join her, the blonde spread the apricot brocade over the bed, exclaiming over it. There were silk ribbons, velvet ribbons, fine lawn chemisettes, silky stockings, pantalettes, and yards and yards of more wonderful material.

"Where did you get all this?" Willow cried, holding up elbow-length gloves and trying one on. Tanya laughed. "California, naturally."

"Oh my!" Willow held up a muslin evening gown trimmed in Chantilly lace, and Sarah's eyes went wide as Willow pressed it against herself and looked at her reflection in the mirror.

"Wow!" Sarah exclaimed, toppling a needleworked bag. "You would look just like a princess if you wore that pretty dress, Aunty Willow!"

Tanya looked at Willow and nodded. "You can have it."

Standing before the cheval mirror, Willow felt her breath catch slightly as she blinked at her sister. "I can *what?*"

"I said, You can have that cream muslin gown."

Willow gasped, "It looks like a wedding gown almost. I love it. Where would I wear it, though?"

Sarah said with a giggle, "You and Uncle Talon can get married again! Oh, wowee!" She jumped up and down on the bed amongst the beautiful things scattered everywhere.

Tanya didn't look too happy. "Sarah, You're messing things up and you're going to tear one of those delicate dresses or shawls."

"I'm sorry, Mommy." But Sarah was still grinning, with one finger touching her front teeth like an imp. "Do you want me to go downstairs and see if Miss Pekoe is going to make tea and cakes?"

"Yes, Sarah. That would be nice. Be a love now, and go so that Mommy and Willow can talk."

She bounced off the bed, sliding to the edge and coming up like a spring unsprung. "I'm going to go find Jorge, too!"

"No, Sarah!" cried Willow.

Tanya looked at Willow, her eyebrows raised. "What's *this* all about?" Tanya had known there was something troubling her sister, and she had wanted to talk, just waiting for Sarah to go downstairs. Willow had been watching Sarah like a hawk.

"Oh! I almost forgot," Sarah said, turning to her mother. "Aunty Willow doesn't want me to go out to the barn by myself. That's where Jorge is. She said I had to stay inside all day and sew. It's so nice outside, though. Is this some kind of secret? Are we going to have a party later?"

"Party?" Tanya thought that sounded like a good idea. She turned to Willow. "A party. Yes, Sarah. Go now. We have to . . . make plans for the party. Maybe." Tanya shook her head. "I'll think about it."

After Sarah had left, promising Willow she wouldn't go outside, Tanya went over and shut the door. She looked at the dark wood for several seconds before turning around to face her sister. "Now," she said, "what is this all about?"

"The dress first." Willow pointed. "I want to know why you want to get rid of such a beautiful gown. Does it have something to do with Ashe, sis? Did he buy it for you? Oh . . . I'll bet you were going to get married again, do it up big, huh?"

Tanya drew a deep breath, thinking of Ashe, of his tender endearments that last tragic morning, of the love she shared with him before he had been taken from her forever, his drowned body never recovered; she hadn't even been able to bring his body back from California and give Ashe a proper burial. Now there were only broken dreams and she had thought she would die with the pain of her aching heart. Yet, she thanked God for Almanzo every morning when she got up to face another day. He was so good to her.

"Yes, Willow. I was. I mean, Ashe and I had planned to do just that, have a second wedding. We . . . we never really had a proper wedding and it would have been so beautiful. It was what we both wanted, a wedding in springtime before . . . before he went away. Like Jasse says, To be with Jesus. Jasse is so good, Willow. She says I'll be with Ashe in heaven someday."

Willow grinned impishly. "With Almanzo, too? The *three* of you?"

Tanya glanced up, startled. "Willow! I . . . I never thought of such a thing."

Tanya's sister kept grinning as she pulled on the other long white glove. "I bet you did, Sis. Yup, I'll just bet those were your exact thoughts when Almanzo looked deeply into your eyes with those dark ones of his and said that he still loves you. Do you feel as if he can see into your soul when you meet his eyes?"

"Really, Willow, I don't think you should be so . . . so . . ." her voice trailed off in a whispery search for a word.

"Bold?" Willow giggled, then dropped her arms to her lap suddenly. "Sis, I have to talk to you about something real important. No one else can know about it, either."

"I knew it. I could tell you had something eating away at you and you just couldn't wait to tell me. Yet something is keeping you from telling me your secret. What's troubling you, Willow? You never could keep anything from your big sister. Spill the beans, come on."

Seated close to Tanya on the bed, Willow told her about the mysterious woman and what she wanted. Tanya looked angry, then alarmed. At last she gasped, "Willow, no one will take Sundance from us. They can't do that. This is Brandon land." She stared at her sister's bent head in growing concern. "This is awful. They have little Michael, these women?"

"Yes, women. Bad women, gold diggers. Not all men. Can you believe it? And I saw Mikey this morning by Strawberry Creek."

"You—*what?*" Tanya reached for the throat of her very proper blue-striped muslin. "I can't believe this is happening. You saw him? Your child, your son? You should have been able to take your own son." Tanya sounded flustered. "Why didn't you run after him, and, and . . . bring him home?"

"I could not. Because, dear sister, he was with *that* woman."

The little foxes, that spoil the vines.
—OLD TESTAMENT, *Song of Solomon*

Chapter Nineteen

In the predawn darkness, walking and feeling dejected, Willow paused on a small rise of hill. She was recalling the time she had lived in Black Fox's camp and Talon Clay—his Indian name was Lakota at that time—had made her a slave to Wolf-Eyes-Woman. She had had to fetch and carry until Talon's father, Nightwalker, had come along to rescue her. She had been furious at Lakota for his bad treatment and had stood at the cleft in the high wall overlooking the valley. She had gazed out over the uneven ripples of buffalo grass in the distance and the shrublike mesquite tree blowing gray-green beneath the October sun. Here was Comancheria! To the west, cacti had sprouted out of the sandy earth, their dangerously hard thorns and growths pointing in every direction like so many road signs gone crazy. Nightwalker, Talon Clay's real father, had told her that somewhere, way back, one of his great-great-grandmothers had been a white woman. She had been fair-haired like herself and Talon. She had had eyes as green as grass. Her name had been Helsi, and she had sailed from the Old World, only to be captured by a

Sioux chief. Talon's Indian ancestors had come from mixed breeds, brothers and sisters, cousins, uncles, and aunts of Nightwalker's. Nightwalker had added that they were not what was called "blue-blooded" and laughed.

As the sun rose above the horizon, Willow continued to walk up and down the little green hills of Sundance, recalling what she had said to Nightwalker after that. She had told Nightwalker that she loved her family back at Sundance very much ...

"Tanya, Sammy, myself, we are a mixture of the Scandinavian countries and some other nationality I can't remember. Blue-bloods are uppity anyhow, and I'm glad we're not like that. I would really dislike having to be totally English, you know, from England?" Nightwalker had nodded his understanding. "My sister Tanya, who has been to school in the East, says that the higher class people talk through the nose and peer down at you if you talk like you haven't attended some fancy finishing school. Reckon they'd really have a laugh if they tried to hold a conversation with the likes of me!"

Nightwalker had laughed at her youthful words, a happy sound that had rolled up from his deep chest. And then he had said something she would never forget, something she had never heard before she had come to Comancheria:

These roads that are away ahead will stay with me through life and after ...

Willow hugged her arms around herself and wished with all her heart that one day she and Talon Clay and baby Michael could be a family and live happily forever. But she feared that it wasn't to be. She and Talon had argued again this morning and the tensions were really riding high. He had shouted at her, *A branch that doesn't bend breaks.* What did he mean? It was more like *he* was that branch, Willow thought as she walked and walked, angry and tormented. Would they never be happy?

She knew one thing positively . . . and it filled every nerve in Willow's slender frame: She was going to get her child back and then they would take it from there!

One with the midnight wind, Willow rode fast on Breeze, galloped to a sudden halt, then slid down onto the soft, moist ground. She hid Breeze behind some scrubby bushes, then crept toward the house on the property of Saw Grass.

It was dark, but there were thousands of huge stars in the vast Texas sky. The moon had a misty halo circling it and it looked almost blue. The darkness was just what she needed to snoop on the Tuckers . . . and just maybe some other people, too!

There was *one* in particular Willow was hoping to see. Maybe two, but she had a sneaking suspicion that they did not keep Mikey here. She might be wrong about everything. Nat Lacey was probably hiding out somewhere else, not here at all. She still had that feeling that the woman was closer than she had at first believed.

This was dangerous work, she realized. And yet, the mystery had to be solved and she was relentlessly compelled to push ahead. She must start here, at Saw Grass, before she could move on to searching out other avenues that had gained her attention and curiosity. Like the old deserted line shack in the thick stand of trees on the southern edge of Saw Grass, which stood about a half-mile from the house itself and nowhere near Sundance property; that was way on the other side. Talon said he and the men had investigated the shack, but she wondered how many times and how often. It could be that the culprits were not always there, or they had a guard posted who was well concealed at some point. Next time she rode that way, she would not merely pass the secluded line shack by.

Willow had chosen Breeze for her late-night ride, since that horse was not likely to make any noise. Breeze was very quiet at night, unlike Star, Istas, Dove, Magic, or the others she usually rode. They snorted or made neighing sounds at the slightest nighttime noises.

Creeping toward the area surrounding the house and flattening herself against the first large cottonwood she came to, Willow listened for sounds that would alert her to anyone who was standing outside or walking from one building to another. Were her eyes playing tricks on her, or did she just see a shadow move behind her, Willow asked herself. A shadow, yes, like a huge black cat.

Instinctively, Willow swung to her left, for the sense of danger seemed to issue from that direction. And was that a hiss! She waited for another movement or sound. She had her Toledo steel knife. Endurance and cunning were her other weapons. She was pigheaded, too, loaded with patience and determination to discover her son's whereabouts.

About to move to another vantage point—an even larger cottonwood—and rigid with concentration, Willow found herself yanked back just as she was about to flee to the next tree. She tried to swallow but found her mouth was dry.

There was a man holding onto her! She had thought him a cat!

Dagblasted! She'd been caught!

About to turn toward her captor, Willow heard him mutter, "Do not faint this time. It is only me. I mean you no harm."

Hank Rountree. *Hawk!*

Peeling one hand from her waist, the other from her mouth, he smiled roguishly as Willow shook her head. "Why are you following me?" She glared at him in the dim moonlight, her mind still reverberating from the savage anticipation of danger. "Are you *crazy?* Where have you been? I haven't seen you at Sundance for several weeks. Why do you follow me now? *I thought you were a dangerous cat!*"

Pressing her to the tree as they heard a sound, Hawk whispered in Willow's ear, "I have been around. You just cannot see me all the time. I move with the shadows."

"There," Willow warned. "I see a man."

"I know he is there." She didn't have to warn him. "His name is Bob Fox. His cousin is Little Fox and a man named Winder."

"How do you know them?"

"I just do. You need not know how." Hawk's eyes narrowed into the darkness like probing black needles. "They work for these people."

"The Tuckers?" Willow was very curious now.

"Them. And others."

"You're just like Almanzo," she hissed into the dark surrounding them. "Have you met him?"

Hawk chuckled softly. "Of course. We have known

367

each other off and on for years. And no, I am not crazy."

"You still did not answer my first question, Hawk." She remembered that he liked being called Hawk. "Ouch, you're standing on my foot."

"Sorry."

"What, I asked, are you doing here?"

An oddly comforting smile curved lips unused to such exercise. "I am following you. This is true. I wanted to make sure you would be safe. I did kill a man for you once before. If I had not, he might have killed you. Now you are courting danger again. This time you could get into more trouble. Yes, even with your neighbors who you think are safe."

Willow almost snorted. She had never thought the Tuckers safe! "Them? Huh!"

"It is dangerous for you to ride out at night with so much danger around these parts."

The corner of Willow's mouth rose. *Now* he tells her. What about when she had ridden alone on the trail? Hadn't he thought of that? Then again, the old saying bore some truth at times, she supposed: *It is safer on the trail most times than it is close to your own home.* More dangerous things seem to happen on one's own property, or while visiting a neighbor. There were even . . . she hated to think it . . . *casualties.*

Willow almost laughed when Hawk looked at her so seriously. "Don't worry, Hawk." She pulled her gaze from the house. Saw Grass at night. She had never visited at night before. "Say, shouldn't you be out searching for your wife and children? Oh, that's right, you told me you've been searching far and wide."

How many secrets could she trust Hawk with? Would

he run to tell Talon if she let him in on the one about Nat Lacey and Mikey? Why was he still hanging around Sundance?

Oh Lordy! Nat Lacey. That was the name of the dance hall girl who had jilted Hawk! What to do? *What to do?* Should she speak?

"Hawk," she began slowly, trying to choose her words carefully, "Why are you still around Sundance? Is there some special reason? Or do you just like us?"

Hawk chuckled. "I like you. You are like no other woman. The others at Sundance are good people also. If I did not have a task I would go and look some more for my family. Right now I am watching out for you and *your* family." He looked forlorn. "Mine might be lost forever."

Hawk could get Mikey back for her! She knew he could. He was big and strong and wise. Then again, so was her husband, and Talon would not appreciate her choosing to tell Hawk first!

"Hawk," she again proceeded slowly. "How smart are you?" Her eyes met his under the midnight moonlight. "How much do you know?"

"More than you think, little one. The sheriff also knows much about me; I must walk my lonely trail with caution and quiet feet."

Willow whirled, her face alert, eyes darting around as her fear returned. Her voice was muffled to an intense whisper.

"Hawk! Wait; I have to tell you something."

"You may. Later."

With that, Hawk melted back into the shadows and she stood alone once again. She was looking at the

369

house, seeing no shadows indicating anyone moved about inside.

Then the shot rang out.

Willow was again riding as one with the wind. She kept glancing over her shoulder to see if Hawk was following. He was nowhere in sight. She was worried about him. Had he come by foot or horseback? She knew Indians could run far and not get tired. There had only been one shot. Had Hawk taken that bullet? Was he lying back there dead or dying, while she was running for her life?

Carefully, Willow turned her horse back.

Sneaking up, having left Breeze back several hundred yards, Willow heard men's voices. When she saw them, she halted in her creeping pace, catching a sudden shallow breath. They were walking around where she and Hawk had stood earlier, looking down at the ground. One man scuffled his boots in the dirt, as if covering up something. Willow waited, concealed in the scrubby bushes, hoping she had enough cover.

"Hey, Fox," one of the men said, "let's go. No one will be able to tell. We'll cover it up in the morning if there's any traces left."

Cover what up? Willow wondered. Blood? And whose blood? Hawk's?

After they left, Willow crept toward the area the men had been combing. Removing a pair of fawn colored gloves from her pocket, she donned them and pushed aside the dirt where they had done the covering up. The light of the pale silver moon couldn't tell her what that dark stain was on her fingers, but she was pretty sure it was, in fact, blood.

At home, on closer inspection under the light, Willow saw the dark red stains. She stared at it. *Hawk's blood.* What was she going to do now?

Tanya and Almanzo were out walking the gallery in the moonlight once again. "Look at me, Tanya." It was a beautiful night and he lifted her chin with a forefinger, delving into her gorgeous blue eyes. "I am not going to do anything you do not want me to. I just love to be with you." As he shrugged, he added, "Nothing more than to look into your eyes, hear you talk, see your smile, know that I can make you happy, somehow, some way."

Tanya did not believe all he said. Almanzo's eyes said so much more; she knew he wanted to claim her as his very own, intimately. "You are kind and generous to say these things, especially knowing as you do that my husband recently passed away. It has not been easy for me. I want to return your affection, but it is much too early. You look as if you don't think so. I love Ashe and always will, even though he has died. His spirit resides with me still."

"I am not asking you to forget your deceased love, Tanya. Only give me a chance to help you to heal. I want to do that very much. Do you think that I am completely over Kachina's passing? No, I am not. I still mourn every day. She was so beautiful and kind. I do not cut my flesh with a knife nor do I wail to the heavens. This I do not believe in." He smiled into her eyes gently. "I am not a crazy savage as you might have thought a few times in the past."

"I never thought that, Almanzo," she told him sweetly.

"I think you did. Your eyes spoke. When they called me Mustang Man and I rode in on my wild horse, you stood at the portal of Sundance and stared at me as if afraid. You had only seen me dressed as a *caballero* before. That other time I looked very much the savage; I was told this by other men."

How could she admit that yes, he made her afraid back then? And now? Ashe had never caused her to feel these wild sensations; with Almanzo, if she gave in she did not know how she would respond. But just what was it he would do with her? She would never make love without marriage vows.

Almanzo was reading her well. If he were to capture Tanya's heart, she would come to him with total abandonment. Her lovely blue eyes said much.

She was right, however. Though he had always loved her, he still retained a pure and holy remembrance of his and Kachina's love. Her memory had not dimmed; he only loved Kachina more in her passing. This did not mean he couldn't love another with his heart as fully as he loved the Indian woman. As for loving with their bodies, it was too soon; a year would be proper to pass in mourning before anything took place.

"We will always be friends, Almanzo." She laughed softly and took his hand. "You have made me feel secure; I hope you never have to leave."

"I will stay always, Tanya. Always, for you." He hugged her around the waist and pulled her toward the house. "I have to go out to the range and stay with the new cattle tonight; I don't want any more to get stolen than already has been. First, we will go and find that playful daughter of yours and see if she will read to us again. It is very romantic to hear her read from the Book of Solomon."

Tanya laughed. "I know."

If not ever to be lovers, Tanya and Almanzo realized they would always remain best of friends. All they needed now was to help each other heal. They would not forget their dearly departed but relieve the intense sadness by gently remembering the happier times.

At the moment, if they knew what Tanya's sister was up to, they would be terribly alarmed at her daring deeds of the evening!

A liar needs a good memory.
                    —*Quintilian*

Chapter Twenty

Hawk had been shot!

What now? Willow hurried along, a soft breeze lifting the tendrils of hair that had escaped from the single blond braid extending down her back. She knew she couldn't just leave it at that. How to—? *Almanzo—he would help!* Jesse, too, and Frank, the two newer ranch hands. She couldn't enlist her husband's help. If she did and Lacey found out, she'd harm or kill Talon or do something awful to her son. Willow knew she had been warned and better tread carefully with that pit viper!

She had to keep her secret from Talon Clay.

Hurrying to the little house on the other side of the main dwelling, splashing across the creek and trudging up the small hill, Willow threw open the door. She remembered the night she had ridden in, dusty and weary, flinging herself on the bed where Talon had found her and joined her in a night of ecstasy.

She hoped he wouldn't find her again! At least, not until she had gotten this dangerous task over and done.

Willow walked through the few rooms, seeing the puncheon bench drawn up in front of the fire they'd made on chilly evenings. She knew the crane would still squeak if she swung the heavy pot or kettle off the fire. If there was a fire. And if there was soup.

Getting everything ready and the bed made, Willow hurried to find Almanzo, and, for some reason, she decided not to enlist the aid of the two broncbusters, Jesse and Frank.

When all was done she went to the barn. She mounted Breeze and rode to find Almanzo, knowing he had stayed out on the range with the new cattle that had been purchased that spring. She found him just coming up out of his bedroll.

"Almanzo!" she said excitedly. "You have to help." She spread her ungloved hands. "Please. Come with me. It's very important."

"What is it, little one?" His dark eyes took in her disheveled appearance and the lavender blur under her lower lids, revealing that she was stressed and needed sleep badly. "Ah, something is wrong? Have you been out looking for your son without telling Talon Clay?"

"No, Almanzo. At least, not in the past several hours. Something else has come up." She saw that dawn was just lighting the eastern edge of sky to a glowing orange in the distance. "You have to come. This time it's Hawk. He's been shot."

Willow and Almanzo crept up to the place where she had heard the shot ring out. "It happened here. I know someone shot Hawk . . . there, *there,* is the blood!"

"Hush." Almanzo turned to her with his finger to his mouth. "Someone is going to hear."

"You're darn tootin' someone is!"

Whirling to face an angry-looking Talon Clay, Willow found all she could do was gulp at the fierce look of him. His eyes were like green fire. His jaw was rigid. His shoulders squared hard ... and his hands were clenched into fists.

"What the hell is going on here?" Talon ground out between his teeth, shoving aside the plumelike branches of a willow tree. "I wake up and find my sneaky little wife has left again. What are you doing now, may I ask?" His green eyes smoldered as he looked straight at her.

Willow's gaze fell to Talon's tough, stony thighs, and for a moment she recalled a day not too long ago when he'd thrust her against the wall and made wild, passionate love to her. Her voice, when it emerged, was wavering and uncertain. "L-Looking for blood."

"Blood?" Talon swept an arm wide, indicating the dawning orange-pink sky as he stared at Willow poised in the shadows. "At this time of morning, you're looking for ... *blood?*" Then he became alarmed and his heart gave a jolt against his ribs. "Lord, don't tell me it's Mikey's blood."

With her next breath stuck in her throat, Willow peered at the wild look of Talon Clay. What was she going to tell him now? She'd have to fabricate something, because she surely was not going to tell him the whole truth. "I ... I thought I saw Jorge running down the lane in the moonlight and, and, I got dressed and hurried out the house to go catch him. I was afraid maybe Sarah was running with—"

"Stop!" Talon Clay held up his hand. The cords were standing out in the weathered, tanned column of his neck. "That is a fairy tale if ever I heard one. Come on, Willow, can't you make up a better one?"

"Dagblasted, Talon Clay! We can't just stand here jawin' like this while a man could be bleeding to death . . . where is Sammy?" Willow craned her neck; she was worried about her brother being the next one bush-whacked by a bullet. "I thought I saw him behind you just a moment ago?"

"Yeah, he's with me," Talon said, and, flatly ignoring her indignant outburst, he went on to fire at her, "Now what's this all about." His look went to his Indian friend. "Almanzo, you know what's going on?"

All of a sudden Sammy appeared. "I been searching the area after you mentioned blood. There's a trail here . . . it goes—" Sammy pointed suddenly—"over there!"

They stared collectively at the huge old barn leaning sadly to one side, as if it had been in this condition for years. Talon knew it had; he'd slept in it many a time when he had lived with the Tuckers. Now there was a trail of blood leading up to it!

Kicking her boot around in the decomposed foliage, Willow looked down at the freshly coagulated blood. She shuddered and looked up to see Talon staring at her. And then she saw *them* out of the corner of her eye.

"Look there!" Willow hissed into the predawn light, her breath coming out in cool, airy puffs. "Those men, they're trying to cover up the trail."

Feeling a steely grip on her shoulders, Willow looked back to see Talon, his mouth a tight line. "Whose blood, Willow?"

She gulped. "Hawk. It's his blood."

His eyes narrowed; there was no time to question her further. "Hawk's blood? You certain of that?"

She nodded, saying, "Pretty sure." It must be, but she wasn't going to tell Talon all of it now.

His grip was still on Willow's shoulders as Talon breathed in her ear the words she'd been so afraid she'd hear: "Does this have anything to do with our son?"

"That's what I'm trying to find out, Talon." Well, that was the truth!

"I thought so."

Taking his gun from his holster, Talon moved slowly and cautiously toward the back of the dilapidated barn. Even more carefully and quietly, Almanzo trailed on Indian-light feet.

Willow stayed behind with Sammy. She'd seen the warning in Talon Clay's eyes—and she didn't want to push her luck!

Hawk was waiting for any one of the gunslingers to come back inside the barn. He was ready for them this time. There was a knife concealed beneath his pants, tied with a leather thong to his leg, and he had freed himself from the ropes they had bound about his ankles and wrists. Stupid men! They hadn't even frisked him down to see if he carried a weapon.

He had lost a lot of blood, but thank God he could still understand what had happened and what was going on, and why they had left him to bleed to death. Why hadn't they seen Willow? Or had they spotted her standing near that cottonwood and captured her? Did they have her even now? He didn't think so, or else they would have been talking about her, while he lay here quietly making them believe he was unconscious. The words they had spoken as they gathered around a small lantern did not make much sense to him. But he knew this one thing: If he did not get away soon they would come back to kill him.

I am ready for you, Hawk was chanting to himself. The first one that entered was going to receive a surprise—a deadly one!

Creeping into the barn cautiously after crawling inside an opening barely large enough for him to squeeze through, Talon Clay made his way on cat feet. He could see Hawk lying stiffly on a pile of hay, and there were trickles of blood making a trail, looking like red needles in a haystack poking out every which way.

Just as Talon neared the haystack, Hawk leaped from the bloody bed and came at Talon with a wickedly shining blade. "I have you now. You will not escape. *Aiyeee!*" His cry sang low as he flew at a man he thought was coming to kill him.

"Oh God—he thinks—" Talon didn't finish, all he saw was the blonde come slashing toward his throat. Hawk was good and if he didn't get out of the way of that slashing knife he was going to be dead meat. *"Unnngh!"* Talon leapt out of harm's flashing silver path. "Hawk . . . it's me! Hank . . . Hank Rountree . . . me . . . Talon Clay . . . *Ow!*"

Hawk blinked. Talon Clay? He bent down as Talon flew to get out of his way and went spinning at the haystack; he bumped it hard, holding onto his bloodied arm. Hawk caught one of Talon's knees as it rose to jab him in the groin by accident.

"Hawk! *Eiy!* Rountree!" Almanzo yelled as he made it through the opening just in time to see Hawk peering down at the slash he had made through Talon Clay's red checkered shirt. "You have the wrong man!"

All three whirled at the same time as they heard the four men crashing through the doors, coming at them with guns flashing from their holsters in the lantern light. Talon, Almanzo, and Hawk hit the chaffy floor. What ensued as the gunslingers kept coming was the mightiest fistfight ever as Talon prepared to relieve them of their weapons. Talon chose the biggest attacker, and the two men struggled, slamming, crushing, and battering each other, while Almanzo and Hawk took on the other three.

Bob Fox stared at Talon Clay with hatred in his eyes as they broke apart for a second. He despised anything to do with Texas Rangers; he knew Talon Clay Brandon was one and he was going to kill him if he could. Just then he saw the blonde burst into the huge barn and his eyes glittered with lust. She was a pretty piece, Bob thought, and if he could do away with the Brandon man and his companions he would be that much farther ahead in helping Garnet get what she wanted—and what he was beginning to want. He would be paid handsomely by his Boss Lady.

"You killed Carl Tucker!" Bob Fox hissed, his voice thick with anger.

"No!" Willow cried, seeing the extra weapon Fox had swiftly whipped from his belt. She ran toward him at an angle, to keep his attention away from Talon Clay. Bob flung her aside like a toy, sending her crashing to the floor. "She was good when I had 'er."

Talon was in a rage now. Willow had struck her head

on an iron farm implement and lay quietly, her blond braid sticking out at a crazy angle. Her mouth twitched and then she moved no more.

"Bastard! Lying, no good bastard!" Talon flew at Fox. He lashed out with his fist, catching Fox flush in the face so that he staggered back and fell. Talon walked over to him.

Bob Fox was mad now. It didn't matter that he had been bested before by Texas Rangers. This slim, furious Ranger before him had called him everything he hated in himself, and had knocked him down, to boot.

With a growl of rage, Fox got to his feet and faced Talon. "I know where your kid is, Brandon, and you're never goin' to see him alive again. You kill me and you'll never know where to find him. You could try to make me talk, but I'd rather die than tell you sonofabitchin' Rangers anything." He heard the blonde moan and try to sit up. "How does she compare to her mother in the sack, huh, Brandon?"

At that moment Talon struck out again with the swiftness of a snake's tongue, and again Fox went down. Talon leaped on top of him and they became a tangle of flailing arms and legs. It was a bitter fight, with no cursing, no sound except the grunting and the smack of fists on flesh. Even the others had stopped fighting to watch.

Talon fought like a maniac. No one dared touch his wife! Astraddle Fox, he slugged blow after blow into Fox's face, until that giant of man, goaded to desperation, heaved himself to his feet, shaking Talon off. His face was bloody, and there was the light of murder in his eyes.

Fox tried to clinch with Talon, and in angry contempt, Talon let him. They wrestled, locked in an iron embrace, but Talon pumped a dozen blows into Fox's midriff before the bigger man wanted to break. But Talon would not let him break; he followed him with implacable anger, his lean shoulder muscles corded with the overhand blows he looped into Fox's face. And with the blind anger of a bull, Fox fought back. When one of his ponderous blows landed, it would lift Talon off his feet and set him back a yard, but each time Talon would charge anew, fighting with the deadly fury of a Ranger gone mad.

"Talon!" Willow screamed as she gained her foothold; the lantern Fox had been carrying was toppled and the fire spread in the puddle the spilled oil had formed.

"Get out ... G-get out!" Talon shouted, his breath coming in short gasps.

Round and round the fire they circled now, and it was Fox, in spite of superior weight, who was giving ground. With the dogged bewilderment of a cornered bear backing from hounds, he tried to protect himself, but couldn't. His slowness left him prey to Talon's lightning blows, and as each one landed on his raw face, he staggered more heavily.

In one last rally, he lowered his head, braced his feet in the dirt-and-chaff floor, and slugged wildly at the marauding figure before him. Another bale of hay caught fire just then, but Talon, blind with rage, drove blow after blow at those thick, protecting arms, and then in a fury of frustration, he dived in and clinched with Fox. The big man wrapped his arms around Talon, trying to smother him, but Talon, legs braced broadly, hunched his shoulders and heaved mightily. Fox left the ground, and still heaving, Talon toppled him over backwards. Almost before Fox sprawled on his back, Talon was at him again, straddling him. Time after time, his fists raised as if he were pounding with a hammer, Talon slugged down at that face.

"Talon!" Willow screamed, trying to stop him. The fire was spreading and getting closer all the time.

"I said . . . get the heck out . . . Willow!"

"I never listen, Talon, remember?" But she knew *he* was not listening to *her*. He was angry and frustrated— this man Fox had said the wrong thing about their child and about herself! She hoped and prayed he would not slay the man, even though Fox was no good.

Abruptly, Fox's arms ceased to move and sank down by his side, but still Talon kept hitting him, his blows hard and savage, merciless, countless. At last, struggling and cursing and kicking, he had to be dragged off by Almanzo and Hawk, who had a hard time holding him until he came to his senses and calmed down. Talon stood there, weaving on his feet, his shirt torn to ribbons, his face bloody, his body bruised and battered. Bob had given a good fight.

But Fox was completely out. His cousin Little Fox slapped him, punched him, rolled his head, but the man remained limp as a rag. Little Fox, who was not so little at all, looked over at the Ranger. "You have killed him. You have killed my cousin."

"The fire's spreading!" Willow shouted, wondering if all the men had gone mad. "Get him out! Stop standing around and get everyone out!" She coughed and choked in the noxious smoke and flame.

Talon Clay shouted, "Get the bastard to his feet."

Willow ran outside to the spring and filled her hat with water and brought it back. She doused water in Fox's face. Still he did not move. "Lord, I think he might be dead." She coughed again and Talon grabbed her arm when she gagged from the acrid smoke, shoving her outside. "Forget the bastard. He's one of the men who kidnapped our son! Damn it, Willow! Stop looking out for crazy sonofabitches and think about us!"

"What is that supposed to mean?" she snapped back, her fiery face illuminated to a red hue.

Inside the barn Fox moaned. With his arm flung up, Almanzo stood up and backed off, and slowly Fox rose to a sitting position. For a long minute, while the rest of them watched him, Bob Fox stared at the fire with the glassy eyes of a man who is only partially conscious.

Talon ran over to a window-like opening that gave his eyes a better view than the blazing door.

"You're right," Talon told Willow, seeing the man being helped to his feet. "I need him alive to lead me to our son."

"Us, Talon, lead *us.*" She watched him climb in through the huge square, wondering if he had gone crazy.

Talon strode over to Fox and hoisted him to his unsteady feet. What clothes were remaining on Fox were covered with blood and soot. His face was distorted with welts and bruises, and his lips were shapeless ribbons of flesh. Talon slapped him in the face until he flinched and raised an arm, then Talon released him and backed off. Soon they had moved Fox out into the yard. Talon was about to say something when he heard a woman's voice.

"Put out the fire, boys!"

Everyone turned to see the woman with the shotgun hoisted to her shoulder. Garnet walked down from the wooden stairs and stopped in the middle of the yard.

She jerked her head when the three remaining men hopped to her command at last.

"Nat Lacey," Willow said. "I knew it, just knew her hidey-hole was over here at Saw Grass."

Tearing his eyes from the woman with the low-brimmed hat, Talon looked at Willow. "What are you talking about? You know this woman, Willow?"

"Sure do." She tore her eyes from the woman with the shotgun. "I might as well tell you. You're going to find out anyway."

"Do not!"

Willow jerked her head toward Hawk. "No?" Did he say *Do not?* She studied Hawk and tried to find the reason for his outburst. She saw nothing but a stoic Indian face.

"No," he said. "You have no idea."

Blinking at that, Willow turned back to Talon. What was she supposed to say now? Hawk was warning her to remain silent. But silent about what? How much did Hawk know? Had he been searching things out while he'd been sneaking around Sundance, never in plain view?

"What's this all about and what did Hawk say?" Talon snapped at Willow. "Where's my son?" He jerked his head. "Who's this woman?"

Hawk watched them. Little did they know that he had been guarding and watching out for their son, keeping him from coming to harm. He had tracked their movements like six Indians instead of one. This had been the Indian name of his childhood: Little Six. There was not a move the outlaws made without him knowing. Michael had been safe all this time in the line shack, but his parents had not known anything. He had tried to slow Willow's movements this very night.

And it was too soon to let them in on the secret just yet. Hawk was biding his time. When everything was resolved and Michael was safe, he would move on. His task in the White Man's Walk was soon over. The bad men had done away with the real Nat Lacey. He had watched as the man Bob Fox and his cousin Little Fox had slain her. They had been worse than Indians in their killing. They had enjoyed watching her suffer. She had lived a bad life and had perished without mercy, for she had shown no one else this in her life. She had destroyed the lives of happily married couples. She had even confessed to him after they had made love that she had once buried a rabbit alive and dug it up when it was dead. Her death in the river had not been less merciless; they had cut her to doll rags and let her blood run fast. First Bob and Little Fox had violated her. When they had left her for the vultures Hawk had taken her body and buried it. Then he had prayed over the grave that his wife and children would be returned by the Great Spirit. A life of a bad woman for three lives. His sin with the woman had been paid for dearly and thoroughly. Now he must not interfere with others' Walk-in-Life.

Just as Talon was about to come closer to the woman with the shotgun, she re-hoisted the long gray object to her shoulder. "Come any closer, dude, and I'll blow your handsome head to smithereens!"

Talon halted and stood staring at the woman. There was something familiar about her. What had Willow called her? Lacey? He hadn't caught the first name.

"Get off Saw Grass," she ordered, shifting her eyes to

the man whose name she knew was Desert Hawk. "You, too."

Hawk knew her real name, but he was not about to correct her and spoil the woman's game. No. He wanted her to fall into a trap of her own making: many outlaws wanted her—to die.

"Where are the Tuckers?" Talon asked the woman. "And who are these men?"

"What's it to you?" Garnet asked. "You a Ranger or something?"

"Yup. That's just what I am. And I'll just bet you know it, too. That and a lot of other things." His gaze slid over to the gunmen putting out the last of the fire; the barn had been damaged badly and no doubt would fall in at any moment. "I aim to find out what's going on around here." He wiped his bleeding nose on his red-checked sleeve.

The woman with the shotgun sneered. "Go right ahead, lawman. Your friend Hank Rountree was snooping around here and I told my men to get him. Of course, I didn't know it was Hank at the time. Your wife was snooping, too; did you know that?" She glanced at Willow and insinuated, "They must have come here together."

"We did not!" Willow exploded, shoving a strand of hair out of her eyes. Her eyes were "talking," asking *Where is my son? What have you done with him?* But she couldn't actually say it. Hawk had warned her.

Again the woman with the shotgun addressed Hawk. "I know you. You've done some jobs for me. Don't think I can't remember back that far. You all better hightail it out of here—before you bleed to death all over my yard!"

"Where are the Tuckers?" Talon pressed. *"Your yard?"*

"As long as they're gone, it is. Gone to New Orleans. Visitin' with some folks there. None of your business, Ranger so you and your family just better mosey along."

Talon knew a liar and a cheat when he saw one. "Just got to get my gun. Lost it in the tussle."

"I said, *Get your butt going.*"

Daringly, Willow ran over and snatched a gun from the ground. She held it up. "This yours, Talon?"

"Yup. That's it."

"Then let's go." She tossed her head. "It's way past breakfast time and I'm starving!"

Talon turned once before they departed, his voice a deep growl. "Better show up with my son by sundown or else the sheriff will be knocking at your door tomorrow—" Suddenly he shook his aching head distractedly—"Whoever the heck you really are—" Under his breath he said, *"Some* animal's mother."

Garnet watched them go into the cottonwoods and fetch their horses. When she heard the departing tattoo of hooves she went to find Winder and the Foxes.

It was time to do some more dirty work *and* find out who else had been snooping around Saw Grass!

The wild hawk stood with the
  down on his beak,
And stared, with his foot on the
  prey.
                    —*Alfred, Lord Tennyson*

Chapter Twenty-One

Willow had planned to bring Hawk to the little house so he could recuperate there if he had been shot bad. It was Talon who needed the nursing, however; he could hardly walk when they returned to Sundance. He was bloody and bruised. Willow cleaned him up, fed him soup, kissed his weary face, and then put him to bed. He held her hand as he was falling asleep. She tiptoed out, knowing he needed the rest more than she. He had fought so hard and valiantly for her honor.

She sat up with Hawk and Almanzo in the kitchen, on the puncheon benches, and decided to stay with them until it was time to go to bed. "Are you sure that gunshot wound doesn't need tending?" she asked Hawk.

"It's only a flesh wound," he replied. "I have to be going."

Almanzo said, "For a flesh wound you bleed like a stuck pig." He laughed.

"I had too much blood, I guess."

Tanya walked in, carrying two baskets of food. "Tell me all that has happened. I don't want to miss a thing." She began to place the food on plates, knowing

Almanzo's eyes followed her every move. "I've brought fried chicken, buttered biscuits, and just about everything else you can imagine."

The men ate hungrily while Willow, nibbling a few bites, related the happenings of the night before and that morning. "I'm going to see if Talon wants a chicken leg. I heard him stirring in the bedroom."

"Leave him be," Almanzo said. "You should go to bed. You have not slept in a day."

"I can't. I was going to, but I'm worried now and won't be able to sleep. Do you think Mikey will be returned?" She told them about the times she had met "Nat Lacey" by the creek out back of Le Petit, deciding it was safe to tell it now because everyone seemed to know. "She warned me not to tell anyone or else something would happen to Talon or Mikey."

"She sounds terrible!" Tanya exclaimed. "What kind of a woman would be so cruel? We should get the sheriff to bring a posse over there."

"What are they going to do?" Almanzo asked. "Go there and kill them all for doing bad things to people and hiding the boy? This is kidnapping, true, but who can prove it? Then there will be no one to tell what happened to the boy if we get them taken care of so soon."

Hawk sat still. He wanted to speak but he could not say anything. It was not time. The woman who *called* herself Nat Lacey had to be caught, alive. She was Garnet Haywood—and she had a big secret. It must be learned so that others would not suffer from her hatred and deceit; this woman was sly and had escaped before; he had learned much listening outside doors. Also, there were others in her gang that needed to be found out. *All of them,* he thought with steely determination, *or no one at all.* "I will go now," he said, rising from the bench. "I have to be outside."

Talon Clay could finally walk back to Le Petit without wincing in pain if he rose and tried to move. At home, dark oak in the Spanish style, large, deep chairs, and cream-white drapes gave him a cheery welcome. He sank into one of those chairs after lying abed in the guest room downstairs. Willow had napped a while and was wearing her amber India lawn dress, remembering how often her husband had said, "I love you in that dress."

They were waiting. Waiting for the woman to bring their son back to them.

The hours ticked along. And so did the muscle in Talon Clay's cheek.

Talon got up and paced every time the old grandfather clock in the hall began a new hour, then sat for a spell. Suddenly he snarled, "Damn and tarnation! Why am I pacing and sitting when my son is out there somewhere and I finally know who's got him. I have to do something about it." He slapped his knees and jumped up. "Ouch!" he cried and winced. "I'm not going to do this anymore. I'm through waiting."

"Sammy!"

Talon turned to look at Willow, then he realized what had alarmed her so. "Sammy. Lordy be, he never returned with us." Talon ran his hands through his hair. "He disappeared. He was with me this morning, wasn't he?"

"Of course. I saw him. He was right behind you. Where do you think he is now?"

"I'll just bet they took him prisoner." Talon raced across the room for his gun and shell-belt, grimacing at his bruises all the way. "I'm going to town to contact some of my Ranger buddies."

"Talon—you can't go to town!" Willow hurried toward him, putting a hand on his arm. "Most of the Rangers have joined the war. You haven't joined because you're searching for your son. Besides, you don't have to go if you don't want to." She prayed that he would not leave her again.

"Oh, sweet love." His hand pressed her cheek tenderly. "I'd never leave you. You're right, this is an emergency and my family needs me more right now. I'm going to give up Rangering to stay home and run a ranch. Shoot, we got two houses to keep up now. And the little house needs some fixin' up, too: the roof leaks, the doors and windows sag, and much more."

"We'll need to sell some things because—" Her eyes widened. "Where is Tanya getting her money? Has she tried selling horses to the Army?"

"Don't get so excited, Willow. Almanzo and myself, we're taking care of everything. I got plenty in 'special' banks all over Texas. You worry too much. No, you're not going to talk me out of it this time. I'm going over to Saw Grass, not to town just yet. This is downright crazy. There's got to be someone, like the Sheriff, who can help us. I'd like to go over and kill the woman myself!"

Willow hated seeing Talon this helpless. Yet, there wasn't much they could do. So many had joined the war. The nearby towns were almost deserted, young men and old. The law was busy with this or that. What they needed was a huge posse, to surround the outlaws.

"I'm not going to war, Willow. Remember I said that and stop frowning."

"Talon, I'm not going to stop you if you want to join Terry's Rangers." She smiled winsomely. "Just promise one thing."

"What's that, my love?"

"You won't go until our son is back home again."

Talon shook his blond head. "Don't you know I promised you that weeks ago? Where have you been? I know it's been a terrible strain on you. It has on me, too."

"Talon, if you try to get Mikey back, she might do something to harm him before you can get to him."

"I realize that." Talon put his gunbelt on. "Where do you think they might be keeping him?" He didn't mention to her how familiar the woman had been to him, merely because he was afraid he might have been abed with her in one of the whorehouses he used to frequent.

Just then Almanzo burst in the front door; he hardly ever entered by the front. Most of the wranglers came to the back when they wanted to speak with Talon Clay. So he was really in a big hurry, they could tell.

"There's trouble." Almanzo was already reaching for Talon's leather vest from the hook; he handed it to him. "You'll need this."

"Right. I can put extra bullets in the pockets."

Dumbstruck, Willow watched them go. "Don't forget to find out about Sammy!" she called after them. Turning away from the door, she dropped her jaw. "Lordy, am I in a dither! What am I doing?" She ran to grab a jacket, since the afternoons were growing a bit cooler. "There's trouble—? *What* trouble?!"

Whirling, Willow clamped her jaw shut, grabbed a bridle, and went after Breeze in the corral.

"What did you say?" Willow leaned across her saddle to tap Almanzo when Talon paid her no mind. "What did he say? Something about Sarah?"

Talon was talking to the men he'd formed into a searching party, ordering half of them into the southern branch of woods, while the others would take the northern hills to search out every hill and cranny. He and Almanzo would take the east and west forks of the creeks.

"What's happened?" Willow snapped, becoming impatient and angry. Her voice rose to a very high pitch. "Would somebody please tell me? What's this about Sarah? And did I hear someone mention Jorge?"

"Calm down, Willow," Talon said, then did a double take. "What are you doing here, woman?"

"Shut up, Talon." Willow's jaws were clenched so hard she could have cracked nuts with her teeth. "If you or someone else doesn't tell me something I'm going to scream at the top of my lungs!"

Nudging each other, Frank and Jesse chuckled. On the inside, however, they were deeply anxious at this change of events. Exchanging significant eye contact, they decided what to do. Frank nodded and jerked his head.

"Sarah is missing. Tanya said she's been gone since early this morning." Talon grimaced as he twisted in his saddle, then frowned when he saw Tanya riding their way, dressed in Western gear. They hadn't seen her on a horse in a long while and she looked beautiful and determined. Talon's brow lowered as he asked, "What are you doing here, Tanya? We can take care of this. You women go on back to the house and wait. We'll get Sarah back in no time. She went chasing that big mutt is all."

"Really?" Tanya's tawny brows rose as her gaze swept around. "Why do you need all these men then? Just to find a girl and a dog?" Her blue eyes narrowed. "I'm going looking for my daughter and no man is going to stop me."

Willow gasped. "Wait! Sarah has been gone all day, you say?"

"Yes," Tanya said, her voice quavering.

"Wait here," Willow said, turning her horse. "I'm going to find Juanita and ask her if she's seen the dog. She was supposed to watch Jorge and feed him, but she didn't like it that he was kept in the barn."

"I've already questioned Juanita," Tanya said, her jaw squared in frustration. "She knows nothing. But she almost fainted at the news."

Frank kept a deadpan expression. He was not telling anyone he had let the dog out himself. He knew he had started something that might have some pretty nasty consequences, all because he felt sorry for the dog whining to get out—and now the girl had followed him. Little Sarah had mentioned something about "Mikey and Jorge" to old Clem. Did the dog have something to do with the boy his boss was holding? If that was the case, he was in deep horsetucky.

"Come on, Tanya, let's go!" Willow called to her sister, tossing her head with fire in her eyes, defying any man to try and stop them. "We must find Sarah before she ends up like Mikey! Maybe we'll find Jorge and Sarah in the same place!"

Oh-oh, Frank thought. He looked at Jesse, who just shook his head. Their gooses just might be cooked now—and real good.

"Damn it, Willow!" Talon shouted, whipping his hat off. "You come back here, woman!" He cursed loudly. "Women. Don't they ever think before they jump right in?"

Almanzo chuckled. "Now they have *two* heads instead of one."

"Let's go!" Talon shouted, then stopped at the ring of men looking at the master of Sundance. "What are you men sitting around with your rumps growing cobwebs on your saddles for? Let's get the hell going!"

When the first blast of the shotgun came rocketing out of the dusk into the back yard, Winder heaved to his feet, a pack of cards still clenched in his left fist. "That's a shotgun," he murmured in the dark cabin. He looked out the window, saw movement in the area of the scrubby pines, and, pulling his gun from its holster, he raced to the little room below, Little Fox behind him.

"The kid's still sleepin'," he whispered. He looked out the window again and in the half-light, he could make out a figure on the far right side of the pines. "Look, there's another one. This one's ridin' . . . I think."

Little Fox saw a lighter patch in the darkness. It was the rider's face as he looked over his shoulder. "Who is it?"

"You mean 'they.' Looks like women to me."

"Naw. It couldn't be women."

"Could it be Garnet?"

"Naw. She's back at Tucker's, sleeping. This is more than one. The Tucker women went to N'Orleans." He blinked eyes as black as his soul. "Why'd she shoot in the air out back?"

"Make us scairt, that's why." Winder spat onto the wood-and-dirt floor. "Maybe they'll go away if we don't say anything."

"I'd like to have a woman."

"What for, Foxy? To kill or to jump 'er bones?" Winder hee-hawed.

"Hey, be quiet, you're gonna wake the kid."

"Where's Ned Thomas? Wasn't he supposed to be coming out here to spell one of us?"

"It's Ned *Thompkins,* Foxy."

"Don't call me Foxy. I'm Little Fox." He thumped his chest importantly. "Listen, the boy's awake. Things are getting bad for us. I should take the boy to the village where I grew up. The chief would pay me real good for a handsome lad like this."

"No, damn it! Garnet would slice you—and me—into tiny pieces."

Little Fox guffawed. "She is only a woman. Just like those two out there. I know who these women are. I have spied on them. Just yesterday morning, she came to Saw Grass."

"Yeah? You thinks that's her out there?"

"I do. I believe I see yellow hair in the half-light that comes before dark."

Little Fox spoke again, "Look! Something is happening! Who is that rider? Is it ... Ned Thomas."

"*Thompkins,* I told you."

"Tanya, what are you doing with that shotgun?" Willow asked, trying to catch her breath after the blast. "You'll only alert them."

"I want them to know I'm coming and I want my daughter."

"Oh, there's a rider coming. No, Tanya, what are you doing? Don't shoot . . . Tanya, you don't know who it is!"

"It's not one of our horses, I can see that. This man passed our house before and he was snooping around."

In the still seconds that dragged by, Willow knew Tanya was making her calculations. She was on fire with fear and anger and hatred.

"Tanya . . . no!"

Willow tried knocking the shotgun from Tanya's hands, but she had already pulled the trigger. The shotgun made a violent blossom of orange in the semi-dark, and the horse's knees folded; he fell with a violence that caused the ground to thud like thunder. The rider was thrown forward over his mount's neck and he landed heavily on all fours, not thirty feet from the line shack. The horse's hindquarters swung up in a crazy cartwheel of momentum and then crashed across the rider's boots, pinning him to the ground. The horse rolled onto the rider and no sound escaped the man.

"He's been crushed!" Willow cried, trying to take the shotgun away from Tanya, but she held fast.

"I'm going to get them all, Willow. Otherwise they will wipe us from the grounds of Sundance, every last one of us."

Willow gulped. "You don't know what you're saying,

400

sis. It's all been too much for you. First Ashe, then hearing abut my son. Now your own Sarah disappears. But I think she only chased Jorge and got lost. Let's go back, Tanya, I think you've killed that man. In fact, I think I should go see."

"No, Willow, look!" Tanya whispered in a hiss, grabbing for Talon's shirt Willow wore over her dress. "There's a man coming out of the shack."

"He's going to shoot. Tanya, let's go!"

The shot rang out and Willow ducked, grabbing Tanya's shoulder and making her sink down as they rode beneath the pines, trying to get away before another bark resounded from the man's weapon. Running their horses back the way they'd come, Willow was the first to slow Breeze down to a trot.

"This is becoming all-out war," Tanya said, putting another slug into her shotgun. Pa's own shotgun, she thought. Tears sprang to her eyes. She'd almost shot Ashe—or wanted to—that day he'd come back to Sundance as a Texas Ranger.

Willow laughed. "You're making it a bigger war, Tanya. You're the first one who shot. You know, I think that was Ned Thompkins you shot. He was nice to me when I rode with the Green Mountain bunch."

"Oh, sure. And he was taking you to the Boss Lady who would have used you for a hostage, too!"

Hostage, Willow thought. Why hadn't Nat Lacey done that? She could have had her kidnapped that day all the men had surrounded her. And yesterday when . . . no, today . . . this morning, when she had brought help to Hawk. How long ago it seemed. They could have shot all of them. Oh . . . no, then they would not have gotten the deed without having to tear the whole house apart.

"Tanya. Lordy, I bet the deed is in the secret room at Sundance. All I have to do is bring it to Nat Lacey and she'll give Mikey to me—and Sarah, if she's got her now, too."

"Oh no, Willow. Ashe boarded up that room, that wall with the secret room in it. I mean, he wainscotted over that."

Willow's eyes twinkled mysteriously. "Yes— but he didn't do it over the fireplace!"

"The secret room is behind there?"

"Of course, Tanya. Think. Remember my telling you about it and all the pretty dresses of our mother's I found in there, along with the locket?"

"Garnet." Tanya frowned. "Our mother."

"I don't think so," said a male voice.

Tanya and Willow gasped. Turning their horses at the same time, Willow and Tanya stared at a man who was bleeding all over himself. His face was bruised and his eye swollen almost entirely closed.

"Ned?" Willow said. "Is it you?"

"It's me." He looked at the gorgeous redhead. "Why did you shoot me?"

Tanya bit her lip. "I'm sorry. I don't know you and— well, I'm looking for my daughter and if you're part of this gang, then you should be dead!"

He smiled weakly and looked to Willow. "What I said regarding Garnet, I meant."

"You said *I don't think so.* What did you mean?"

"Yes," Tanya said breathlessly. "What were you going to add? It's about our mother."

"Again," he said. "I don't think so."

"She's not our mother?" Willow asked excitedly.

Just then a gun exploded and Ned Thompkins jerked, reached out, then fell over dead across his saddle.

"Let's get out of here, Tanya! That shot was probably meant for us."

As they rode fast and furiously, not slowing down until they reached the road, Tanya turned to Willow with a dead serious look in her blue eyes. "I don't think so."

Willow moaned. "Not you, too. What do you mean?"

"I don't think that shot was meant for one of us. I believe whoever pulled the trigger *wanted* Thompkins dead."

"Ah," Willow agreed. "So he wouldn't spill the rest of the beans."

"Right."

"Come on, Jorge. Let's go into that house over there before it gets real dark and we can't see anything."

Jorge didn't even bark. He just sniffed the ground, excitedly wagging his huge, fluffy tail.

Sarah stopped all of a sudden. "Look, Jorge. There's two men coming out of that building. Let's go and talk to them. Maybe they can tell us how to get home." Sarah felt a tug on her arm and looked down. "What's wrong, Jorge? Why are you pulling me down?" She fell into a heap next to the big dog. "What are we going to do, boy? Wait till they go away?"

A soft whining and a wet lick was her answer. Every time Sarah tried to stand, Jorge yanked her back down and almost sat on top of her. She was frowning at the dog when she heard the sound of horses riding near—two of them—and then they disappeared over the low hill.

"Let's go, Jorge! They're gone now!" Sarah tugged at Jorge's long hair and he trotted right beside her, licking her hand every so often. "I hope there's some food in there. We missed supper. Aren't you hungry, Jorge?" For answer, he woofed softly and nuzzled her hand with his wet nose. "I guess you thought they were bad men, huh?"

Woof!

Child let me grasp your hand,
  Child let me grasp your hand.
You shall live,
  You shall live!
Says the father.
  A'te he'ye lo.
                    —*Ghost Dance Song*

Chapter Twenty-Two

Small grubby hands reached out for the dog.

"Jorge—" the voice was breathless and tiny—"Oh, boy, you brought Jorge!"

"It's dark in here," Sarah said in a shivery voice. "How can you see?"

"You get used to it," Mikey said, then blinked at Sarah. "How do you know my dog? Gosh, are you an angel?"

"No, Mikey. I'm not an angel. I'm just a girl, Sarah. I know you're Uncle Talon's and Aunty Willow's lost baby, though."

"I'm not a baby!" He chuckled, holding up four chubby fingers. "I'm *this* many."

"You got eyes just like your daddy, Talon Clay. Green eyes. But yours are a whole lot bigger."

"Who's Talon?" Mikey tipped his tawny head. "I don't have a daddy." He screwed up his mouth. "I don't think I don't." He giggled as Jorge licked his face thoroughly. "Boy, am I happy to see you, doggie!"

"Well, you *do* have a daddy. You do." Sarah pulled Mikey up from the room beneath the floor. "It's just an

405

old hole down there. How could you stand it? You look all right to me, though. Come on, Mikey, grab the rope. You're getting up out of there."

"Whew!" Mikey looked back down into the dark, dank hole. "I sure wanted to get outta there." He looked around. "Well, where's my daddy?"

"He's not here. He's out looking for me and Jorge though, I bet. Mother, too. Your mother's Willow."

Mikey nodded, still holding onto Jorge. "I know. But she don't want me no more." Tears were in his eyes and he dashed them aside furiously with the back of one hand. "The mens told me Mama stopped loving me."

"Oh no, she didn't. That's not true, Mikey. Your mother loves you very, very much. Come on, we're getting out of here before the bad men come back."

"Bad men?" Mikey blinked. "What's them?"

"They're the ones who shouldn't've taken you away from Aunty Willow."

Breathless and excited, Mikey exclaimed, "I heard a *bang!*"

"When?" Sarah shivered as she peeked around the door into the dark outside. "Oh no, it's too dark out there. It wasn't this dark when I got here."

Mikey giggled softly. "It's always dark here. I can see with my eyes in the dark. See?"

"Oh, Mikey, I can't see what you see. Those bad people must not have been too nasty to you, huh?"

"Nasty?" Mikey looked blankly into Sarah's face. "They was nice sometimes. I got good things to eat sometimes. I'm real hungry. Are you, Sarah?" He tugged her hand.

"Yes. But I think we got to wait till morning to find the road. Jorge and I ran by it in the bushes, though. We didn't want to have any bad men find us. Jorge sniffed and sniffed, for days and days, and he found you just like an old bloodhound. But we had to stay a ways off the road all the time."

Mikey laughed. "I know how to find the road."

"You do? In the dark?"

"Uh-hum, I peeked out of my tie-ups every time." He began to get whiny. "But I'm tired of the game now. I want to see Mommy and—who's that other one?"

"Daddy, Mikey. Daddy. Talon."

"Yeah. I want to see him, too."

"You will. I promise. First, we have to find our way back in the dark. What was the bang you heard?"

Mikey shrugged. "I dunno. I heard it, that's all. Them guys were always talking about shoot-'em-ups."

Ruffling Mikey's blond head of hair, Sarah said, "You know what? You're pretty smart for being just a little bitty kid."

"I know."

"We have to go back, Mikey. It's too dark out here. I can't find the way." Sarah looked up at the moon and stars, thousands of twinkling objects, but so far away, and the moon just a "slice of yeller" in the night. "We gotta go back in there and *ugh!* go down in that dark room in the ground."

In a sing-song voice, Mikey said, "Those men're gonna come back."

"We'll have to take our chances." She patted Jorge. "You have to be good and quiet, boy. You can't make a sound. No. Don't whine like that. I said—*Hush!*"

Down in the underground room was a tiny cot with

plenty of blankets. The two children curled up with the dog adding his own warmth between their shivering bodies.

They were all very quiet.

The children were awakened some time in the middle of the night. "Hey, you! Boy, are you hungry down there? Awake?"

"Do not bother the boy while he sleeps." Hawk felt a change in the place; something had been taken away—or added. More people? Did he smell an animal? He sure did. Fur. Lots of it.

Stone, from the Green Mountain hideout at Rountree, looked closely at the Indian in white man's clothing. "How do I know you're really working for us? You might be working against us. How can I trust you? You come sneaking up on me in the night and tell me you're working for Nat Lacey." He studied the man again as he lighted a lantern. "That's one thing made me believe you, though, when you said you worked for her, by the borrowed name. She don't go by her real name. You look awfully familiar to me, dude. Sure we didn't work together before at the hideout?"

I owned the place, you idiot, Hawk wanted to shout.

"You might be right," Hawk said. "I have been there. Now *you* look familiar to me." He jerked his head toward the hole. "The Brandon kid is doing fine. I checked him earlier before Little Fox and Winder left." Winder was no more. The other one, Little Fox, got away. Hawk knew that Little Fox had not identified him, for he had worn some other clothes he had stashed in the bunkhouse at Sundance. "Give me the food. I will feed the boy. I did so this morning."

"You did?" Stone still looked at the big Indian with a remnant of suspicion. "Tell me: What is the password?"

"Open Sesame." Hawk had gotten the words from Garnet herself when he had done some jobs for her at the ghost town. "Do you believe me now?" Hawk asked himself why he just didn't kill the man and be done with it. He had already gotten rid of Winder and that was going to make the Boss Lady wonder where one of her favorites had disappeared to; all she could do was wonder because she'd never find his body. He was too close to make any mistakes now. He must tread carefully.

"Yeah," Stone acceded. "You know too much to be an outsider. Go ahead, give the kid his food. I've got to get something from my saddle anyway and relieve myself over by the trees. Be sure there's some of that grub left over. Don't eat it all yourself. I'm hungry."

Whatever happened now, Hawk was thinking, he must not be seen by the Rawhide Bunch or the Green Mountain Gang or Garnet—Lacey, she now calls herself—because some were familiar with him, so familiar that even a distant glance at his features would enable most of them to spot him. But not this one by the name of Stone; he'd never seen Hawk before.

I will kill him now, Hawk decided. That will make one less man—again. He knew Garnet had many gunslingers.

There was a large handkerchief of thin cotton in his pocket, which he knotted about his face, drawing it up to the bridge of his nose and tying it at the nape of his neck. This secured him well enough from recognition if another of this gang should come along. Until they actually laid hands on him and stripped the mask away, he would simply be an unknown man. But who was going to best him in a fight? No one, he told himself.

Now that he was masked, he moved out of the line shack, slowly, with infinite precision, making so many pauses that it was almost as though he were attempting to deceive the "night eye" of the heavens with his cat-like movements.

Hawk forgot his love of life, his dread of a future without his beloved family, and once more he was only the consummate killer, prowling in the darkness, his eyes lighted like a cat's.

The children heard the ancient boards creak above their heads. "Shh, Mikey; Jorge. Someone's up there. More'n one. I hear two men talking."

"What are they sayin'?" Mikey asked as he popped his head out of the pile of blankets and dog fur. "Can we go home now? I wanna go home. I'm hungry and it's getting cold."

"I know, Mikey. The nights are cooler now that it's September. I hear that Indian talking. He was at Sundance the other day; I saw him."

"Indian?"

"Yeah. I'll tell you about him later, but now I want you to get back under those blankets with Jorge and keep quiet."

Mikey did—and then popped up again shortly. "I smell food. I'm really hungry, Sary. Can I have some food? I don't like this game anymore. I saw Mommy yesterday and I wanna go see her again."

"Yesterday?" Sarah wondered. It could not have been yesterday. "Oh, I know what you mean, Mikey. When babies say yesterday it could mean two weeks ago."

Mikey pouted. "I'm not a baby." He held up four fingers—

"I know. I know." Sarah was getting scared. Those men, one the Indian, were talking an awful long time. "Now someone's going outside, Mikey." They waited to hear more; time passed. "Someone's coming in again. Shh, Jorge, stop that whining," Sarah ended with a whisper as the footfalls grew louder. "He's right above us."

"Oh, good. Food." Mikey sprang up from bed and, defying Sarah's whispered shout, he ran to stand beneath the hole under the wide floorboards. "I'm hungry—" he shouted before Sarah's hand clamped over his mouth.

Sarah saw more light as the long, thick boards came away. "Oh-oh, now we're in trouble." She glanced over her shoulder and saw Jorge come bounding over to the circle of pale light streaming down.

"You may come up," Hawk called down, sticking his hand out for the child to grab hold. "I have food. It is still warm. Come, take my hand."

"NO, MIKEY!"

Sarah swallowed hard as the lantern light came nearer her face and above her was the face of *that* Indian. Was he a friend or a bad man? She decided he was not all that good, taking in the bronze shadows that danced on the Indian's face as the flame glowed and glimmered. His lips were pressed in a thin, grim line. His eyebrows were dark and drawn low. His nose was a slash in his face. His long black hair was tied at the nape with a strip of leather. If Sarah had been a grown woman, she would have thought him quite fierce and handsome. She *still* thought he was fierce.

Neither of the children made an attempt to speak, but carefully watched the Indian's every move. He rose to full height, towering majestically above the two children. He then said, "A dog, too?"

That's when Sarah spoke before thinking. "That's Jorge. Can he come up, too?" When she finished talking, she clamped a hand tight over her mouth, the other over her eyes. "I'm sorry," she said, peeking up at him between split fingers.

"No need to be sorry," Hawk said, smiling.

Sarah smiled back. The Indian looked much better when he smiled. It changed his scary look, making him boyish and friendly. "Do I know you?"

Lifting the children out of the hole, he answered Sarah as he set Mikey on the uneven floor behind him. His voice was low and soft, "You have seen me at your home. I know your family, everything about them. How did you get here?" He nodded toward the hole. "And with the dog?"

Mikey interrupted. "That's Jorge. He's not a dog. He's a boy."

Sarah screwed up the corner of her mouth. "Of course he's a dog, Mikey." She looked back up at the Indian. "Sometimes Mikey says things funny."

"I know." Hawk said gently. "I have children of my own."

"You do?" Sarah blinked powder-blue eyes. "Are you going to bring them to Sundance? What were you doing with the bad men? I heard you talking to one. He sounded mean. You talked different then. You sound nicer now."

Hawk bent down. "That's because your company is so much more pleasant, Blue Eyes."

Sarah giggled. "I like that name. Is it going to be my Indian name?" She looked over at Mikey, already devouring the contents of the baskets.

Hawk said *yes* in Apache. She laughed again.

"When you are a grown woman the Indians would give you the name Morning Rain."

Walking over to join Mikey before he ate all the food, Sarah said, "I like that, too. What's your name?" she asked as she nibbled on a chicken leg.

"Hawk."

"Just Hawk?"

"No. It is Desert Hawk." He joined them on the low bench and reached for a biscuit. Glancing over to the hole where the dog was barking and trying to jump out, Hawk said, "The dog sounds angry. I mean Jorge."

"He wants to get out. Will you help him out?"

"Only if he does not bite me." Hawk looked down into the trusting eyes of the girl. "Will you help?"

With Sarah's coaching Jorge allowed the Indian to help him out of the hole. As soon as he was up he wanted to get outside. "Oh-oh, he's gotta be let out the door. He won't go far; he'll be right back."

"At first light I will take you home," Hawk said, having decided to get rid of the rest of the returning Green Mountain Bunch all by himself and then ride away quietly.

"Home!" Mikey cried, running at Hawk and looping his arm around the big man's neck. Scooping Sarah up

413

on the other side, he sat down with them to finish the food. "Jorge is back. He's hungry, too!" Mikey exclaimed.

"Then we shall feed him."

Sarah looked up at Hawk. "Who made all this food?"

About to say "witch," Hawk decided to tell the truth, "It must have been someone over at the Tucker's dwelling."

Hawk wondered if it would be impossible to get rid of all the bad people for the Sundance family.

He nodded. Perhaps. All the more worthy of deep reflection on the matter. For what is worthwhile in this earth except the accomplishment of the impossible?

On Monday morning, before Hawk returned to Sundance with his glorious surprise, a lawyer showed up by the name of Hy Bannon. He knocked at the door almost before the crack of dawn to show Talon Clay the will which made Garnet Haywood Brandon heir to the ranch. He sat there in his tacky clothes and tie, explaining everything to the new master of Sundance as the lovely blonde moved into the room.

"This here explains it all," he said in a nasal voice. The lawyer looked at Willow Brandon, then went on. He disclosed how Pete Brandon had changed his will six months before he died, cutting off Talon Clay and Ashe and naming his wife, Garnet Haywood Brandon, sole inheritor of the estate. Almost whispering, the lawyer said he thought there was a terrible reason why Mr. Brandon did not wish his second son to inherit his holdings.

Talon Clay shot up out of his chair. "That's crap! And you said *second son;* do you realize that, Mr. Bannon?"

"Yes, well," Bannon said nervously, "meaning you, I would suppose. Second, I did say. You tell me your brother is dead?" He addressed the blond Ranger's back as he paced.

Talon flipped around to face the lawyer. "What? I never said that. How did you find out? There ain't nobody else who knows."

Bannon shifted uneasily. "Not even the folk in the nearby towns?"

Talon could not be sure about that. Willow went to stand in back of Talon's chair as he sat down again, watching the lawyer like a hawk. "Go on," he ordered.

Bannon said that Pete Brandon had been in a big rush to change his will and leave all his possessions and holdings to his wife. "Seems another woman had come here to Sundance before the Hayes children—" He nodded at Willow, then at the redhead and the young man, as they, too, came into the room. "Before y'all got here. She stayed here and died here."

Willow and Tanya looked at each other with huge, bewildered eyes. Sammy, too. Willow asked the lawyer, "What woman? There was no other woman beside Garnet herself, Martha, and now Tanya."

"Her name was Margaret."

"What?!"

"Yes," he said, taking in a deep breath before going on. "Seems she was the real mother to the—" he cleared his throat—"Hayes children."

415

Sammy blinked in shock. "That's your middle name, Sis." He looked around. "Sis?"

Everyone looked down.

Willow Margaret Hayes-Brandon had fainted.

"Weave we the woof. The thread is spun.
The web is wove. The work is done.
                              —*Gray*

Chapter Twenty-Three

"She left a diary," Bannon went on after Talon had revived Willow.

"Diary," Willow muttered, trying to sit up. She took a sip of the water Tanya had gotten for her, then brushed the glass and Tanya's hand aside. "Journal, you mean," she said and quickly rose to face Bannon. "Think, think," she muttered as she paced.

"What are you doing, Willow?" Talon questioned, trying to get her to sit down. She was making him nervous, too. "What is it you're trying to remember?" He frowned then. "Garnet kept a journal? Yes, you're right! I remember one."

Willow spun about. "I bet it was Margaret's journal and not Garnet's. It meant nothing to me years ago. There were some words in there about 'fearing death at someone's hand.' I do recall something of that nature." She looked at Tanya and Sammy, who both appeared to be in as great a state of shock as she was. "Our mother . . . Margaret. What was she like? What did she look like?"

Talon was staring at the lawyer as if he didn't trust

him, and a muscle in his cheek twitched. "I don't have time to be jawin' with any lawyers. I'm going to the Tuckers and get this damn mystery over and done with." He slammed the door, his words floating back angrily, "I'm going to get my son and that woman be damned!"

The lawyer was frowning in confusion and Willow turned to set him right. "You have to understand, Mr. Bannon, why Talon Clay's acting that way. Our son was kidnapped."

"I heard about that."

"You did?" Tanya asked, rushing across the room. "They've taken my daughter, too. We can't find her." Tanya stood wringing her hands in her handkerchief. Finally she sat down and turned her face away from the lawyer. "This is all very tangled," she moaned. And dear Lord, she thought bitterly, *I almost killed a man!*

"Sounds like some demented minds at work here," the lawyer declared. When the blonde turned a questioning glance on him, he sped on, "No, no, I did not mean y'all present right here, right now. I am speaking about those who have kidnapped your little loved ones."

About to sit on the loveseat, Willow shot up, talking excitedly. "Come with me. I have something to show you." When the lawyer hadn't moved, she said, "You, too, Mr. Bannon. We're going to the Brandon cemetery to lay some ghosts to rest."

Bending down near the wooden cross, Willow traced her fingers across the broken and disconnected letters. "See here, the name has been messed with. Someone has crossed out some letters."

Hy Bannon shook his head.

Tanya frowned and kept fretting, praying that her beloved child would soon be found. There would be two missing children if Sarah was not brought back to Sundance.

Sammy said, "What are you trying to say, Sis?"

"All right," Willow began, pacing back and forth, her shadow lying across the grave marker. "Someone has deceived the mourners who come here, or else they can't spell."

"I still don't—"

Cutting Bannon off, Willow pointed her finger. "Garnet and Margaret. I have a strong feeling they were sisters. That would make Garnet our aunt, not our mother. Look here: Someone has scratched out the letters 'M'; 'G'; and the second 'R'. The letters remaining on the cross are 'A'; 'R'; 'A'; 'E'; 'T'. Notice this now: The second 'A' is out of place."

Bannon was nodding. "A-R-A-E-T," he said. "Hardly a name that makes any sense."

"Right," Willow said. "But leave out the second 'a' and add a 'g' at the beginning and an 'n' where that 'a', the second one, is."

"That would be *Garnet,*" Bannon said. "You are very right," he told her. "The one who practiced to deceive forgot to delete the second 'a', thinking he or she was being clever. She wanted everyone to believe this was her grave marker."

"Of course!" cried Sammy and Tanya at once.

"You've solved the Sundance mystery," said Hy Bannon.

Willow whirled and gaped at the lawyer. "You know about it, too?"

He nodded. "I've been trying to figure this out for

419

years. Young woman," he addressed Willow, "you have probably saved Brandon land from the evil clutches of Garnet Haywood." He looked down at the grave and back up at Willow. "I wonder about one thing: Where does *Haywood* come from?"

Shrugging, Willow made a supposition. "No doubt from her first husband."

Bannon frowned. "Or second, or third, or fourth."

"How true." Raking her fingers through her hair, Willow said, "Are you prepared to go get the sheriff, Mr. Bannon?"

"Of course. Meanwhile, you tell that Ranger husband of yours to go over to Tuckers' and make the arrest immediately."

"You know she's there?"

Bannon shoved his wire-rimmed glasses up. "I'm very nosy, Mrs. Brandon. I've been sneaking around here for weeks to solve this. Actually, I've come and gone for years." He nodded when Tanya acknowledged him with wide eyes. "Garnet Haywood even thought I was a traveling vendor. You know, there's a lot of them phony ones trying to make a fast buck since the war started. And it's going to get worse; people will get mighty hungry in Texas before it's over. The Federal blockade forced an immediate economic revolution, and the departure of the men threw the burden of supplying food and clothing on women and slaves. It also threw the plantations back on their own resources."

"Are there *that* many plantations in Texas, Mr. Bannon?" Sammy asked.

"Plantation families in Texas work to spin cloth for uniforms. I can hardly approach a plantation manse now without hearing the sound of wheels or looms. Big plantations and isolated settlements have established shops to try to make such necessities as hoes, knives, and shirts."

"From scratch?" Tanya asked, craning her neck for any sign of the hands returning with Sarah and Jorge.

"Oh, yes. You see, before the war the most progressive planters had been buying their tools and slave clothing from the Northern factories."

"Our blacks are free," said Sammy. "Always been; always will be."

Willow looked at Tanya. "We can make uniforms at home, Sis. Women are used to labor, but field work, I believe, would exceed our strength and skill, if all the men left. This is one of our problems in forming a good posse to search for our son—" Willow spread her hands—"so many men are up and leaving, even our ranch hands. Just the other day Frank and Jesse said they were going to join the Stars and Bars. Those villains who tried forcing our men to leave thought we'd believe it was by their own doing. How stupid of them!"

"You know what, Sis?" Sammy looked at Willow. "I think those two were working for that Boss Lady at the Tuckers'." He looked at the lawyer. "Nat Lacey she calls herself. She sent the Tuckers away to New Orleans. Even gave them the money."

"How do you know that, Sammy?" Tanya asked.

"I did some snooping. You know where I think Talon Clay's headed out to now? I think he's gone over to that line shack on the other side of Tuckers'. Just might be Mikey's there. I'm goin' right now!"

With that Sammy sped away to fetch his horse. Three pairs of eyes watched him go. Almanzo was walking up the short cemetery hill but the redhead hardly saw the handsome man, so deep were her thoughts.

"*Sarah,*" Tanya whispered with a thoughtful frown. "She's no doubt there, too, then. Trailed snoopy Jorge. The hiding place . . . we were right there last night, Willow!"

Willow shouted, "I know it!"

Hy Bannon nodded. "You know what else? I did even further snooping myself. Your Nat Lacey just might be Garnet Haywood."

Willow snapped her fingers. "I think you got it, lawyer!"

The sight of them was beautiful. Three humans were walking along the road with a fluffy, large dog. They walked in "stairs", the lowest one being the dog's back, then Mikey's head, Sarah, and the tallest, the Indian called Hawk.

Riding alongside Almanzo, Talon felt tears sting his eyes as his gaze settled on the smallest child. Hypnotized, he could only stare at him. His son! How wonderful he was!

Then he was off his horse and running towards the child. Hawk moved . . . holding up his hand to Talon Clay, warning him not to frighten the boy with his sudden, fierce joy. Talon slowed, shifting his eyes back to Mikey and slowly letting them drift over the lad from head to foot. He is perfect, Talon thought, rapt with exhilaration and curiosity.

Sarah was whispering something in Mikey's ear and the boy nodded with sudden happiness. Almanzo chuckled and Hawk disappeared into the background, softly on cat feet.

Take it slow, Talon kept reminding himself over and over.

Walking up to the boy slowly, Talon scooped Michael up in his arms and the child looked at him in bewilderment for a time. Then he gave the man's beard-rough cheek an affectionate pat. "Daddy," he said, giving Talon a one-arm hug. Flinging out his arm, he added, "There's *Jorge!*"

Willow dropped the reins when she saw them coming, and Breeze tossed a large silky head and whinnied. His eyes sparkling, Talon came down off his horse and handed Mikey over to Willow; she gazed into her husband's eyes and whispered, "Oh, Talon."

Leaving everyone where they were, Talon and his little family walked the distance to their home and closed the doors, wanting to be alone. Talon turned mother and child in his arms and hugged them both fiercely. It was not long before there was a rap on the door. Willow looked up at Talon. "Who could that be?"

"Is jes' me."

"Juanita," Willow exclaimed. "She'll be very disappointed if we don't let her in."

"She won't cry if we don't, will she?"

"Yes." Willow nodded.

Juanita joined the happy family and that night she was singing happily in the kitchen, once again with her "babies," Michael Angelo and Jorge.

* * *

Alone later, Willow and Talon finally found time for each other when Mikey had been put to bed for the night. Willow turned to Talon after setting down the tortoiseshell hairbrush, running her hand over the beautiful hand mirror accompanying the set. "I could sleep forever," she said with a tired yawn. "The summer has been a wild one and I wonder how long it will take to settle down and find some badly needed peace."

"Come here," Talon said. "Sit beside me, my passionate vixen, before we drop into that bed like dead soldiers."

Willow laughed softly, then halted suddenly, laying her head on his shoulder. "What are we going to do now, Talon?"

"About what?" he asked, his lips brushing her hair. "Our family? Garnet . . . or Nat Lacey? True, that one has to be dealt with. I'm just wondering how to go about it. But we had better work fast. As soon as she discovers our son is missing, she'll be looking for him. She has lost her hostage. I suppose now she'll just disappear as she did before when her sister—"

"Sister?" Willow looked at him and straightened. "What do you know about that?"

"You know that knock on the door a while ago?" he asked and she nodded. "It was Hy Bannon. He filled me in and asked what we should do about the woman, the Boss Lady of the badmen." He grimaced, wondering how he could ever have been in love with her; then again, he'd only been a young lad. "You know, I'm beginning to wonder if that tiny portrait you have in the locket is not really your mother, and Garnet had stolen it from her. She probably stole all those dresses from

Margaret, too. Though sisters, they must have looked like *twin* sisters."

"It makes me so happy to know my mother was a good person, not anything like Garnet Haywood."

Talon said with a shrug, "How do we know what Margaret was like? She must have come to Sundance shortly after I went to stay with the Tuckers. I wish I knew what was written in that lost journal."

"You and me both." Willow sighed, feeling sleepy. "One day we might know the entire Sundance mystery. But at least *some* ghosts have been laid to rest."

"Should we string Garnet Haywood up? They still do that in some wild west towns, you know."

Willow shook her head. "I think we should just wait and see what she does. She's not going to stop here without her hostage. The number of her gunslingers is growing slimmer. The gang will soon be dispersed, no doubt. Some of the patriotic ones—if such are possible—will probably leave to join the war, too. She'll be left alone on the Tucker place until the ladies return."

"Ladies!" Talon hooted. "You call Janice Ranae and Hester *ladies?*" He snarled, "More like wicked women. That Garnet, she's a doozy, though. She wanted to make it all seem like the truth. One day she planned to come sashaying into Sundance, when she thought it was safe enough. She must have heard about my brother's death. She was always afraid of Ashe—I couldn't understand why. It was not only that he had become a Texas Ranger. Now she knows he's gone, she dares to come closer to Sundance, even going so far as to move into the Tuckers'. My brother was smarter than I was. He steered clear of Garnet. He knew her for the lying, cheating, no-good woman she was. Is." Talon snorted and jerked his head. "How could I ever have thought—believed, excuse me—that she was the mother of the Hayes children?"

"Offspring, you mean. We're all kind of grown up now, Talon."

"Lord—" Talon faced Willow—"forgive me again, Willow. I put you through hell, all because of my imaginary love for a wanton witch."

"I forgive you, Talon." Willow yawned and lay down on the bed. "But now I want to get some sleep."

"Good night, Willow."

" 'Night . . . Talon."

In the morning, the lawyer surprised them by bringing the deed over to Petit Sundance; Tanya wanted it this way. The lawyer said Tanya wanted to make sure it did not fall into the wrong hands. "If you know what she means," Bannon ended with a wink.

Later that afternoon, while Talon was out with Almanzo, Willow wandered through the house with Mikey, showing him this and that. She laughed and played with her son for hours. When Mikey was down for a nap—he needed to catch up on sorely-needed sleep—Willow discovered the lost journal.

Holding her skirts high so she wouldn't trip over them, she climbed the precarious staircase and rummaged through the attic. There were broken bits of furniture and books and newspapers stacked everywhere. Sighing, she straightened. Her eyes drifted back and forth, scanning nooks and crannies. Might as well leave, she thought. What's this? Her hem caught on a treacherous loose board. Removing the old broken plank, she looked down and gasped, a swirl of images spinning in her brain like leaves caught in a dust devil.

The journal!

Willow felt a tingle whip through her. This had to be her mother's journal. There it was. The name: Margaret Elizabeth Brandon.

"My dear Mother."

Taking it with her, she raced over to an old, low trunk and sat down. She bit her lip to halt the tears that shimmered in her eyes. It was no use. She read some things her mother had recorded and cried until she could cry no more. She had no plans to show Talon just yet, maybe never; some things were to be held secret in the special places of one's heart.

Holding the journal close to her breast, Willow whispered, "She was my mother." She felt closer to Margaret than her brother and sister because, even though Tanya and Sammy knew about Margaret, they seemed content to leave it at that. They'd all had hurt feelings to deal with and maybe their time would come later. For now, she decided to leave sleeping giants alone.

The silvery Texas moon beamed down over Sundance and the winter owls hooted in the wood. Willow and Talon were in their bedroom making love. She had been dreaming about it, and when she came slowly awake she felt him touching her, over and over, here, there, everywhere. She became bold herself and began to touch him back.

Breathless kisses. Sweet embraces. Hot touches. Growing even hotter and hotter. Blazing-sun-hot. Her opened lips widened slightly to welcome the seeking parry of his tongue. The kiss was as fragile as spring rain at first, then grew more demanding and delicious.

Gathering her to him firmly, he hugged her until she could feel the hard beating of his heart and the ample strength of his arms around her. They accepted the gift of love that was theirs, giving to each other, and taking with mutual understanding. Their breathing came quicker when they at last pulled apart, his eyes shining and lingering on her moist, soft mouth that awaited his return, waited to be claimed once more. The ardor built between them, breaking down any barriers that might remain to thwart the complete fulfillment of their love.

"Talon—" Willow spoke very softly. His name sounded like an endearment.

"My woman," he acknowledged just as softly. "I hear and I obey."

This murmured remark made her laugh with joy unspeakable.

She felt that familiar tight curling and unfurling inside that left her longing for more and more. She was like a morning glory unfolding its petals to exquisite bloom. She arched toward him and he thought her body was so beautiful.

"I'm going to gobble you up," he murmured.

"Eat your fill," she whispered back.

He drank in her passion, hungry for more, seeing it in her eyes, feeling it in her tender touches. Her soft moans of pleasure drove him crazy. She did love him and want him. He wanted to protect her always, to keep her safe and sound in his embrace. Fingers eager to touch loosened the bodice of her blouse and the tiny bit of clothing fell to the floor, waiting to be joined by other larger bits. Deftly he released the buttons that held her riding skirt and it slipped away with the other clothes. His fingers stroked her soft young skin and he could have shouted for joy when he realized she was working with the buttons on his shirt; it hung open to her gaze in moments.

He was growing impatient and shrugged out of his shirt. Pulling her close, he held her.

Impatiently he set her away and hastened to remove the rest of his clothing. Unable to wait one more moment he took her back in his embrace and their bodies joined as they fell to the bed in slow motion.

Their lovemaking was a joyous reunion, like coming home. In her arms, he found everything he'd ever desired. Driven by his love for her and the needs of his body, he buried himself in her velvet warmth, slamming powerfully against her inner thighs. Intensifying the experience, Willow wrapped her legs around him and welcomed his love.

After touching her for the thousandth time, he breathed into her ear, "Am I pleasing you?"

"*Are* you!" It wasn't a question. She moaned, shivered, laughed heartily. "Do birds have wings?"

Moving together and back . . . shuddering from the throes of passion that leapt through them. As Talon felt the sweet answers from deep within his wife, her legs clenched around him when her climax began. Her eyes sparkled. His eyes closed painfully tight. The resulting explosion was mutual, predestined, and complete.

Willow closed her eyes and sighed. There was such joy on her face.

Talon fell asleep, smiling from ear to ear like a grinning idiot.

Sundance was peaceful this night.

For ye shall go out with joy,
And be led forth with peace:
The mountains and the hills shall break
forth before you into singing, and all
the trees of the field shall clap their hands.

—*Isaiah 55:12*

Chapter Twenty-Four

"I didn't want them to hurt my son. That is why I proceeded with caution and didn't fall into their trap. I bided my time after the shooting of Hawk and discovering that the Rawhide Gang was hiding Mikey. When I beat up one of the Fox men, I think that made their boss—" he hated saying the name *Garnet* too often— "more careful. It slowed her down. She was afraid of what we would do next."

Talon finished talking and looked at his friends and family. Almanzo nodded; this was smart thinking. "You waited. Just like Hawk. Now your son is alive." He looked out to the line of cottonwoods where he usually saw Hawk lurking. "By the way, where is that cunning Indian? I believe he had an eye out for the boy all this time. He was waiting to see what everyone would do. I believe he could have brought the boy back to us sooner, yet he was wise to take care."

"That lawyer was snooping around, too. I think he knew more than he was letting on," Willow offered, spreading the creamy skirts of her dress as she sat on

431

the loveseat. "Our son had a protector all this time and we didn't know it."

"You look like an angel today, love," Talon remarked and nods of agreement went around the room. They sat in Tanya's parlor, which had recently been turned into a room for sewing soldiers' uniforms.

With a small laugh, Willow said, "Hawk is the real angel. Our guardian angel. I hope he finds Summer Wind and his sons. Hawk is a good man. But dangerous to cross."

Sammy nodded. *"Mikey's* guardian angel."

"Oh, no," Tanya said, Sarah at her side. *"This* is the real angel." Smiling up at Almanzo, she hugged her daughter. "She had something to do with saving Mikey's life."

Miss Pekoe shook her kerchiefed head as she walked into the room with watered-down tea. "You's all wrong," she said. "Here come de *real angel* right now!" She leaned over to peer into the hall as she waited for the pair of mischief makers.

They all heard a great thudding of paws and running feet as big Jorge and Mikey ran down the hall and entered the room, muddy footprints trailing behind. The naughty duo careened right into a pile of books and newspapers that had been stacked for removal. Miss Pekoe slapped a hand over her mouth as she gaped at the precious papers all dirty with mud.

"Oh, Lawsy! Ah plumb forgot to take dat water bucket Ah jes' filled this morning away from dat fresh hump of dirt at de side of de house. Oh—oh. Jes look at you two!"

Everyone was laughing, even the lawyer who had come along the hall bringing up the rear. "My, my. This place has sure undergone a significant change since *these* two appeared." He laughed. "All for the better, I'd say!" But then, he saw Talon Clay Brandon and he looked undecided suddenly.

Although Talon's mouth was in a thin line as he looked at his son there was a sparkle of adoration in his eyes. He got up from the chair he'd been sitting in and Mikey's eyes turned round. "Oh-oh, Jorge," he said with his mouth a circle. "Here comes Daddy!" With a squeal he hightailed it out of there and went running along the hall looking for Juanita, who would not look as fierce as "Daddy" when she discovered his mischief.

"Humph!" Miss Pekoe rolled her eyes as she straightened from the now-tidy pile of books and newspapers. "Tha's some boy!" she exclaimed, returning to the kitchen where food was getting scarce because staples were gradually declining since the war began.

"Ahem!" Hy Bannon said, clearing his throat. "I've some news." He waved a sheaf of papers in front of them to get their attention. He looked up as Tanya made a move. "No. Don't get up. You should stay, too, Mrs. Brandon."

Hy Bannon went on. "I have news for y'all. There's been some greedy cattle rustling in the area, between here and Emerald, Texas. I have been discussing matters with a secret agent from the U.S. government and he has determined Garnet's Rawhide Gang to be the culprits. She made the worst mistake of her life by showing up and demanding what she did." He looked pointedly at Willow; Garnet had made the demand that Willow find that deed. "The agent will be around with a few other fellows—if you get my drift—and they will round up Garnet and her gang. She won't even receive an injunction. She has no defense. She should have known that the law of self-preservation is the strongest one recognized in this raw, young country where a mother's and father's love for a son—or daughter—gives them the right to protect their family with guns." He looked to Tanya, knowing she had shot a man.

"Anything else?" Sammy asked, knowing there was more.

Out of habit, Bannon cleared his throat. "Garnet Haywood Brandon is also wanted for murder."

Sammy walked in, shouting, "Yippee-yahoo!"

"Yay!" Sarah said with a cheer.

Everyone went still. Willow asked, "Whose murder?"

"Leave the room, Sarah," Tanya ordered her daughter.

"Ohhh, Mommy." Sarah groaned. "I love these kinds of stories. Everything is just getting good."

"This one's no story, Sarah," Talon said. "Run along like your mother said."

Her face lit up like Christmas. "I'll go find Mikey and Jorge."

When she was gone, all heads swiveled in the lawyer's direction.

"She's wanted for the murder of one *Margaret Elizabeth Brandon.*"

All of a sudden, Talon whipped his head around to his wife. "Willow—" he snapped—"Don't you go faintin' again."

She didn't heed his order. Willow was on the floor before you could finish saying "hot Texas chili."

Just then Almanzo burst into the room, asking Talon to come with him immediately. "The posse is here," he told the lawyer. Bannon stood, saying, "Already?" and

Almanzo nodded, hurrying Talon along. "You're a Ranger, Talon, and they need you. I'm coming along."

Tanya gasped. She knew Almanzo would be riding into fierce danger—gunfire would be exchanged and she was worried for him. Her love for Ashe had never dimmed; yet, her affection for Almanzo had grown considerably and she didn't want him hurt. He had helped her so much.

"Please tend to my wife," Talon announced to anyone listening, joining Almanzo and rushing to his mount.

"What happened to Willow?" Almanzo asked, leaping onto his horse.

"The usual. She fainted."

"You look worried, my friend." Almanzo reached over to touch Talon's elbow. "She will be fine. Tanya will take care of her." His dark eyes glowed with love for the beautiful redhead. "The posse is waiting up the road. We must go."

Talon frowned as they rode. "How can they possibly be here already?"

"The posse has been waiting for this opportunity to get the Rawhide and Green Mountain gangs." His eyes sparkled. "I believe our outlaw Desert Hawk had something to do with leading them here; they've been after him, too. But he is long gone."

The posse soon appeared in the form of a dust cloud coming from the road. Only one thing could raise that much dust and that *was* a posse. As the riders took shape, Talon counted fifteen men. He recognized a few of them as lawmen he had met in San Antonio and San Angelo. They were all business now as they greeted one another. Their plans were made swiftly.

They rode well armed. Each man had a rifle and

many used the small-bore, five-shot Colt revolver. Several carried a pair of dragoon pistols in scabbards. The older guns were United States issue, Colt's patent, and they came with scabbards, mold, and flask.

Two of the lawmen lit out south over the low hills to scout the area and lie outside the place. Arriving at Tucker's ranch, the posse hid in the barn away from the main building. Checking the house, Talon and Almanzo had found it empty with definite signs that the occupants had left temporarily and would be returning. Talon and Almanzo hurried out to join the lawmen in the barn. They had just gotten settled when Bob Fox, Frank, and Jesse appeared. Fox rode in the lead, his horse pointed toward a corn crib near the barn where the posse waited, along with Talon and Almanzo.

As the three outlaws approached, a posse man popped up from the crib and fired, accidentally killing Fox's horse. The outlaw grabbed his rifle and opened fire. Jesse offered Fox a stirrup but Fox refused to be moved: he kept firing blindly and insanely at the barn until his rifle was empty. Then he mounted behind Jesse.

"They're getting away!" Talon yelled, jumping up from his hiding place. "Look, there's more coming!"

Sure enough, ten more men rode into the ranch, among them a gunslinger by the name of Laredo. He was skinny with bright red hair sticking out beneath the sides of an odd blue cowboy hat; Talon paid this no mind—he had other, more important matters that needed tending. Talon wanted to get the first three. Frank was riding in front of Jesse, who turned his horse, heading south. The horse, nicked by a bullet, jumped and caused Fox to lose his hat. Dropping off the horse, he went back for it while clutching his rifle in one hand. After picking up the hat and putting it on, Fox held his Winchester in both hands, lifting it over his head and shouting curses at the posse.

That was a bad mistake.

Talon's rifle cracked. Fox fell, dead.

The two lawmen who had lain low outside the ranch dispatched with Frank and Jesse. Talon rejoined the posse, and bullets kicked dust around them and clipped twigs from bushes as the lawmen and outlaws exchanged gunfire.

In the end only one of the outlaws was wounded and taken prisoner. The rest lay dead, scattered all about the Tucker Ranch. The sheriff, feeling he had accomplished enough for one day, returned to town. Three of the lawmen sustained injuries and were brought to Sundance to have their wounds bandaged. They were fed hot soup and were back on the road by the next morning.

No one knew what had happened to Garnet. She was still on the loose.

In the morning, Willow found Talon Clay sound asleep in the hay of the big barn. But not for long. Mikey and Jorge arrived after Willow had, and they began to sniff and poke around the sprawled-out man who looked more like a dead Ranger than a sleeping man.

Opening his eyes, Talon found his wife standing in a shaft of glorious sunlight pouring into the barn. "Wha—?" he said, shielding his head as boy and dog pounced on him with tickles and wet licks. "Whoa! Wait just a durn minute! What is this? The morning welcoming committee?"

"Talon, wake up," Willow said excitedly. "I have a great idea."

"I *am* awake," Talon groaned. "And if your idea is one of your usual ones, I'm goin' back to sleep."

"Oh no, you're not."

Peeping out with one eye, Talon began to rise but the naughty duo wouldn't let him. Talon roared, "Get lost, you two ragamuffins!" To his blinking surprise, the two sped out the door, giggles and yips filling the morning air.

"Well now, wife," Talon said. "What's this grand idea?" He smacked his lips and scratched his muscled ribs with two fingers of each hand. Then he sat with one elbow resting on a hay crib. "I'm listenin'."

"First, I want to know how Garnet Haywood managed to get away. I questioned those wounded lawmen, but they just shrugged and kept sipping their molasses and ground nut coffee. Then I asked Almanzo, and he said I better ask you because you'd want to tell me yourself." Her shoulders shrugged impatiently when he took too long in answering. "Well?"

"She got away. That's it."

Willow gasped. "She *what?* That's all you can say?" Pacing the barn, Willow whirled to a stop in front of her disheveled husband. "After all this . . . the worst outlaw gets away?" Her voice rose to a weak little screech.

Talon moaned and Willow rushed to his side. "Have you been hurt?" she asked, looking him over closely for a wound.

"No!" Talon nabbed her and, lifting her up, he sat her down smack dab on his lap, her legs bent in a wide vee. "Talon Clay! Someone might discover us and see me in this most unladylike position! Let me up! My skirts are riding up my legs!"

"Uhmmm, good. I got you right where I want you, *desperada.*" He undulated his hips and pulled her closer to his hardening body. "Let's make love, right here. Now."

"What?" Willow looked at him as if he'd been shot clear through the head. "Right here? Right now? With the doors open? People passing right by? Kids playing right outside?"

Talon chuckled at her lovely fright and kissed her lips for a long time. She surfaced breathless and blushing from his passionate embrace. As he was letting her go, she brushed her skirts down furiously while at the same time he kept lifting them.

Willow shook her head at his deep laugh and bold wink. "You're incorrigible, depraved, a pervert! You know that?" She giggled even as she made these comments. "But I still love you."

"Say—I have a question to ask you. About that note you sent me while I was in LaGrange—what was this about a divorce?"

"I never said anything about a divorce. Don't you remember we spoke about this on the trail?" He shook his head and she continued, "Well, I never mentioned divorce and haven't the slightest notion where you got that. And we never knew who sent that letter saying cruel things—"

"Such as you being fat and dowdy?"

"Right. I realize now that you would never have done that, Talon."

Staring at the bodice of her yellow blouse, Talon suddenly blurted, "The handwriting wasn't yours, my love.

Not the second set of letters anyway, and I think some-one sneaked into my room because there was a wom-an's colorful Mex shawl in there."

"I wonder who could be so cruel as to write such things? I suppose there are some things we're never go-ing to learn about the kidnapping. But I bet a lot had to do with Hester Tucker wanting to get at you again, and Janice Ranae. Tuckers' revenge, you'd say."

"You believe the Tuckers had something to do with the kidnapping?" he asked. She was silent. He said, "Hester sure was pumping me for information that day I last saw her. Something was up. Wonder why the chicken-turd Tuckers suddenly up and went off to Lou-isiana? Are we always going to have trouble with them?"

Angry for a moment, Willow took a piece of straw and broke it in half. "I'll just bet they did have some-thing to do with Garnet Haywood. Janice Ranae used to visit her when our kidnapper lived here. There was a letter—"

"How do you know that?" Talon's gaze eased over the crests of her breasts and back to her face. "The jour-nal?"

"Yes." She would not say *whose* journal; that was still her secret. "I'll show it to you someday, but not just yet. I'm not finished studying it. I want to know the story inside out before showing it to anyone else."

"There's really not much to tell. Garnet and Margaret were here at Sundance at the same time, if only briefly for Margaret. Was she murdered here? And if so, who is alive to tell about it?"

"Clem?" she wondered aloud.

"He's too old. His mind wanders in and out. You

never know if he's telling the truth or not. She was murdered by Garnet Haywood, her own sister. We don't know if that was your aunt's maiden name or only a name contrived by Garnet. Was she married before she hooked onto my step-pa?"

"We have no idea. The letter to Rob had not truly been signed 'Garnet.' I found another letter in a book—" She would not yet say *which* book—"and traces of the "M" at the beginning of that signature can still be seen! I believe Margaret Hayes did write those letters, not Garnet. Garnet wanted someone to believe she did, in case she got caught pretending to be her own twin sister. Yup, don't look like that, Talon. I believe they were twins, to have looked so much alike."

"You may be right," he conceded. "No wonder Garnet seemed awfully sweet and nice at times when I happened to see her sitting outside, looking sad but peaceful."

"Maybe she wasn't at peace," Willow said. "Because she was really Margaret, the other twin."

"Poor lady, how bewildered and rejected she must have felt when some of us menfolk treated her like the slut her sister Garnet was. She—perhaps it was Margaret, now I think of it—used to smile at me real pretty like and I wanted to step over the flowers and wring her neck."

Willow added, "Wonder if Clem knew there was two of them, twins, at Sundance? And your "Pa," Pete—he surely must have known that Garnet had a twin living with them. How could Garnet hide it? If only we could talk to Pete, but he's long gone. And Margaret herself."

"God—" Talon shook his head miserably—"if only I'd known. I would have kept your sweet lady of a mother alive and happy. Then you would have been reunited with her when you and your Pa came here with your brother and sister." Talon's face darkened. "I'll just bet Garnet had something to do with your Ma and Pa splitting up. Could be Garnet was diddling around with your Pa, too. This might've tore up the marriage because of what Garnet did to make it all seem she was so innocent. She probably made your Pa look like a lecher instead of the steady, hardworking man you said he was. Wish I would have talked to Rob before he died. Heck, I didn't even know you existed back then 'cause I went away and became a stupid outlaw."

Willow couldn't get off the subject. "Maybe that was Margaret in the locket—her picture, not Garnet's. Margaret looks sweeter, I think." Willow still wondered: Why had Margaret and her husband separated? Was her mother searching for her family when she arrived at Sundance? Maybe Margaret and Rob Hayes had been searching for each other all that time. She hated to think that her parents had split up because of Garnet's treachery, but most likely that's what it was.

Talon watched Willow's troubled gaze. "How clever of the little detective. You do your work as thoroughly and intelligently as a Ranger, my love." He laughed and winked.

"You never knew that Pete Brandon was your stepfather, did you? Talon—" she gasped—"Your last name is an Indian one. Not Brandon."

"Of course it's Brandon. My Pa *never* said different. Ashe never did, either. It was just accepted that I was and am a Brandon. We had the same mother, Martha. My name is on that deed—"

Smiling, Willow cut in, "No, it's not." Her voice was

442

sing-song. "Remember—your father cut you out. Was he jealous because he knew his wife, Garnet, was 'teaching a blond-haired boy the ropes'? Or was he resentful and acting out of spite because his first wife, Martha, had fallen in love with her Indian captor? How can your name be on that deed when he cut you out?"

He grinned at her. "My name's on it now. Tanya cut me in. So how do you like them apples? Pretty clever, huh?"

"Oh Talon, Sundance has always been yours. You know that. You helped carve it out. Your mother's blood runs in you and she was a King. Not of the wealthy Kings of Santa Gertrudis, but a King nevertheless. You and your brother have done almost as well. Don't smirk! You have. You and Ashe plunged into ranching with everything you had."

"Right. We bought and raised horses, using them on the ranch and for sale as saddle, pack, and harness animals. We had some pretty good broncbusters."

"Yourself included. Which brings me to my bright idea. Aren't you waiting for me to tell you?" He nodded and she began, "You and Ashe have started this equine breeding program with advantages that many other ranchers in Texas do not have. Thanks to the sale of the mustangs you and Almanzo captured in the Wild Horse Desert, you bought, or Ashe bought, those thoroughbreds from the Hunters of Louisiana, to upgrade the herd in general."

"Right. Our horses can start fast, reach a gallop in fewer strides, and keep up fiery speed for close to a quarter mile."

Excited, Willow went on. "We could call him the Western quarterhorse, combining the features of the rugged Spanish horse and the finer-boned English horse. With high-quality stock we could have more customers than we can handle. Texas ranchers are supplying more cattle for beef to Army posts; they have to feed not only themselves but the Indians the Cavalry defeats and sends to reservations. They sell beef and mounts to the Confederate forces, but it's not nearly enough to make up the difference. We could sustain a horse trade with the Western posts of the U.S. Cavalry."

"You mean breed more of the Hunter horses with Mustangs, and crossbreed with the Mexican horses, too? I see. But we've already beat you to it, love."

Willow snapped, "What do you mean?"

"Almanzo and I have been discussing this very same thing. Horses are smarter and swifter on the hoof than cattle, and easier to round up. On trail drives they would be much better. The horses bring high prices and are in demand among new ranchers and the Army."

"Oh, well. I thought it was a good idea and I still love you, even though you steal—" She giggled when he tickled her playfully in the ribs.

He pulled her back down beside him, gazing into her eyes. "Say that again. And tell me more, Pussywillow, tell me what's going to happen to us."

"I love you."

"I love you, too, even your biggest bright ideas. Now—the rest."

She jumped up, grabbing his hand and trying to lift him. He shook his head, staying right where he was, refusing to budge. "Uh-uh. About us, Willow. You can make it short and sweet."

She laughed and twirled and faced him, shouting, "It's very predictable: *We'll be a family now!*"

Grinning handsomely, he leaped to his feet. He had heard just what he wanted to hear!

Wearing a shawl, Willow slipped outside for a walk to the cemetery before making Talon a favorite meal for his birthday dinner, with Miss Pekoe's expert help. She stopped before the grave marker she'd had Clem fix up: *Margaret Hayes, beloved mother of Tanya, Willow, Sammy.* The afternoon smelled like a day poignantly remembered, briefly, from her past. She had shared the day with someone. Had they held hands? Had someone smiled down at her? Was that someone special? A relative? A parent? Had she been very small? It felt like a "Mother," this reminiscent feeling. Though how could she know? She couldn't remember her real mother. If only one could recapture the past, put it into a box of memories, and take it out on days you wished to enjoy this special kind of love.

Tears came softly. *If only.*

Outside Sundance that night and all across the country at war, campfires burned and stars winked. Margaret had been laid to her peaceful rest. And a woman by the name of Garnet Haywood was making her last trek back to California.

Just that morning they had learned that a gunslinger, Mick Stone, was allowed to take Garnet's body to the old Rountree place to bury it. As it went, an outlaw bunch called Breeds had been hunting Garnet. She hadn't paid up and they decided to take the debt out in blood revenge; they had also learned she was not only

445

a kidnapper but a murderess. Talon said that would have earned them each a rope at the hanging tree, if they could catch these lawless Breeds. "Don't give a good damn," Talon had said to Willow, and gave her a long look. She could understand his wanting to have been the one to turn Garnet in—alive.

Garnet was gone for good. Her wicked aura lingered no more.

Leaving the gallery, Willow went back inside and slowly shut the French doors to pick up the beautiful mirror Talon had given her; she checked her bedtime appearance and carefully laid down the mirror.

Another day at Sundance had ended.

AUTHOR'S NOTE

Many friends have written asking me to write another book about Talon Clay and Willow. The first story in the Sundance Saga, *Texas Tigress,* received so much attention that I felt another book was in order. To please my fans—and myself—I wrote *Captive Caress,* Talon Clay's and Willow's story. More and more letters came and they kept arriving over the years. So many questions about the Sundance Saga have piled up—my fans want to know all about these intriguing characters. Now that I have written a third adventure, *Love's Lost Angel,* dealing with the Hayes family and the Brandons—and the naughty Garnet!—I hope some of my reader's curiosity will have been appeased. At least somewhat. Who knows? There might even be a fourth. Who can tell?

My best till next time,

Sonya

You can write me at: Angel Enterprises, 13628 Square Lake Trail, Stillwater, MN 55082